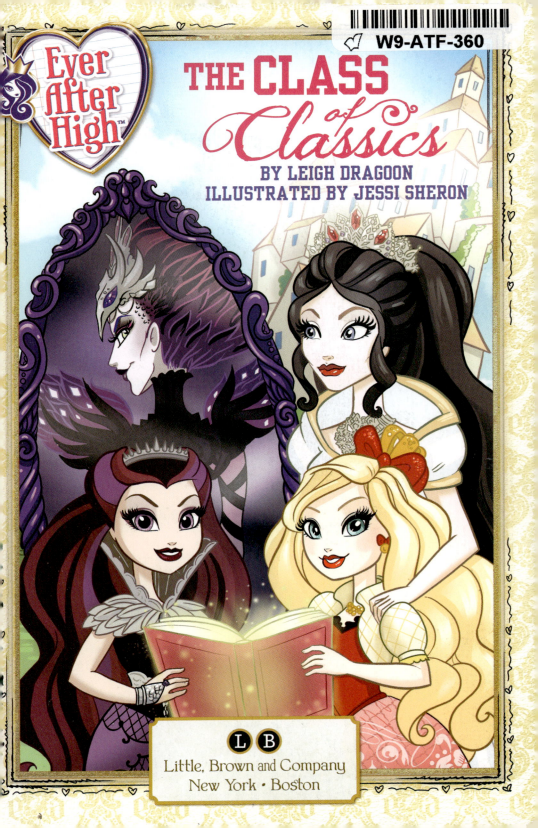

Ever After High™

THE CLASS of Classics

BY LEIGH DRAGOON
ILLUSTRATED BY JESSI SHERON

L B

Little, Brown and Company
New York · Boston

Illustrations by Jessi Sheron

Cover design by Ching N. Chan. Cover illustration by Jessi Sheron.

Little, Brown and Company
Hachette Book Group
1290 Avenue of the Americas, New York, NY 10104
Visit us at lb-kids.com
everafterhigh.com

First Edition: June 2017

Little, Brown and Company is a division of Hachette Book Group, Inc.
The Little, Brown name and logo are trademarks of Hachette Book Group, Inc.

The publisher is not responsible for websites (or their content) that are not owned by the publisher.

Library of Congress Cataloging-in-Publication Data

Names: Dragoon, Leigh, 1976- author | Sheron, Jessi, illustrator.
Title: Ever after high: class of classics: an original graphic novel /
by Leigh Dragoon; illustrations by Jessi Sheron.
Description: First edition. | New York ; Boston: Little, Brown and Company,
2016. | Summary: "When a magical spell goes awry, the teenage children of fairytale classics are
sent into their parents' yearbooks where they learn about the past
and how they came to be who they are today." --Provided by publisher.
Identifiers: LCCN 2016008103 | ISBN 9780316337410 (trade pbk. : alk. paper) |
ISBN 9780316431804 (ebook) | ISBN 9780316436304 (ebook) |
ISBN 9780316436311 (ebook) | ISBN 9780316431798 (library ebook edition)
Subjects: | LCSH: Graphic novels. | CYAC: Graphic novels. |
Characters in literature--Fiction. | Magic--Fiction.
Classification: LCC PZ7.7.D73 Ev 2016 | DDC 741.5/973--dc23
LC record available at https://lccn.loc.gov/2016008103

ISBN: 978-0-316-33741-0 (paperback); 978-0-316-43180-4 (ebook);
978-0-316-43630-4 (ebook); 978-0-316-43631-1 (ebook)

PRINTED IN THE UNITED STATES OF AMERICA

CW

10 9 8 7 6 5 4 3 2 1

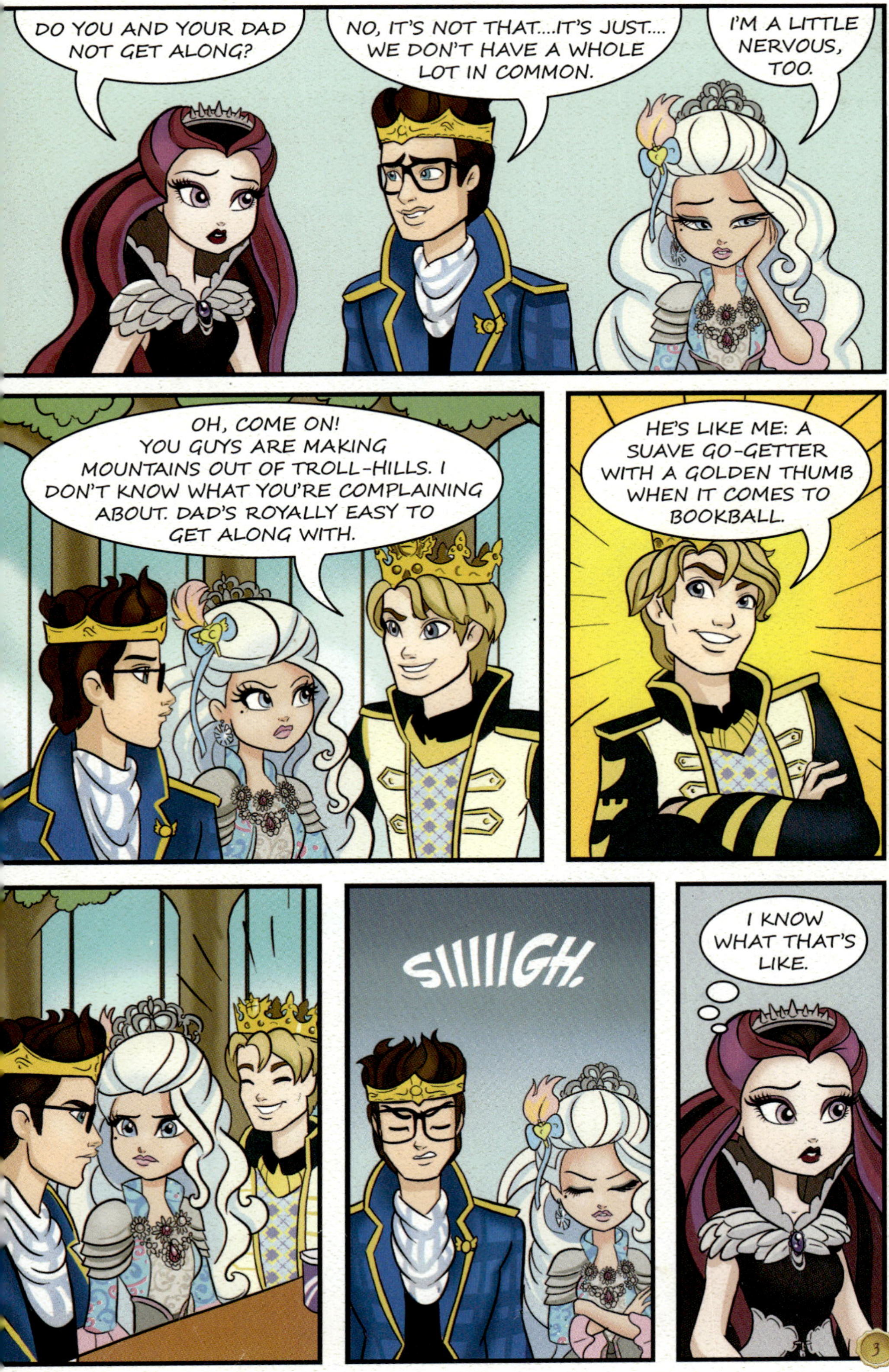
DO YOU AND YOUR DAD NOT GET ALONG?
NO, IT'S NOT THAT....IT'S JUST.... WE DON'T HAVE A WHOLE LOT IN COMMON.
I'M A LITTLE NERVOUS, TOO.
OH, COME ON! YOU GUYS ARE MAKING MOUNTAINS OUT OF TROLL-HILLS. I DON'T KNOW WHAT YOU'RE COMPLAINING ABOUT. DAD'S ROYALLY EASY TO GET ALONG WITH.
HE'S LIKE ME: A SUAVE GO-GETTER WITH A GOLDEN THUMB WHEN IT COMES TO BOOKBALL.
SIIIIIGH.
I KNOW WHAT THAT'S LIKE.

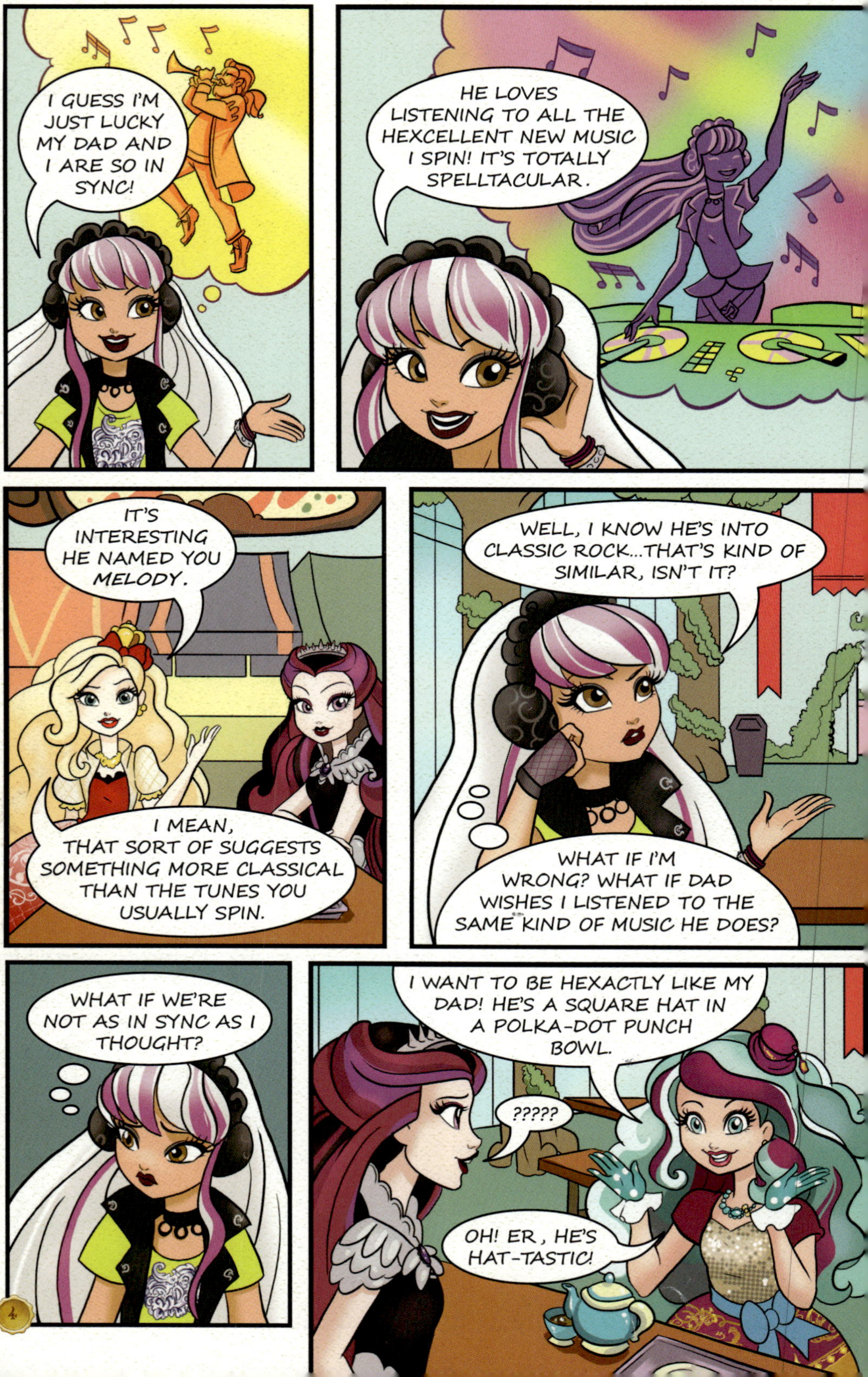
I GUESS I'M JUST LUCKY MY DAD AND I ARE SO IN SYNC!
HE LOVES LISTENING TO ALL THE HEXCELLENT NEW MUSIC I SPIN! IT'S TOTALLY SPELLTACULAR.
IT'S INTERESTING HE NAMED YOU MELODY.
I MEAN, THAT SORT OF SUGGESTS SOMETHING MORE CLASSICAL THAN THE TUNES YOU USUALLY SPIN.
WELL, I KNOW HE'S INTO CLASSIC ROCK...THAT'S KIND OF SIMILAR, ISN'T IT?
WHAT IF I'M WRONG? WHAT IF DAD WISHES I LISTENED TO THE SAME KIND OF MUSIC HE DOES?
WHAT IF WE'RE NOT AS IN SYNC AS I THOUGHT?
I WANT TO BE HEXACTLY LIKE MY DAD! HE'S A SQUARE HAT IN A POLKA-DOT PUNCH BOWL.
?????
OH! ER, HE'S HAT-TASTIC!

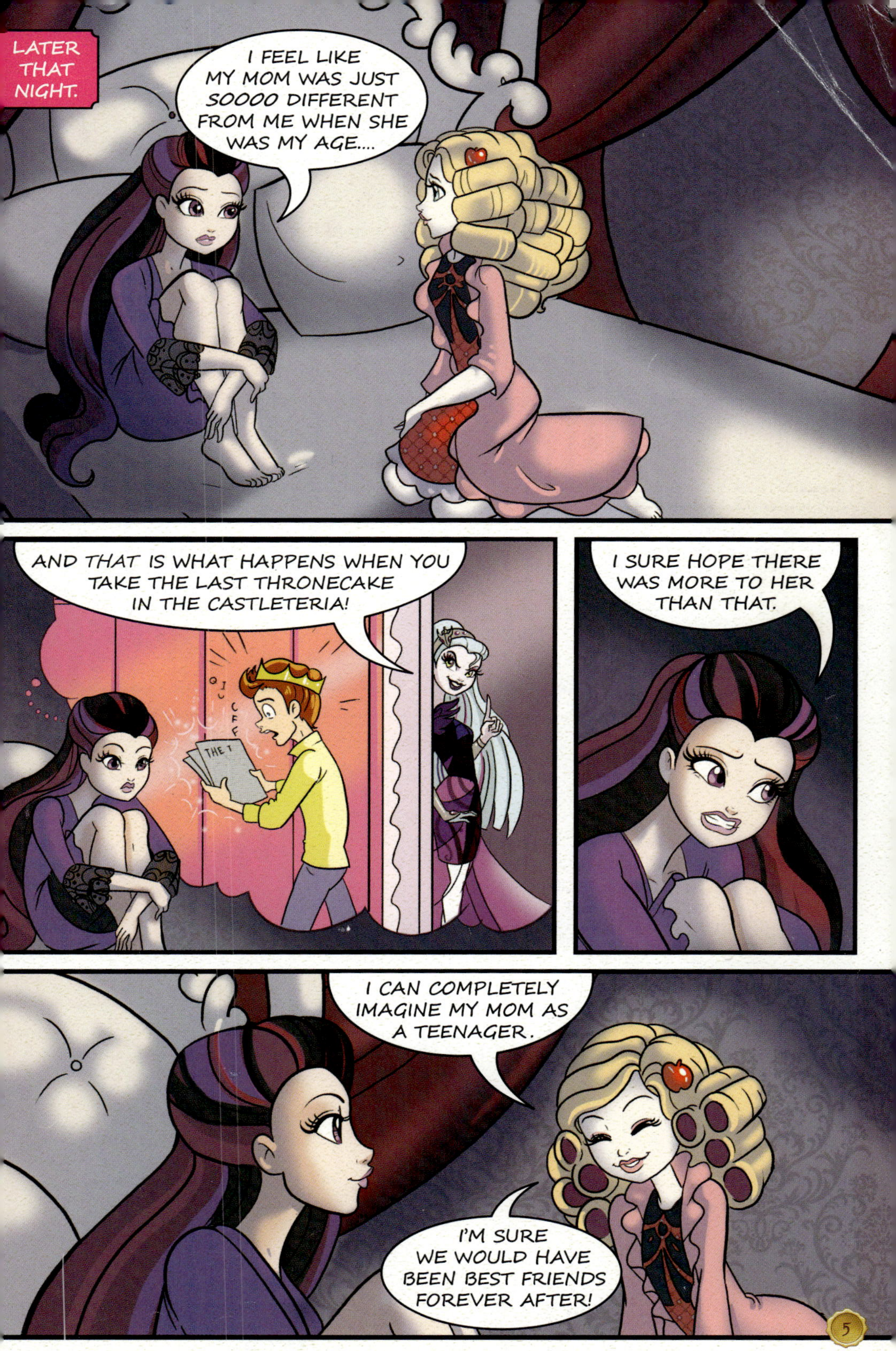
LATER THAT NIGHT.
I FEEL LIKE MY MOM WAS JUST SOOOO DIFFERENT FROM ME WHEN SHE WAS MY AGE....
AND THAT IS WHAT HAPPENS WHEN YOU TAKE THE LAST THRONECAKE IN THE CASTLETERIA!
I SURE HOPE THERE WAS MORE TO HER THAN THAT.
I CAN COMPLETELY IMAGINE MY MOM AS A TEENAGER.
I'M SURE WE WOULD HAVE BEEN BEST FRIENDS FOREVER AFTER!

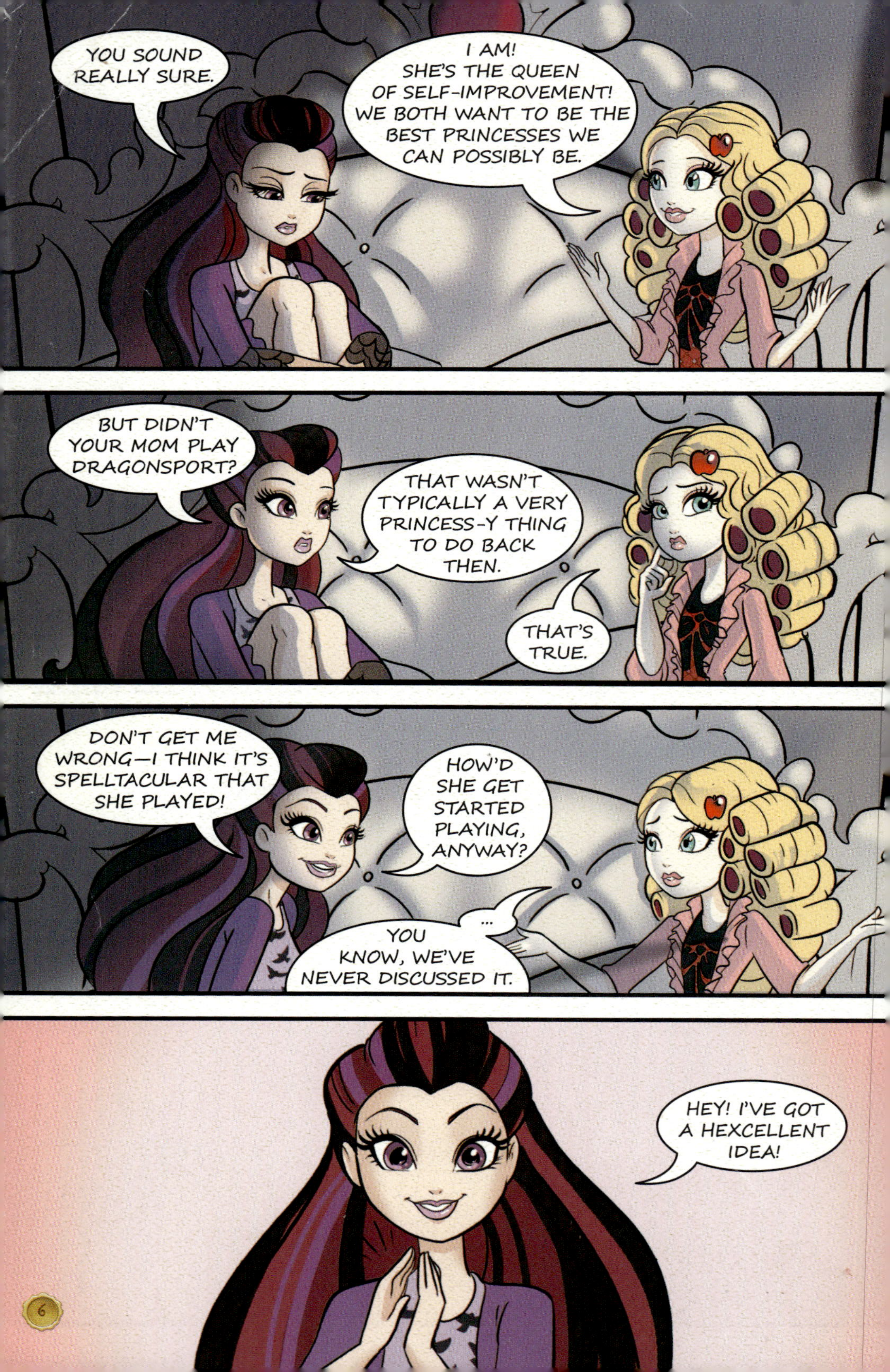
YOU SOUND REALLY SURE.
I AM! SHE'S THE QUEEN OF SELF-IMPROVEMENT! WE BOTH WANT TO BE THE BEST PRINCESSES WE CAN POSSIBLY BE.
BUT DIDN'T YOUR MOM PLAY DRAGONSPORT?
THAT WASN'T TYPICALLY A VERY PRINCESS-Y THING TO DO BACK THEN.
THAT'S TRUE.
DON'T GET ME WRONG—I THINK IT'S SPELLTACULAR THAT SHE PLAYED!
HOW'D SHE GET STARTED PLAYING, ANYWAY?
...
YOU KNOW, WE'VE NEVER DISCUSSED IT.
HEY! I'VE GOT A HEXCELLENT IDEA!
6

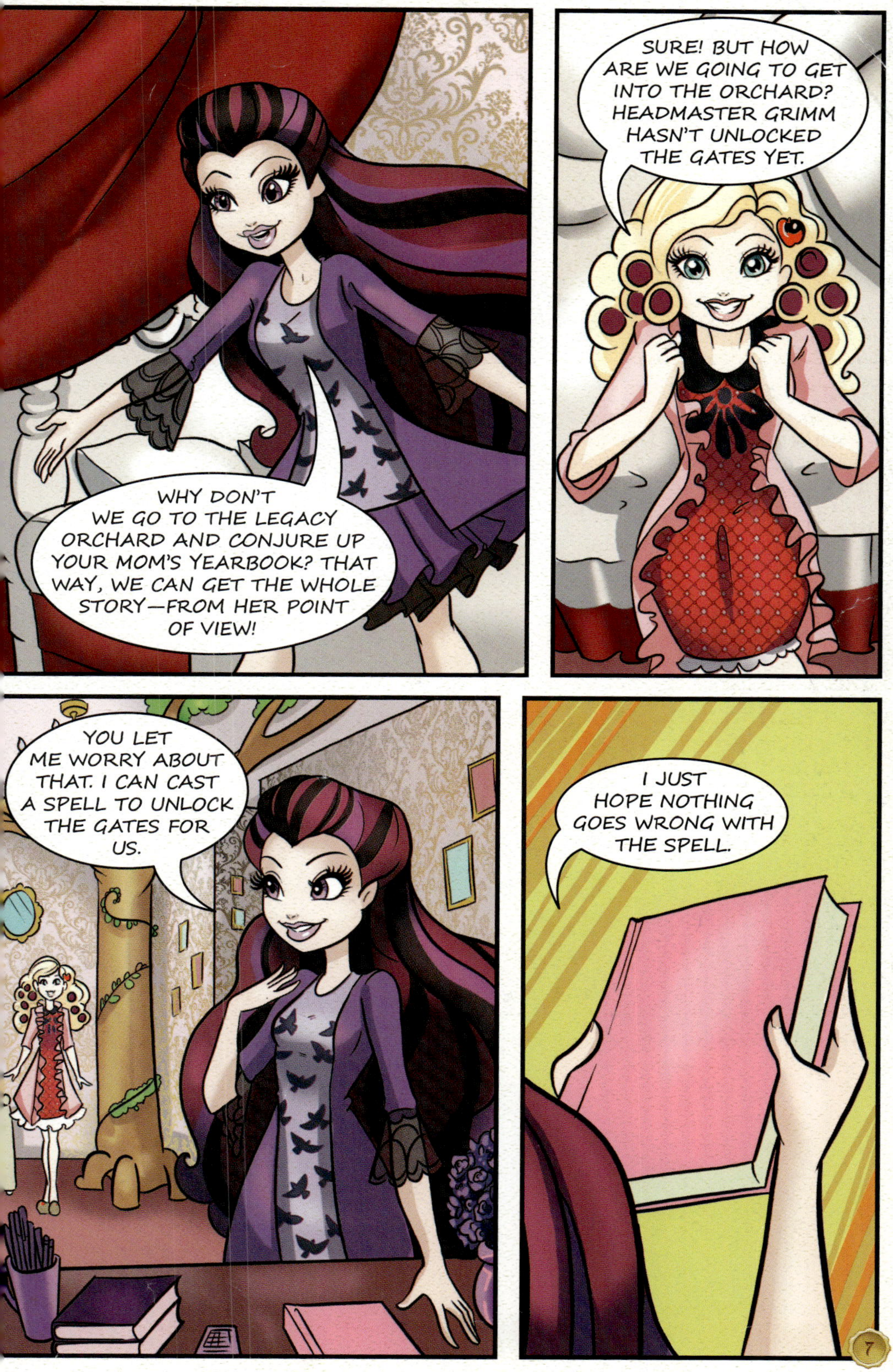
WHY DON'T WE GO TO THE LEGACY ORCHARD AND CONJURE UP YOUR MOM'S YEARBOOK? THAT WAY, WE CAN GET THE WHOLE STORY—FROM HER POINT OF VIEW!
SURE! BUT HOW ARE WE GOING TO GET INTO THE ORCHARD? HEADMASTER GRIMM HASN'T UNLOCKED THE GATES YET.
YOU LET ME WORRY ABOUT THAT. I CAN CAST A SPELL TO UNLOCK THE GATES FOR US.
I JUST HOPE NOTHING GOES WRONG WITH THE SPELL.

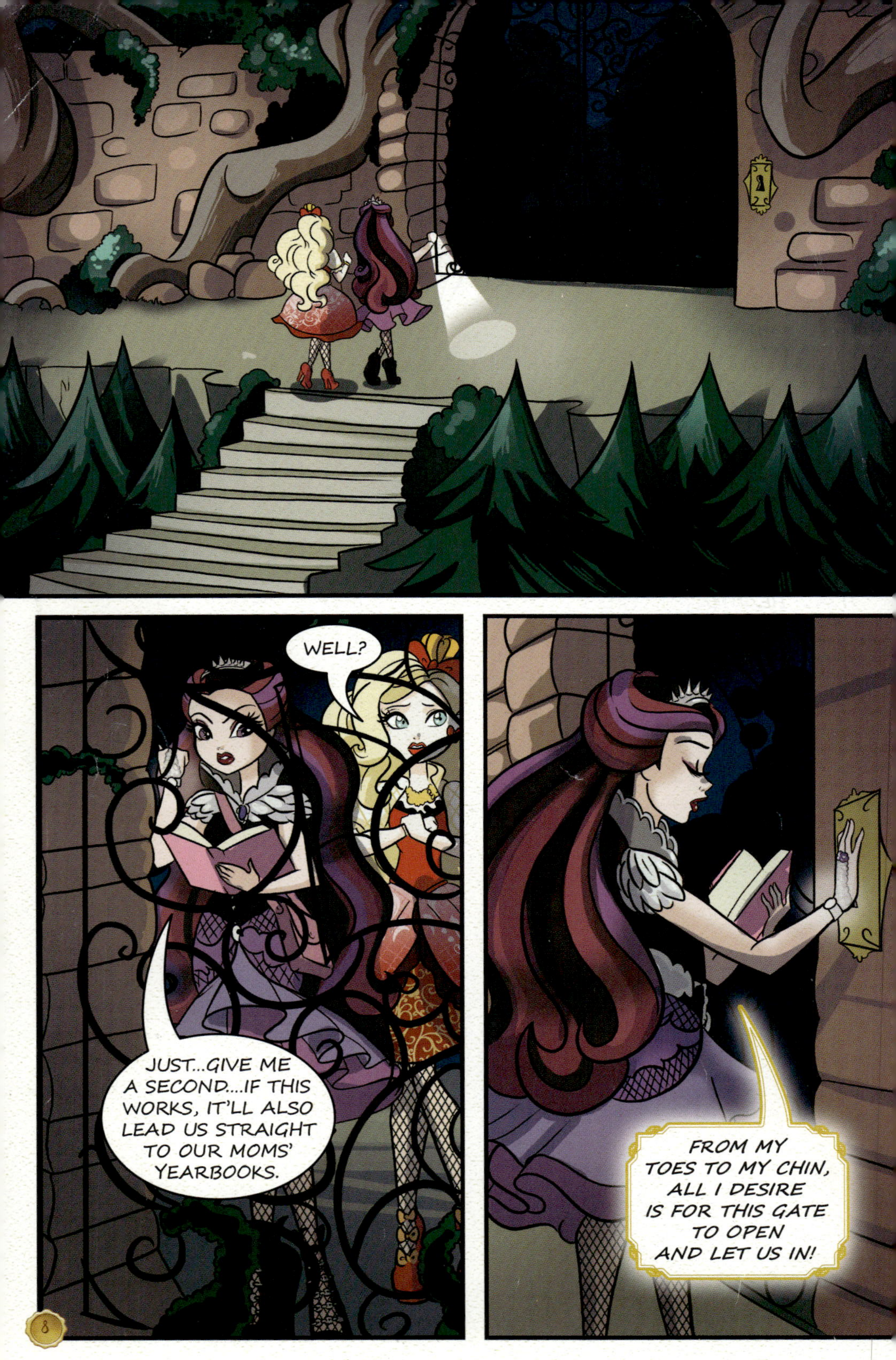
WELL?
JUST...GIVE ME A SECOND....IF THIS WORKS, IT'LL ALSO LEAD US STRAIGHT TO OUR MOMS' YEARBOOKS.
FROM MY TOES TO MY CHIN, ALL I DESIRE IS FOR THIS GATE TO OPEN AND LET US IN!

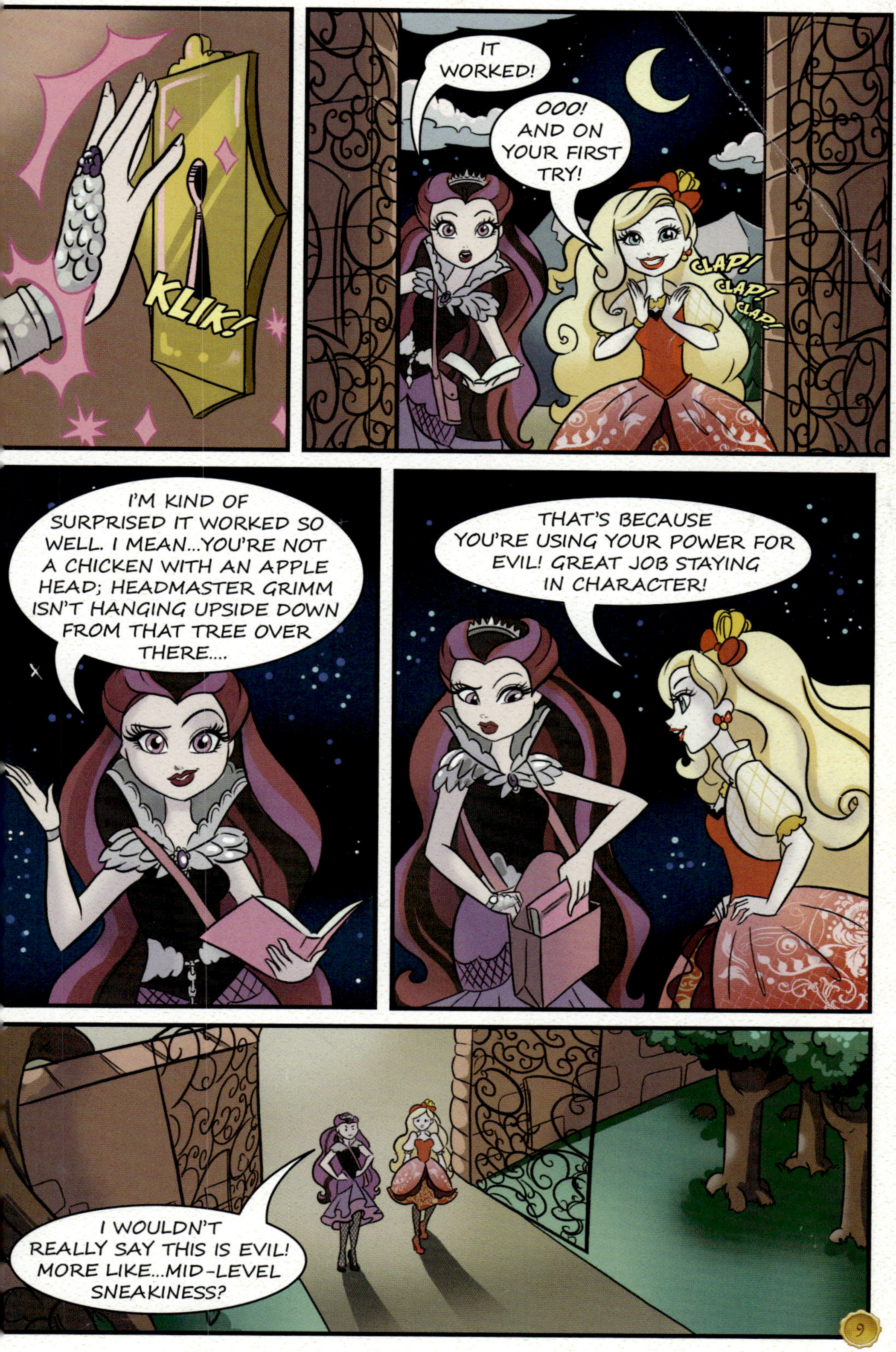
KLIK!
IT WORKED!
OOO! AND ON YOUR FIRST TRY!
CLAP! CLAP! CLAP!
I'M KIND OF SURPRISED IT WORKED SO WELL. I MEAN...YOU'RE NOT A CHICKEN WITH AN APPLE HEAD; HEADMASTER GRIMM ISN'T HANGING UPSIDE DOWN FROM THAT TREE OVER THERE....
THAT'S BECAUSE YOU'RE USING YOUR POWER FOR EVIL! GREAT JOB STAYING IN CHARACTER!
I WOULDN'T REALLY SAY THIS IS EVIL! MORE LIKE...MID-LEVEL SNEAKINESS?

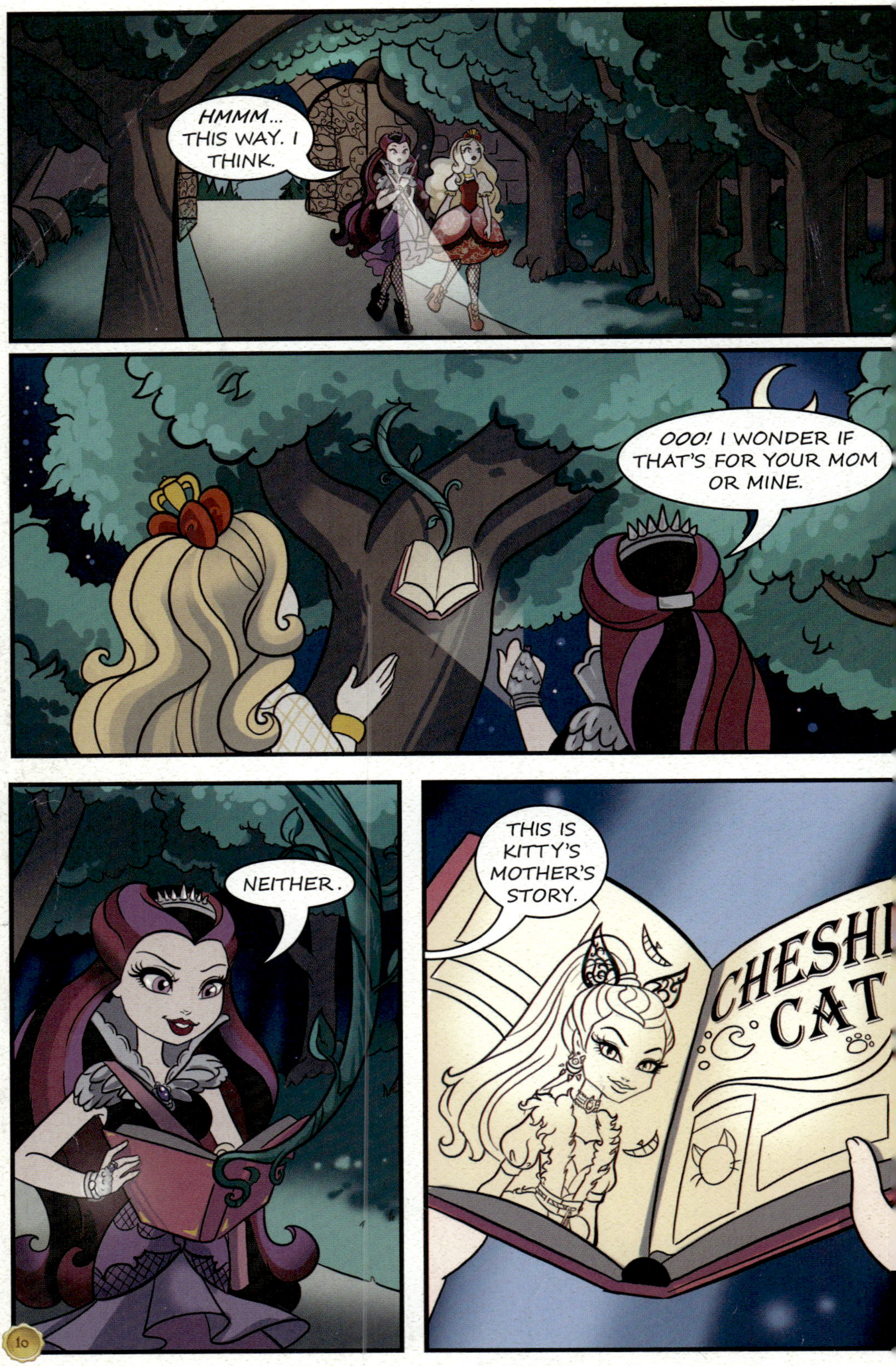
HMMM... THIS WAY. I THINK.
OOO! I WONDER IF THAT'S FOR YOUR MOM OR MINE.
NEITHER.
THIS IS KITTY'S MOTHER'S STORY.
CHESHI CAT

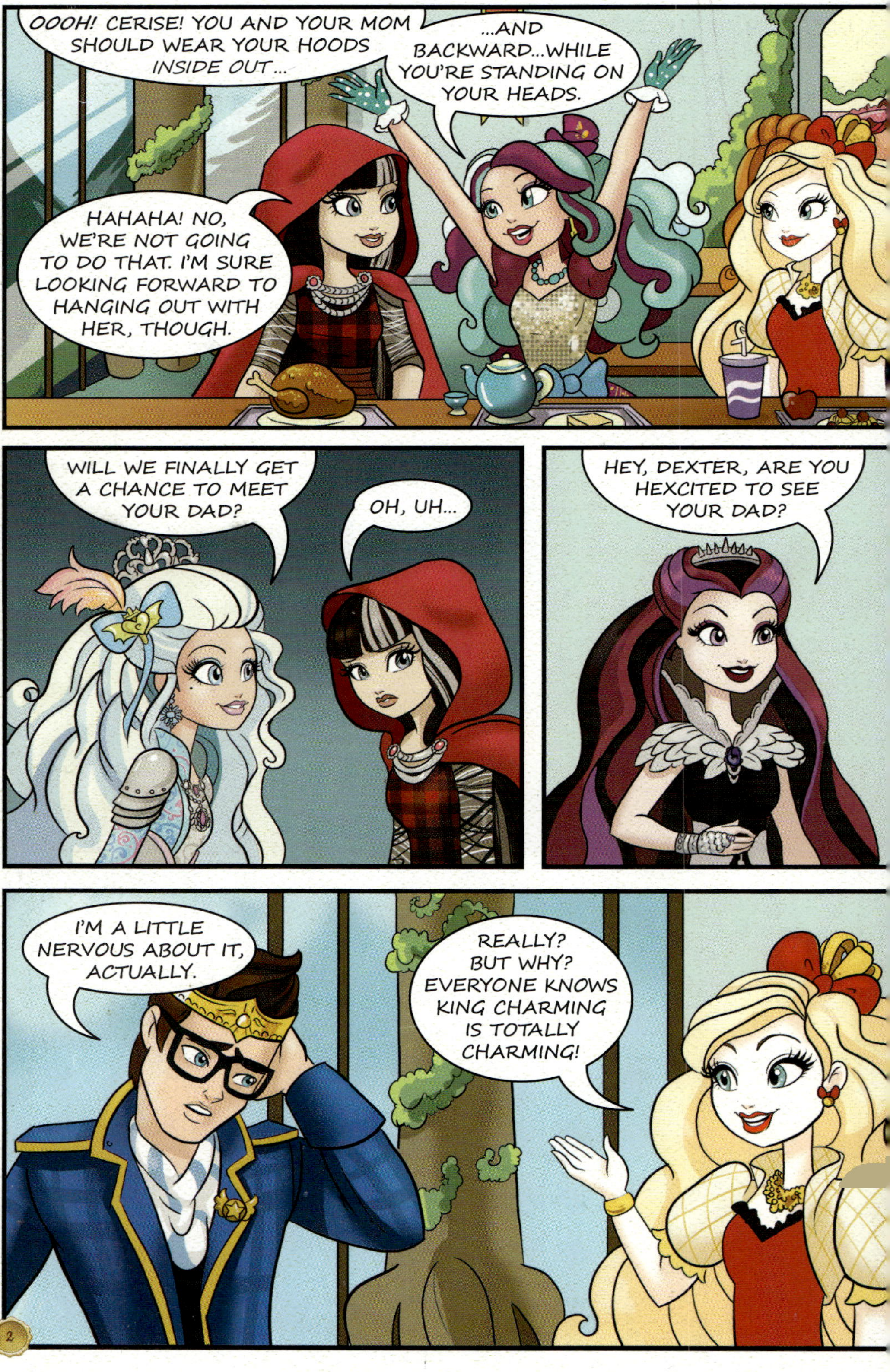
OOOH! CERISE! YOU AND YOUR MOM SHOULD WEAR YOUR HOODS INSIDE OUT...
...AND BACKWARD...WHILE YOU'RE STANDING ON YOUR HEADS.
HAHAHA! NO, WE'RE NOT GOING TO DO THAT. I'M SURE LOOKING FORWARD TO HANGING OUT WITH HER, THOUGH.
WILL WE FINALLY GET A CHANCE TO MEET YOUR DAD?
OH, UH...
HEY, DEXTER, ARE YOU HEXCITED TO SEE YOUR DAD?
I'M A LITTLE NERVOUS ABOUT IT, ACTUALLY.
REALLY? BUT WHY? EVERYONE KNOWS KING CHARMING IS TOTALLY CHARMING!

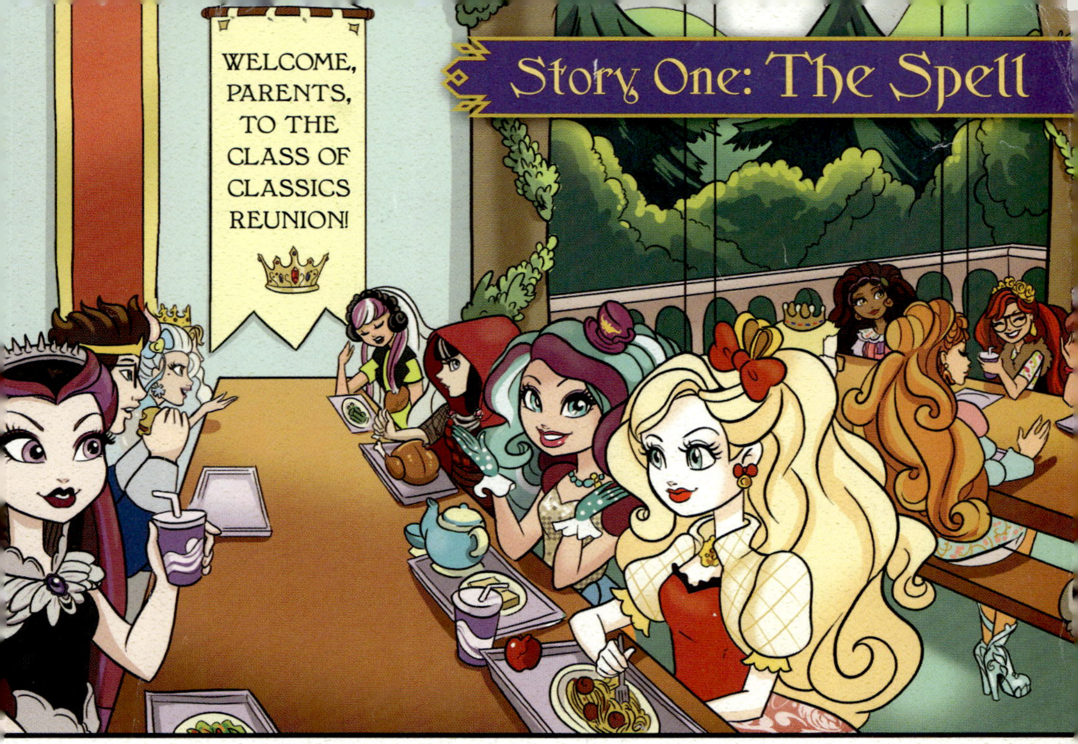
Story One: The Spell
WELCOME, PARENTS, TO THE CLASS OF CLASSICS REUNION!

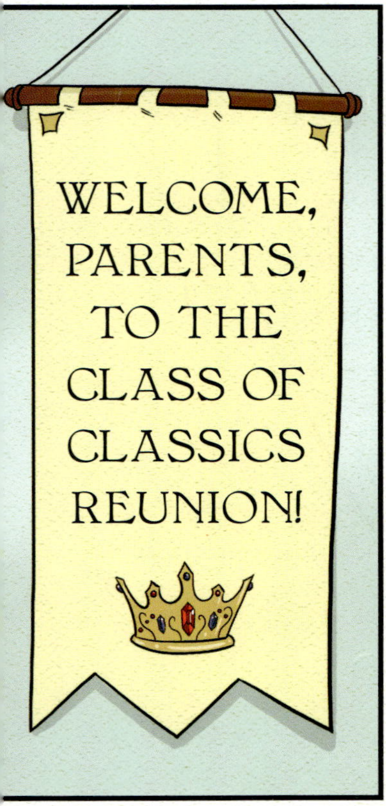
WELCOME, PARENTS, TO THE CLASS OF CLASSICS REUNION!

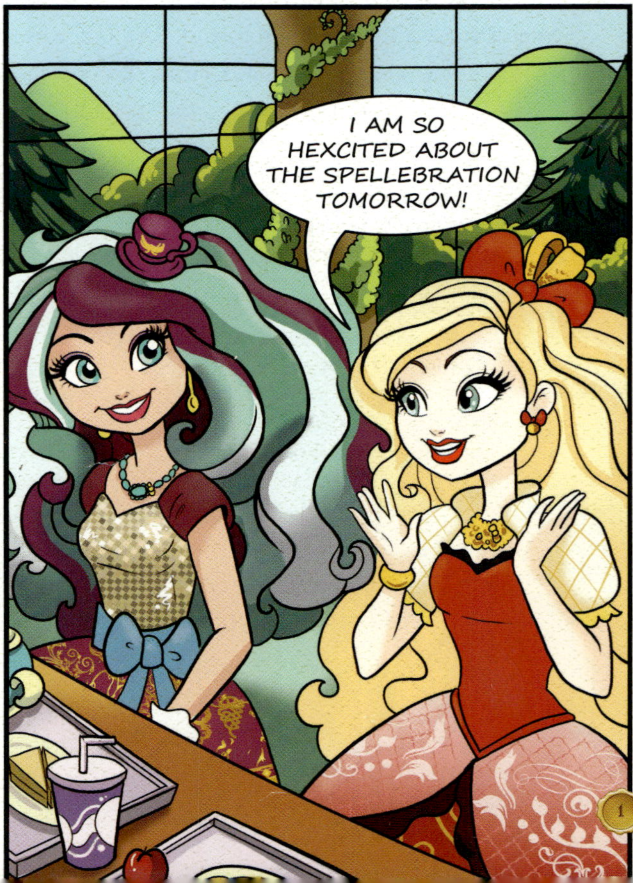
I AM SO HEXCITED ABOUT THE SPELLEBRATION TOMORROW!

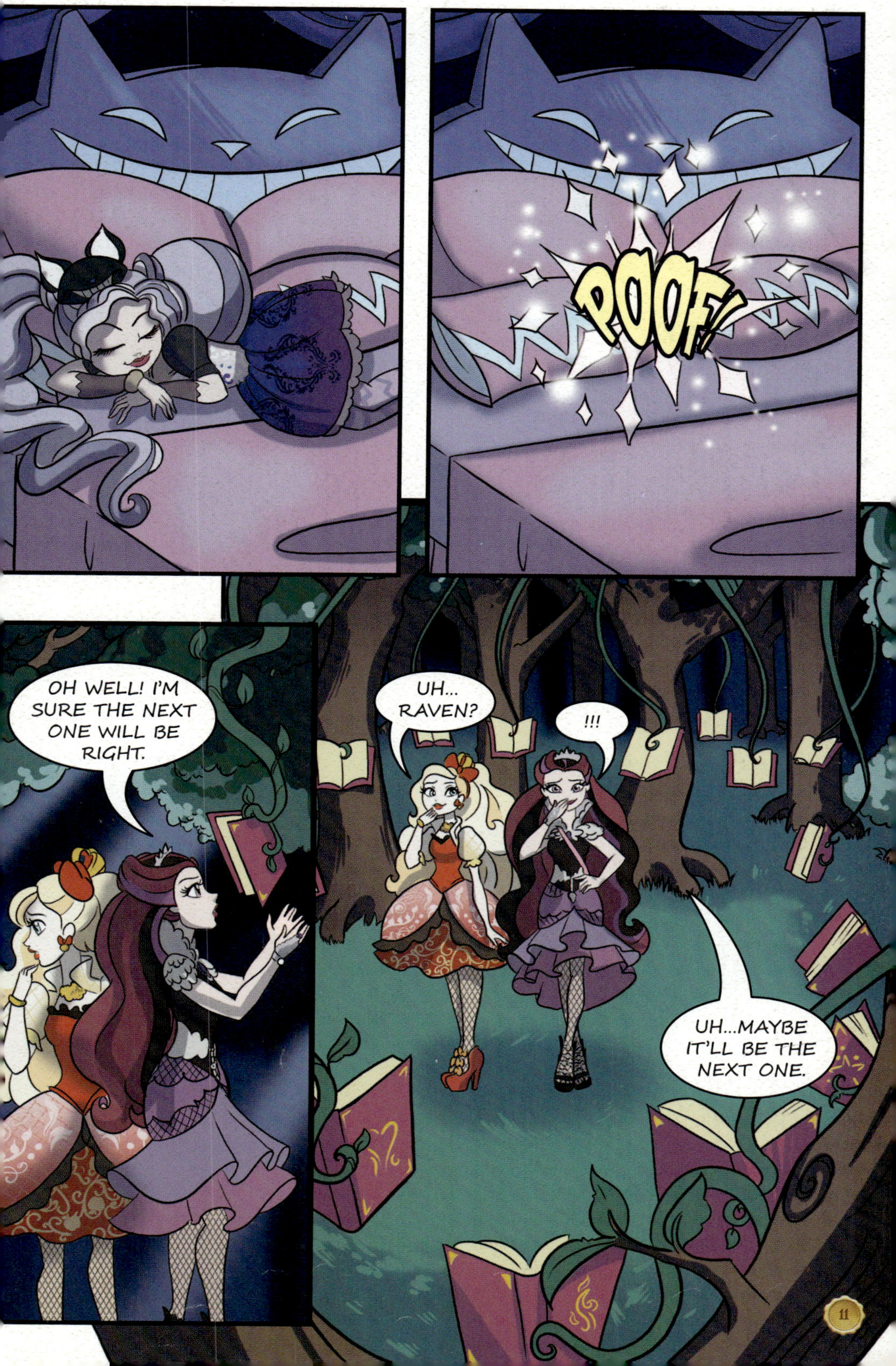
POOF!
OH WELL! I'M SURE THE NEXT ONE WILL BE RIGHT.
UH... RAVEN?
!!!
UH...MAYBE IT'LL BE THE NEXT ONE.

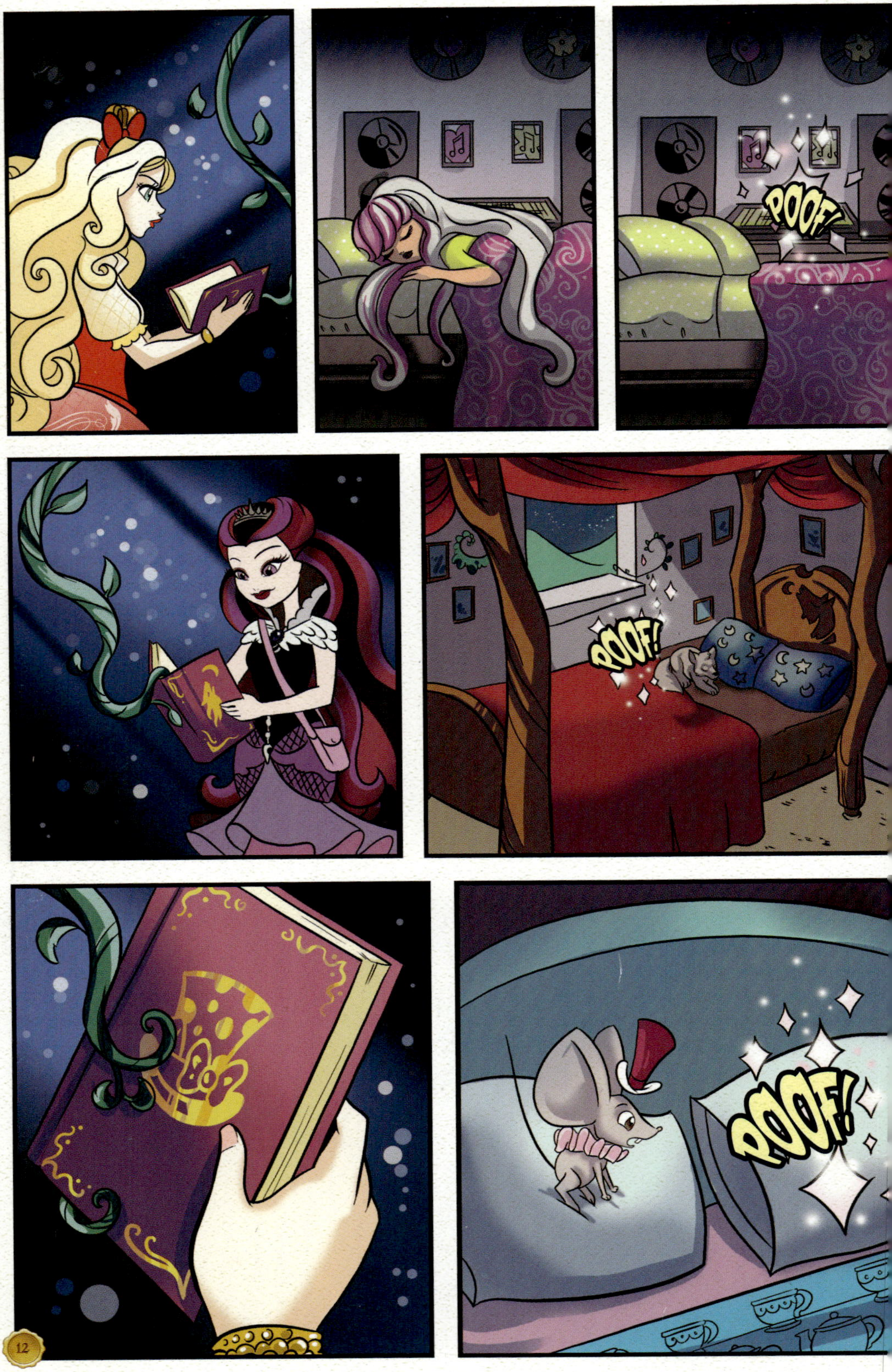
POOF!
POOF!
POOF!

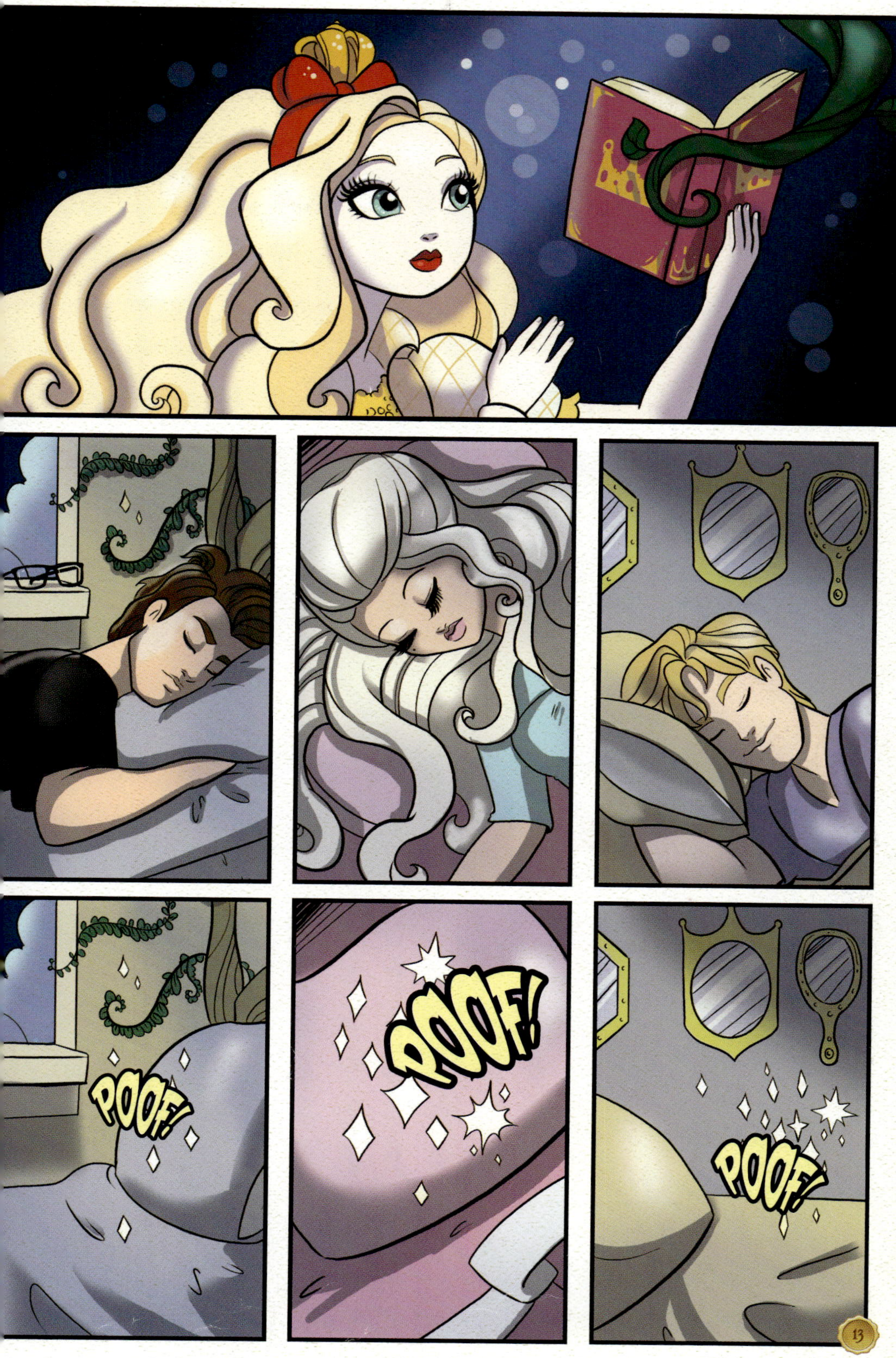
POOF!
POOF!
POOF!

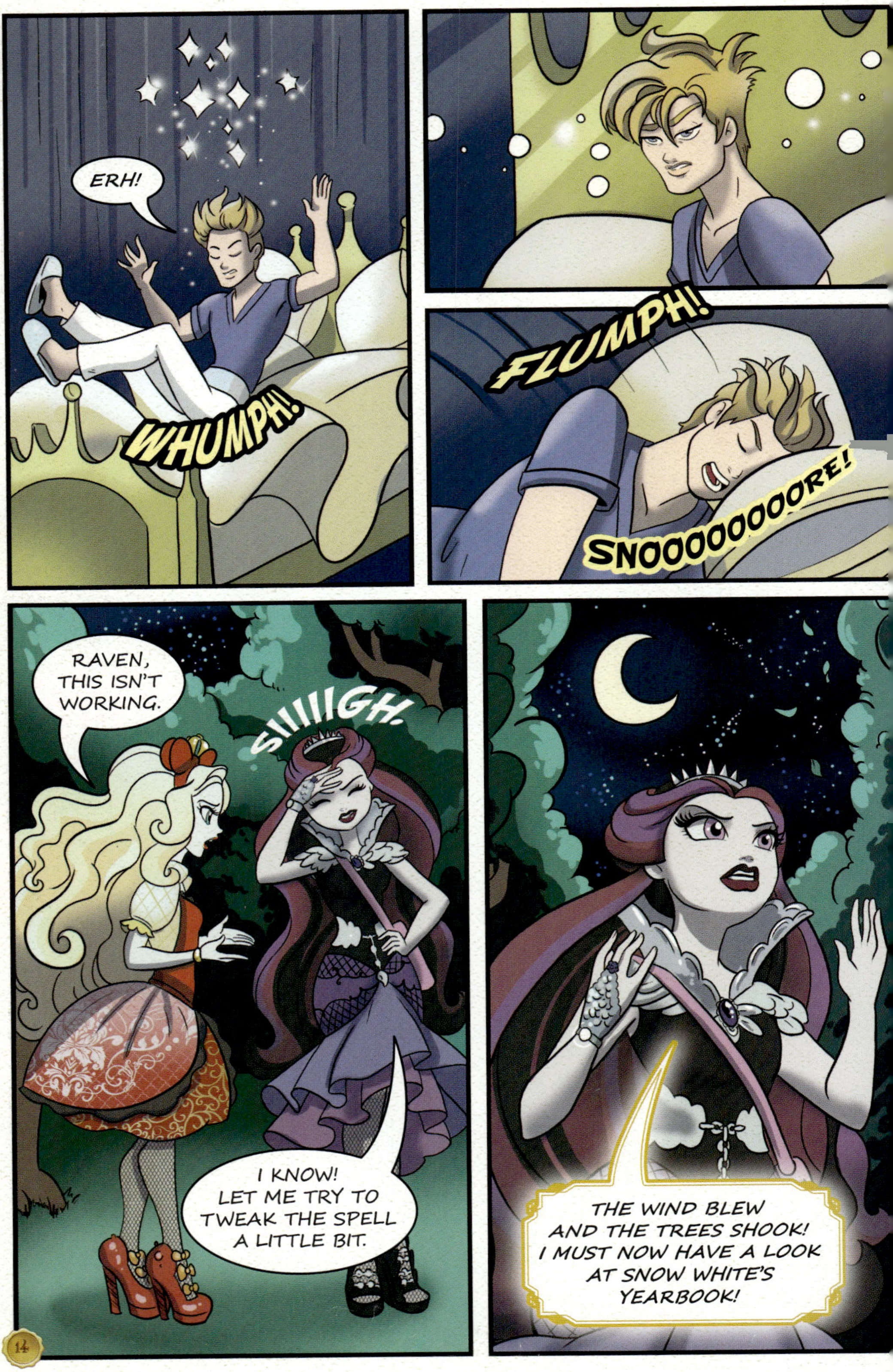
ERH!
WHUMPH!
FLUMPH!
SNOOOOOOOOORE!
RAVEN, THIS ISN'T WORKING.
SIIIIIGH.
I KNOW! LET ME TRY TO TWEAK THE SPELL A LITTLE BIT.
THE WIND BLEW AND THE TREES SHOOK! I MUST NOW HAVE A LOOK AT SNOW WHITE'S YEARBOOK!

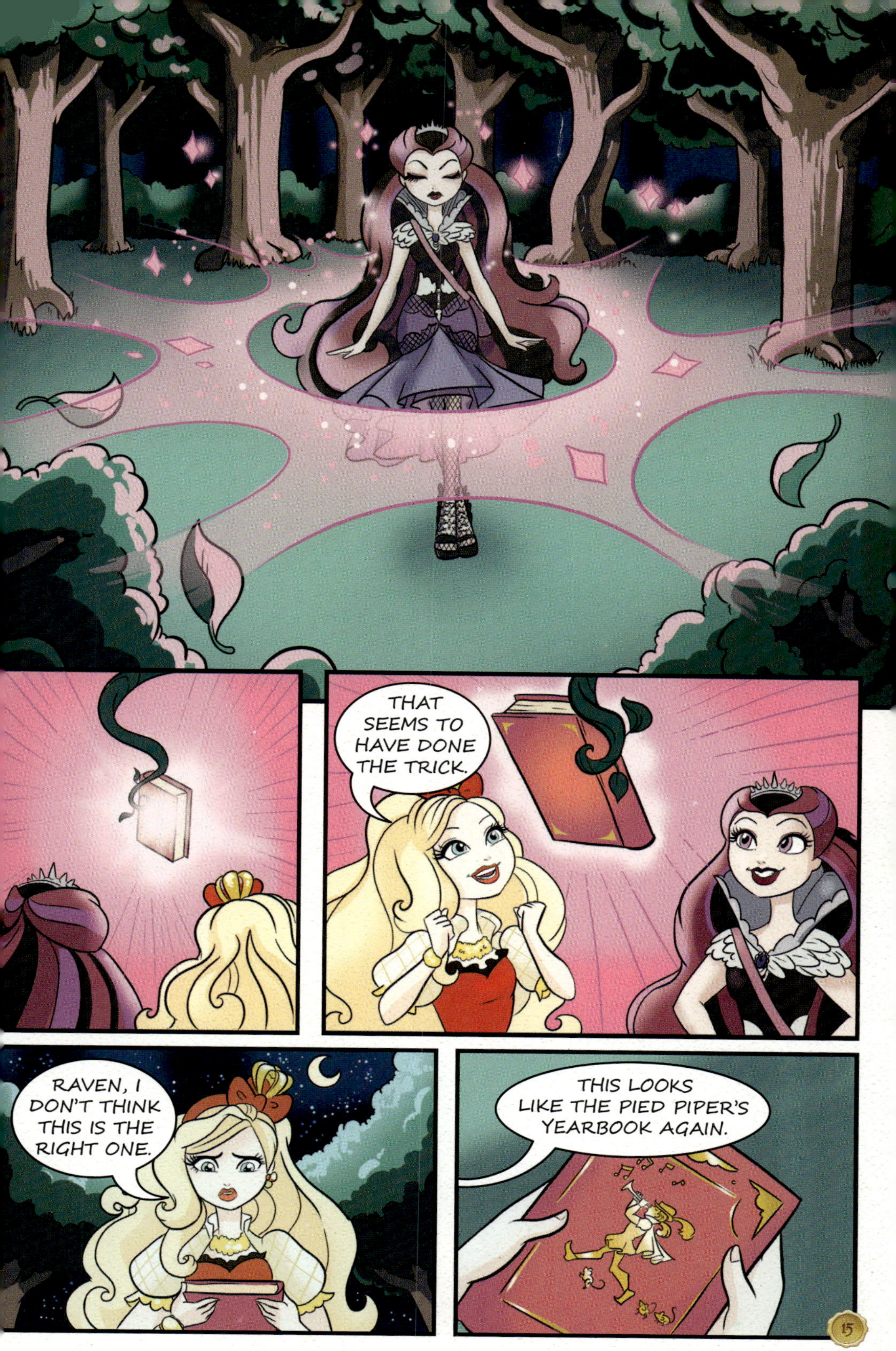
THAT SEEMS TO HAVE DONE THE TRICK.
RAVEN, I DON'T THINK THIS IS THE RIGHT ONE.
THIS LOOKS LIKE THE PIED PIPER'S YEARBOOK AGAIN.

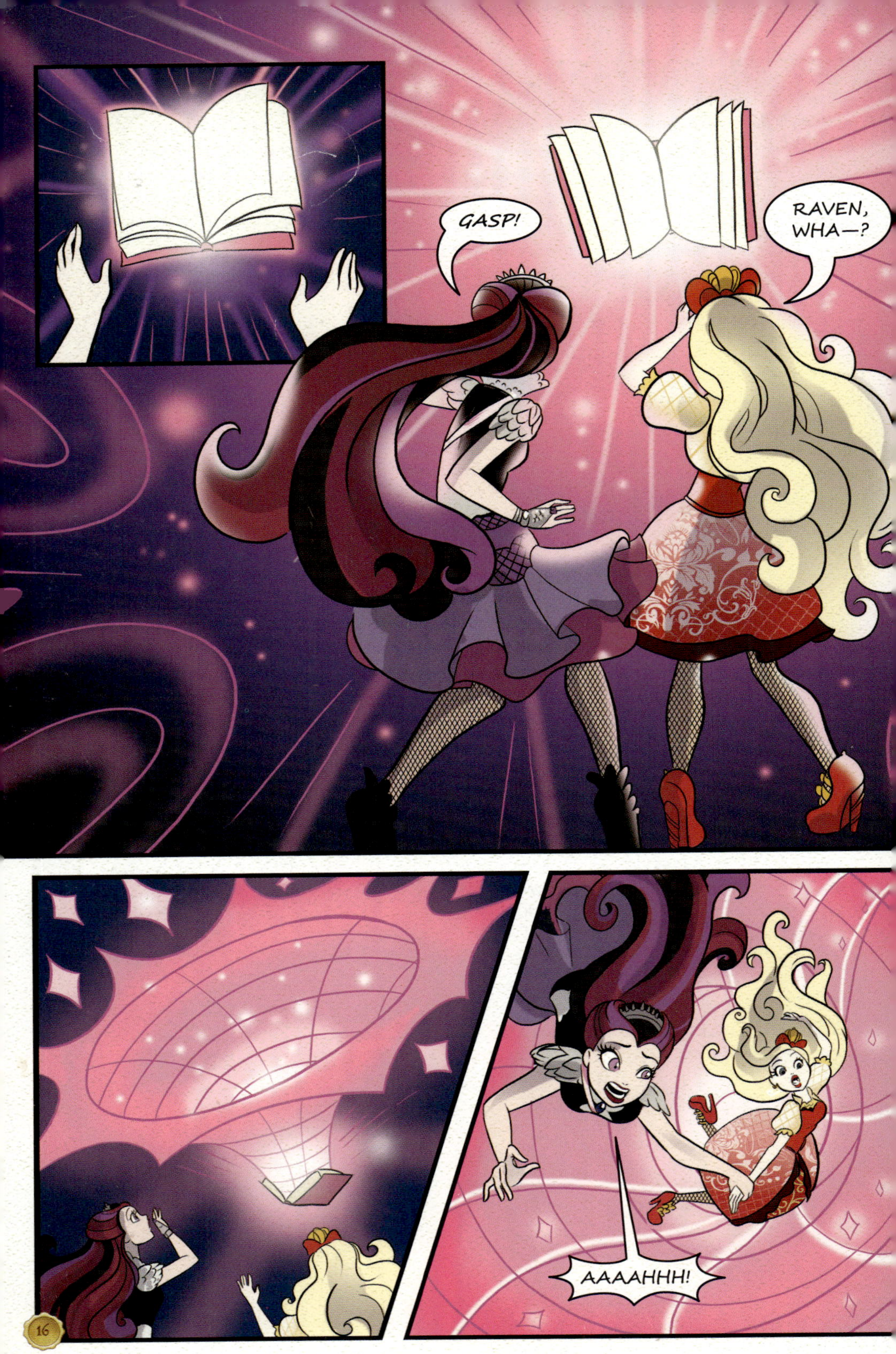
GASP!
RAVEN, WHA—?
AAAAHHH!

Story Two: Pied Piper

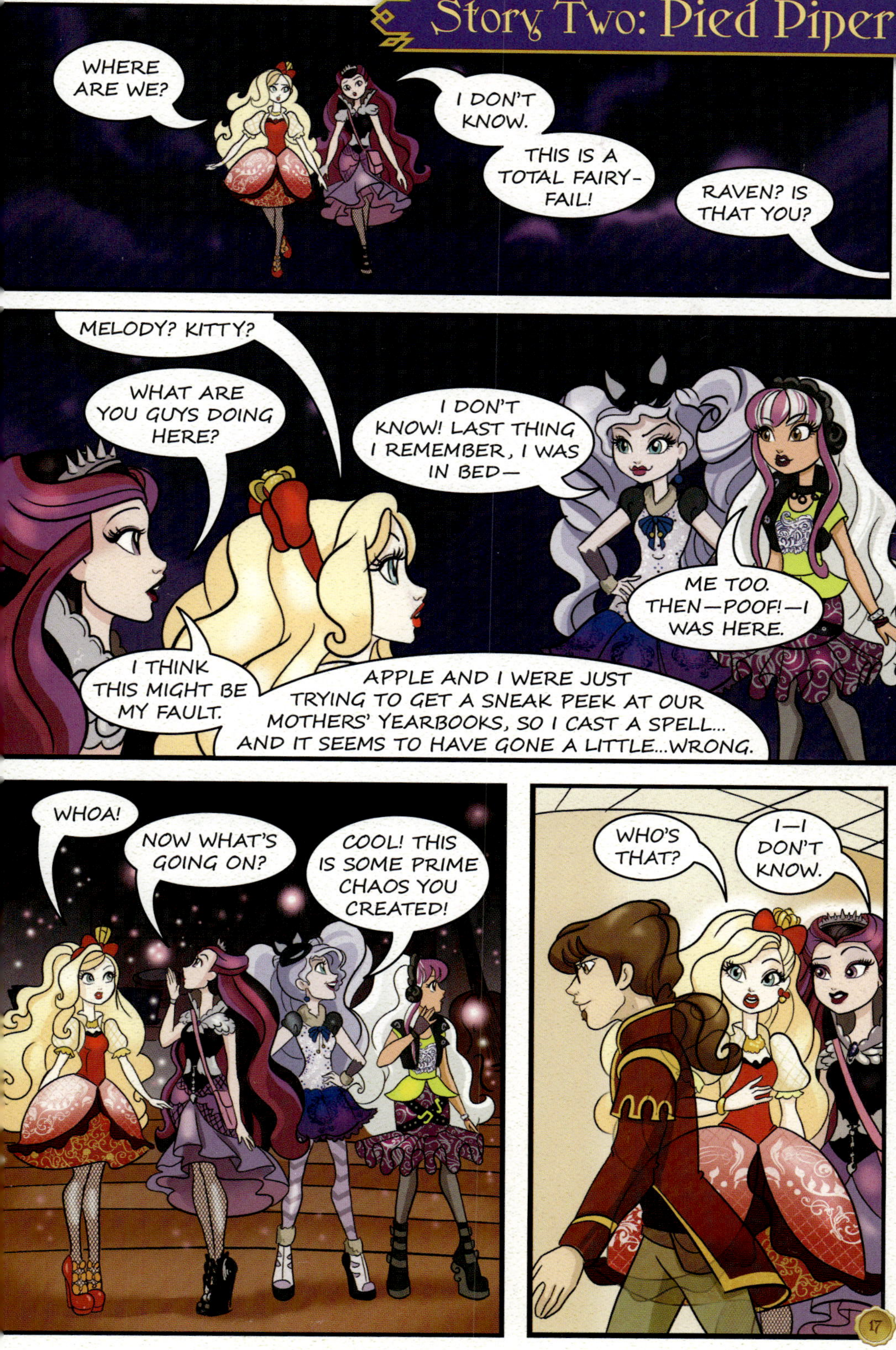
WHERE ARE WE?
I DON'T KNOW.
THIS IS A TOTAL FAIRY-FAIL!
RAVEN? IS THAT YOU?
MELODY? KITTY?
WHAT ARE YOU GUYS DOING HERE?
I DON'T KNOW! LAST THING I REMEMBER, I WAS IN BED—
ME TOO. THEN—POOF!—I WAS HERE.
I THINK THIS MIGHT BE MY FAULT.
APPLE AND I WERE JUST TRYING TO GET A SNEAK PEEK AT OUR MOTHERS' YEARBOOKS, SO I CAST A SPELL... AND IT SEEMS TO HAVE GONE A LITTLE...WRONG.
WHOA!
NOW WHAT'S GOING ON?
COOL! THIS IS SOME PRIME CHAOS YOU CREATED!
WHO'S THAT?
I—I DON'T KNOW.

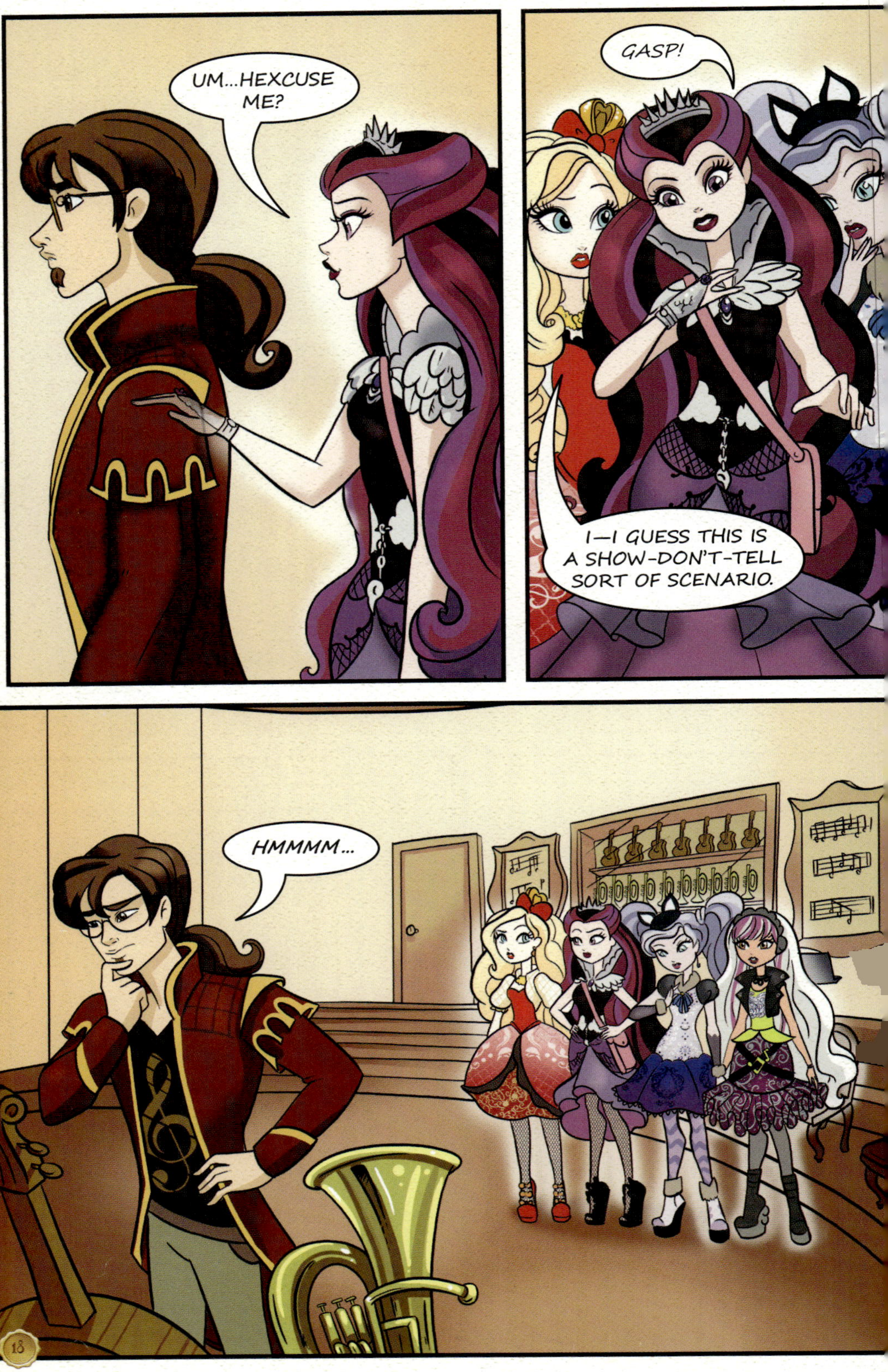
UM...HEXCUSE ME?
GASP!
I—I GUESS THIS IS A SHOW-DON'T-TELL SORT OF SCENARIO.
HMMMM...

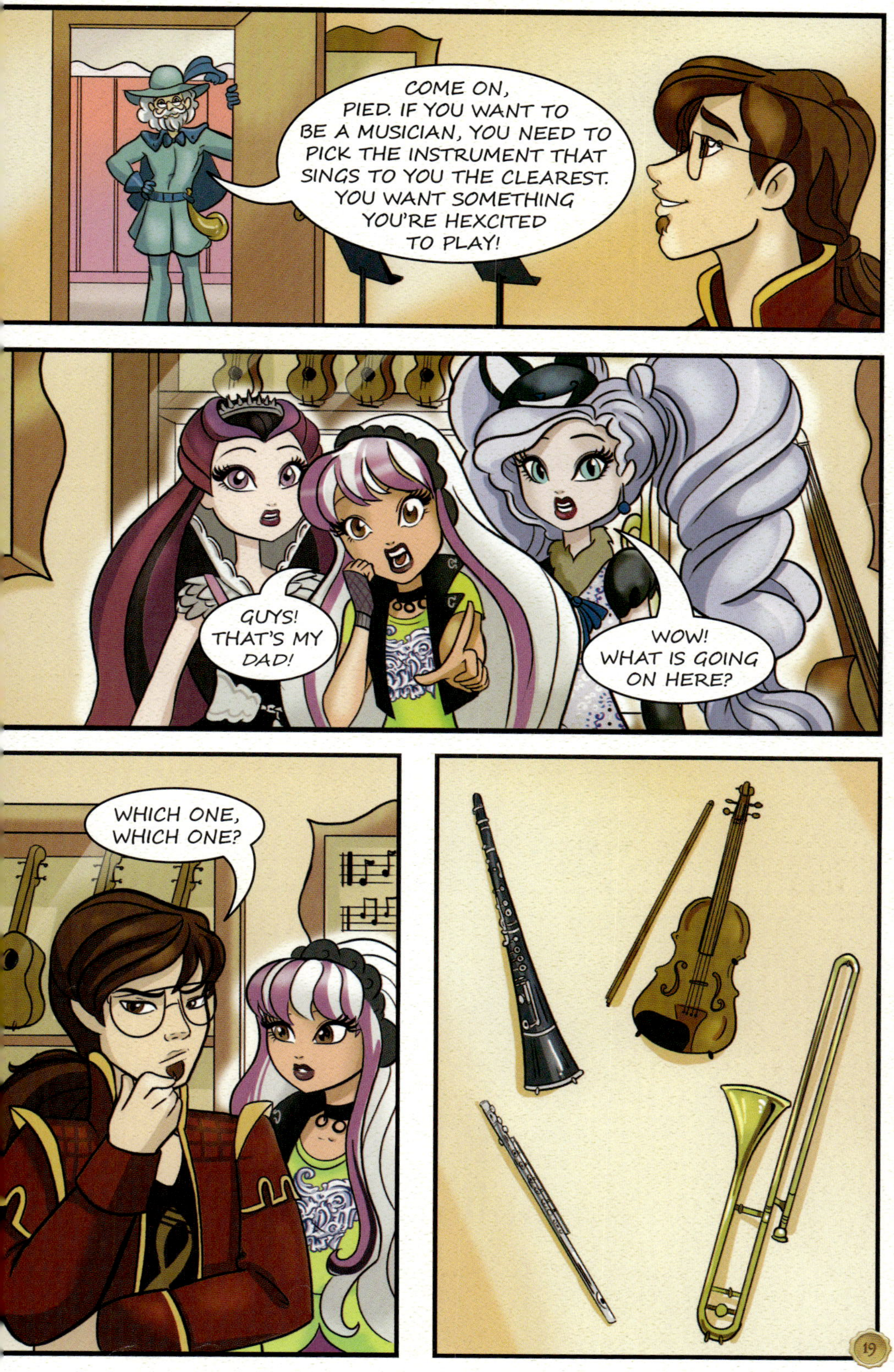
COME ON, PIED. IF YOU WANT TO BE A MUSICIAN, YOU NEED TO PICK THE INSTRUMENT THAT SINGS TO YOU THE CLEAREST. YOU WANT SOMETHING YOU'RE HEXCITED TO PLAY!
GUYS! THAT'S MY DAD!
WOW! WHAT IS GOING ON HERE?
WHICH ONE, WHICH ONE?

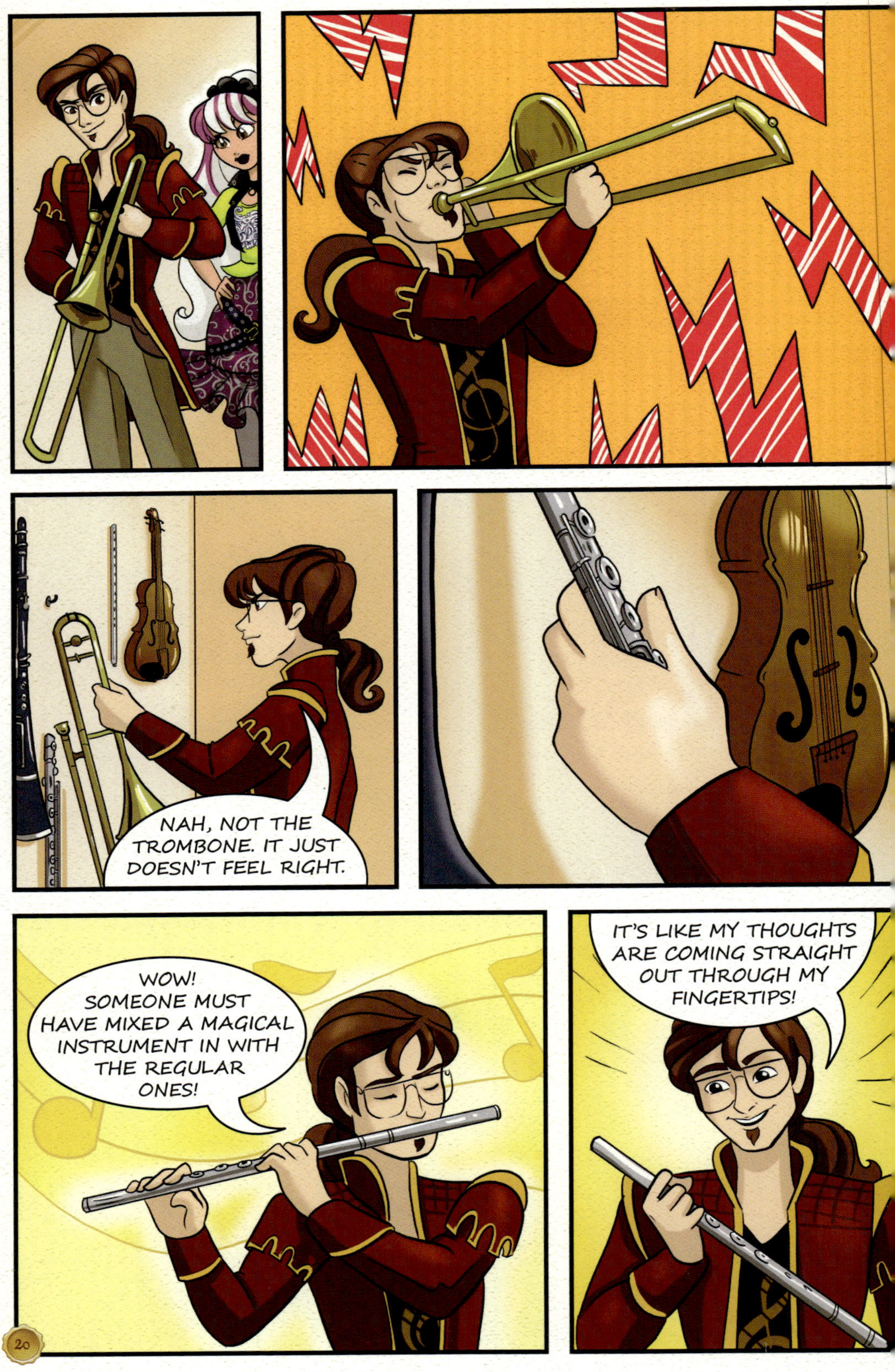
NAH, NOT THE TROMBONE. IT JUST DOESN'T FEEL RIGHT.
WOW! SOMEONE MUST HAVE MIXED A MAGICAL INSTRUMENT IN WITH THE REGULAR ONES!
IT'S LIKE MY THOUGHTS ARE COMING STRAIGHT OUT THROUGH MY FINGERTIPS!

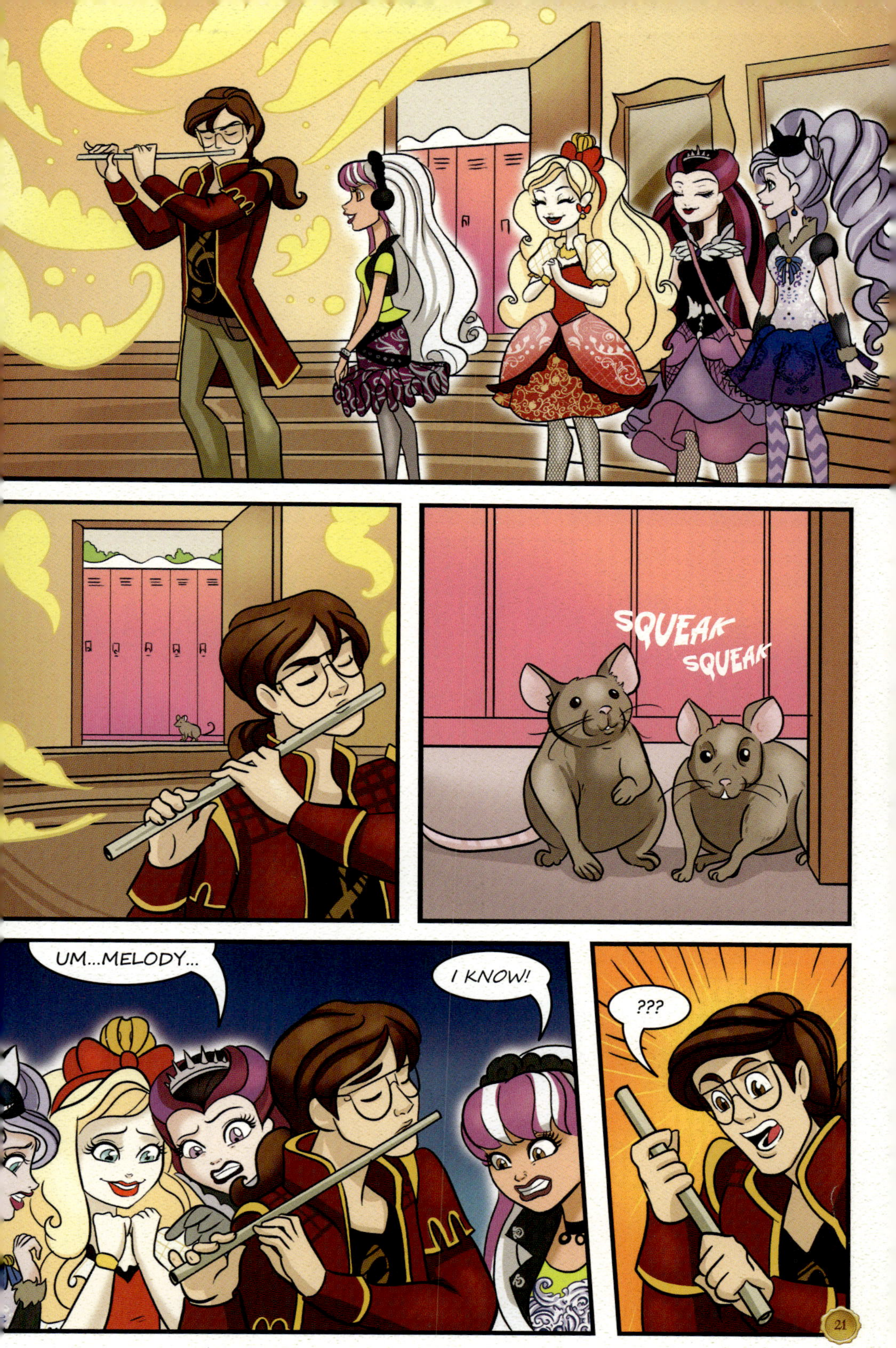
SQUEAK
SQUEAK
UM...MELODY...
I KNOW!
???

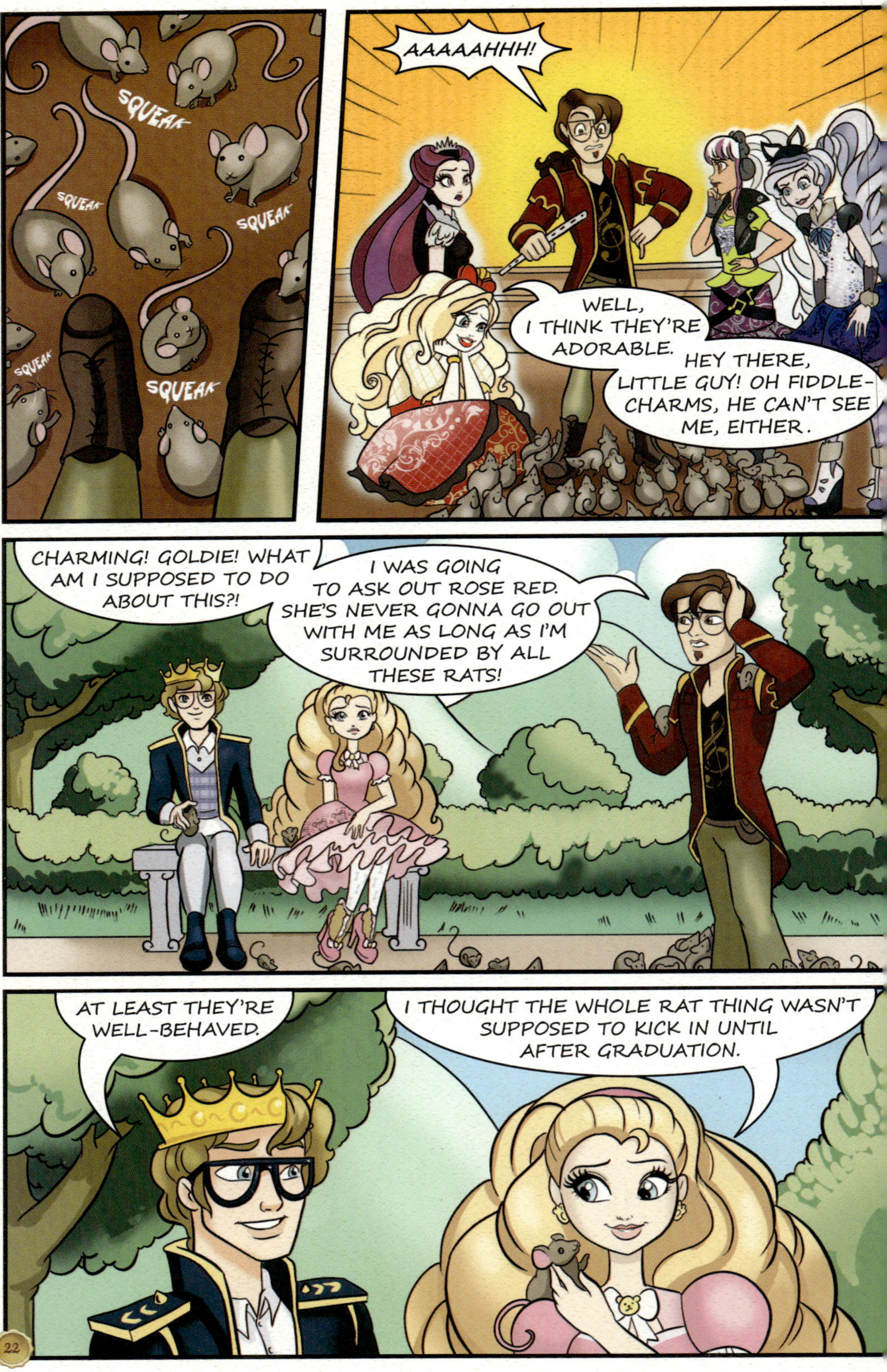
SQUEAK
SQUEAK
SQUEAK
SQUEAK
SQUEAK
AAAAAHHH!
WELL, I THINK THEY'RE ADORABLE.
HEY THERE, LITTLE GUY! OH FIDDLE-CHARMS, HE CAN'T SEE ME, EITHER.
CHARMING! GOLDIE! WHAT AM I SUPPOSED TO DO ABOUT THIS?!
I WAS GOING TO ASK OUT ROSE RED. SHE'S NEVER GONNA GO OUT WITH ME AS LONG AS I'M SURROUNDED BY ALL THESE RATS!
AT LEAST THEY'RE WELL-BEHAVED.
I THOUGHT THE WHOLE RAT THING WASN'T SUPPOSED TO KICK IN UNTIL AFTER GRADUATION.

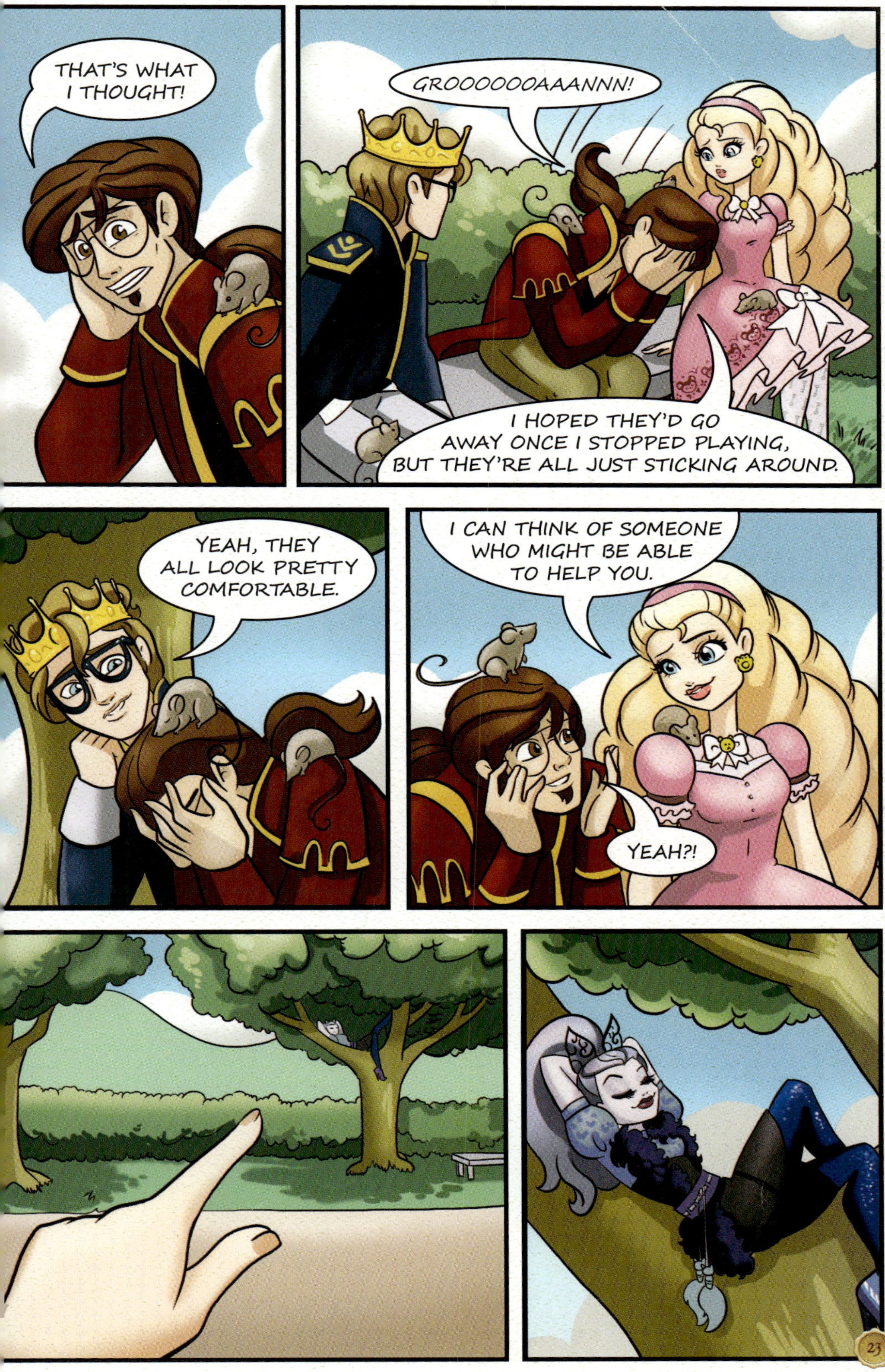
THAT'S WHAT I THOUGHT!
GROOOOOOAAANNN!
I HOPED THEY'D GO AWAY ONCE I STOPPED PLAYING, BUT THEY'RE ALL JUST STICKING AROUND.
YEAH, THEY ALL LOOK PRETTY COMFORTABLE.
I CAN THINK OF SOMEONE WHO MIGHT BE ABLE TO HELP YOU.
YEAH?!

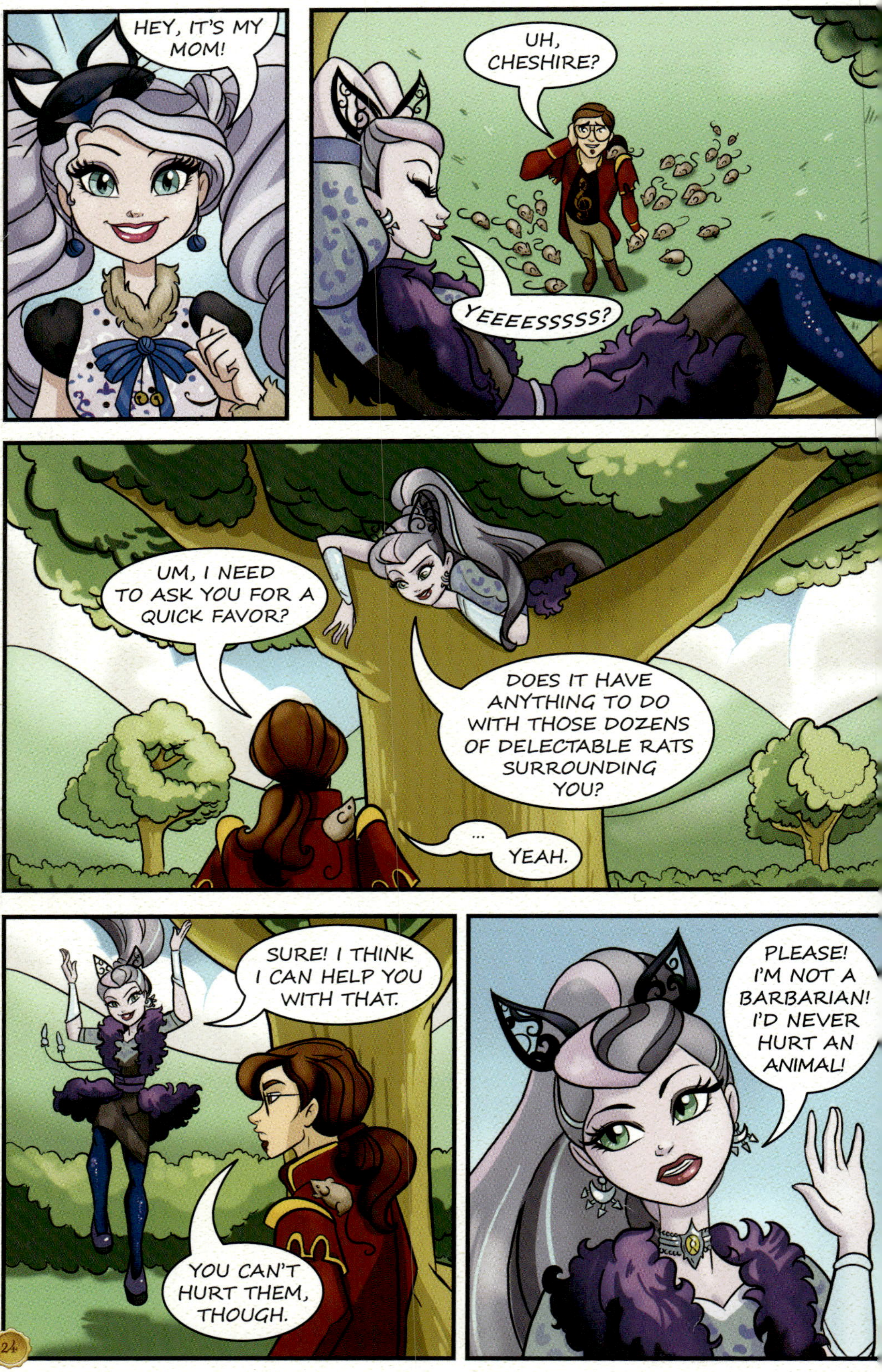
HEY, IT'S MY MOM!
UH, CHESHIRE?
YEEEESSSSS?
UM, I NEED TO ASK YOU FOR A QUICK FAVOR?
DOES IT HAVE ANYTHING TO DO WITH THOSE DOZENS OF DELECTABLE RATS SURROUNDING YOU?
... YEAH.
SURE! I THINK I CAN HELP YOU WITH THAT.
YOU CAN'T HURT THEM, THOUGH.
PLEASE! I'M NOT A BARBARIAN! I'D NEVER HURT AN ANIMAL!

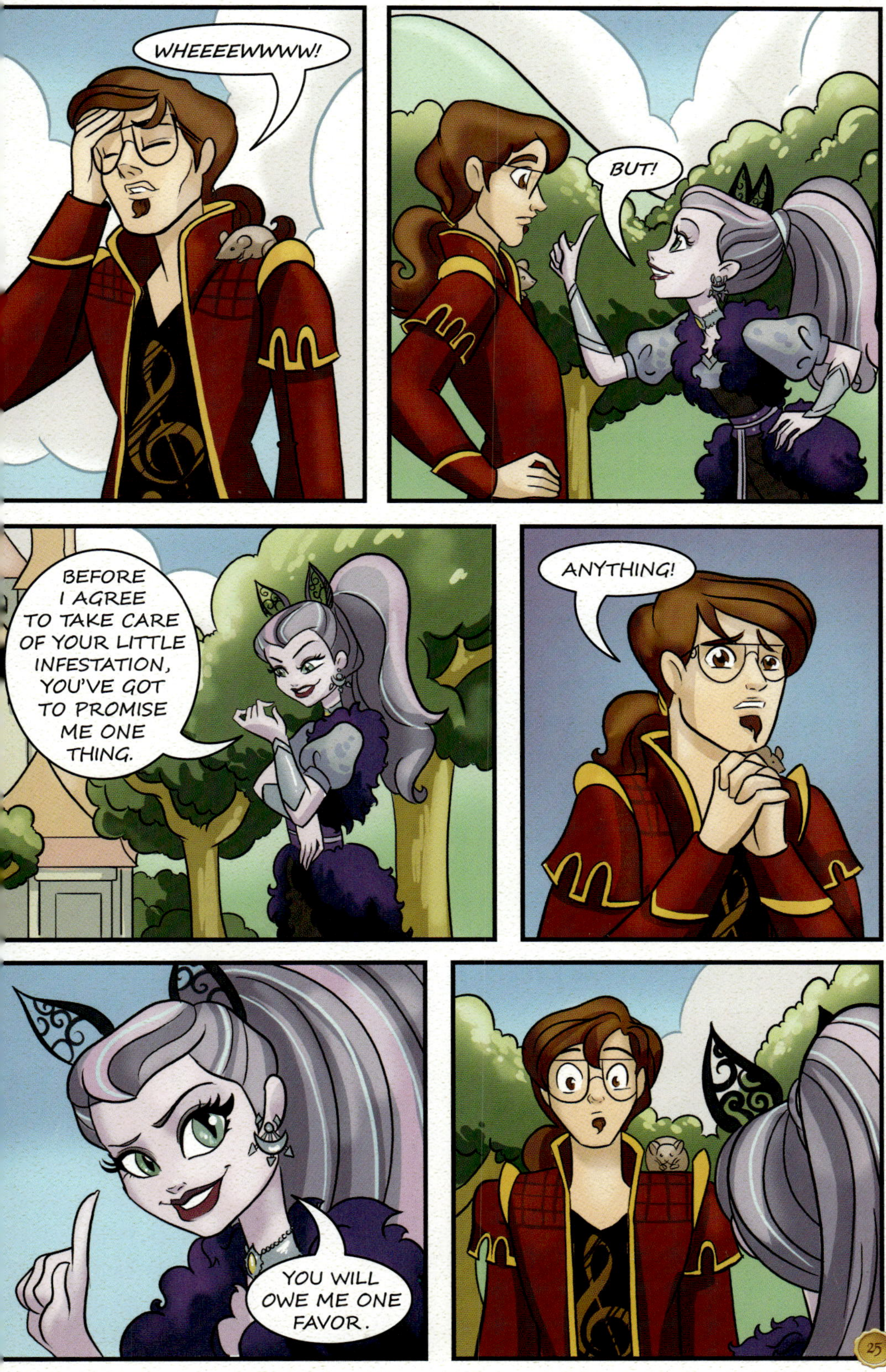
WHEEEEWWWW!
BUT!
BEFORE I AGREE TO TAKE CARE OF YOUR LITTLE INFESTATION, YOU'VE GOT TO PROMISE ME ONE THING.
ANYTHING!
YOU WILL OWE ME ONE FAVOR.

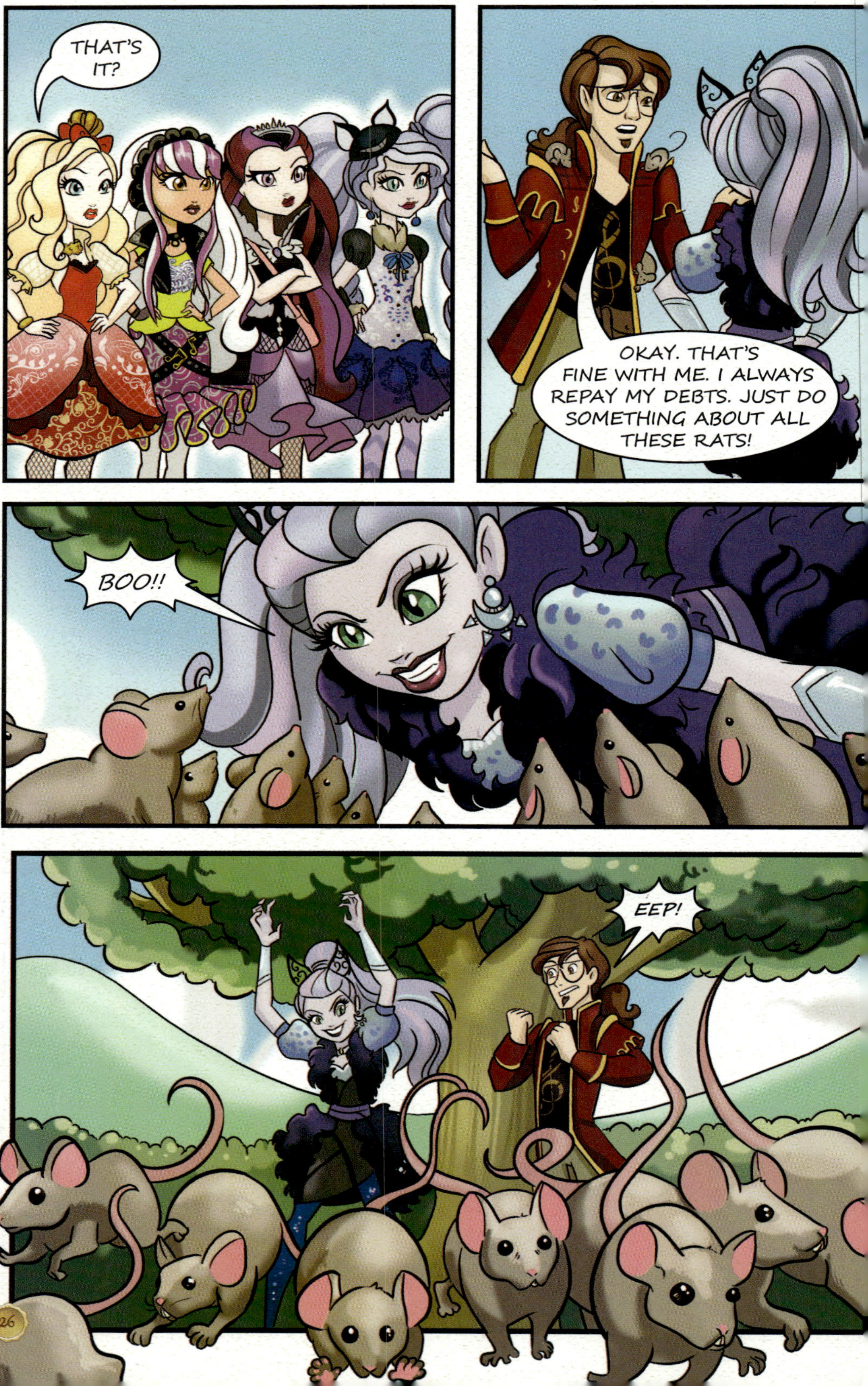
THAT'S IT?
OKAY. THAT'S FINE WITH ME. I ALWAYS REPAY MY DEBTS. JUST DO SOMETHING ABOUT ALL THESE RATS!
BOO!!
EEP!

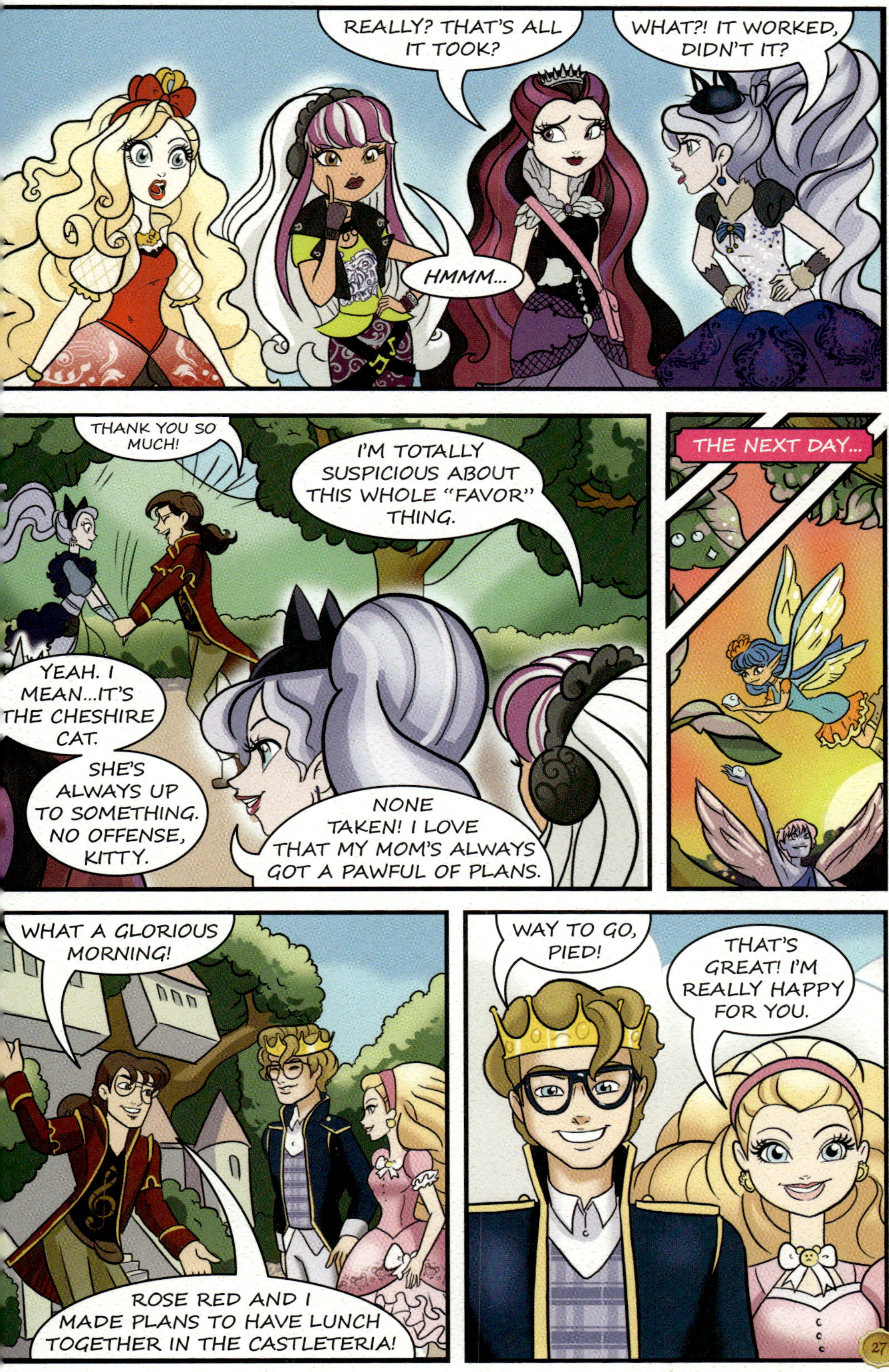

REALLY? THAT'S ALL IT TOOK?
WHAT?! IT WORKED, DIDN'T IT?
HMMM...
THANK YOU SO MUCH!
I'M TOTALLY SUSPICIOUS ABOUT THIS WHOLE "FAVOR" THING.
YEAH. I MEAN...IT'S THE CHESHIRE CAT.
SHE'S ALWAYS UP TO SOMETHING. NO OFFENSE, KITTY.
NONE TAKEN! I LOVE THAT MY MOM'S ALWAYS GOT A PAWFUL OF PLANS.
THE NEXT DAY...
WHAT A GLORIOUS MORNING!
ROSE RED AND I MADE PLANS TO HAVE LUNCH TOGETHER IN THE CASTLETERIA!
WAY TO GO, PIED!
THAT'S GREAT! I'M REALLY HAPPY FOR YOU.

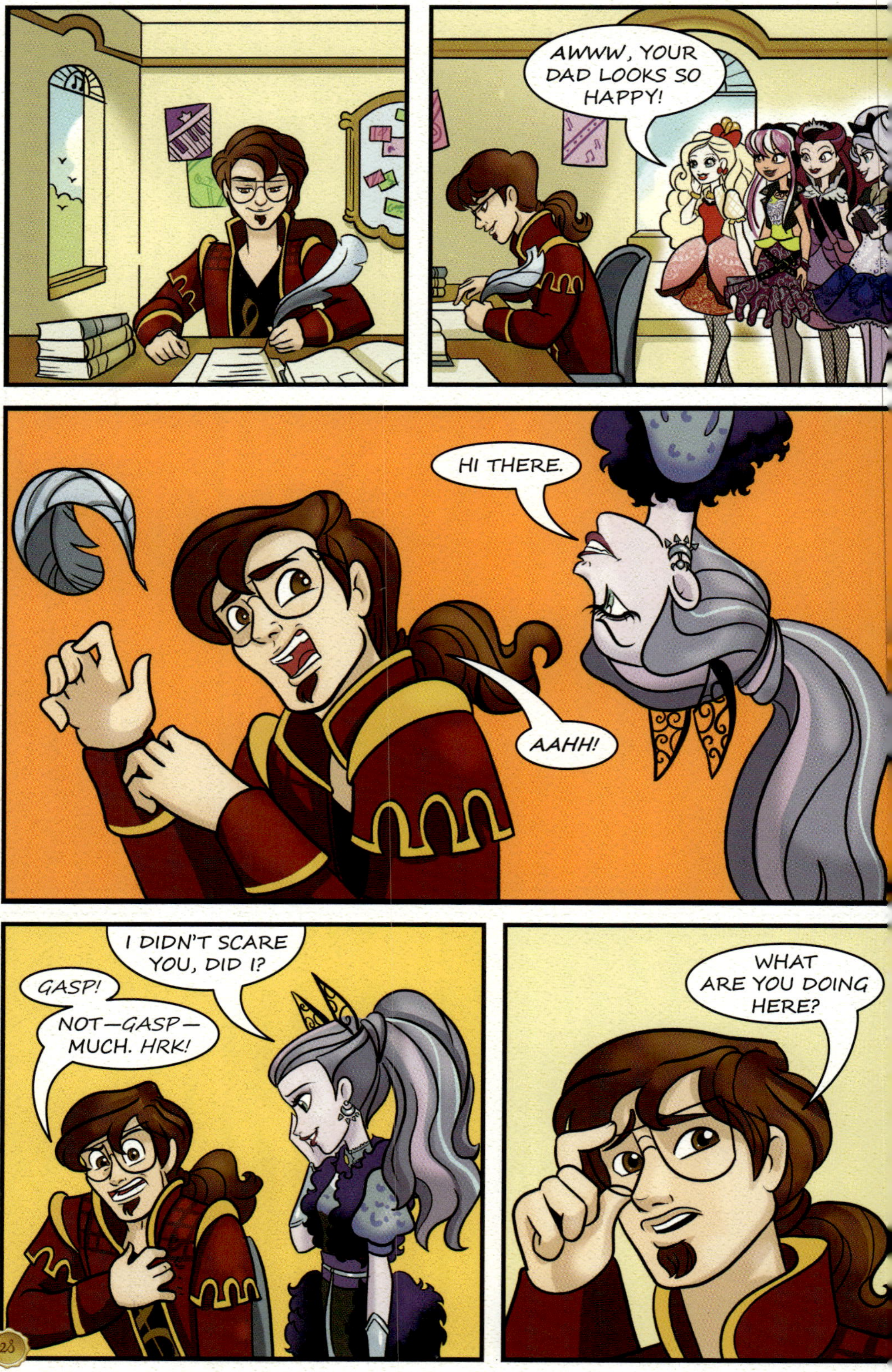
AWWW, YOUR DAD LOOKS SO HAPPY!
HI THERE.
AAHH!
GASP!
NOT—GASP—MUCH. HRK!
I DIDN'T SCARE YOU, DID I?
WHAT ARE YOU DOING HERE?

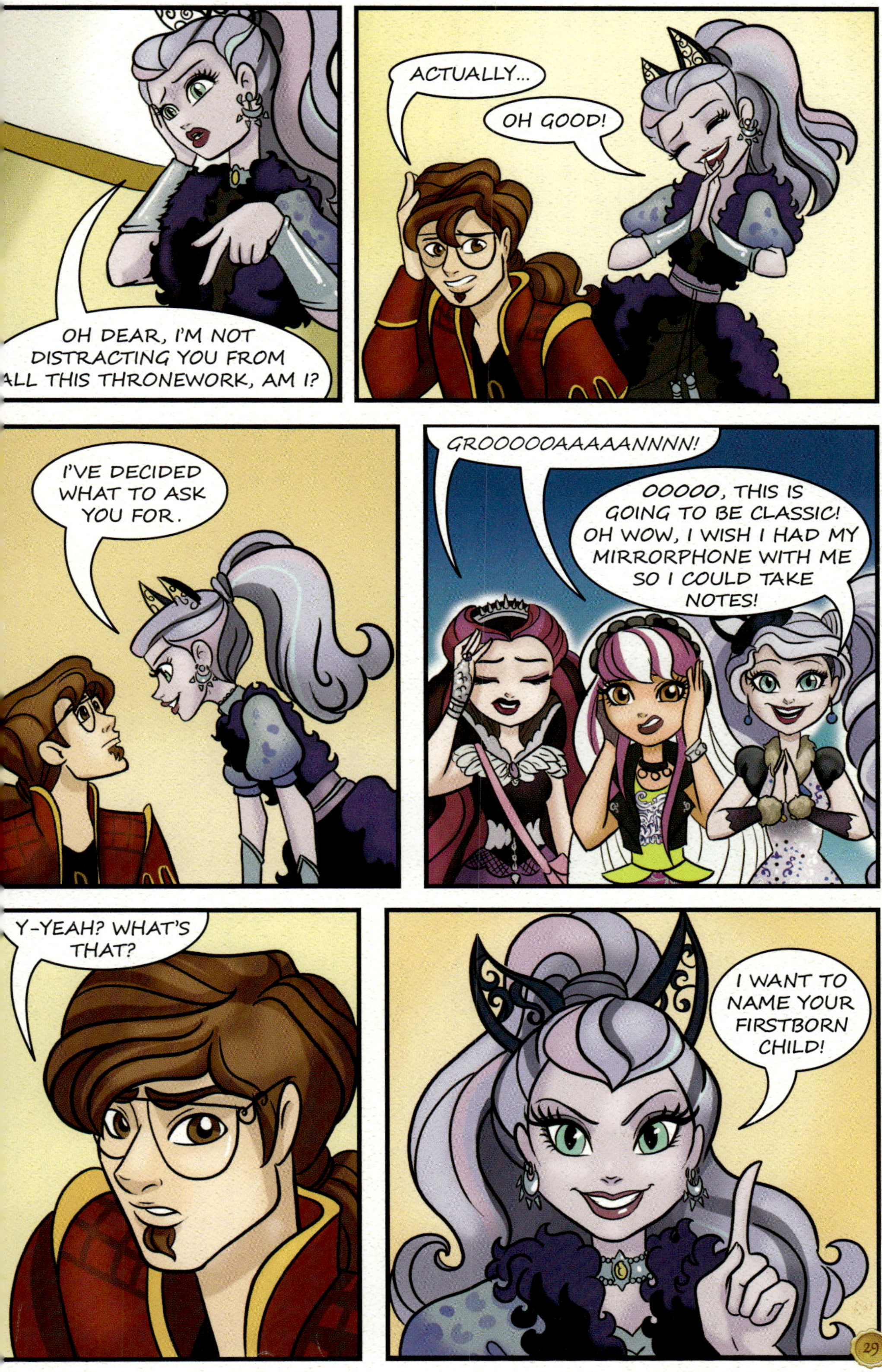
OH DEAR, I'M NOT DISTRACTING YOU FROM ALL THIS THRONEWORK, AM I?
ACTUALLY...
OH GOOD!
I'VE DECIDED WHAT TO ASK YOU FOR.
GROOOOOAAAAANNNN!
OOOOO, THIS IS GOING TO BE CLASSIC! OH WOW, I WISH I HAD MY MIRRORPHONE WITH ME SO I COULD TAKE NOTES!
Y-YEAH? WHAT'S THAT?
I WANT TO NAME YOUR FIRSTBORN CHILD!

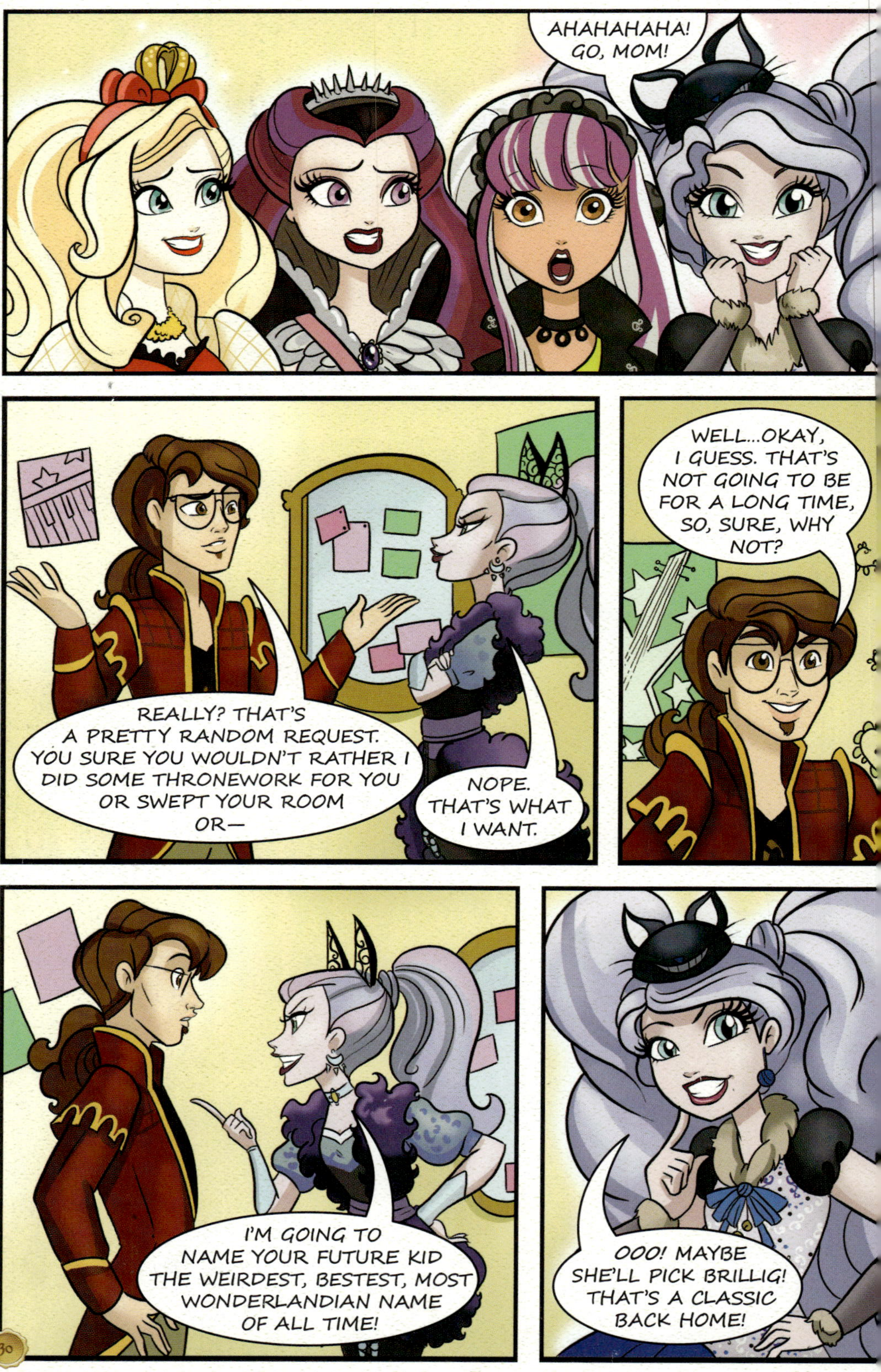
AHAHAHAHA! GO, MOM!
REALLY? THAT'S A PRETTY RANDOM REQUEST. YOU SURE YOU WOULDN'T RATHER I DID SOME THRONEWORK FOR YOU OR SWEPT YOUR ROOM OR—
NOPE. THAT'S WHAT I WANT.
WELL...OKAY, I GUESS. THAT'S NOT GOING TO BE FOR A LONG TIME, SO, SURE, WHY NOT?
I'M GOING TO NAME YOUR FUTURE KID THE WEIRDEST, BESTEST, MOST WONDERLANDIAN NAME OF ALL TIME!
OOO! MAYBE SHE'LL PICK BRILLIG! THAT'S A CLASSIC BACK HOME!

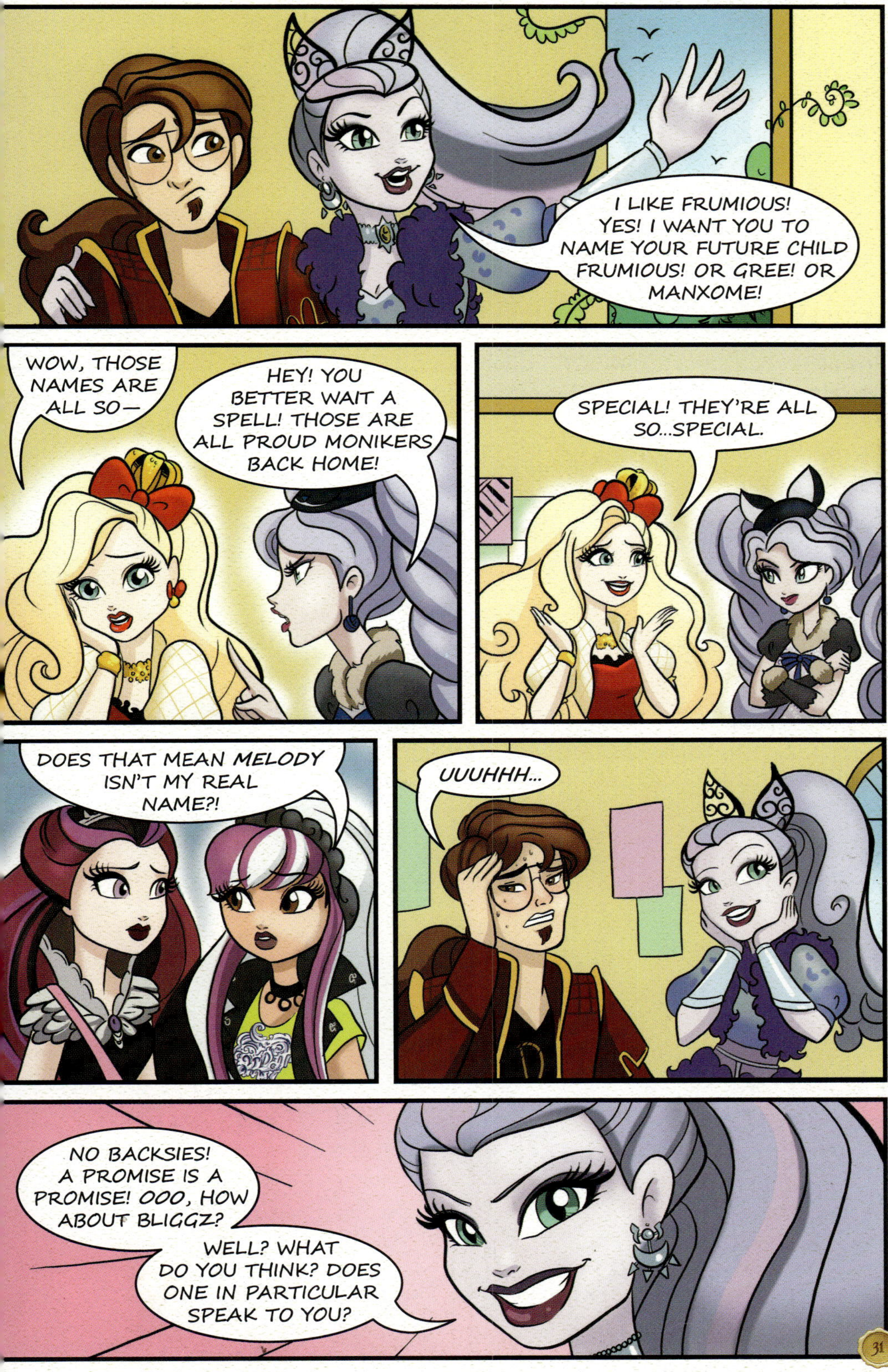
I LIKE FRUMIOUS! YES! I WANT YOU TO NAME YOUR FUTURE CHILD FRUMIOUS! OR GREE! OR MANXOME!
WOW, THOSE NAMES ARE ALL SO—
HEY! YOU BETTER WAIT A SPELL! THOSE ARE ALL PROUD MONIKERS BACK HOME!
SPECIAL! THEY'RE ALL SO...SPECIAL.
DOES THAT MEAN *MELODY* ISN'T MY REAL NAME?!
UUUHHH...
NO BACKSIES! A PROMISE IS A PROMISE! OOO, HOW ABOUT BLIGGZ?
WELL? WHAT DO YOU THINK? DOES ONE IN PARTICULAR SPEAK TO YOU?

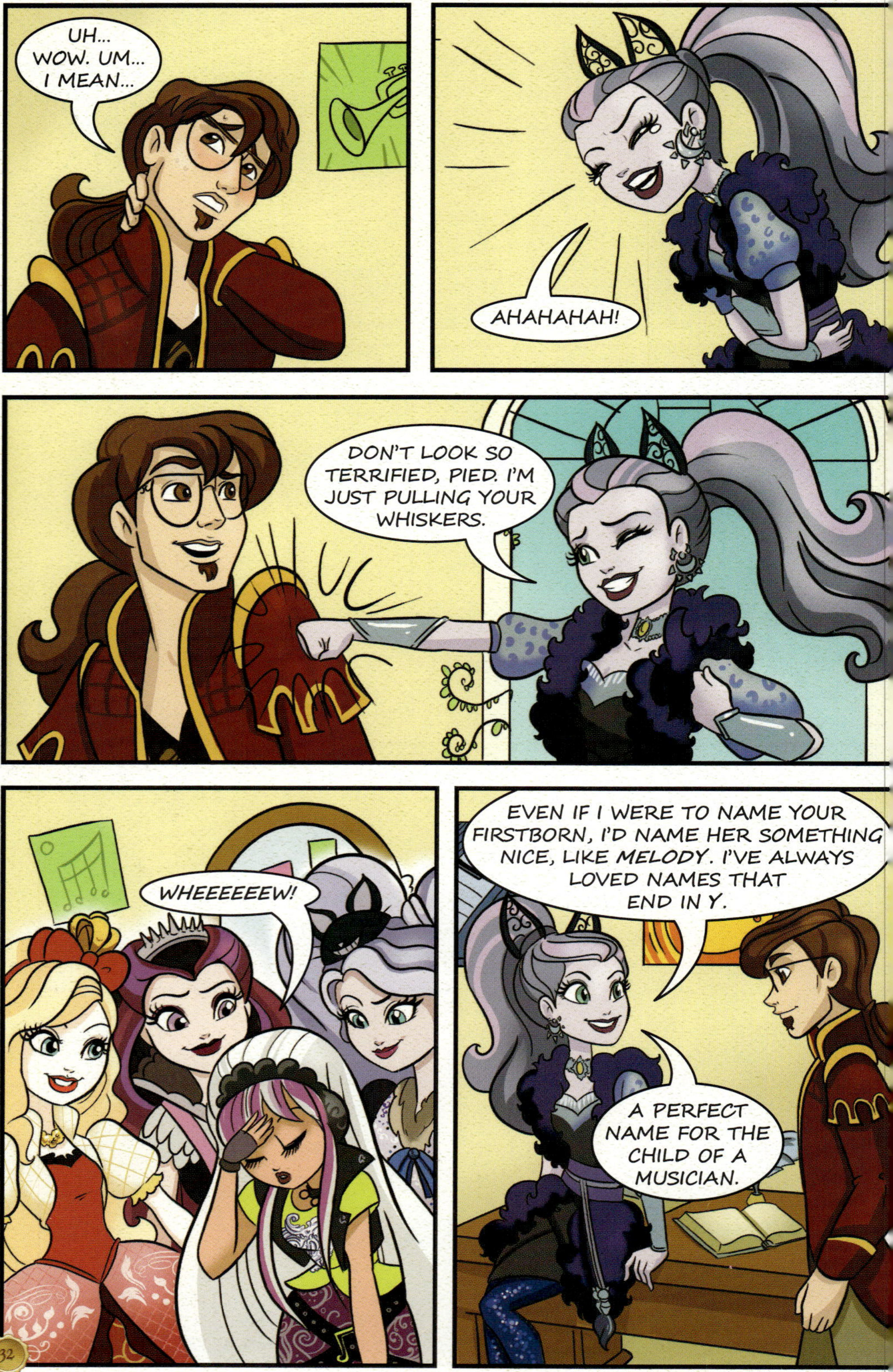
UH... WOW. UM... I MEAN...
AHAHAHAH!
DON'T LOOK SO TERRIFIED, PIED. I'M JUST PULLING YOUR WHISKERS.
WHEEEEEEW!
EVEN IF I WERE TO NAME YOUR FIRSTBORN, I'D NAME HER SOMETHING NICE, LIKE *MELODY*. I'VE ALWAYS LOVED NAMES THAT END IN Y.
A PERFECT NAME FOR THE CHILD OF A MUSICIAN.

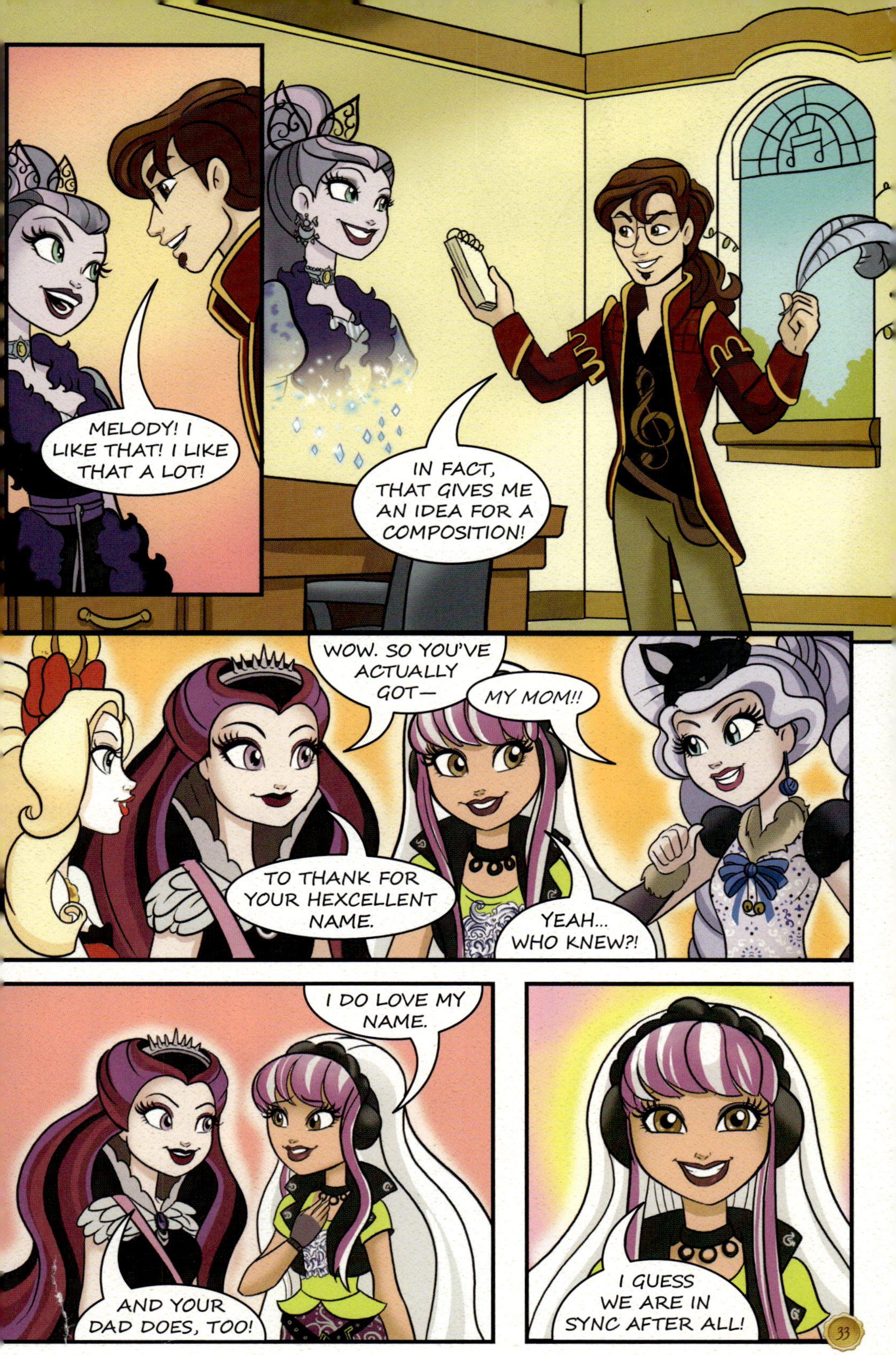
MELODY! I LIKE THAT! I LIKE THAT A LOT!
IN FACT, THAT GIVES ME AN IDEA FOR A COMPOSITION!
WOW. SO YOU'VE ACTUALLY GOT—
MY MOM!!
TO THANK FOR YOUR HEXCELLENT NAME.
YEAH... WHO KNEW?!
I DO LOVE MY NAME.
AND YOUR DAD DOES, TOO!
I GUESS WE ARE IN SYNC AFTER ALL!

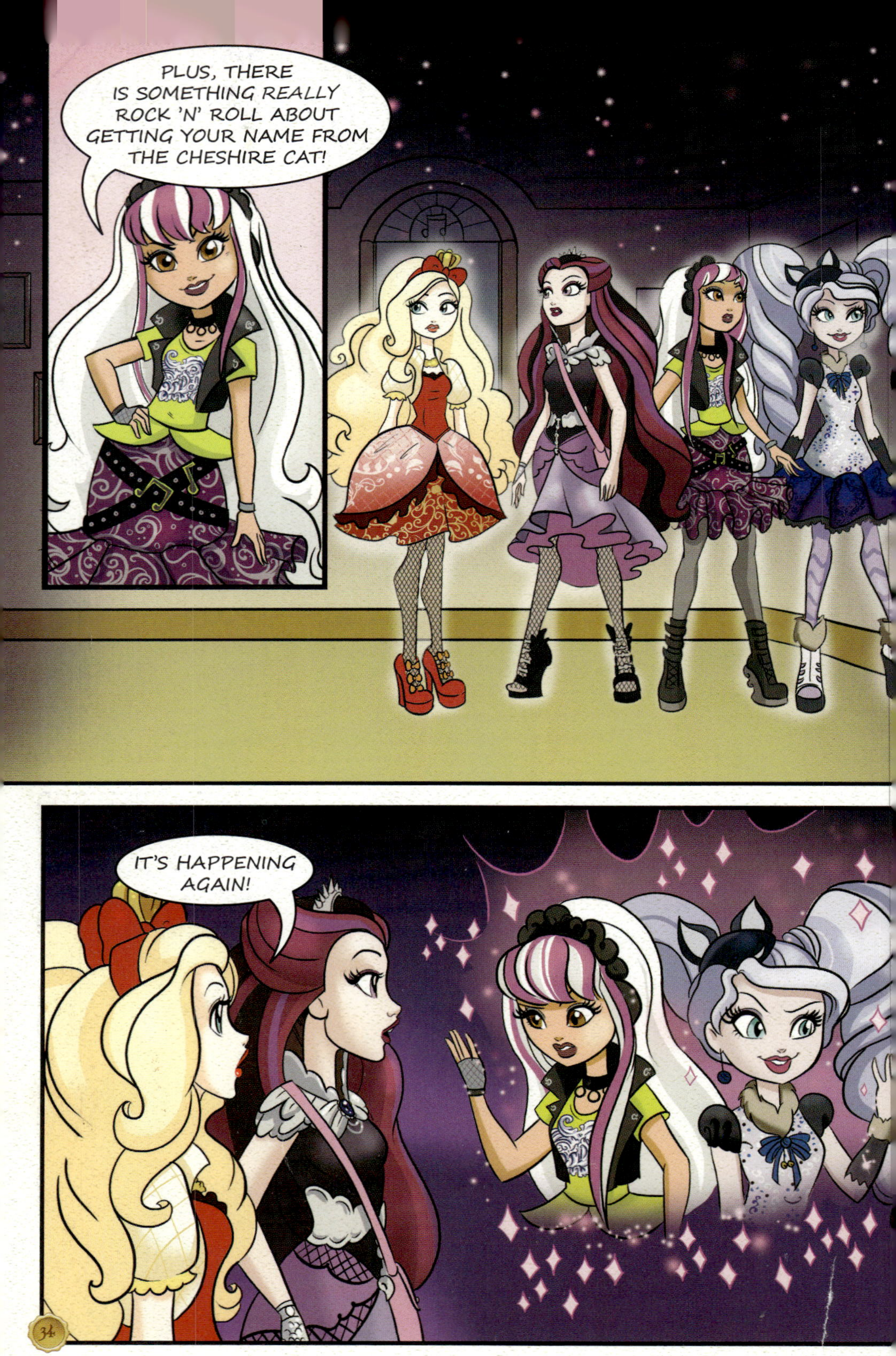
PLUS, THERE IS SOMETHING REALLY ROCK 'N' ROLL ABOUT GETTING YOUR NAME FROM THE CHESHIRE CAT!
IT'S HAPPENING AGAIN!

Story Three: Mad Hatter

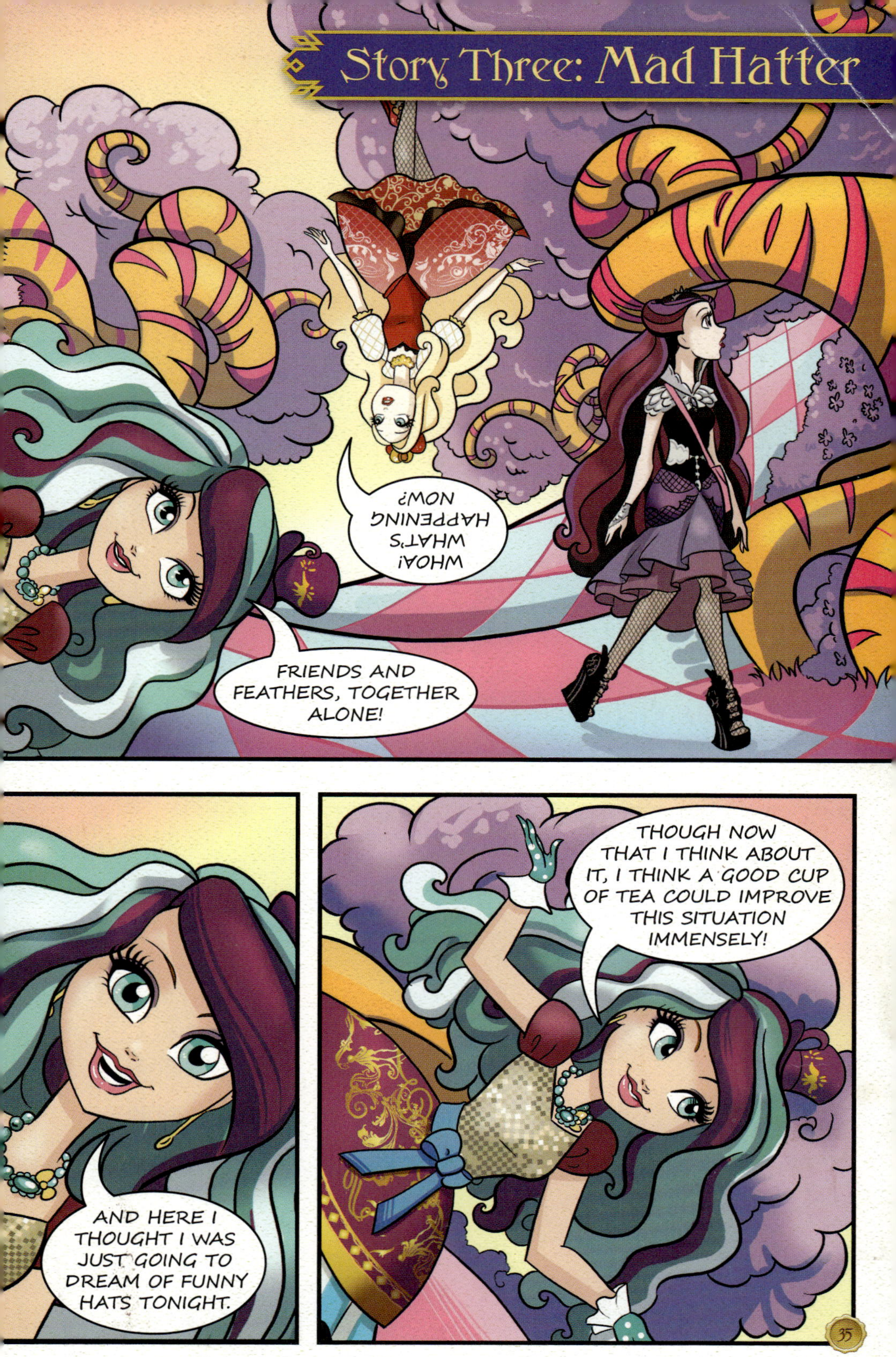

WHOA! WHAT'S HAPPENING NOW?
FRIENDS AND FEATHERS, TOGETHER ALONE!
AND HERE I THOUGHT I WAS JUST GOING TO DREAM OF FUNNY HATS TONIGHT.
THOUGH NOW THAT I THINK ABOUT IT, I THINK A GOOD CUP OF TEA COULD IMPROVE THIS SITUATION IMMENSELY!

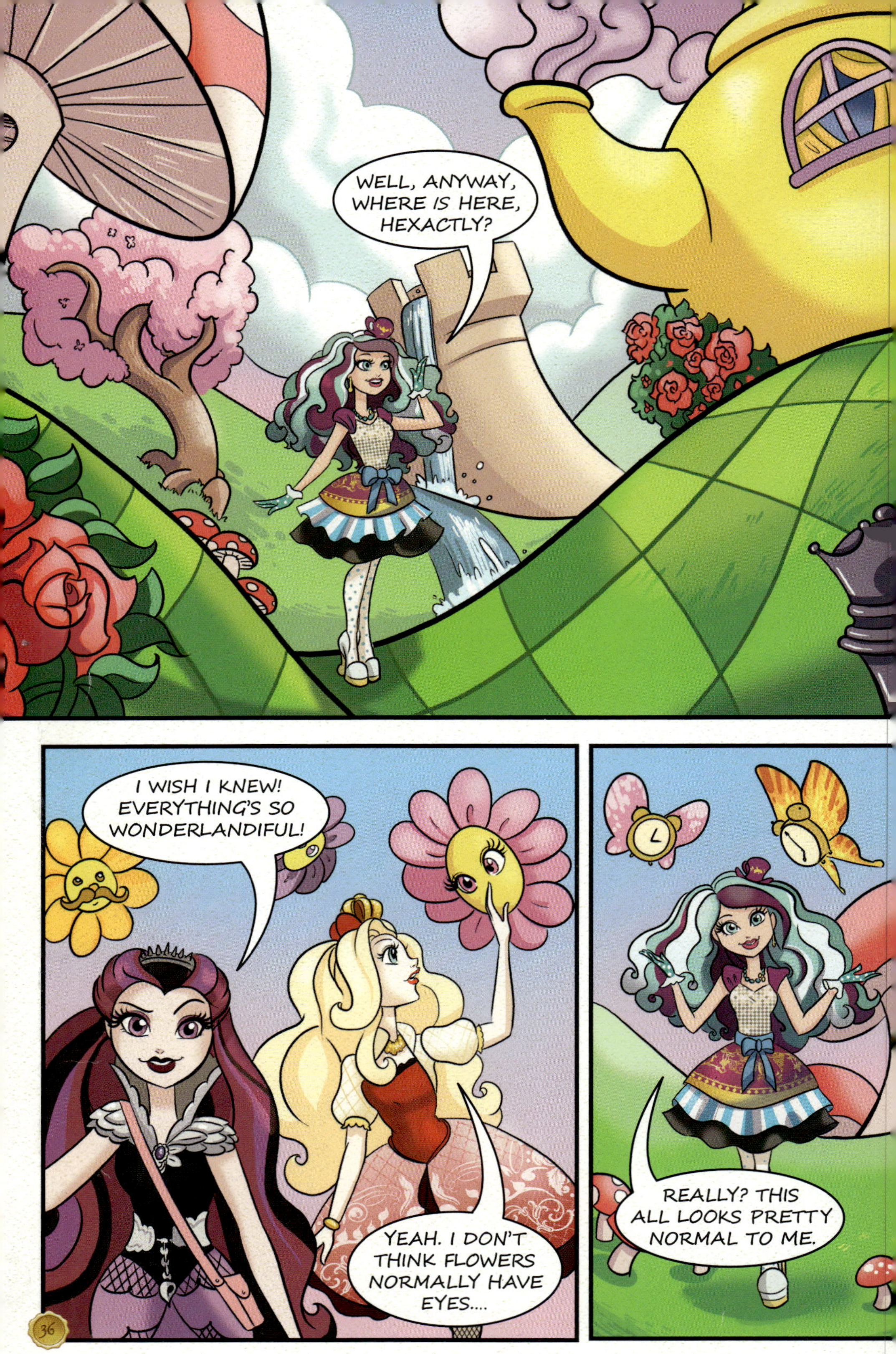
WELL, ANYWAY, WHERE IS HERE, HEXACTLY?
I WISH I KNEW! EVERYTHING'S SO WONDERLANDIFUL!
YEAH. I DON'T THINK FLOWERS NORMALLY HAVE EYES....
REALLY? THIS ALL LOOKS PRETTY NORMAL TO ME.

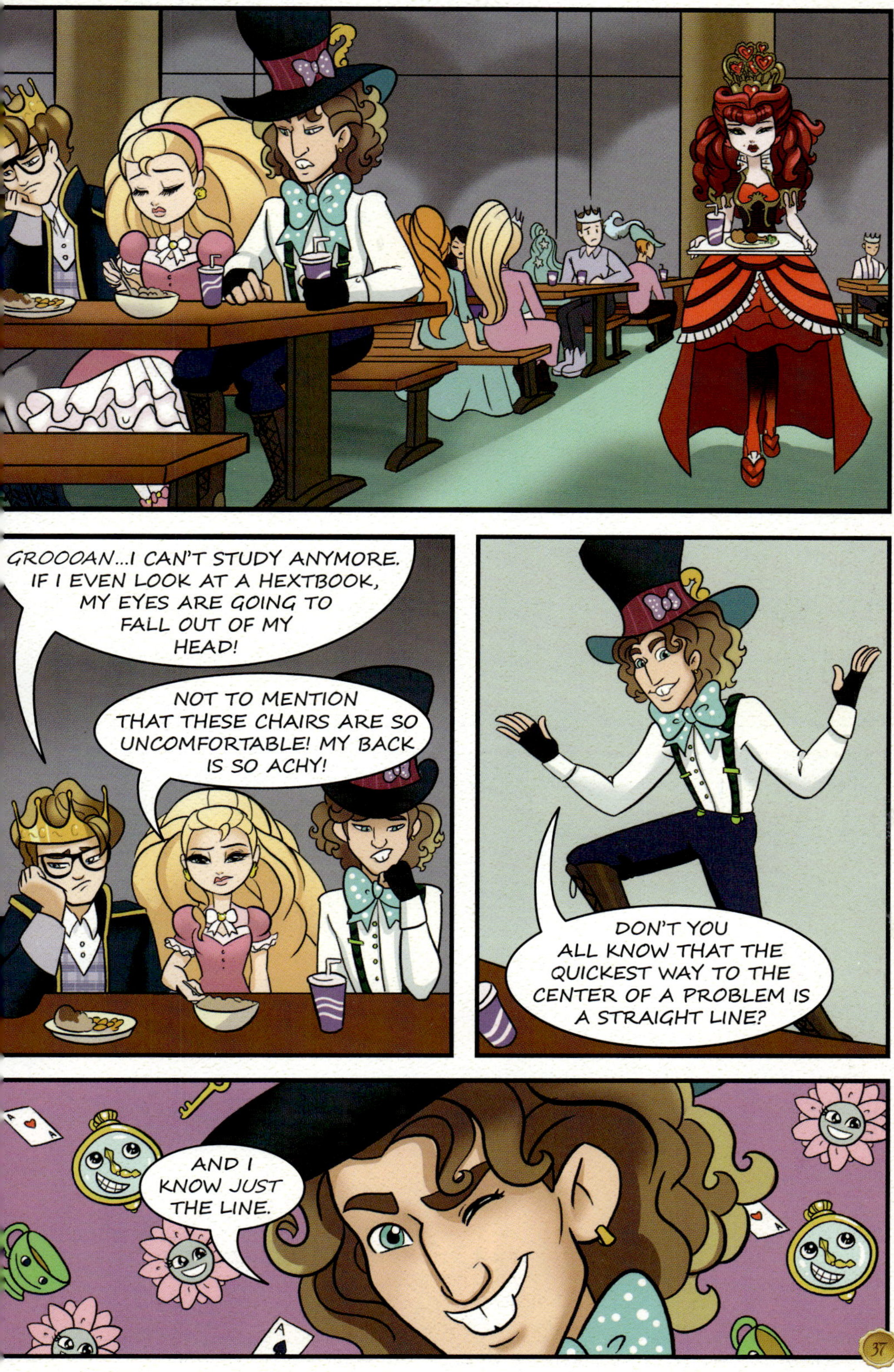
GROOOAN...I CAN'T STUDY ANYMORE. IF I EVEN LOOK AT A HEXTBOOK, MY EYES ARE GOING TO FALL OUT OF MY HEAD!
NOT TO MENTION THAT THESE CHAIRS ARE SO UNCOMFORTABLE! MY BACK IS SO ACHY!
DON'T YOU ALL KNOW THAT THE QUICKEST WAY TO THE CENTER OF A PROBLEM IS A STRAIGHT LINE?
AND I KNOW JUST THE LINE.

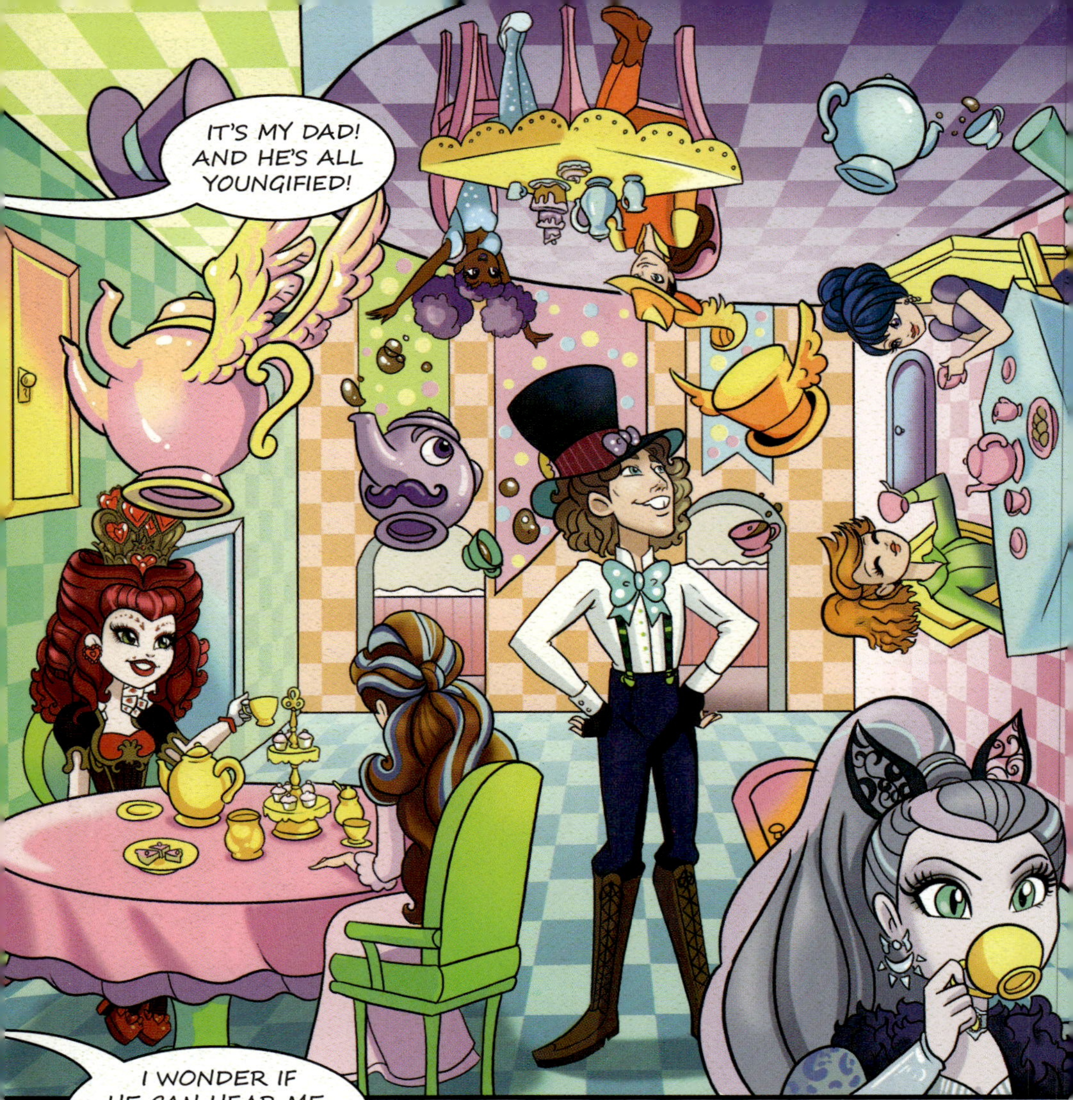
IT'S MY DAD! AND HE'S ALL YOUNGIFIED!

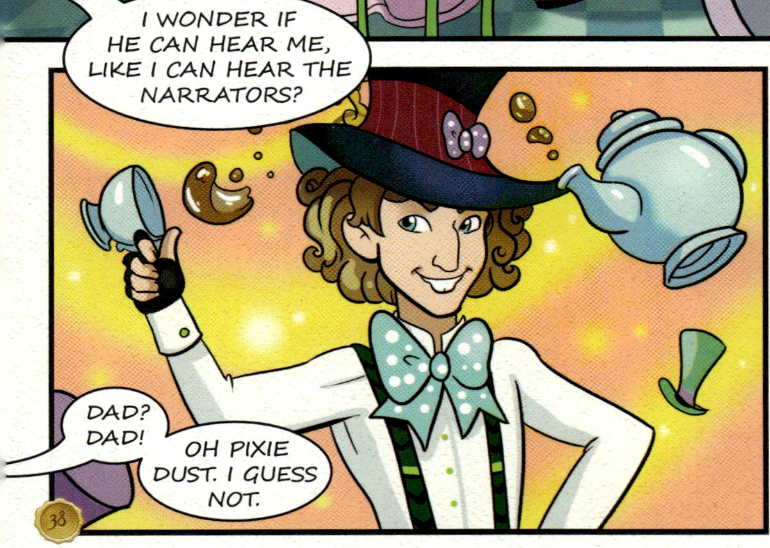
I WONDER IF HE CAN HEAR ME, LIKE I CAN HEAR THE NARRATORS?
DAD? DAD!
OH PIXIE DUST. I GUESS NOT.

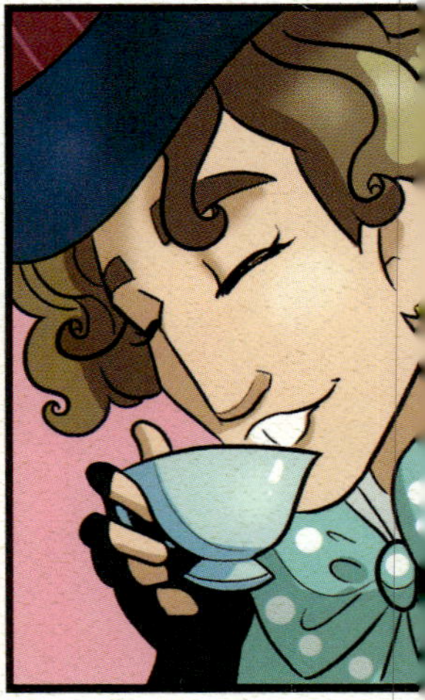

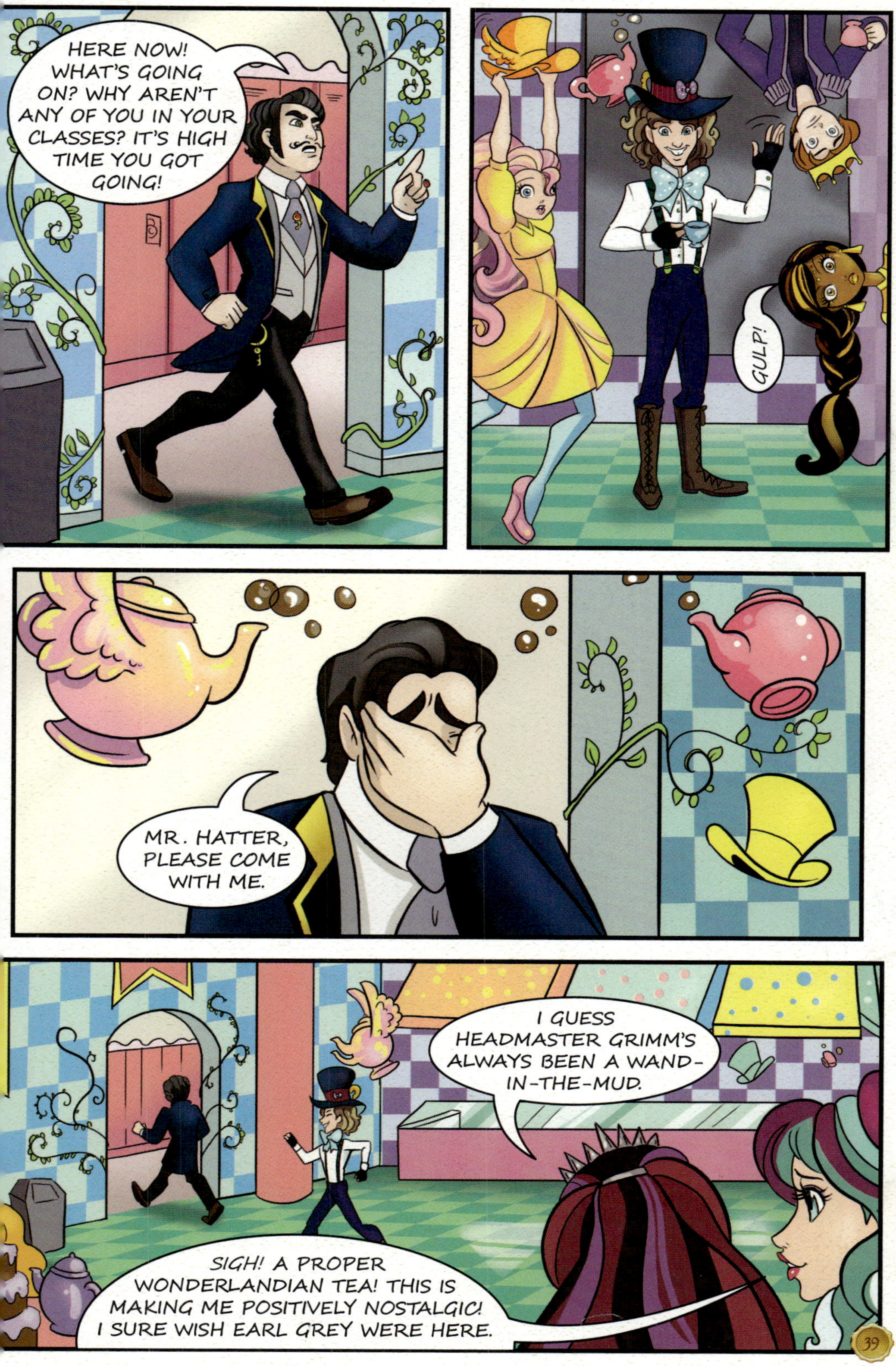
HERE NOW! WHAT'S GOING ON? WHY AREN'T ANY OF YOU IN YOUR CLASSES? IT'S HIGH TIME YOU GOT GOING!
GULP!
MR. HATTER, PLEASE COME WITH ME.
I GUESS HEADMASTER GRIMM'S ALWAYS BEEN A WAND-IN-THE-MUD.
SIGH! A PROPER WONDERLANDIAN TEA! THIS IS MAKING ME POSITIVELY NOSTALGIC! I SURE WISH EARL GREY WERE HERE.

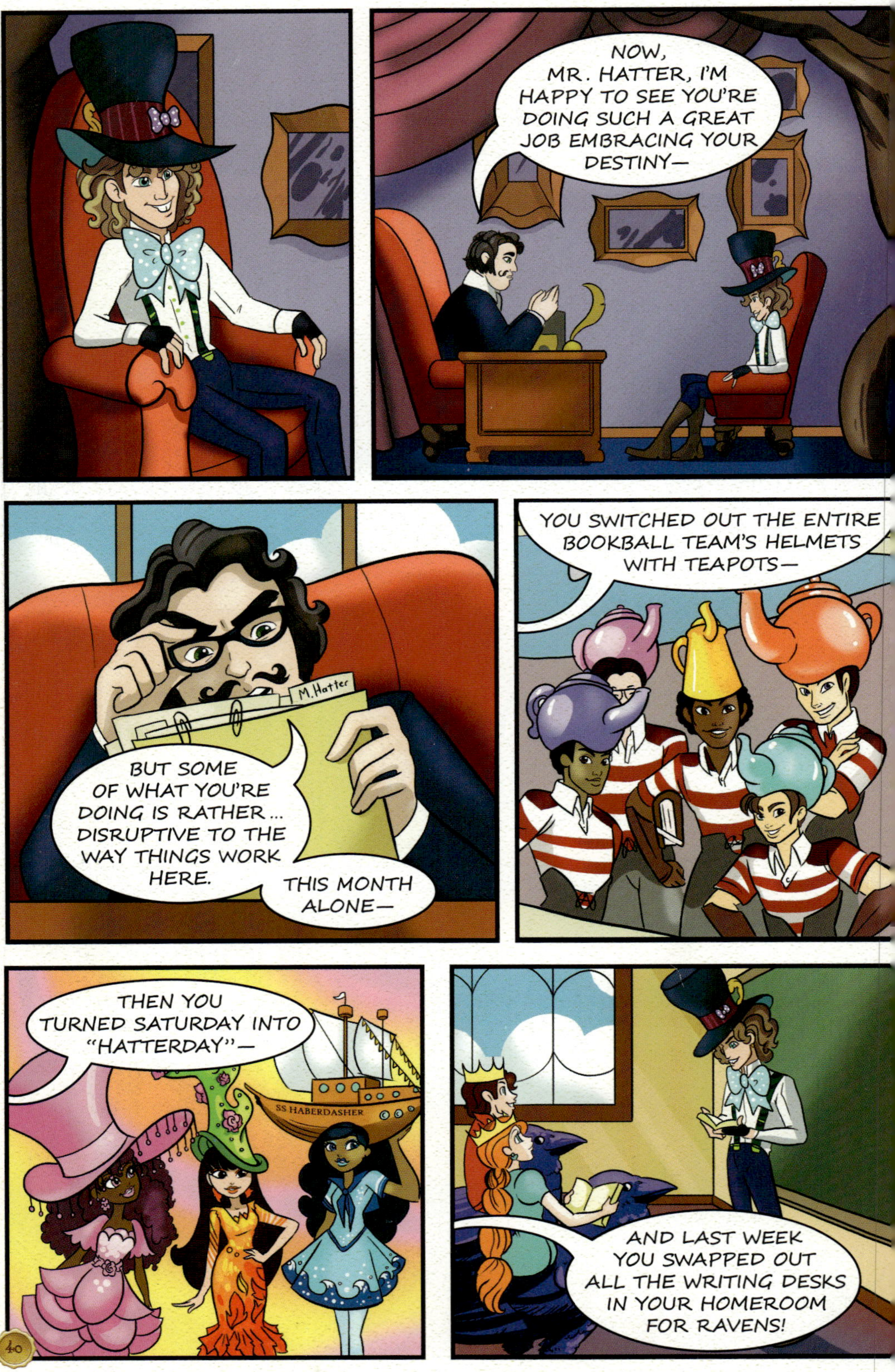
NOW, MR. HATTER, I'M HAPPY TO SEE YOU'RE DOING SUCH A GREAT JOB EMBRACING YOUR DESTINY—
M. Hatter
BUT SOME OF WHAT YOU'RE DOING IS RATHER... DISRUPTIVE TO THE WAY THINGS WORK HERE.
THIS MONTH ALONE—
YOU SWITCHED OUT THE ENTIRE BOOKBALL TEAM'S HELMETS WITH TEAPOTS—
THEN YOU TURNED SATURDAY INTO "HATTERDAY"—
SS HABERDASHER
AND LAST WEEK YOU SWAPPED OUT ALL THE WRITING DESKS IN YOUR HOMEROOM FOR RAVENS!

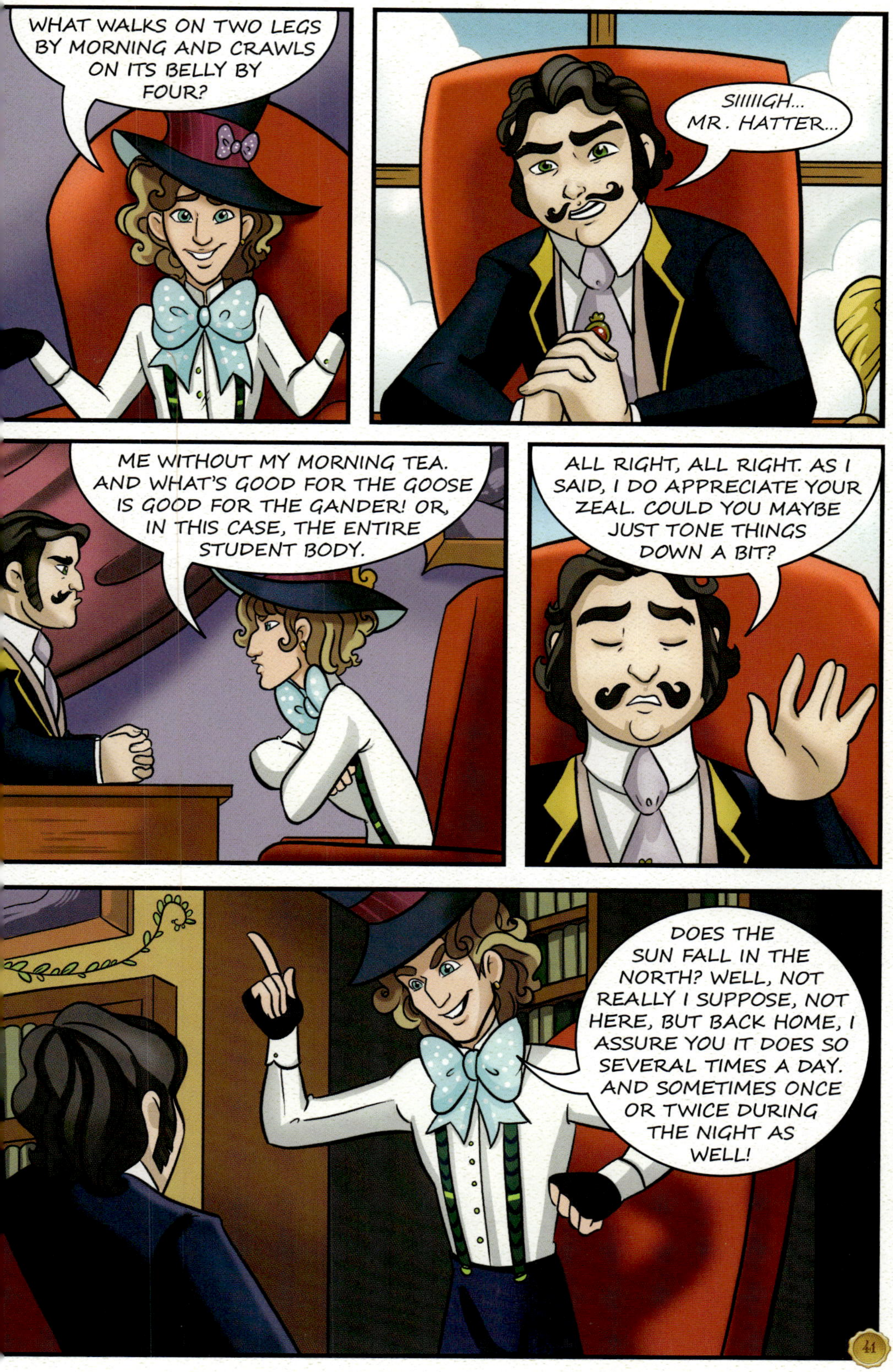
WHAT WALKS ON TWO LEGS BY MORNING AND CRAWLS ON ITS BELLY BY FOUR?
SIIIIGH... MR. HATTER...
ME WITHOUT MY MORNING TEA. AND WHAT'S GOOD FOR THE GOOSE IS GOOD FOR THE GANDER! OR, IN THIS CASE, THE ENTIRE STUDENT BODY.
ALL RIGHT, ALL RIGHT. AS I SAID, I DO APPRECIATE YOUR ZEAL. COULD YOU MAYBE JUST TONE THINGS DOWN A BIT?
DOES THE SUN FALL IN THE NORTH? WELL, NOT REALLY I SUPPOSE, NOT HERE, BUT BACK HOME, I ASSURE YOU IT DOES SO SEVERAL TIMES A DAY. AND SOMETIMES ONCE OR TWICE DURING THE NIGHT AS WELL!

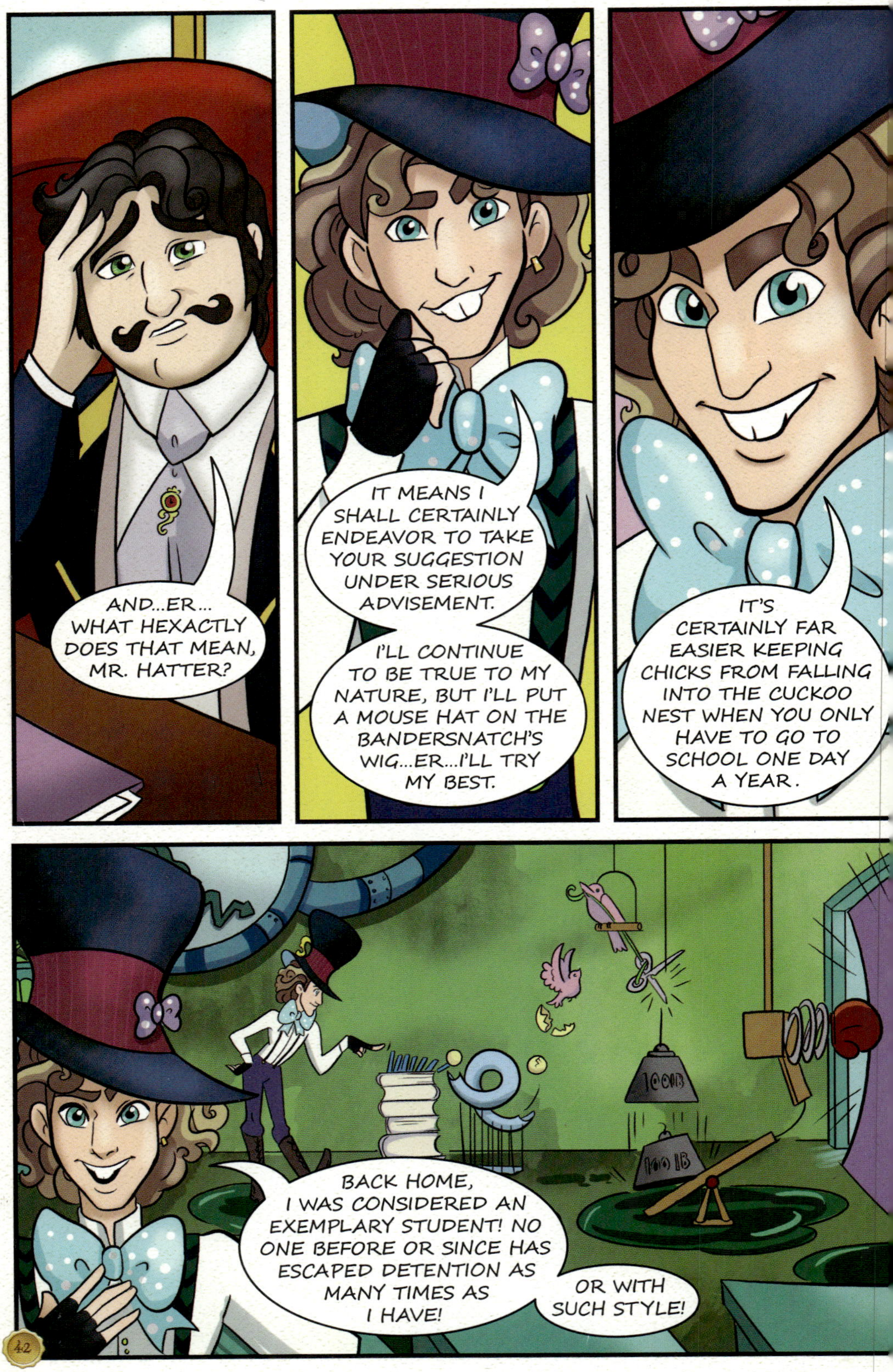
AND...ER... WHAT HEXACTLY DOES THAT MEAN, MR. HATTER?
IT MEANS I SHALL CERTAINLY ENDEAVOR TO TAKE YOUR SUGGESTION UNDER SERIOUS ADVISEMENT.
I'LL CONTINUE TO BE TRUE TO MY NATURE, BUT I'LL PUT A MOUSE HAT ON THE BANDERSNATCH'S WIG...ER...I'LL TRY MY BEST.
IT'S CERTAINLY FAR EASIER KEEPING CHICKS FROM FALLING INTO THE CUCKOO NEST WHEN YOU ONLY HAVE TO GO TO SCHOOL ONE DAY A YEAR.
BACK HOME, I WAS CONSIDERED AN EXEMPLARY STUDENT! NO ONE BEFORE OR SINCE HAS ESCAPED DETENTION AS MANY TIMES AS I HAVE!
OR WITH SUCH STYLE!

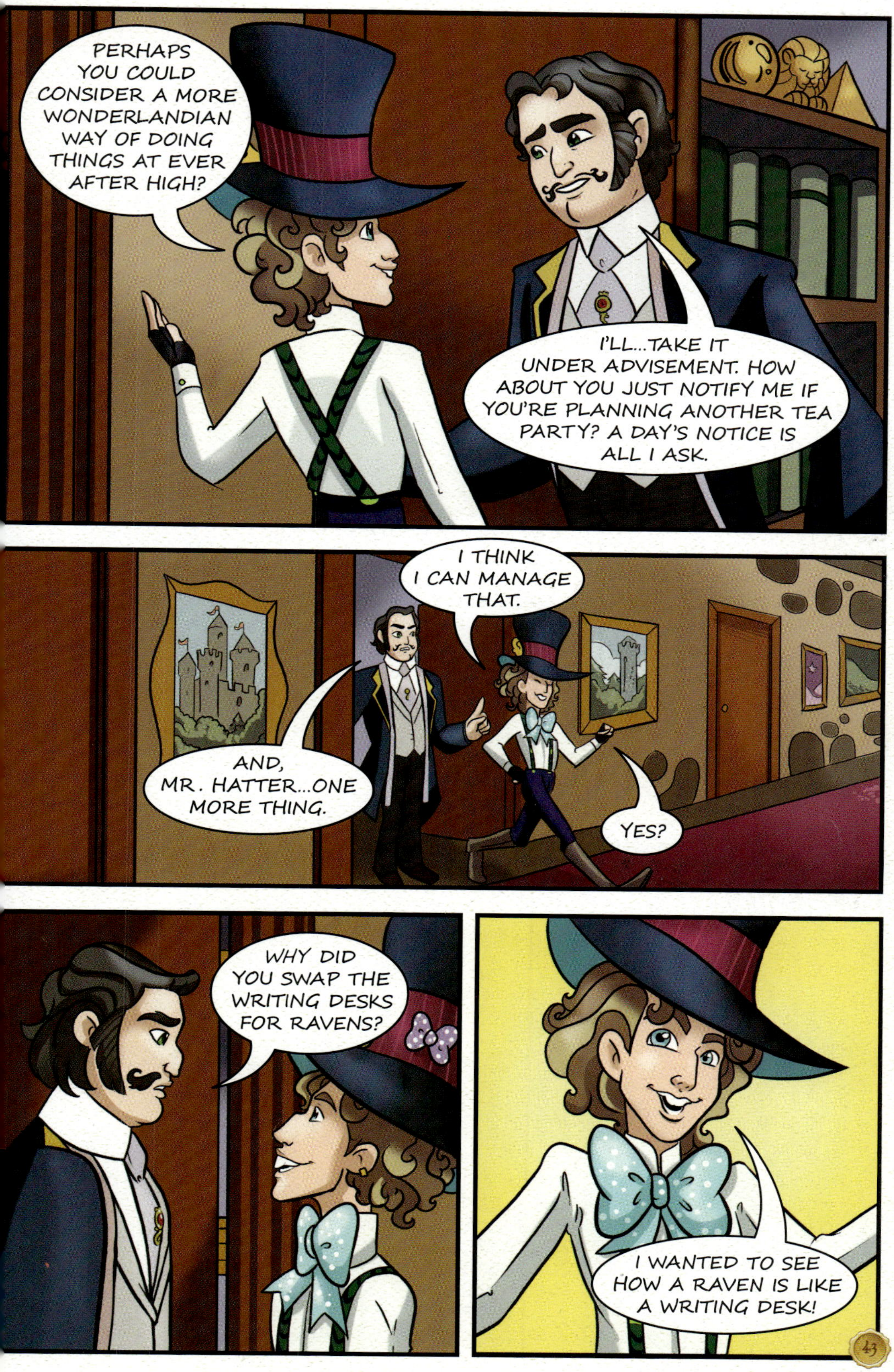
PERHAPS YOU COULD CONSIDER A MORE WONDERLANDIAN WAY OF DOING THINGS AT EVER AFTER HIGH?
I'LL...TAKE IT UNDER ADVISEMENT. HOW ABOUT YOU JUST NOTIFY ME IF YOU'RE PLANNING ANOTHER TEA PARTY? A DAY'S NOTICE IS ALL I ASK.
I THINK I CAN MANAGE THAT.
AND, MR. HATTER...ONE MORE THING.
YES?
WHY DID YOU SWAP THE WRITING DESKS FOR RAVENS?
I WANTED TO SEE HOW A RAVEN IS LIKE A WRITING DESK!

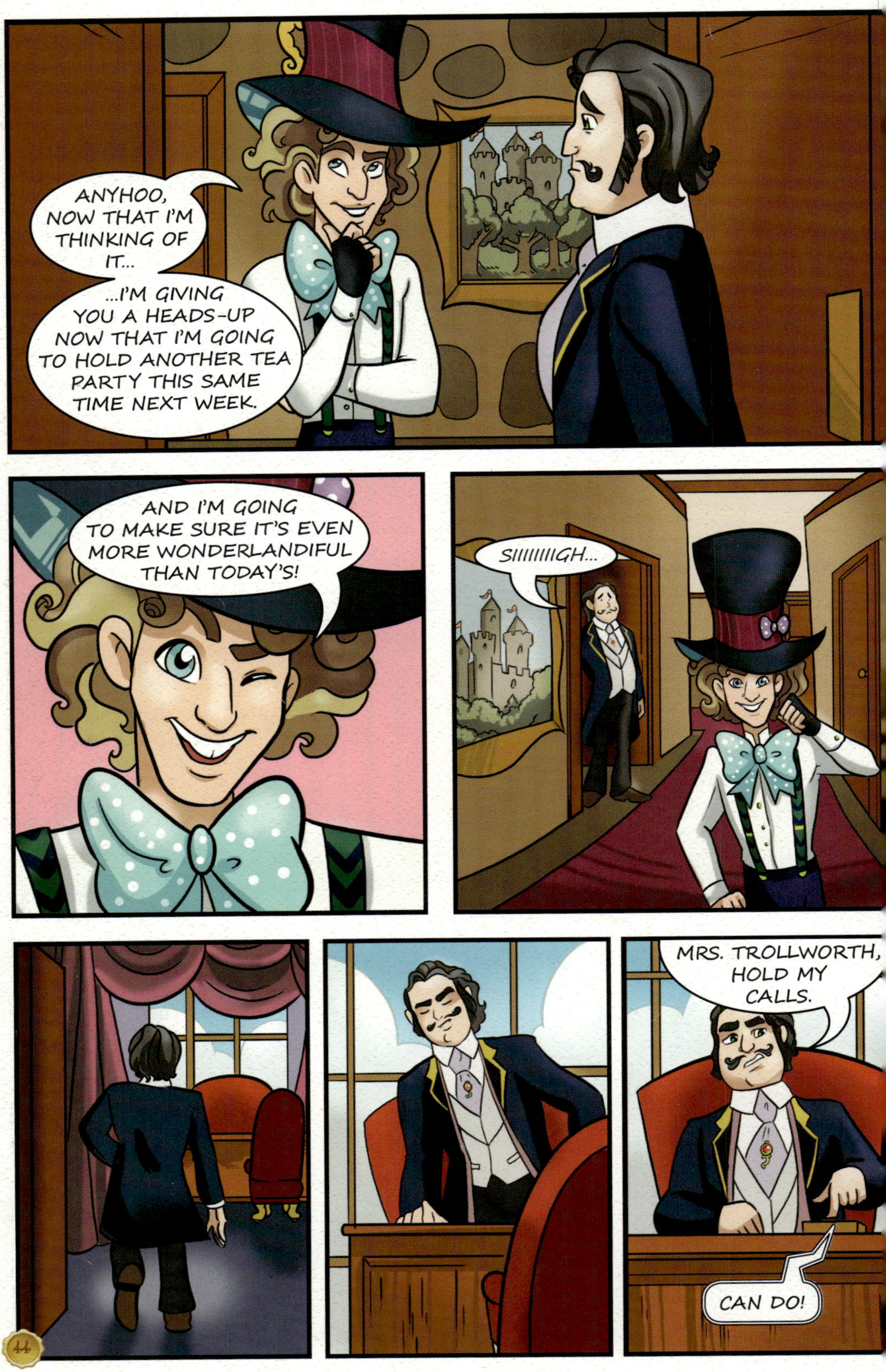
ANYHOO, NOW THAT I'M THINKING OF IT...
...I'M GIVING YOU A HEADS-UP NOW THAT I'M GOING TO HOLD ANOTHER TEA PARTY THIS SAME TIME NEXT WEEK.
AND I'M GOING TO MAKE SURE IT'S EVEN MORE WONDERLANDIFUL THAN TODAY'S!
SIIIIIIIGH...
MRS. TROLLWORTH, HOLD MY CALLS.
CAN DO!

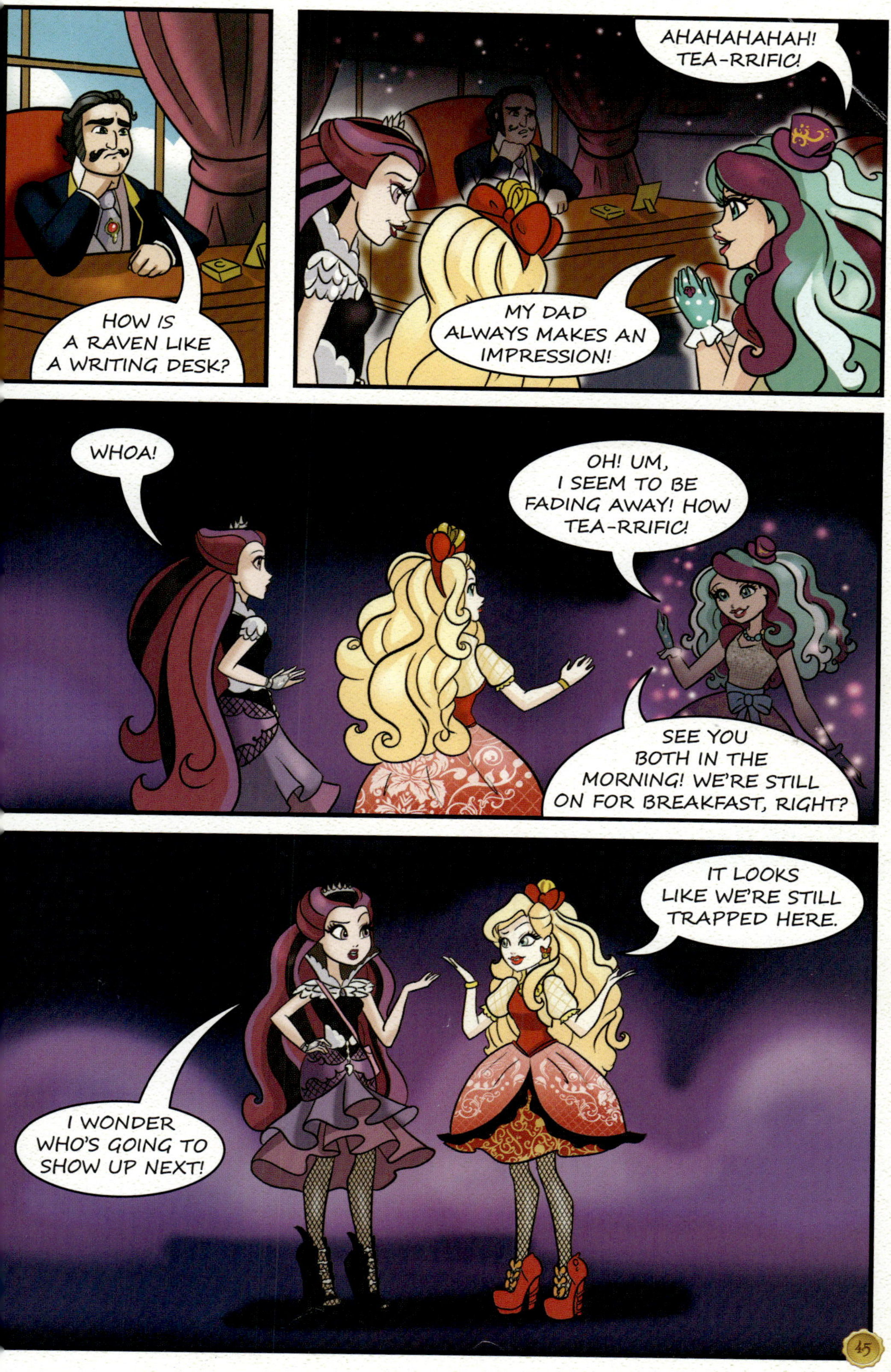
HOW IS A RAVEN LIKE A WRITING DESK?
AHAHAHAHAH! TEA-RRIFIC!
MY DAD ALWAYS MAKES AN IMPRESSION!
WHOA!
OH! UM, I SEEM TO BE FADING AWAY! HOW TEA-RRIFIC!
SEE YOU BOTH IN THE MORNING! WE'RE STILL ON FOR BREAKFAST, RIGHT?
IT LOOKS LIKE WE'RE STILL TRAPPED HERE.
I WONDER WHO'S GOING TO SHOW UP NEXT!

Story Four: Red Riding Hood

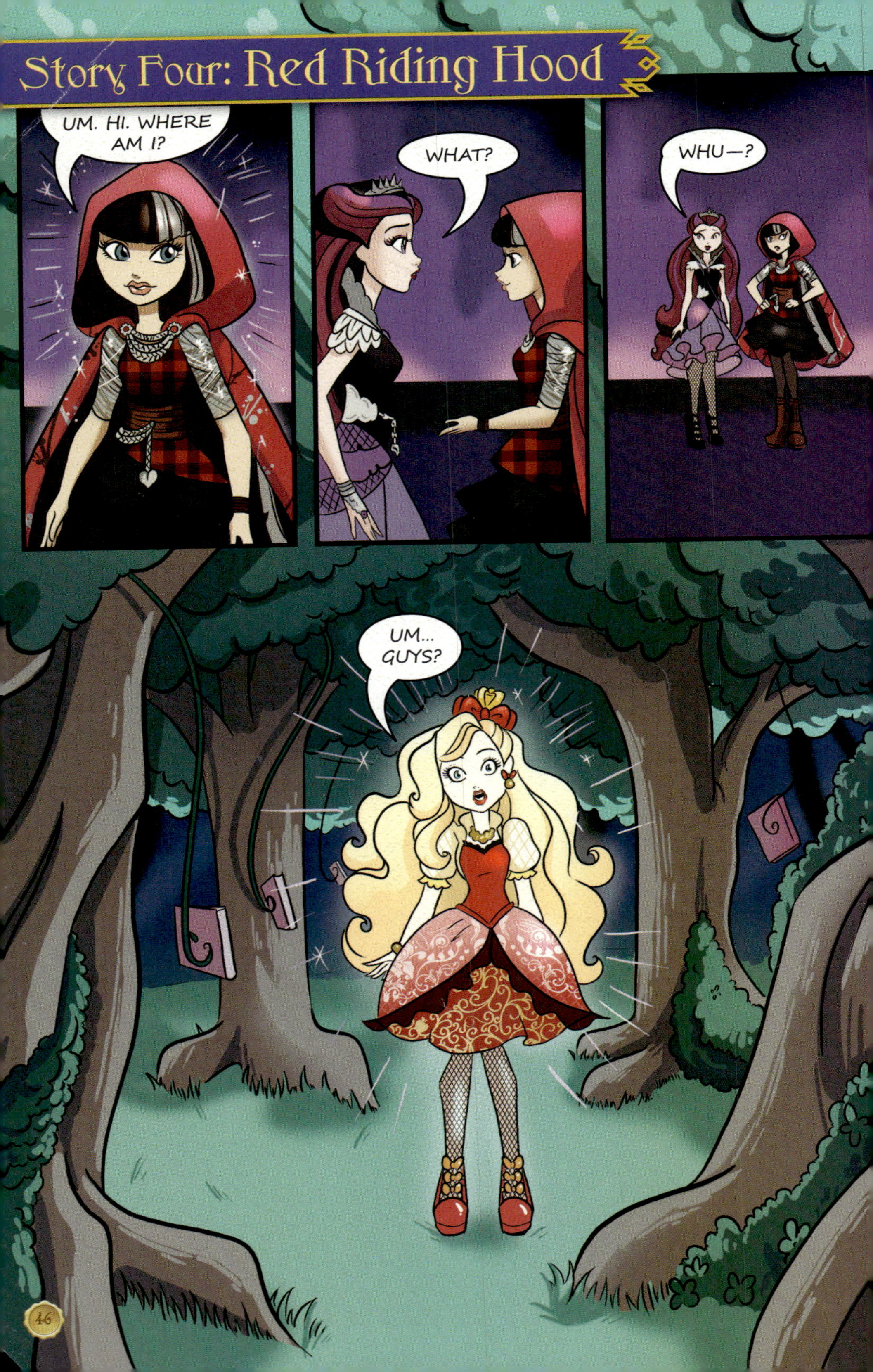
UM. HI. WHERE AM I?
WHAT?
WHU—?
UM... GUYS?

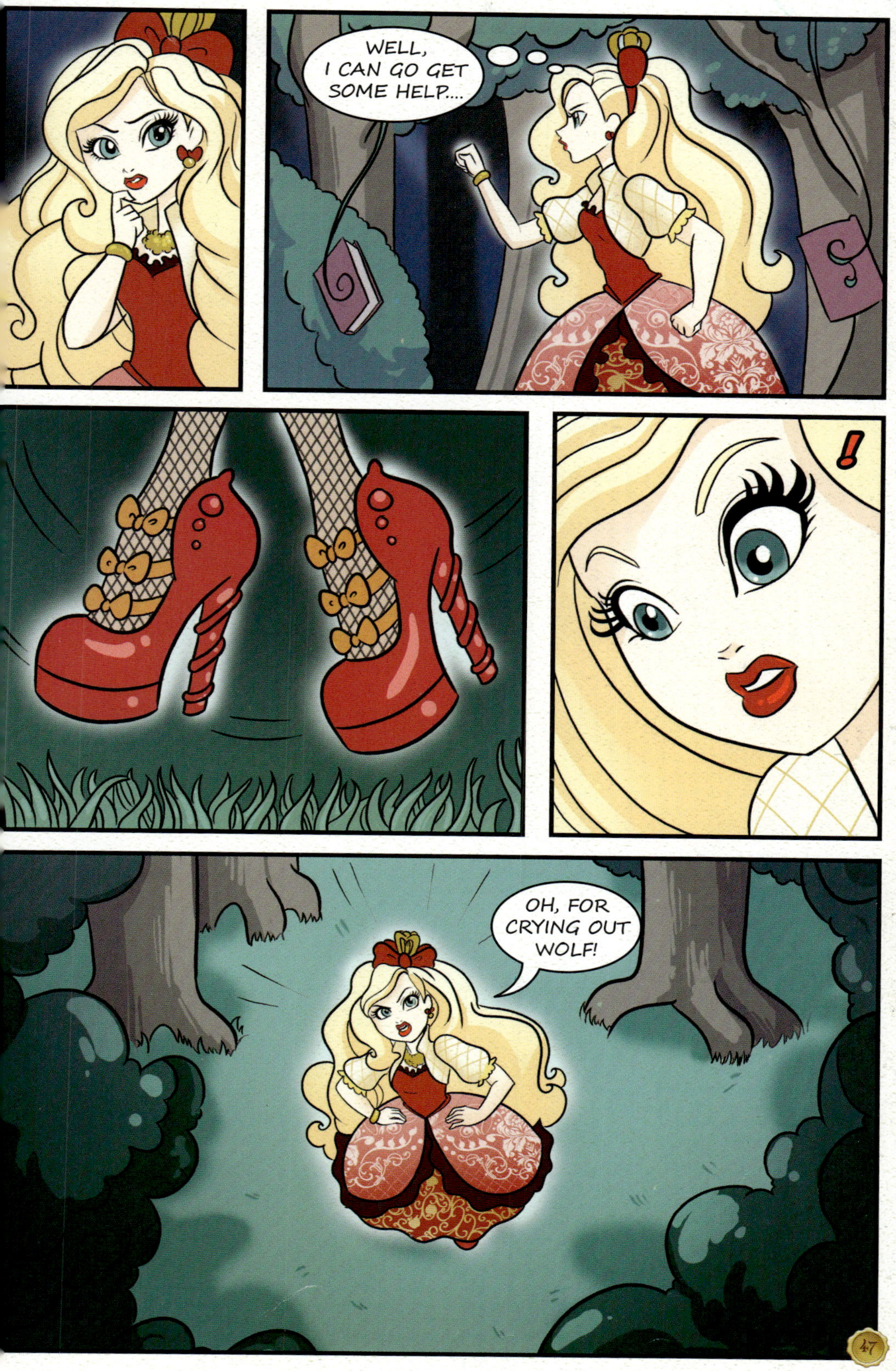
WELL, I CAN GO GET SOME HELP....
!
OH, FOR CRYING OUT WOLF!

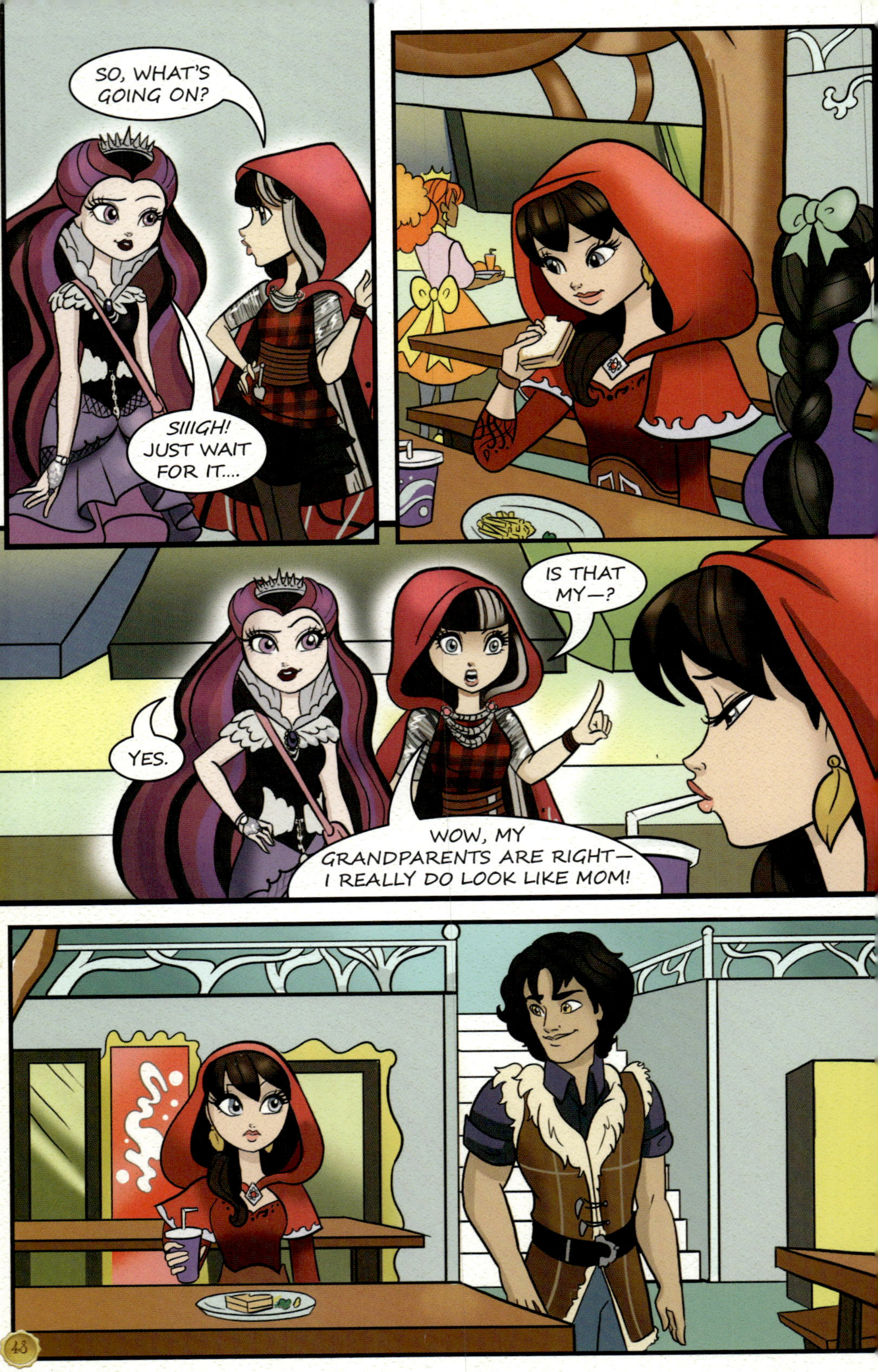

SO, WHAT'S GOING ON?
SIIIGH! JUST WAIT FOR IT....
IS THAT MY—?
YES.
WOW, MY GRANDPARENTS ARE RIGHT— I REALLY DO LOOK LIKE MOM!

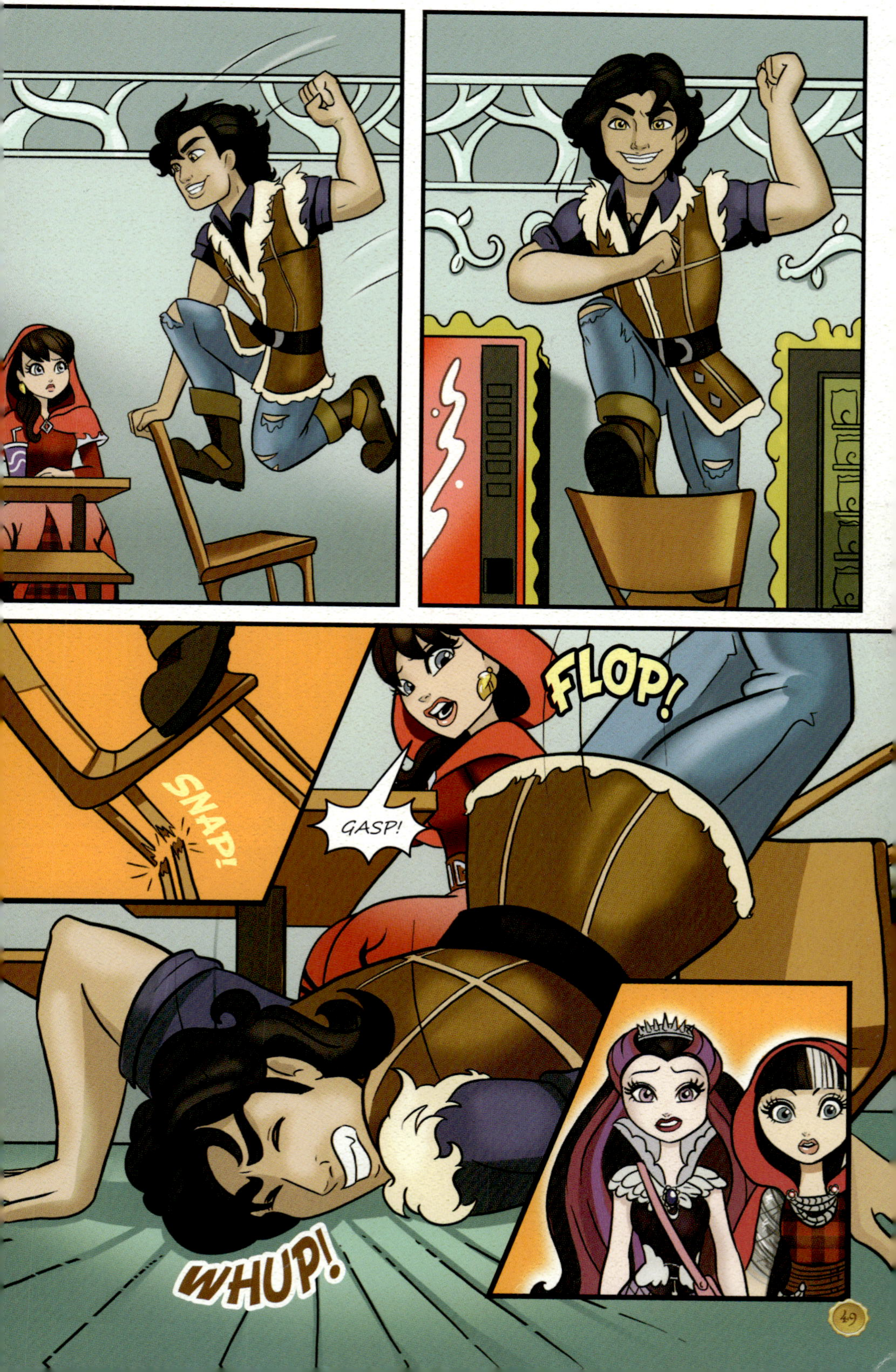
SNAP!
GASP!
FLOP!
WHUP!

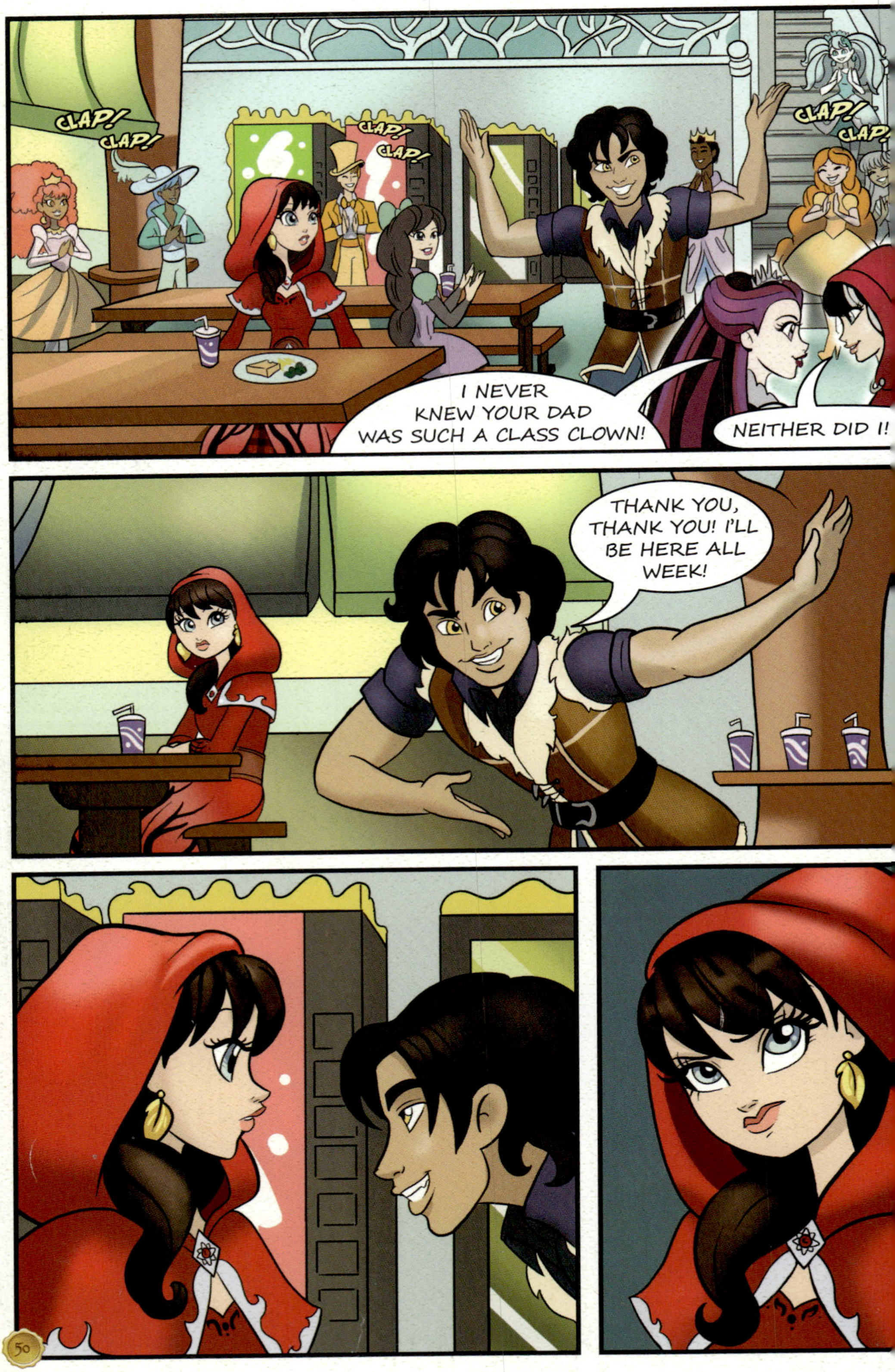
CLAP!
CLAP!
CLAP!
CLAP!
CLAP!
CLAP!
I NEVER KNEW YOUR DAD WAS SUCH A CLASS CLOWN!
NEITHER DID I!
THANK YOU, THANK YOU! I'LL BE HERE ALL WEEK!

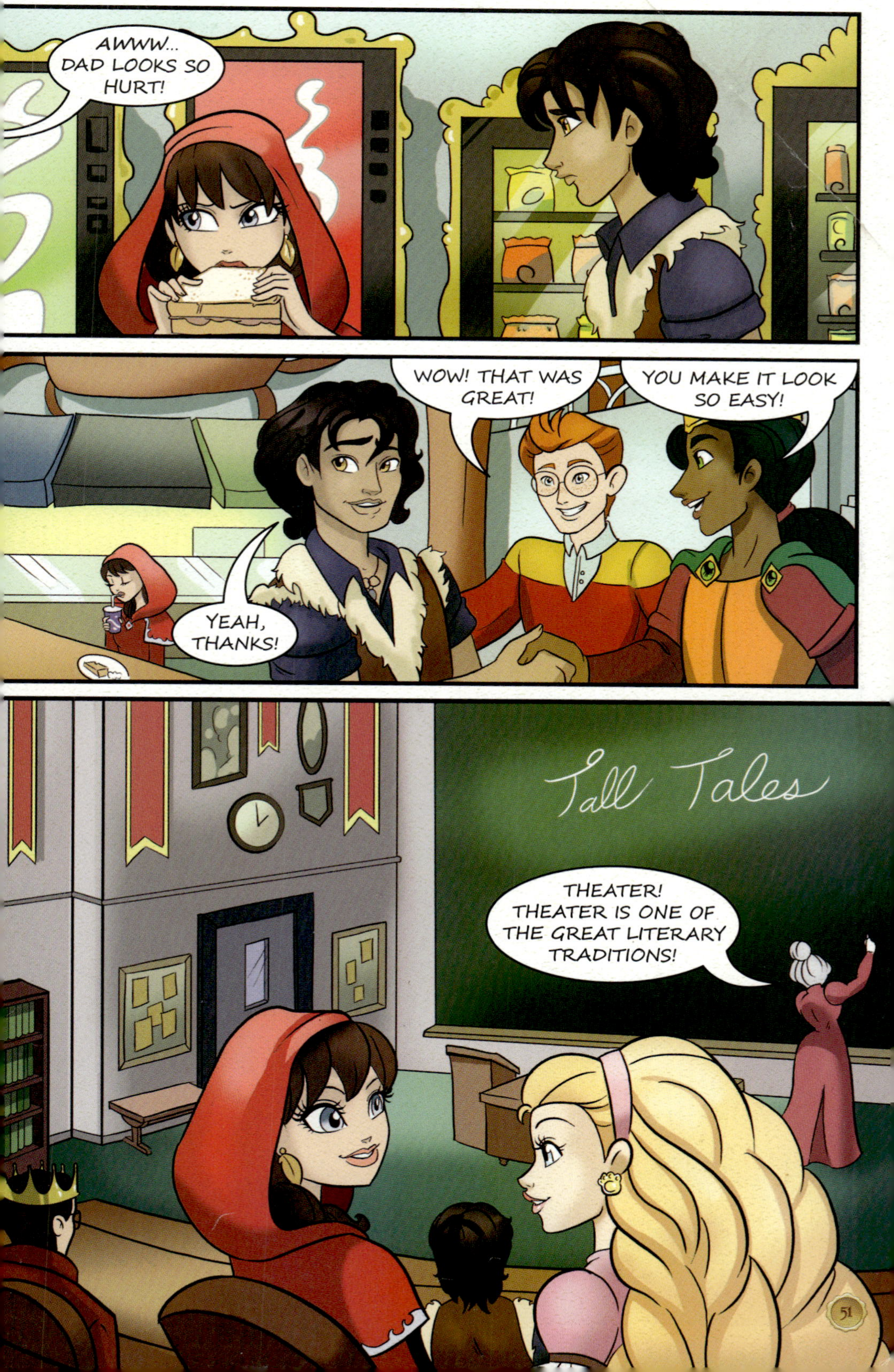
AWWW... DAD LOOKS SO HURT!
WOW! THAT WAS GREAT!
YOU MAKE IT LOOK SO EASY!
YEAH, THANKS!
Tall Tales
THEATER! THEATER IS ONE OF THE GREAT LITERARY TRADITIONS!

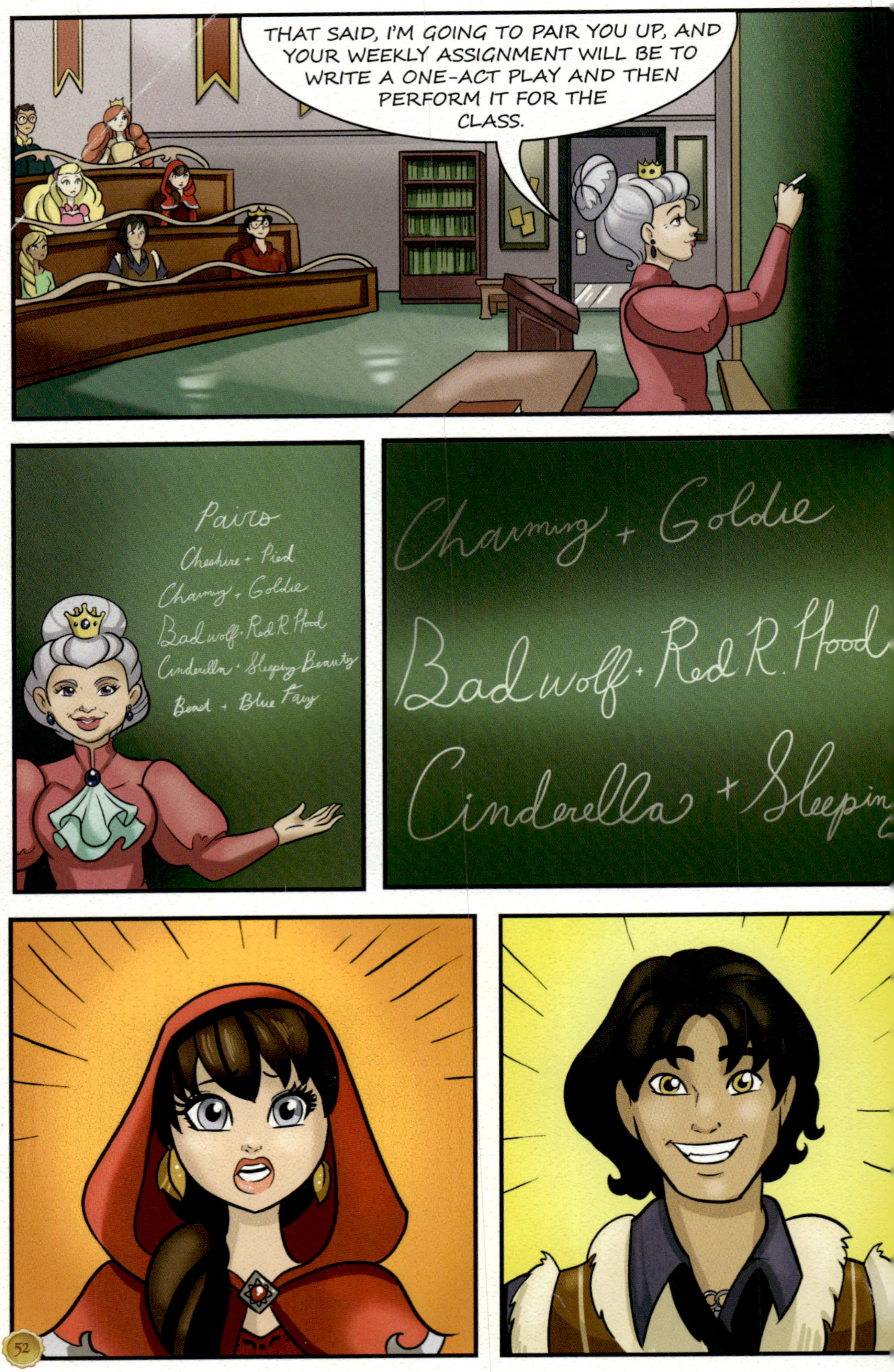
THAT SAID, I'M GOING TO PAIR YOU UP, AND YOUR WEEKLY ASSIGNMENT WILL BE TO WRITE A ONE-ACT PLAY AND THEN PERFORM IT FOR THE CLASS.
Pairs
Cheshire + Pied
Charming + Goldie
Badwolf + Red R. Hood
Cinderella + Sleeping Beauty
Beast + Blue Fairy
Charming + Goldie
Badwolf + Red R. Hood
Cinderella + Sleepin

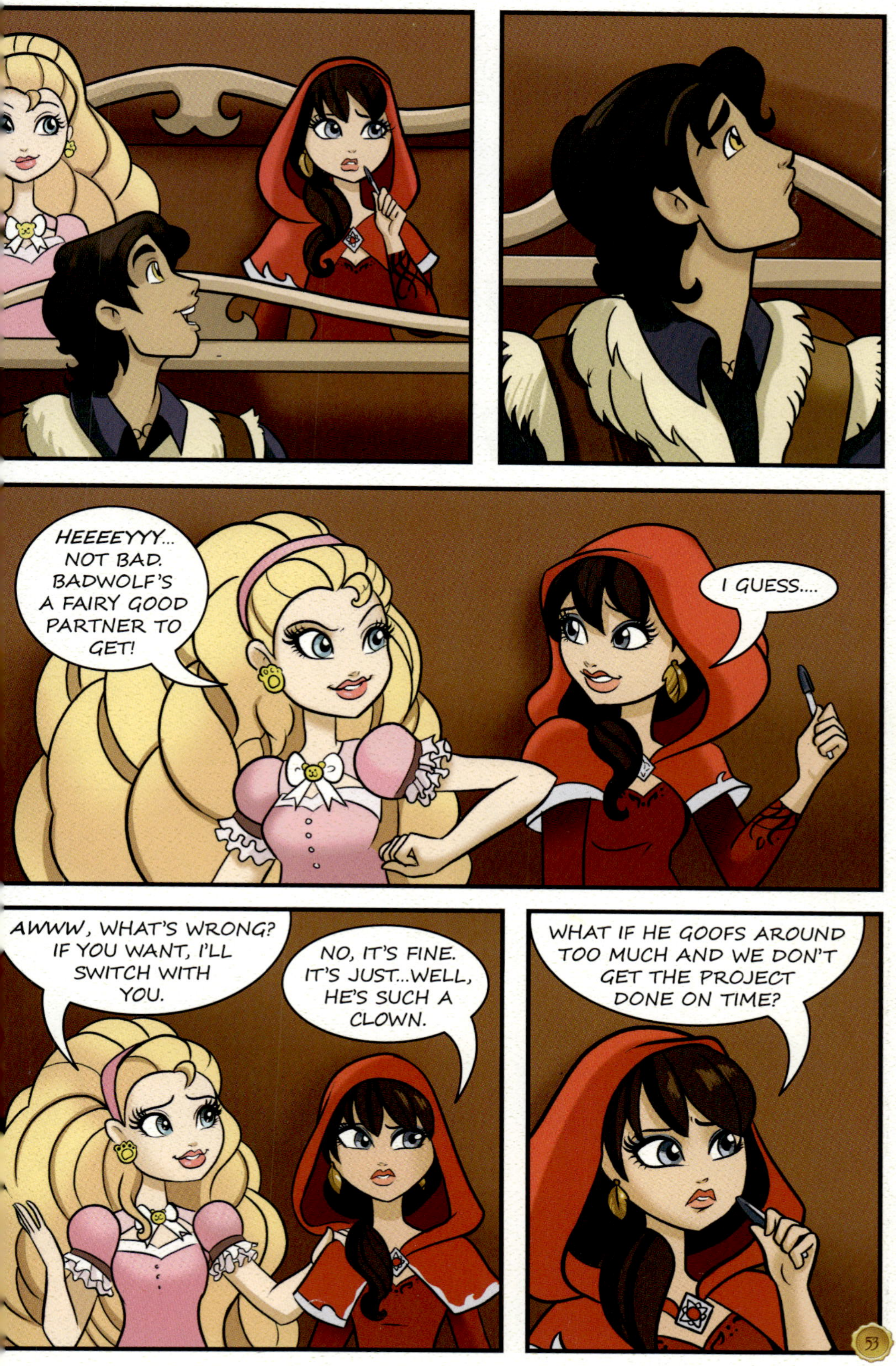
HEEEEYYY... NOT BAD. BADWOLF'S A FAIRY GOOD PARTNER TO GET!
I GUESS....
AWWW, WHAT'S WRONG? IF YOU WANT, I'LL SWITCH WITH YOU.
NO, IT'S FINE. IT'S JUST...WELL, HE'S SUCH A CLOWN.
WHAT IF HE GOOFS AROUND TOO MUCH AND WE DON'T GET THE PROJECT DONE ON TIME?

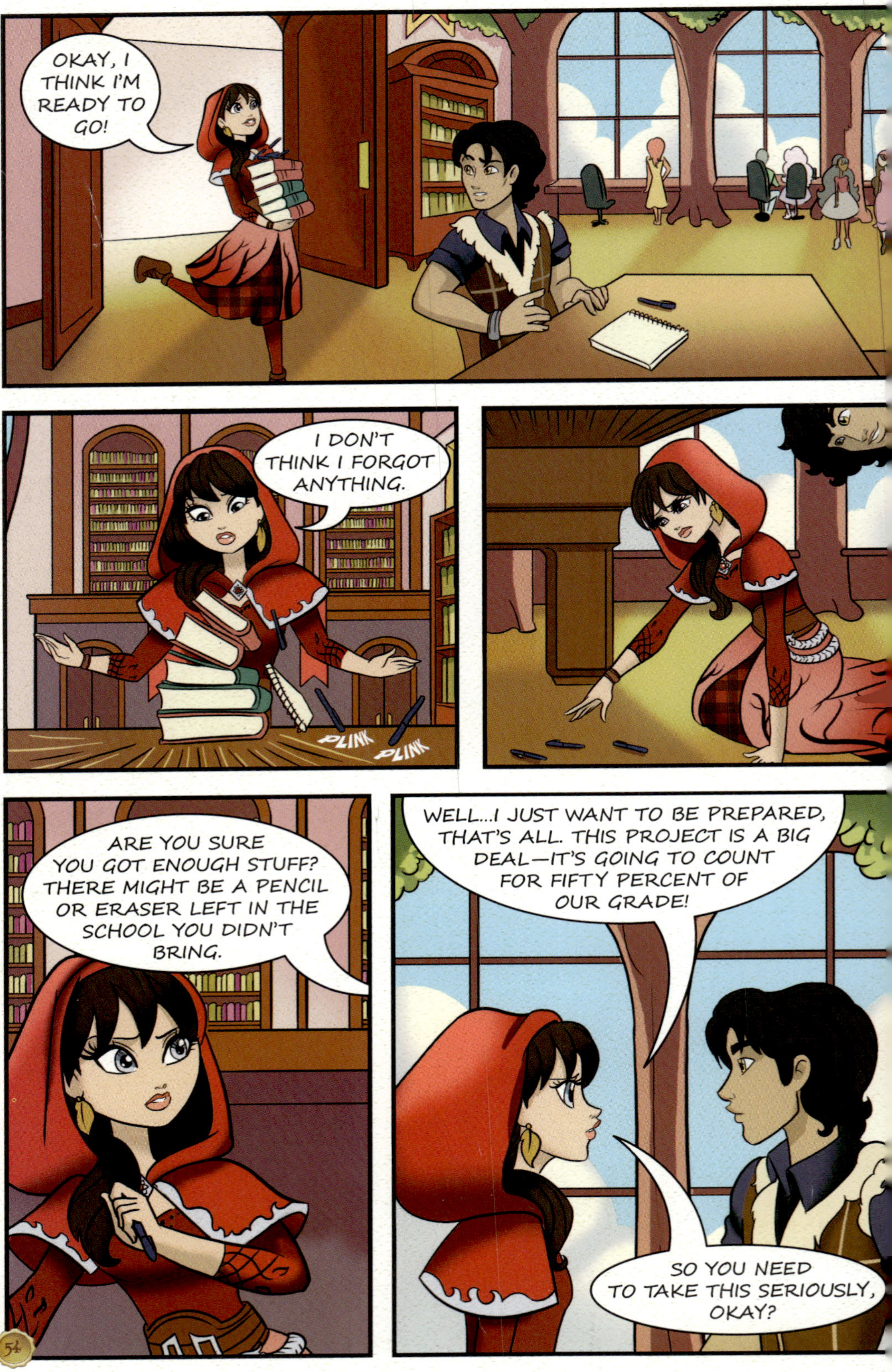
OKAY, I THINK I'M READY TO GO!
I DON'T THINK I FORGOT ANYTHING.
PLINK
PLINK
ARE YOU SURE YOU GOT ENOUGH STUFF? THERE MIGHT BE A PENCIL OR ERASER LEFT IN THE SCHOOL YOU DIDN'T BRING.
WELL...I JUST WANT TO BE PREPARED, THAT'S ALL. THIS PROJECT IS A BIG DEAL—IT'S GOING TO COUNT FOR FIFTY PERCENT OF OUR GRADE!
SO YOU NEED TO TAKE THIS SERIOUSLY, OKAY?

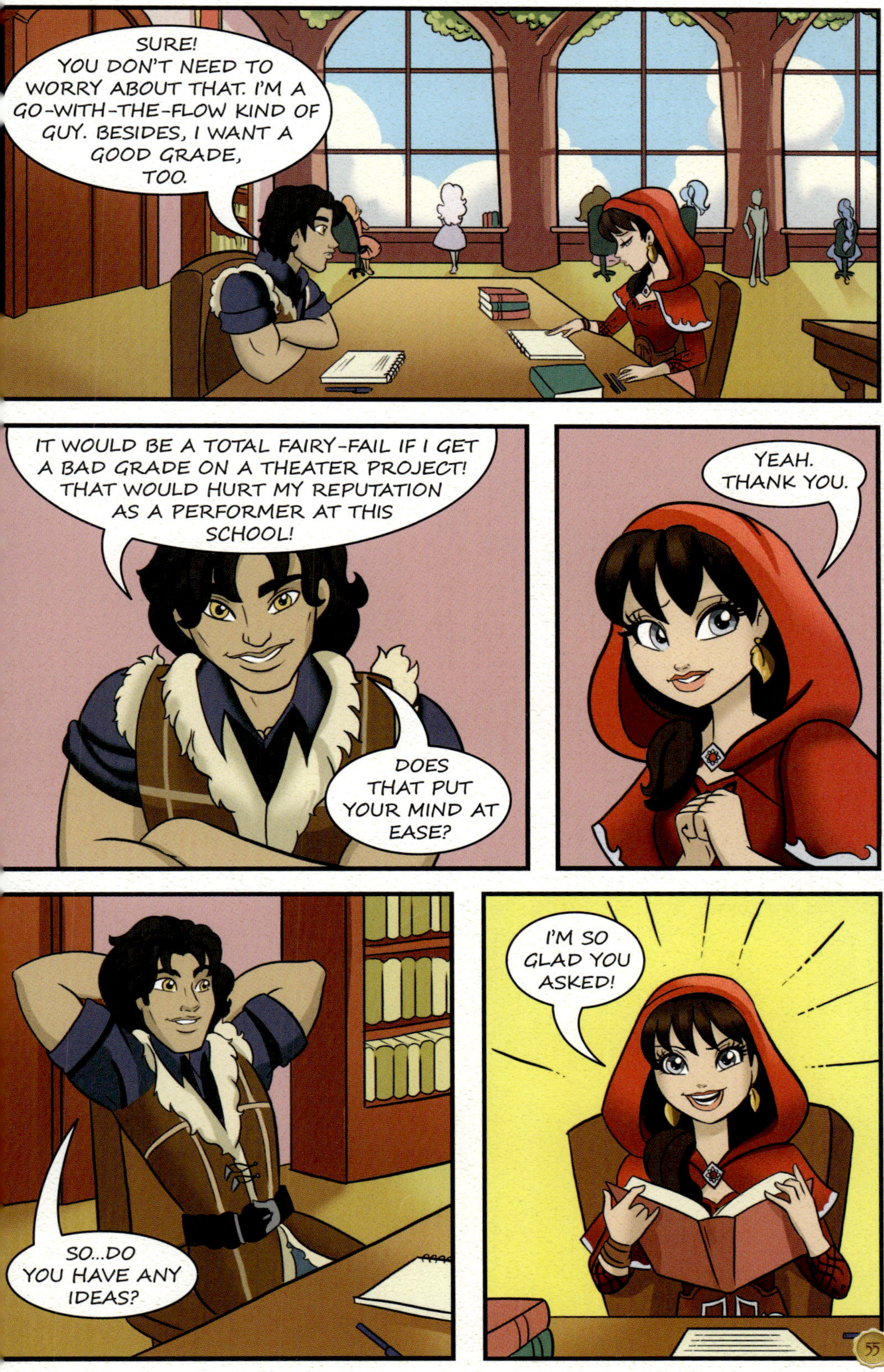
SURE! YOU DON'T NEED TO WORRY ABOUT THAT. I'M A GO-WITH-THE-FLOW KIND OF GUY. BESIDES, I WANT A GOOD GRADE, TOO.
IT WOULD BE A TOTAL FAIRY-FAIL IF I GET A BAD GRADE ON A THEATER PROJECT! THAT WOULD HURT MY REPUTATION AS A PERFORMER AT THIS SCHOOL!
DOES THAT PUT YOUR MIND AT EASE?
YEAH. THANK YOU.
SO...DO YOU HAVE ANY IDEAS?
I'M SO GLAD YOU ASKED!

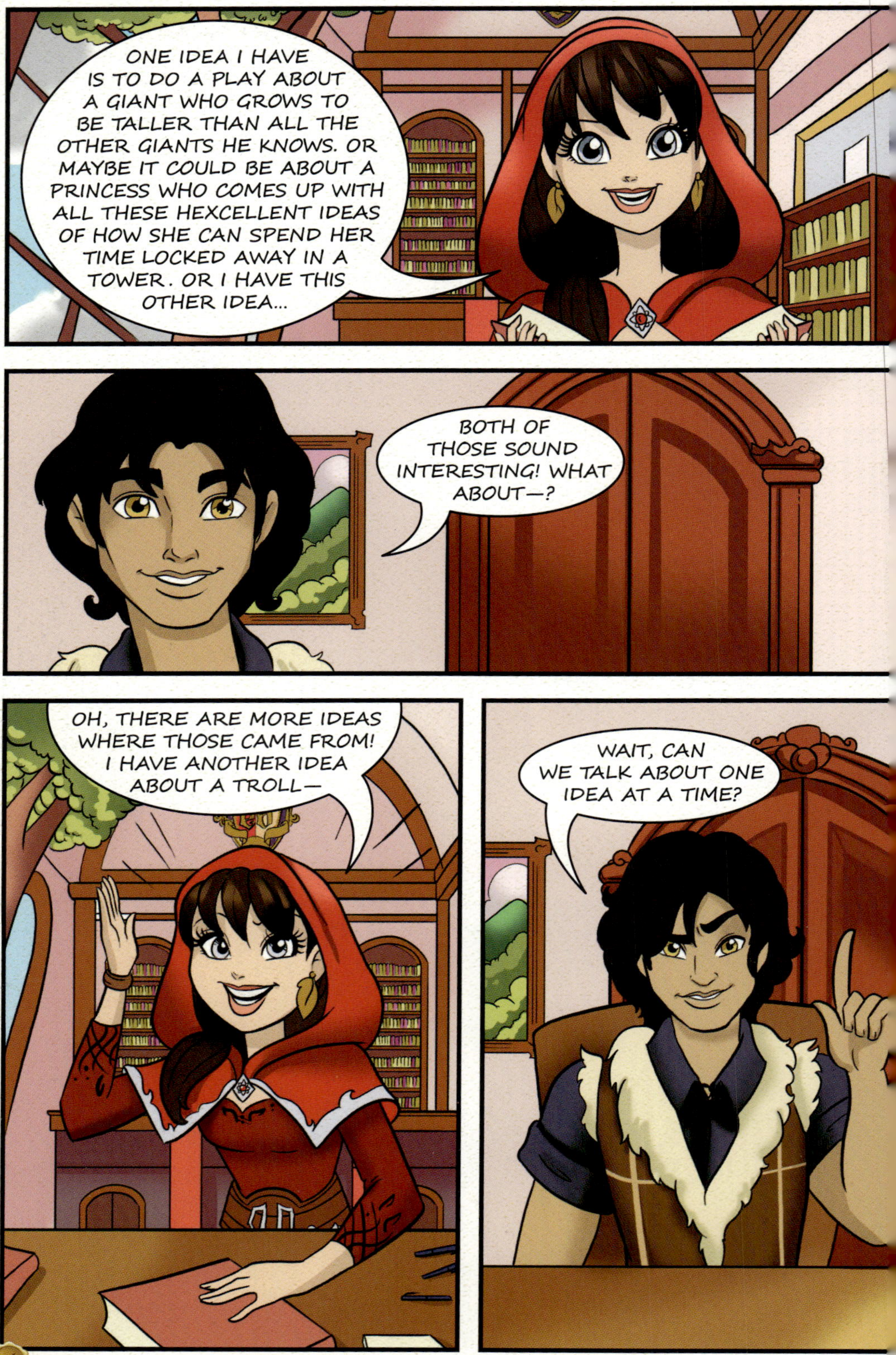
ONE IDEA I HAVE IS TO DO A PLAY ABOUT A GIANT WHO GROWS TO BE TALLER THAN ALL THE OTHER GIANTS HE KNOWS. OR MAYBE IT COULD BE ABOUT A PRINCESS WHO COMES UP WITH ALL THESE HEXCELLENT IDEAS OF HOW SHE CAN SPEND HER TIME LOCKED AWAY IN A TOWER. OR I HAVE THIS OTHER IDEA...
BOTH OF THOSE SOUND INTERESTING! WHAT ABOUT—?
OH, THERE ARE MORE IDEAS WHERE THOSE CAME FROM! I HAVE ANOTHER IDEA ABOUT A TROLL—
WAIT, CAN WE TALK ABOUT ONE IDEA AT A TIME?

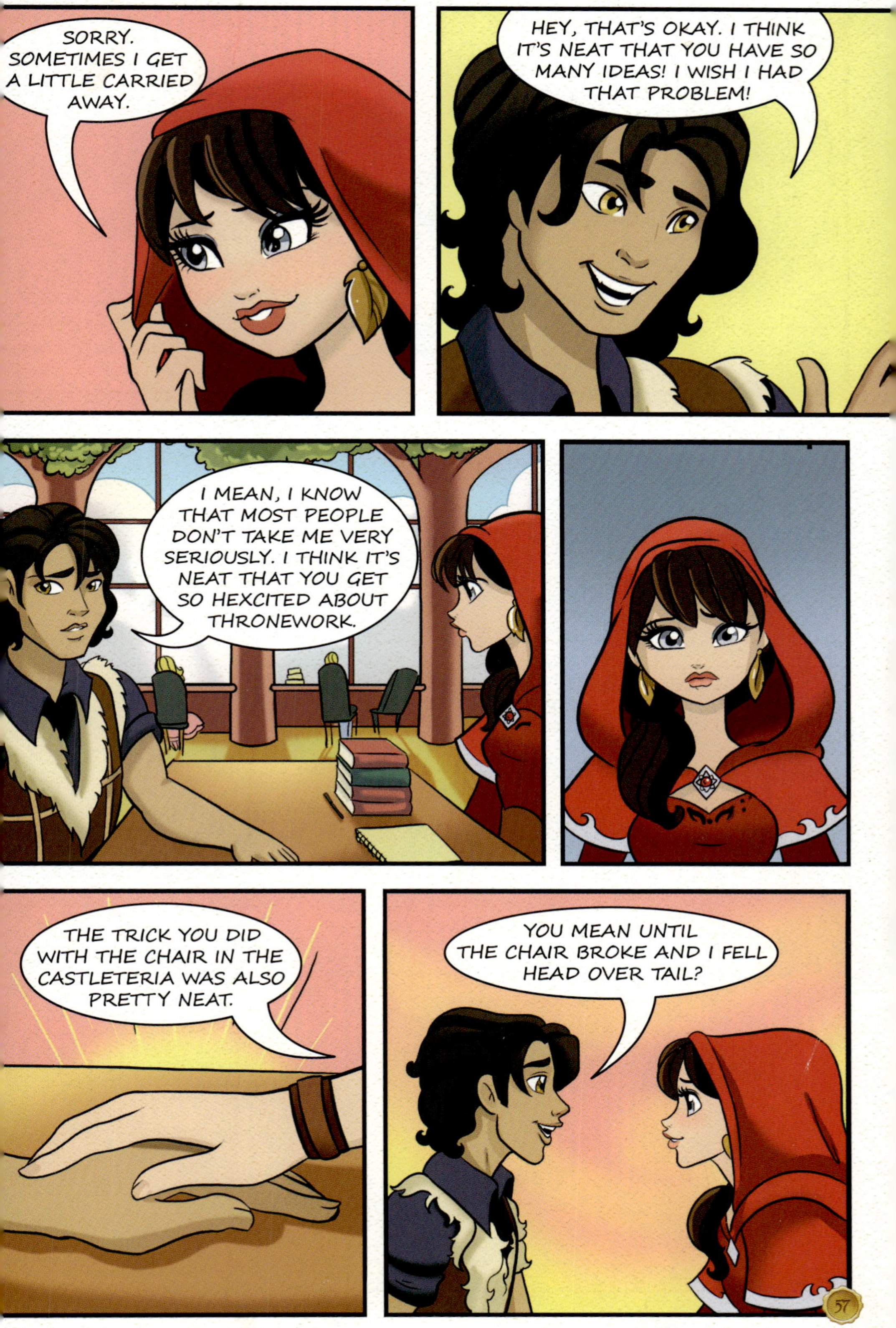
SORRY. SOMETIMES I GET A LITTLE CARRIED AWAY.
HEY, THAT'S OKAY. I THINK IT'S NEAT THAT YOU HAVE SO MANY IDEAS! I WISH I HAD THAT PROBLEM!
I MEAN, I KNOW THAT MOST PEOPLE DON'T TAKE ME VERY SERIOUSLY. I THINK IT'S NEAT THAT YOU GET SO HEXCITED ABOUT THRONEWORK.
THE TRICK YOU DID WITH THE CHAIR IN THE CASTLETERIA WAS ALSO PRETTY NEAT.
YOU MEAN UNTIL THE CHAIR BROKE AND I FELL HEAD OVER TAIL?

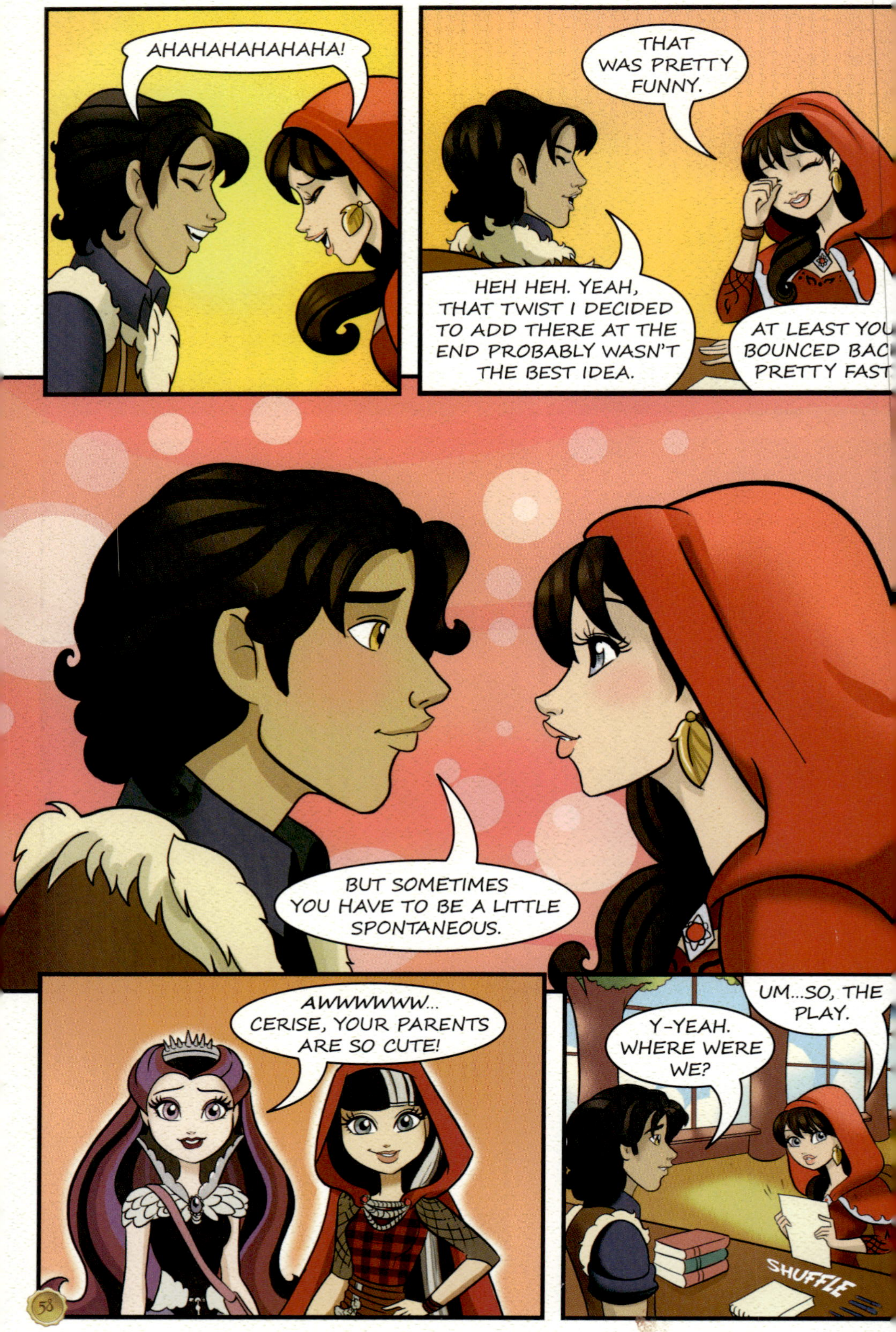
AHAHAHAHAHAHA!
THAT WAS PRETTY FUNNY.
HEH HEH. YEAH, THAT TWIST I DECIDED TO ADD THERE AT THE END PROBABLY WASN'T THE BEST IDEA.
AT LEAST YOU BOUNCED BAC PRETTY FAST
BUT SOMETIMES YOU HAVE TO BE A LITTLE SPONTANEOUS.
AWWWWWW... CERISE, YOUR PARENTS ARE SO CUTE!
UM...SO, THE PLAY.
Y-YEAH. WHERE WERE WE?
SHUFFLE

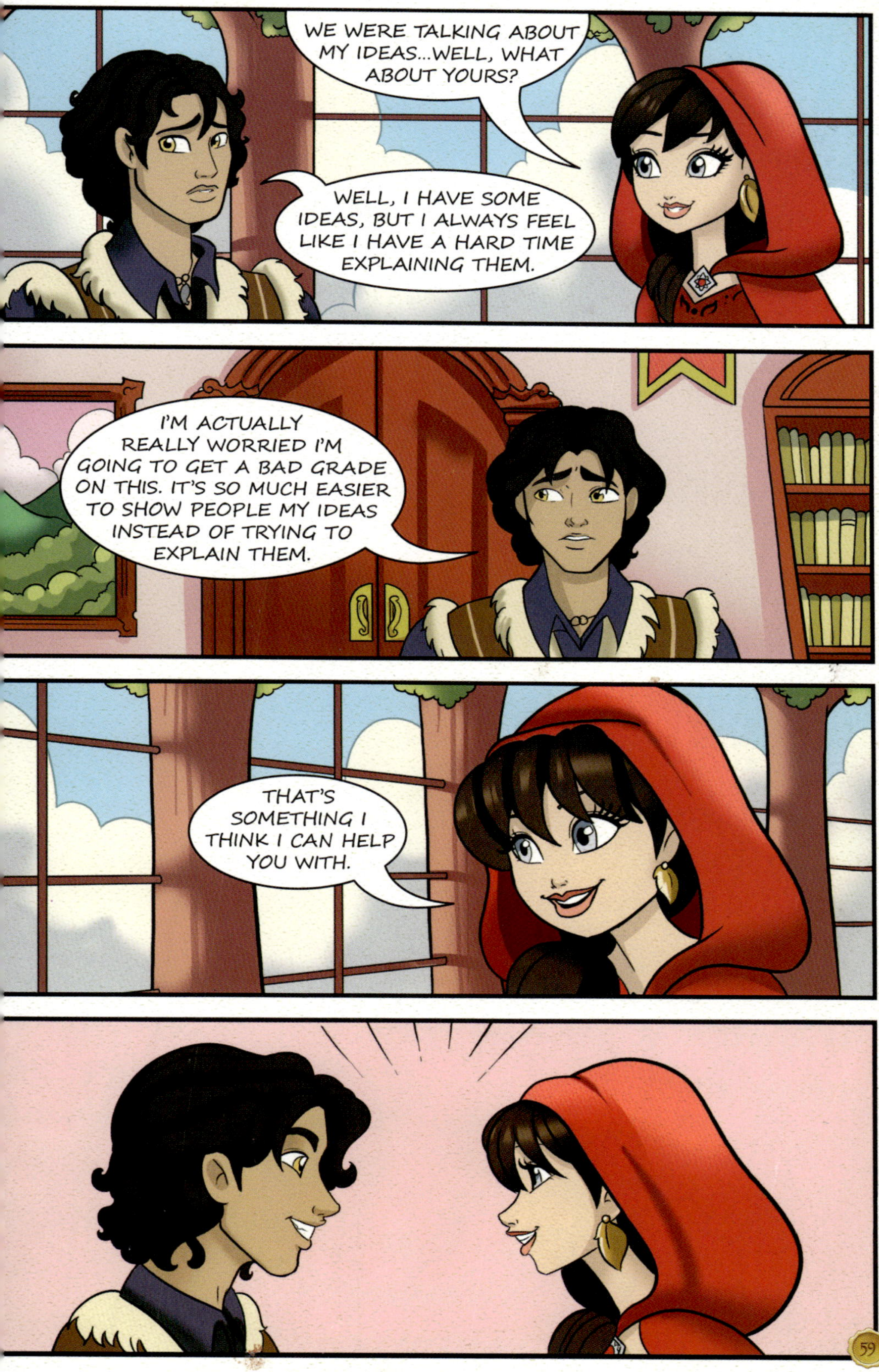
WE WERE TALKING ABOUT MY IDEAS...WELL, WHAT ABOUT YOURS?
WELL, I HAVE SOME IDEAS, BUT I ALWAYS FEEL LIKE I HAVE A HARD TIME EXPLAINING THEM.
I'M ACTUALLY REALLY WORRIED I'M GOING TO GET A BAD GRADE ON THIS. IT'S SO MUCH EASIER TO SHOW PEOPLE MY IDEAS INSTEAD OF TRYING TO EXPLAIN THEM.
THAT'S SOMETHING I THINK I CAN HELP YOU WITH.

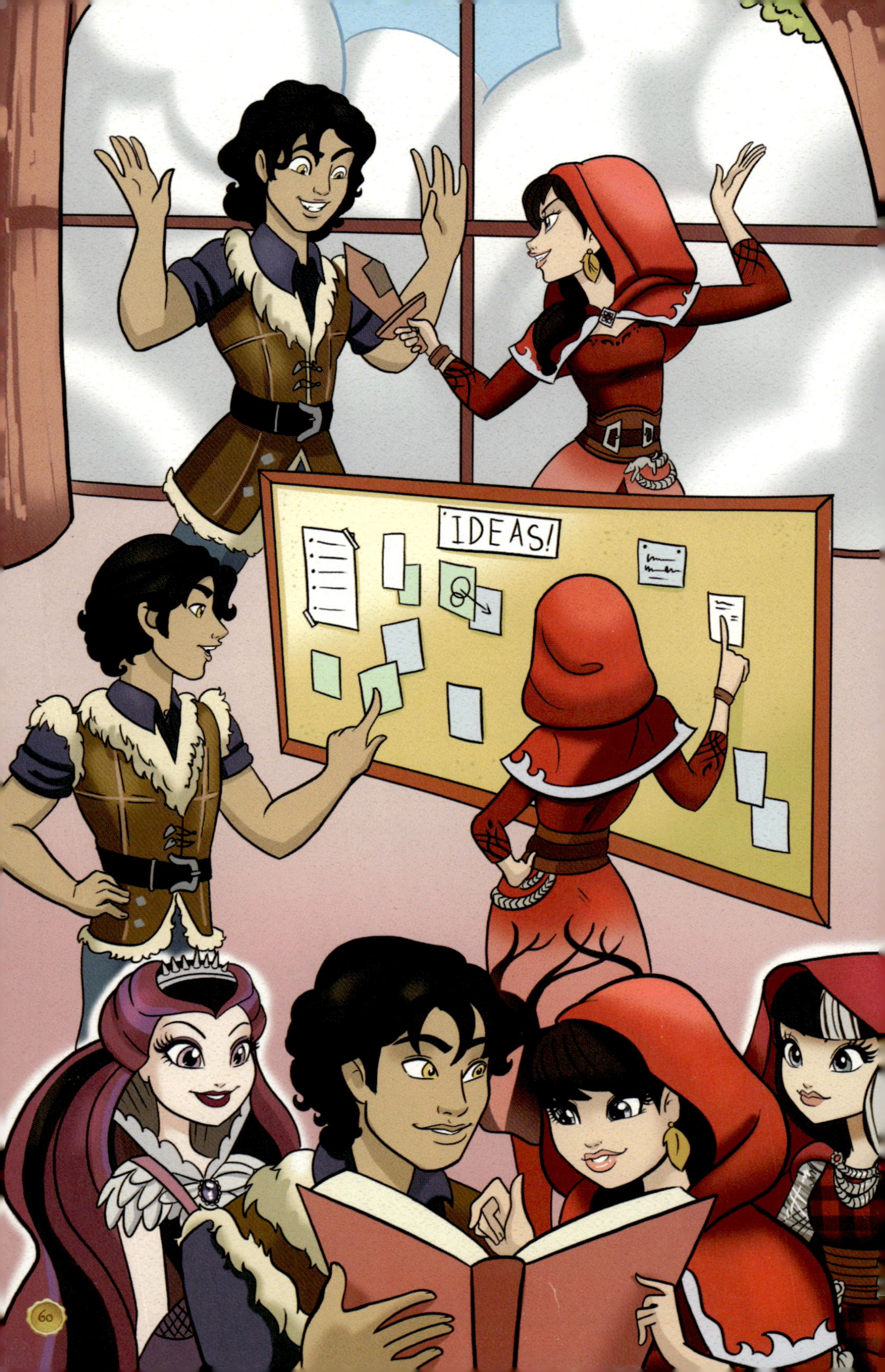
IDEAS!

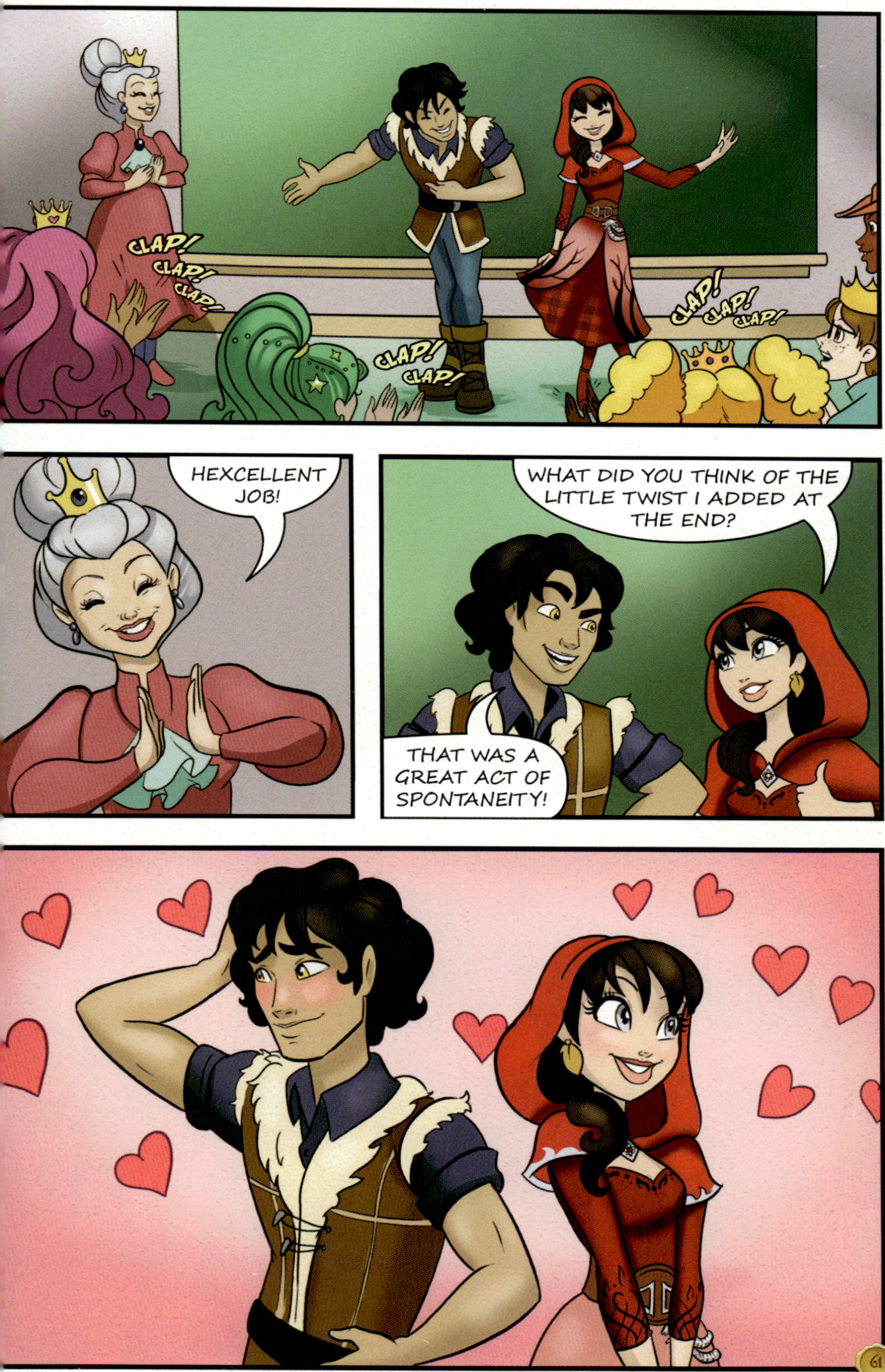
CLAP! CLAP! CLAP!
CLAP! CLAP! CLAP!
CLAP! CLAP!
HEXCELLENT JOB!
WHAT DID YOU THINK OF THE LITTLE TWIST I ADDED AT THE END?
THAT WAS A GREAT ACT OF SPONTANEITY!

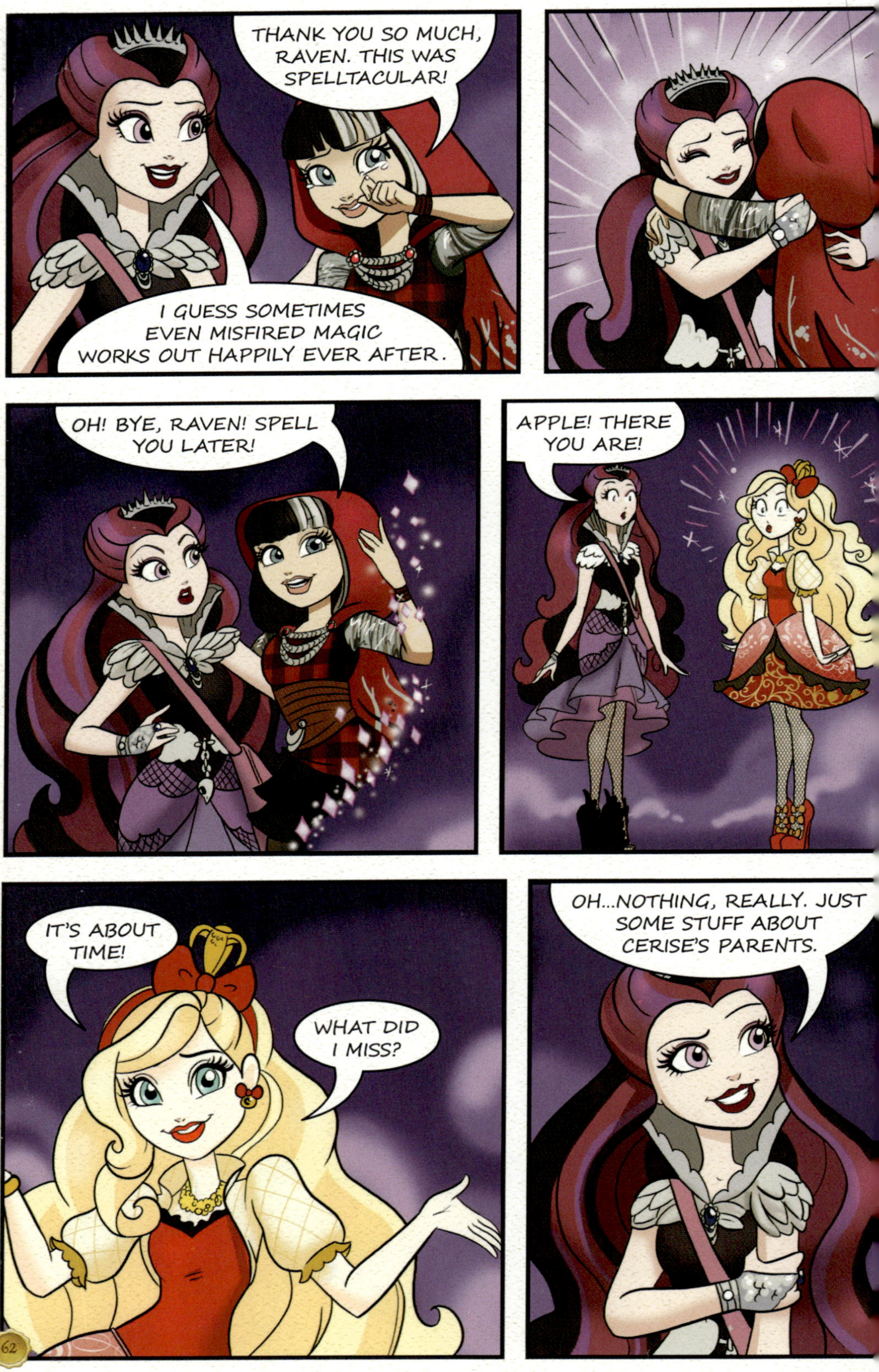
THANK YOU SO MUCH, RAVEN. THIS WAS SPELLTACULAR!
I GUESS SOMETIMES EVEN MISFIRED MAGIC WORKS OUT HAPPILY EVER AFTER.
OH! BYE, RAVEN! SPELL YOU LATER!
APPLE! THERE YOU ARE!
IT'S ABOUT TIME!
WHAT DID I MISS?
OH...NOTHING, REALLY. JUST SOME STUFF ABOUT CERISE'S PARENTS.

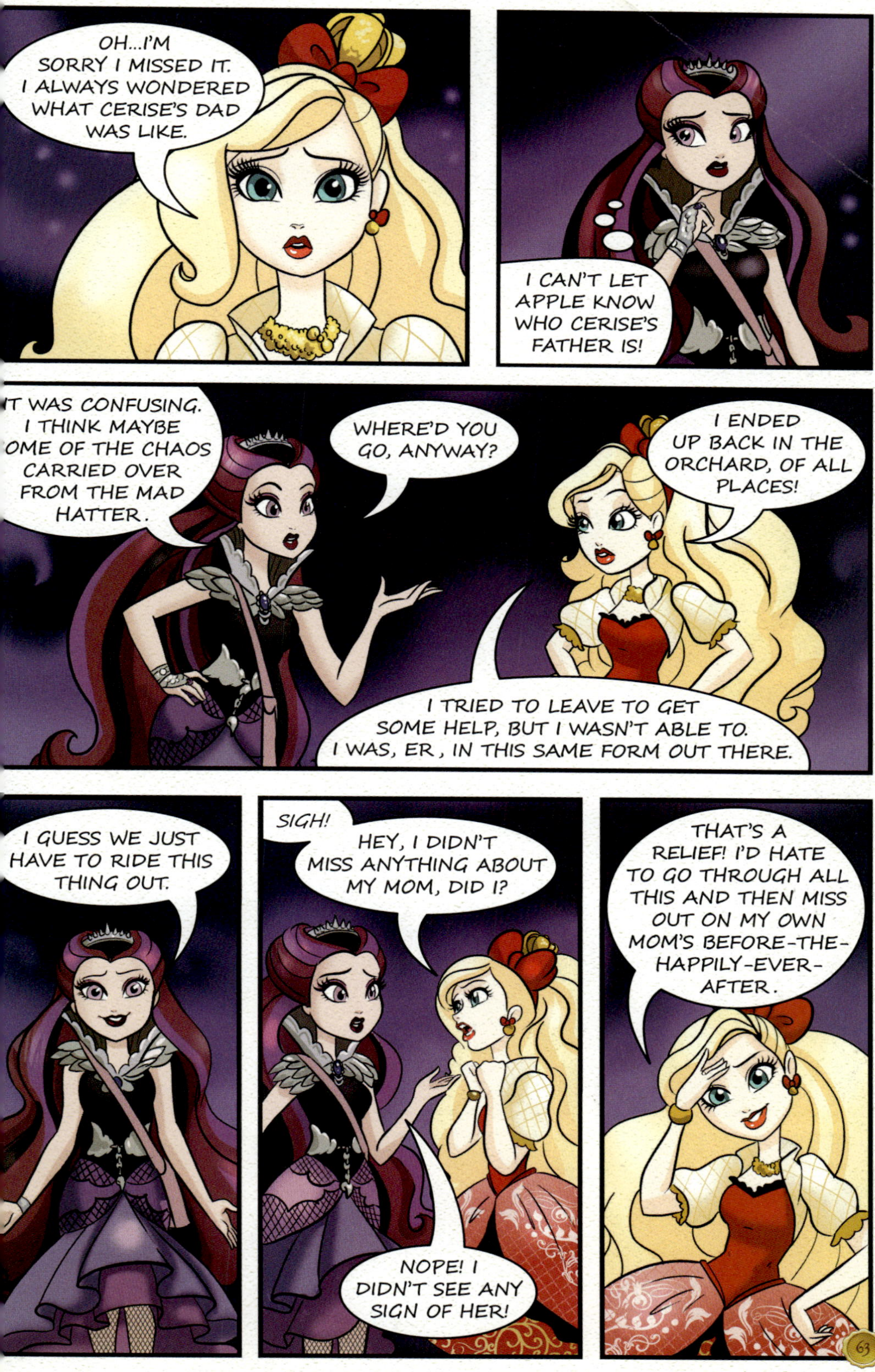
OH...I'M SORRY I MISSED IT. I ALWAYS WONDERED WHAT CERISE'S DAD WAS LIKE.
I CAN'T LET APPLE KNOW WHO CERISE'S FATHER IS!
IT WAS CONFUSING. I THINK MAYBE SOME OF THE CHAOS CARRIED OVER FROM THE MAD HATTER.
WHERE'D YOU GO, ANYWAY?
I ENDED UP BACK IN THE ORCHARD, OF ALL PLACES!
I TRIED TO LEAVE TO GET SOME HELP, BUT I WASN'T ABLE TO. I WAS, ER, IN THIS SAME FORM OUT THERE.
I GUESS WE JUST HAVE TO RIDE THIS THING OUT.
SIGH!
HEY, I DIDN'T MISS ANYTHING ABOUT MY MOM, DID I?
NOPE! I DIDN'T SEE ANY SIGN OF HER!
THAT'S A RELIEF! I'D HATE TO GO THROUGH ALL THIS AND THEN MISS OUT ON MY OWN MOM'S BEFORE-THE-HAPPILY-EVER-AFTER.

Story Five: King Charming

HERE WE GO AGAIN!

HI, RAVEN! HI, APPLE!

WOW, THIS IS A WEIRD DREAM.

UHH... IT'S NOT A DREAM.

WHAT DO YOU MEAN?

I'LL HEXPLAIN SUPER FAST....

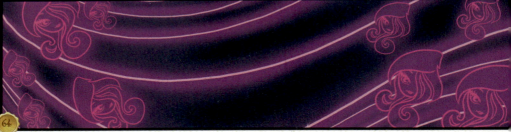

THIS IS SO HEXCITING! WHOSE YEARBOOK DO YOU THINK WE'RE IN, DEX? OUR MOM'S OR OUR DAD'S?

FROM THE LOOK OF THINGS, PROBABLY DAD'S.

THOUGH...I WONDER WHY DARING ISN'T HERE. WHY JUST ME AND DARLING?

MORE WONDERLANDIAN SIDE EFFECTS?

WHAT DO YOU THINK, RAVEN?

HMMM, MAYBE...

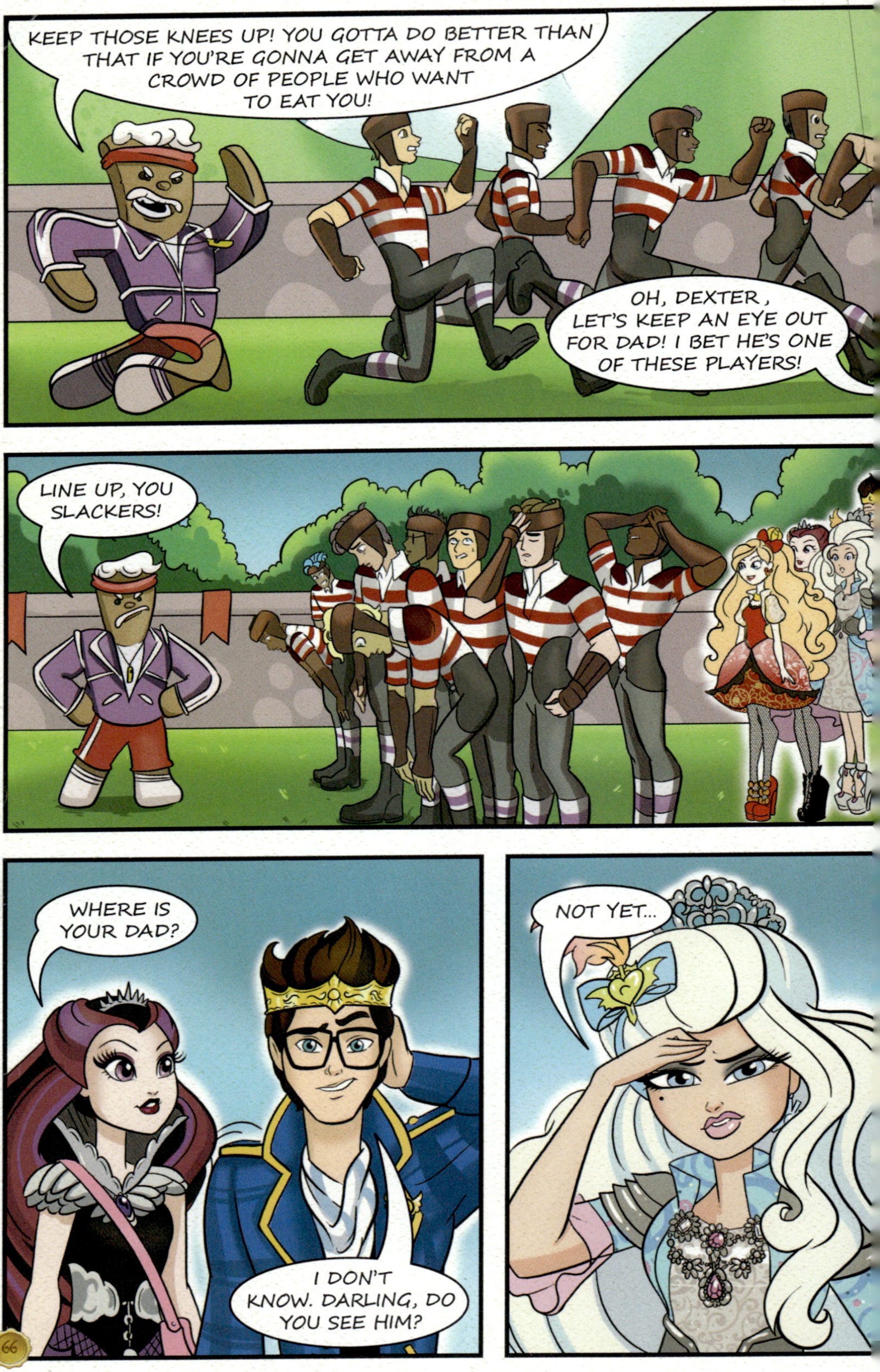
KEEP THOSE KNEES UP! YOU GOTTA DO BETTER THAN THAT IF YOU'RE GONNA GET AWAY FROM A CROWD OF PEOPLE WHO WANT TO EAT YOU!
OH, DEXTER, LET'S KEEP AN EYE OUT FOR DAD! I BET HE'S ONE OF THESE PLAYERS!
LINE UP, YOU SLACKERS!
WHERE IS YOUR DAD?
I DON'T KNOW. DARLING, DO YOU SEE HIM?
NOT YET...

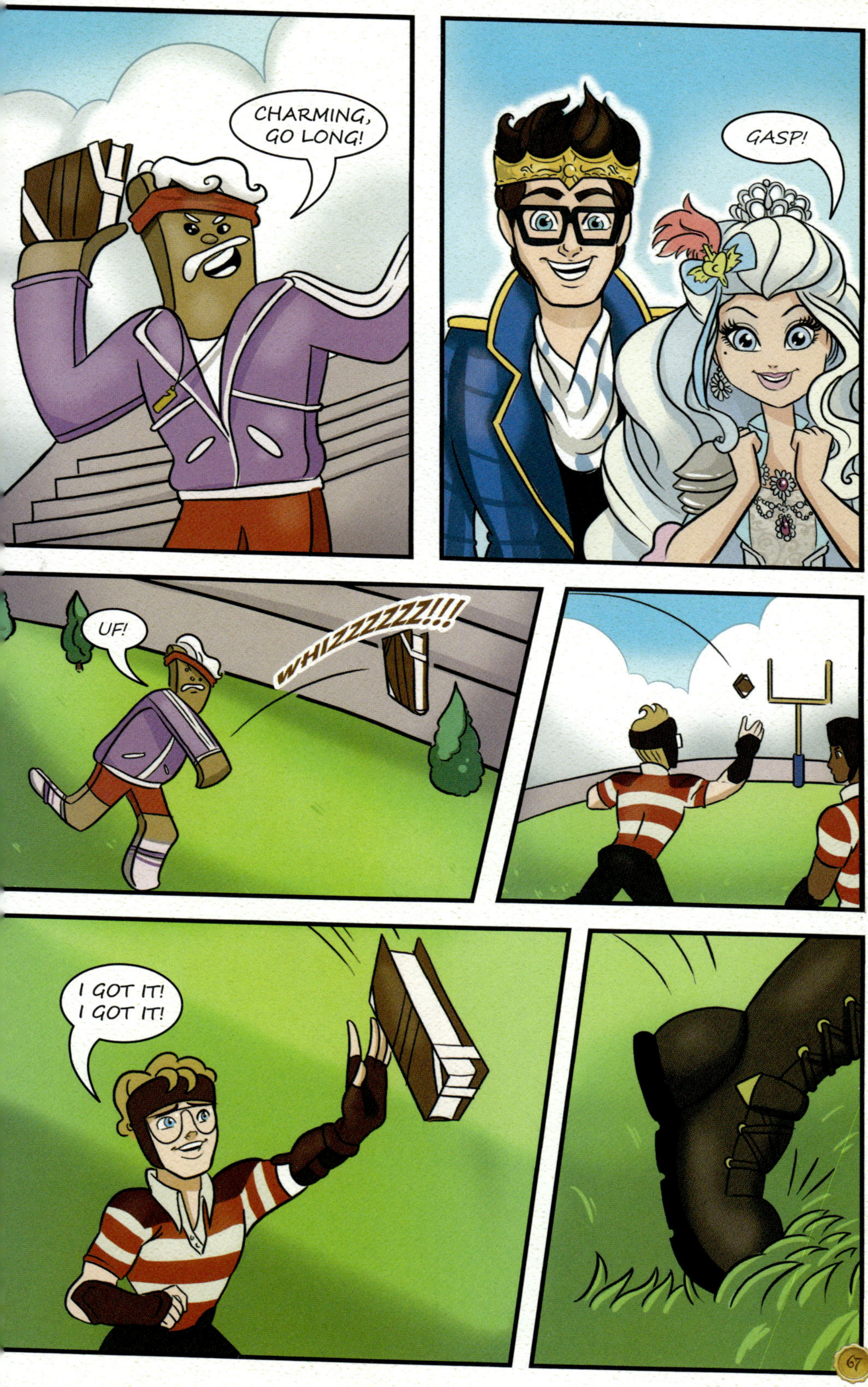
CHARMING, GO LONG!
GASP!
UF!
WHIZZZZZZ!!!
I GOT IT! I GOT IT!

WHUMP!

GROOOOAAANNN...

THUMP

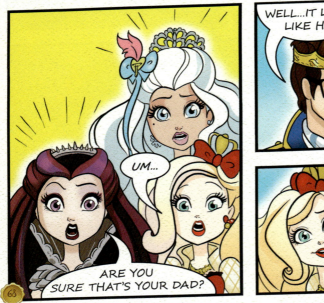

UM...

ARE YOU SURE THAT'S YOUR DAD?

WELL...IT LOOKS LIKE HIM.

HE'S NOT VERY COORDINATED. CAN THAT REALLY BE HIM?

MAYBE HE JUST GOT UP ON THE WRONG SIDE OF THE PAGE TODAY.

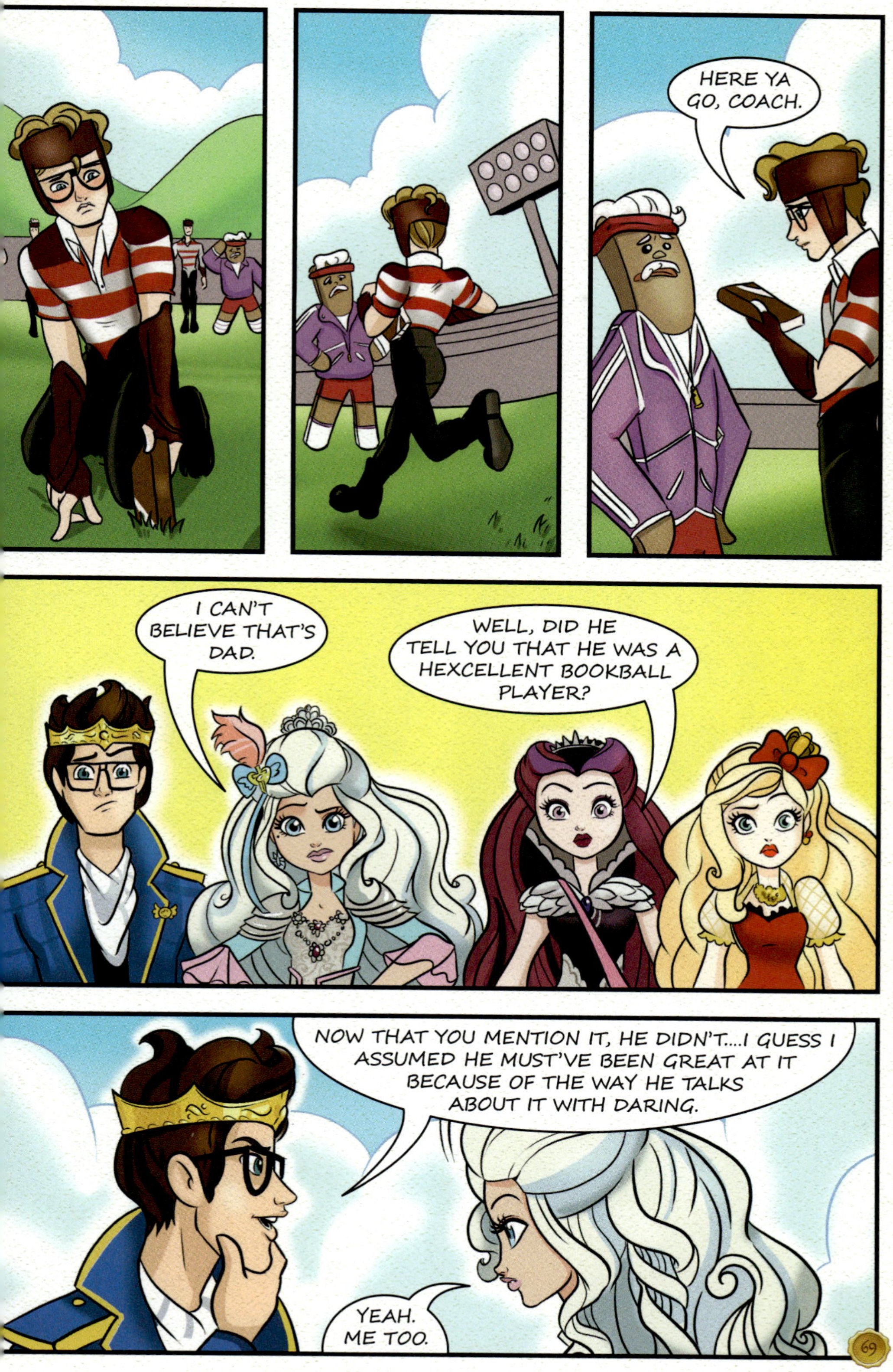
HERE YA GO, COACH.
I CAN'T BELIEVE THAT'S DAD.
WELL, DID HE TELL YOU THAT HE WAS A HEXCELLENT BOOKBALL PLAYER?
NOW THAT YOU MENTION IT, HE DIDN'T....I GUESS I ASSUMED HE MUST'VE BEEN GREAT AT IT BECAUSE OF THE WAY HE TALKS ABOUT IT WITH DARING.
YEAH. ME TOO.

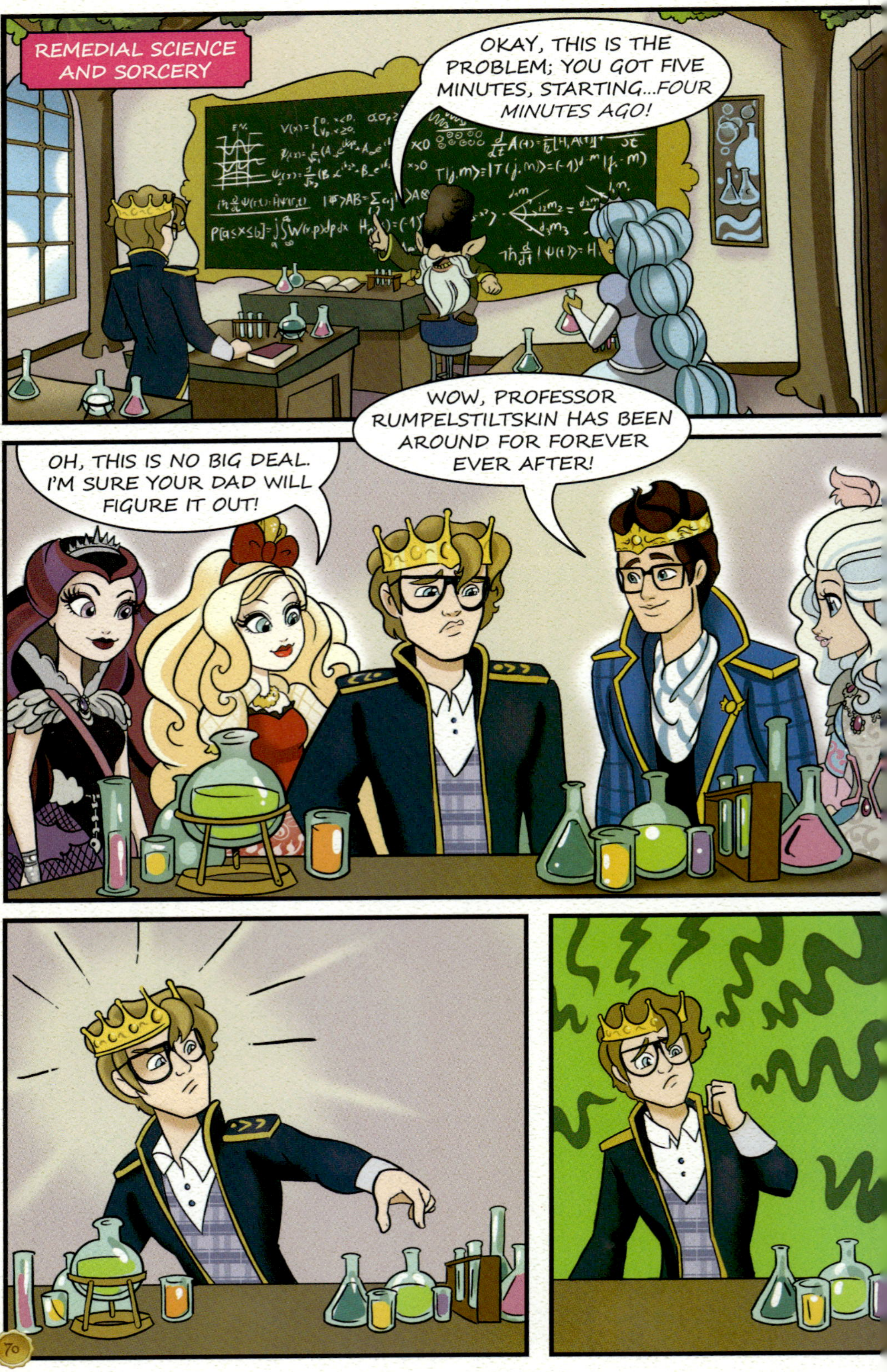
REMEDIAL SCIENCE AND SORCERY
OKAY, THIS IS THE PROBLEM; YOU GOT FIVE MINUTES, STARTING...FOUR MINUTES AGO!
OH, THIS IS NO BIG DEAL. I'M SURE YOUR DAD WILL FIGURE IT OUT!
WOW, PROFESSOR RUMPELSTILTSKIN HAS BEEN AROUND FOR FOREVER EVER AFTER!

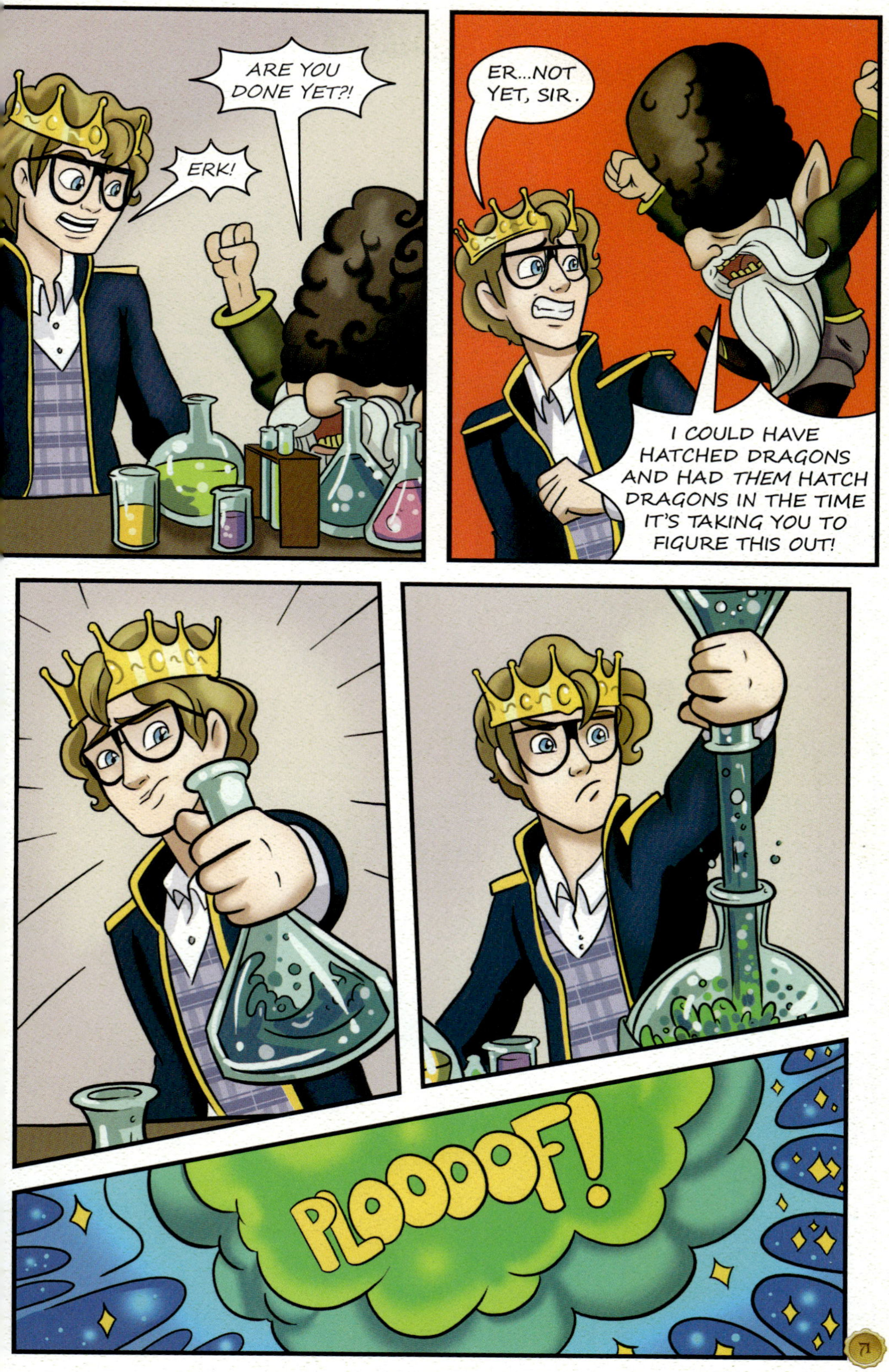
ARE YOU DONE YET?!
ERK!
ER...NOT YET, SIR.
I COULD HAVE HATCHED DRAGONS AND HAD *THEM* HATCH DRAGONS IN THE TIME IT'S TAKING YOU TO FIGURE THIS OUT!
PLOOOOF!

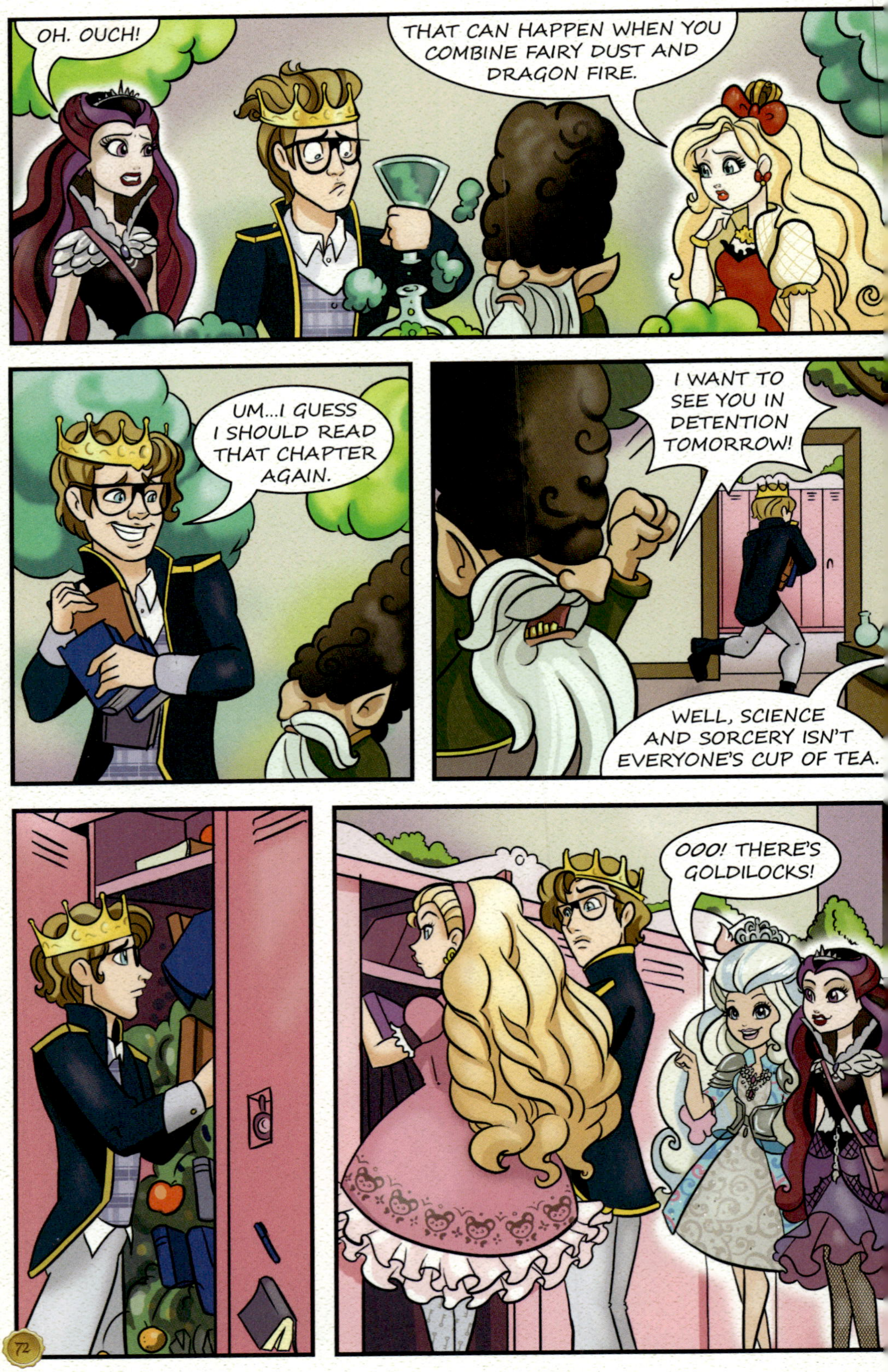
OH. OUCH!
THAT CAN HAPPEN WHEN YOU COMBINE FAIRY DUST AND DRAGON FIRE.
UM...I GUESS I SHOULD READ THAT CHAPTER AGAIN.
I WANT TO SEE YOU IN DETENTION TOMORROW!
WELL, SCIENCE AND SORCERY ISN'T EVERYONE'S CUP OF TEA.
OOO! THERE'S GOLDILOCKS!

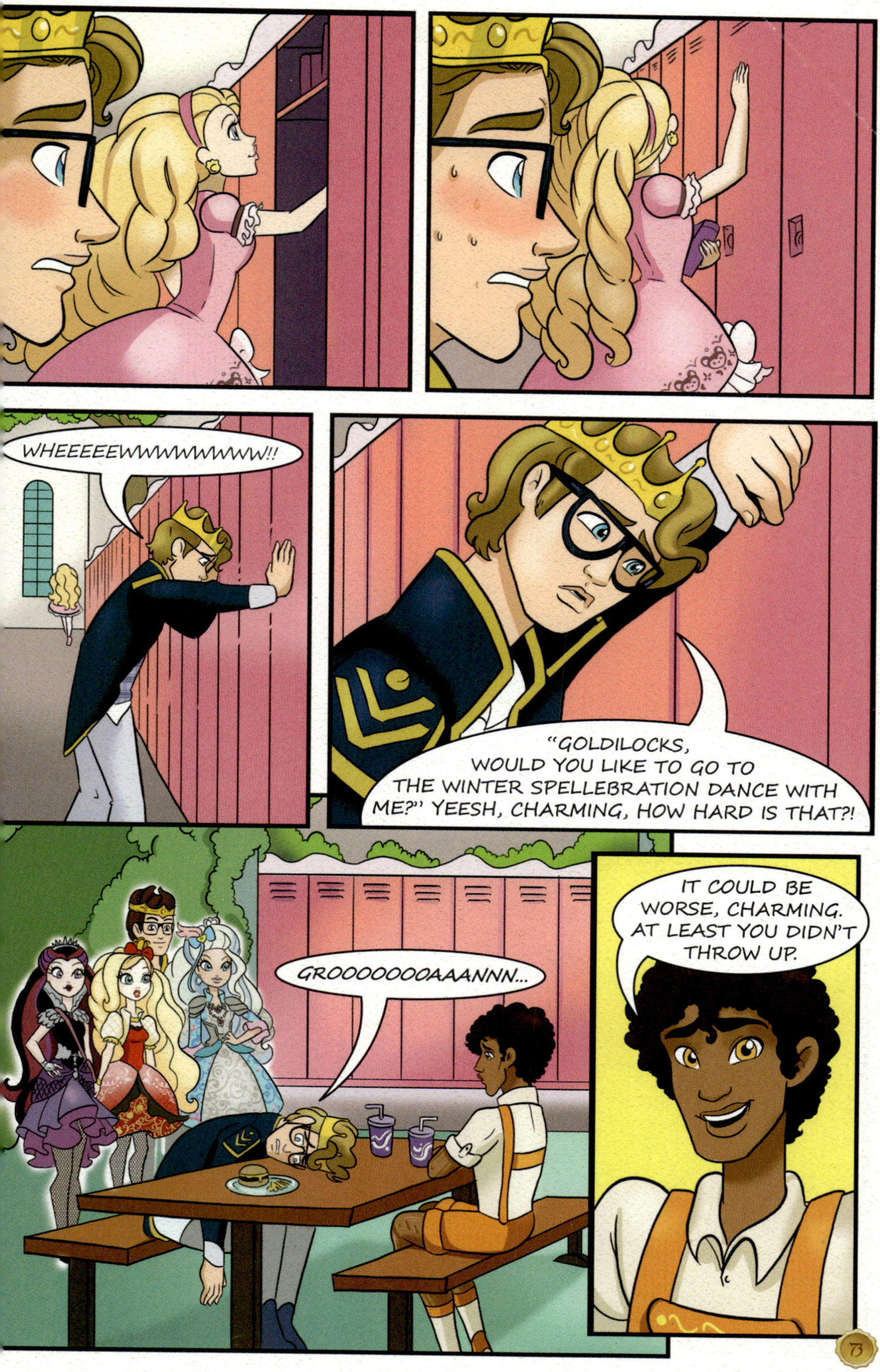
WHEEEEEWWWWWWWW!!
"GOLDILOCKS, WOULD YOU LIKE TO GO TO THE WINTER SPELLEBRATION DANCE WITH ME?" YEESH, CHARMING, HOW HARD IS THAT?!
GROOOOOOOAAANNN...
IT COULD BE WORSE, CHARMING. AT LEAST YOU DIDN'T THROW UP.

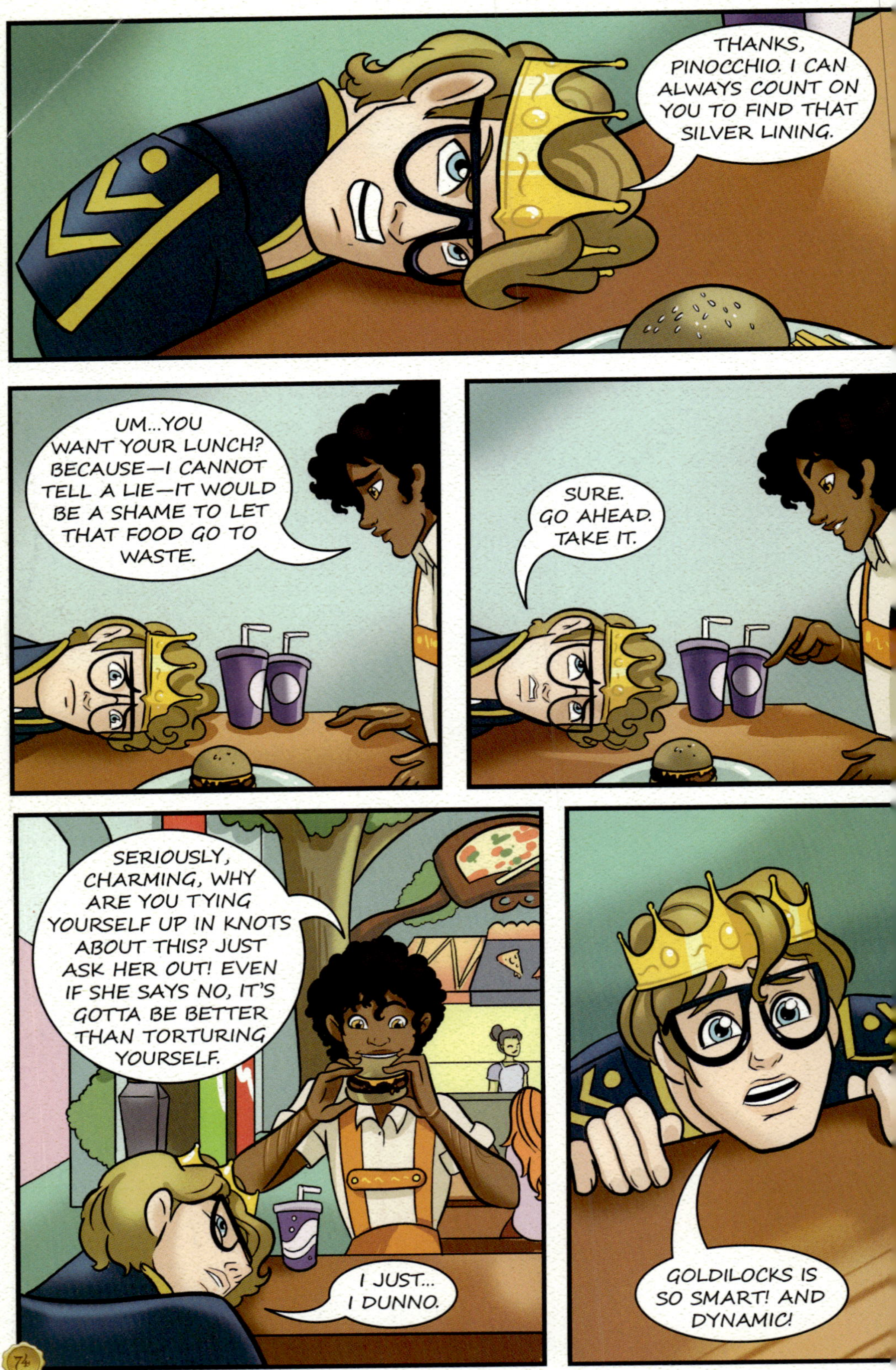
THANKS, PINOCCHIO. I CAN ALWAYS COUNT ON YOU TO FIND THAT SILVER LINING.
UM...YOU WANT YOUR LUNCH? BECAUSE—I CANNOT TELL A LIE—IT WOULD BE A SHAME TO LET THAT FOOD GO TO WASTE.
SURE. GO AHEAD. TAKE IT.
SERIOUSLY, CHARMING, WHY ARE YOU TYING YOURSELF UP IN KNOTS ABOUT THIS? JUST ASK HER OUT! EVEN IF SHE SAYS NO, IT'S GOTTA BE BETTER THAN TORTURING YOURSELF.
I JUST... I DUNNO.
GOLDILOCKS IS SO SMART! AND DYNAMIC!

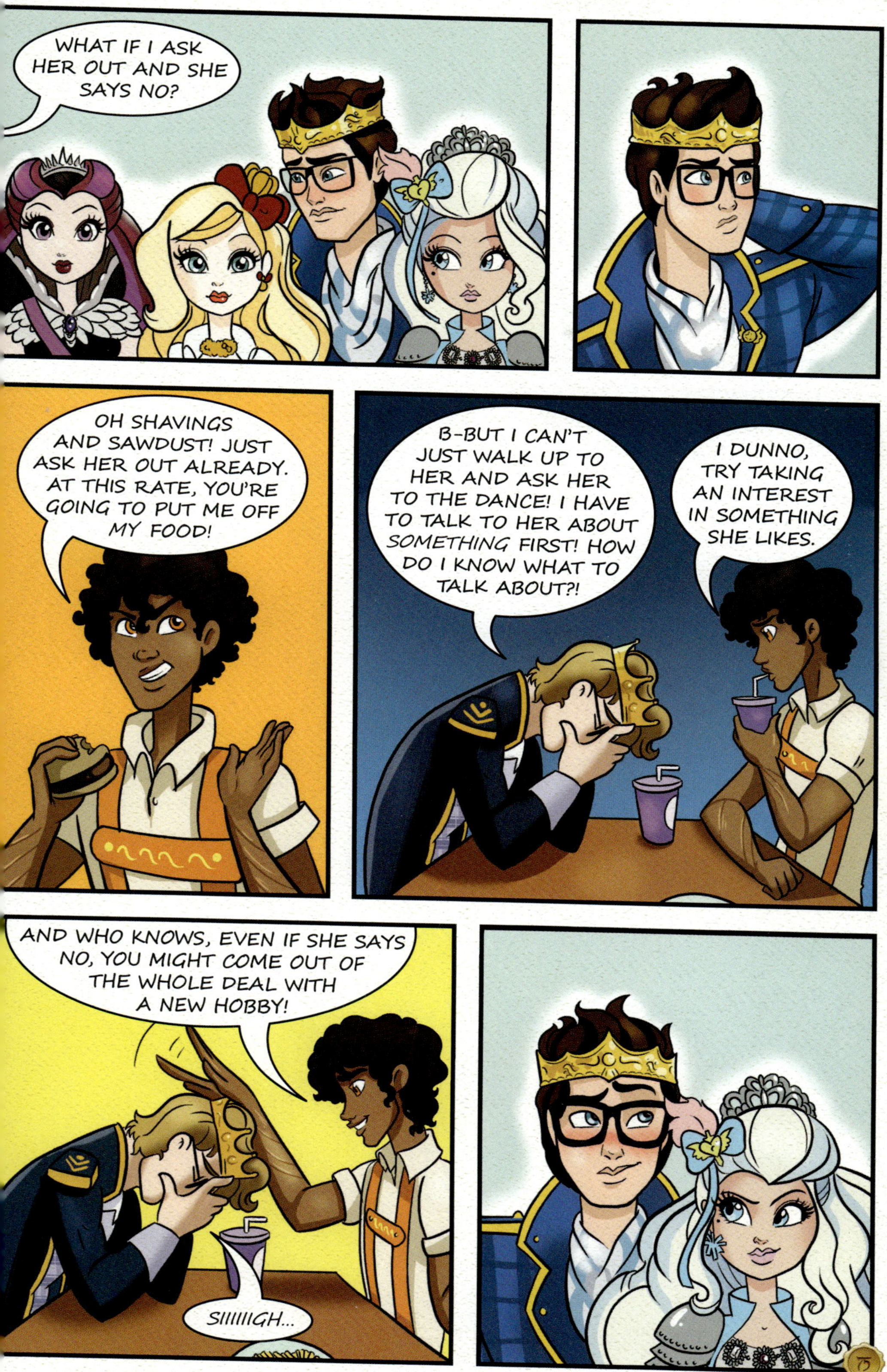
WHAT IF I ASK HER OUT AND SHE SAYS NO?
OH SHAVINGS AND SAWDUST! JUST ASK HER OUT ALREADY. AT THIS RATE, YOU'RE GOING TO PUT ME OFF MY FOOD!
B-BUT I CAN'T JUST WALK UP TO HER AND ASK HER TO THE DANCE! I HAVE TO TALK TO HER ABOUT *SOMETHING* FIRST! HOW DO I KNOW WHAT TO TALK ABOUT?!
I DUNNO, TRY TAKING AN INTEREST IN SOMETHING SHE LIKES.
AND WHO KNOWS, EVEN IF SHE SAYS NO, YOU MIGHT COME OUT OF THE WHOLE DEAL WITH A NEW HOBBY!
SIIIIIGH...

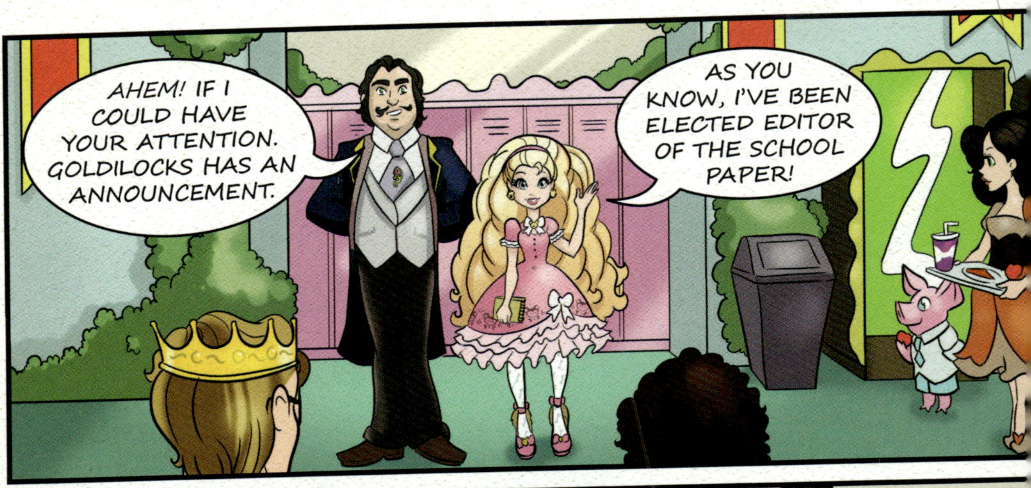
AHEM! IF I COULD HAVE YOUR ATTENTION. GOLDILOCKS HAS AN ANNOUNCEMENT.
AS YOU KNOW, I'VE BEEN ELECTED EDITOR OF THE SCHOOL PAPER!
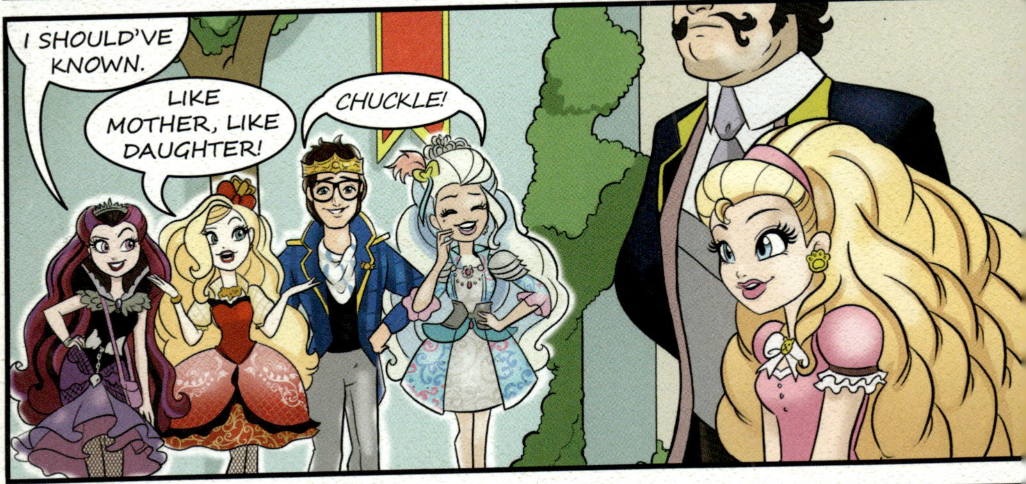
I SHOULD'VE KNOWN.
LIKE MOTHER, LIKE DAUGHTER!
CHUCKLE!
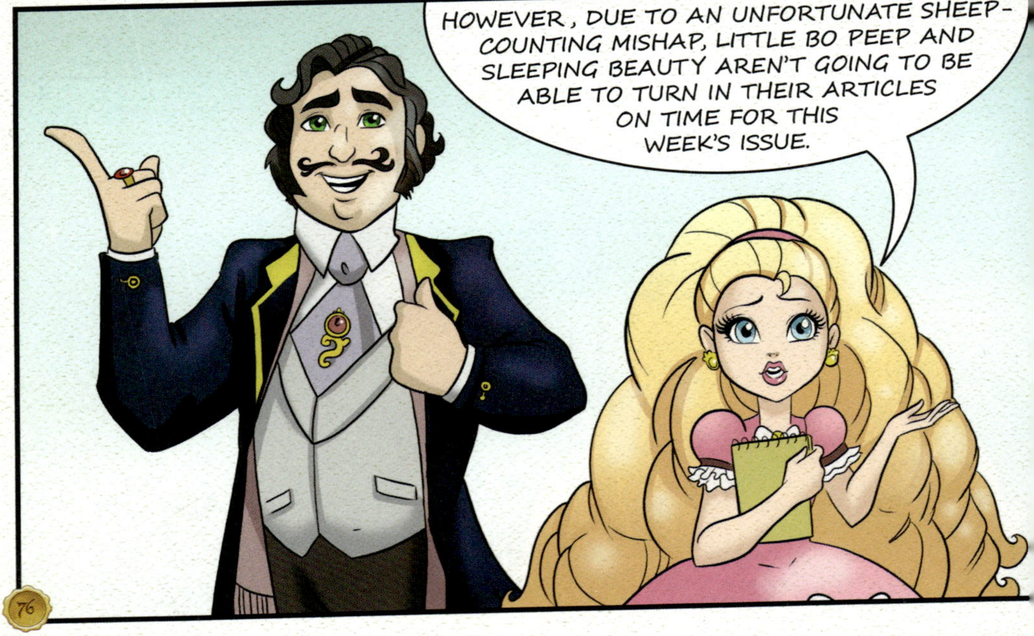
HOWEVER, DUE TO AN UNFORTUNATE SHEEP-COUNTING MISHAP, LITTLE BO PEEP AND SLEEPING BEAUTY AREN'T GOING TO BE ABLE TO TURN IN THEIR ARTICLES ON TIME FOR THIS WEEK'S ISSUE.

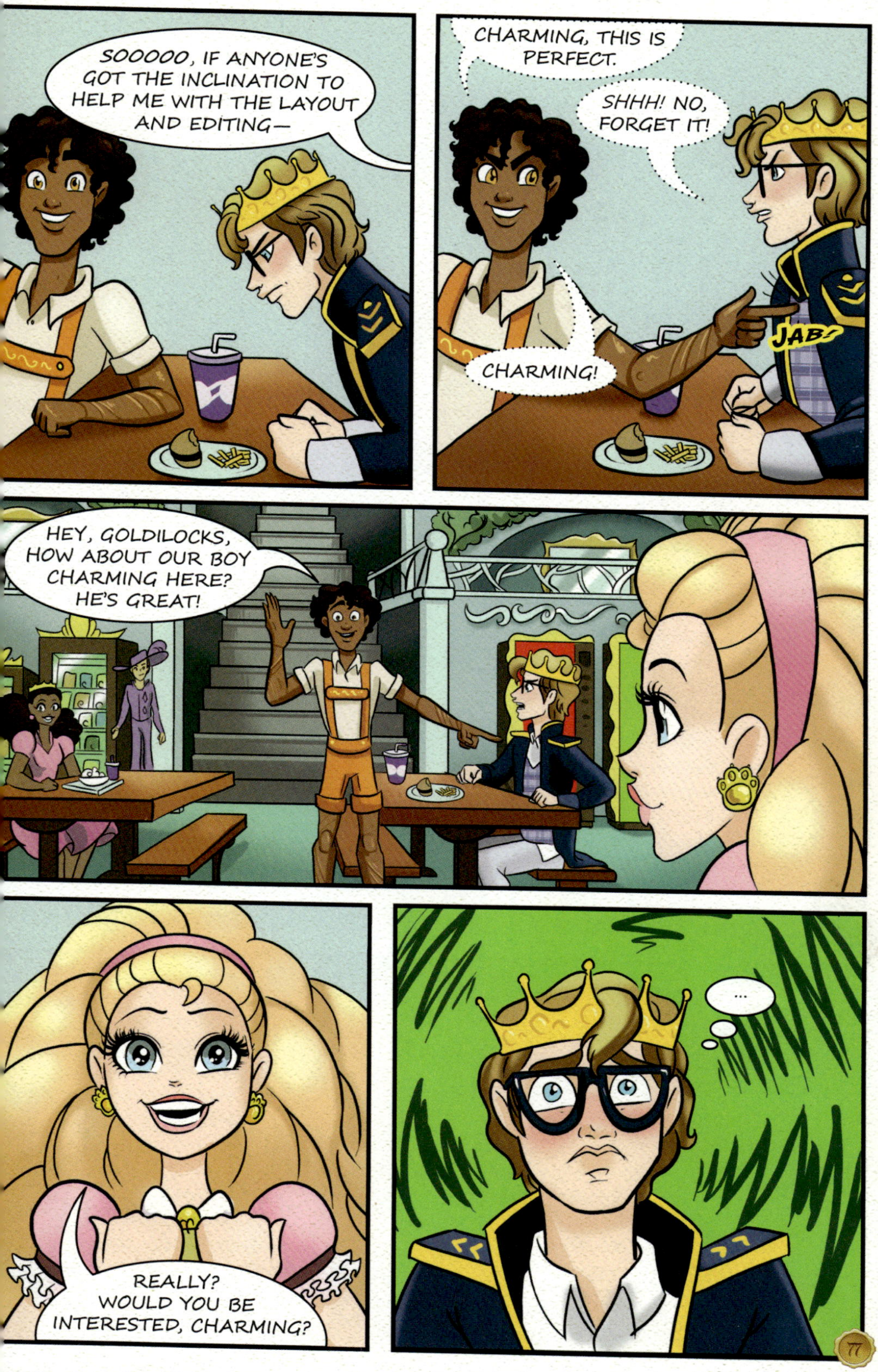
SOOOOO, IF ANYONE'S GOT THE INCLINATION TO HELP ME WITH THE LAYOUT AND EDITING—
CHARMING, THIS IS PERFECT.
SHHH! NO, FORGET IT!
JAB!
CHARMING!
HEY, GOLDILOCKS, HOW ABOUT OUR BOY CHARMING HERE? HE'S GREAT!
REALLY? WOULD YOU BE INTERESTED, CHARMING?
...

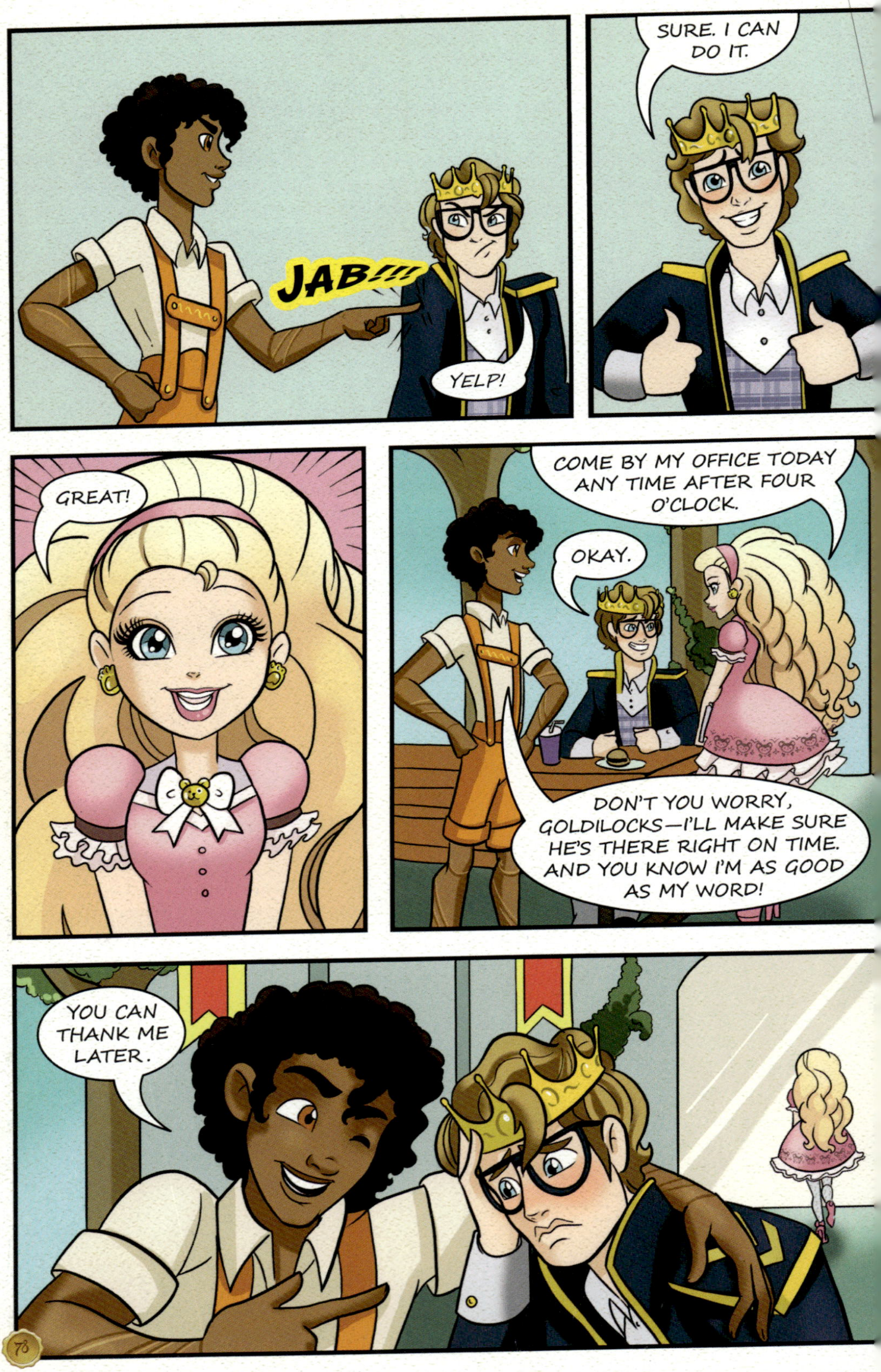
JAB!!!
YELP!
SURE. I CAN DO IT.
GREAT!
COME BY MY OFFICE TODAY ANY TIME AFTER FOUR O'CLOCK.
OKAY.
DON'T YOU WORRY, GOLDILOCKS—I'LL MAKE SURE HE'S THERE RIGHT ON TIME. AND YOU KNOW I'M AS GOOD AS MY WORD!
YOU CAN THANK ME LATER.

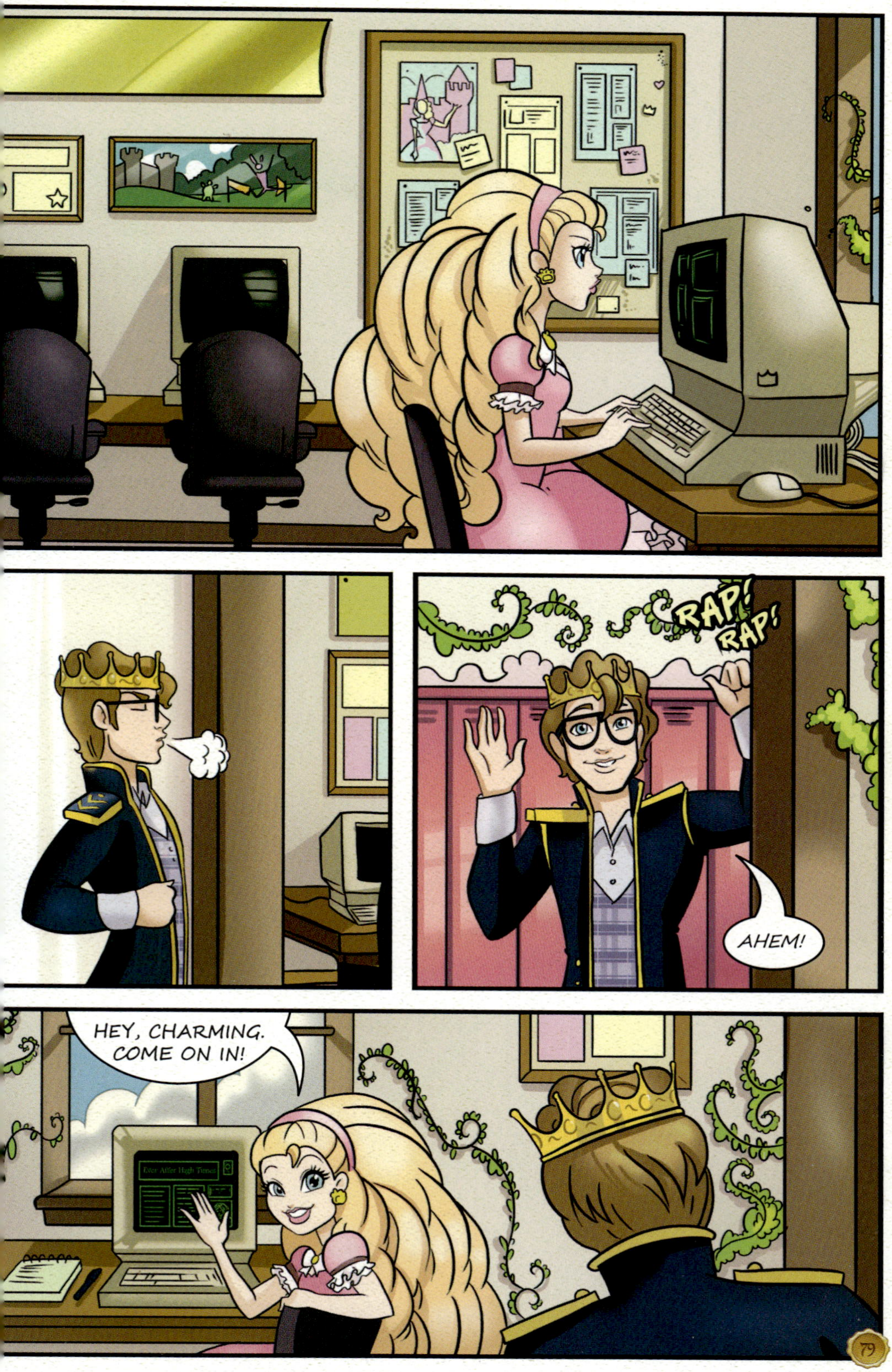
RAP! RAP!
AHEM!
HEY, CHARMING. COME ON IN!
Ever After High Times

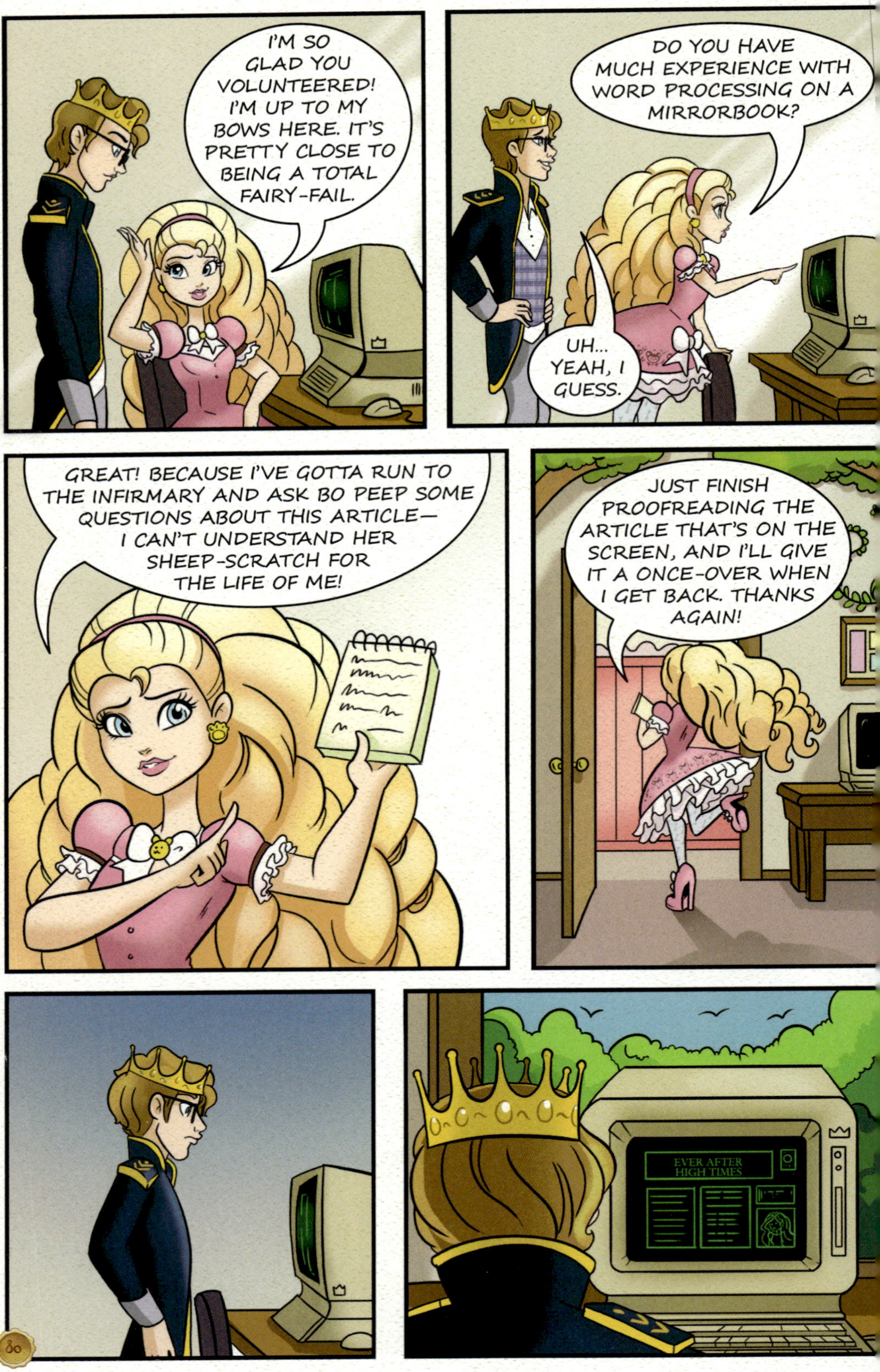
I'M SO GLAD YOU VOLUNTEERED! I'M UP TO MY BOWS HERE. IT'S PRETTY CLOSE TO BEING A TOTAL FAIRY-FAIL.
DO YOU HAVE MUCH EXPERIENCE WITH WORD PROCESSING ON A MIRRORBOOK?
UH... YEAH, I GUESS.
GREAT! BECAUSE I'VE GOTTA RUN TO THE INFIRMARY AND ASK BO PEEP SOME QUESTIONS ABOUT THIS ARTICLE— I CAN'T UNDERSTAND HER SHEEP-SCRATCH FOR THE LIFE OF ME!
JUST FINISH PROOFREADING THE ARTICLE THAT'S ON THE SCREEN, AND I'LL GIVE IT A ONCE-OVER WHEN I GET BACK. THANKS AGAIN!
EVER AFTER HIGH TIMES

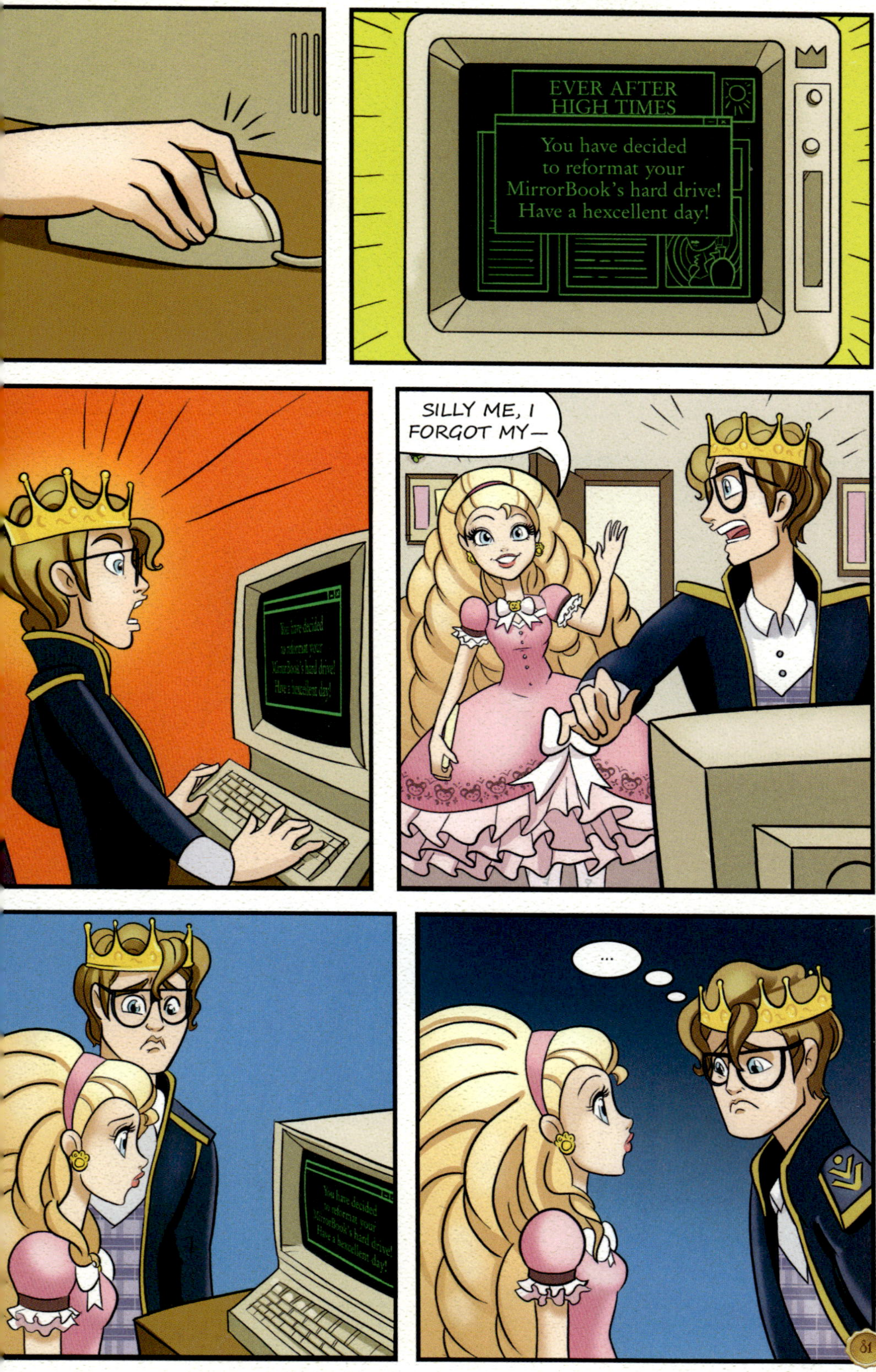
EVER AFTER HIGH TIMES
You have decided to reformat your MirrorBook's hard drive! Have a hexcellent day!
SILLY ME, I FORGOT MY—
...

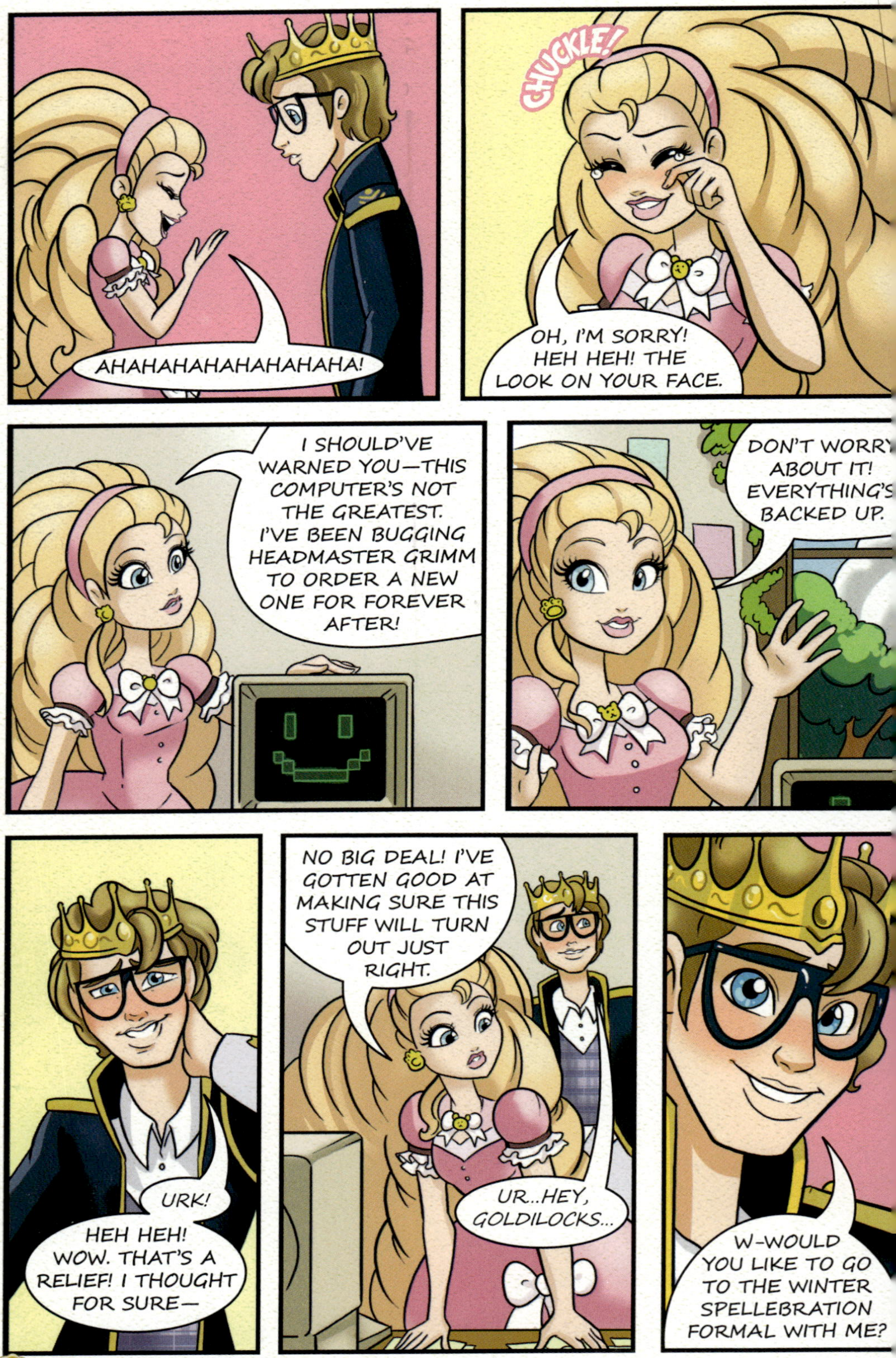
AHAHAHAHAHAHAHAHA!
CHUCKLE!
OH, I'M SORRY! HEH HEH! THE LOOK ON YOUR FACE.
I SHOULD'VE WARNED YOU—THIS COMPUTER'S NOT THE GREATEST. I'VE BEEN BUGGING HEADMASTER GRIMM TO ORDER A NEW ONE FOR FOREVER AFTER!
DON'T WORRY ABOUT IT! EVERYTHING'S BACKED UP.
URK!
HEH HEH! WOW. THAT'S A RELIEF! I THOUGHT FOR SURE—
NO BIG DEAL! I'VE GOTTEN GOOD AT MAKING SURE THIS STUFF WILL TURN OUT JUST RIGHT.
UR...HEY, GOLDILOCKS...
W-WOULD YOU LIKE TO GO TO THE WINTER SPELLEBRATION FORMAL WITH ME?

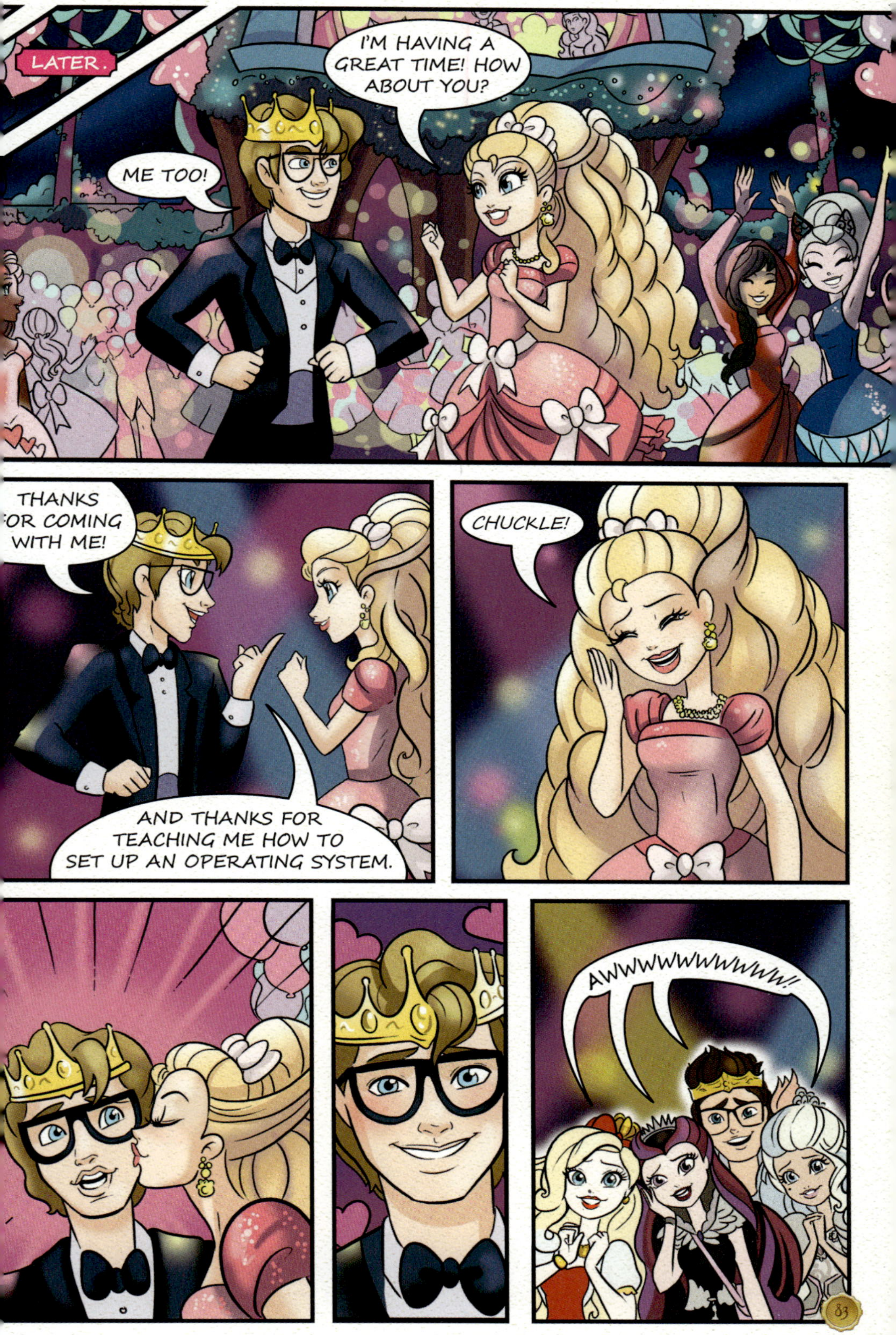
LATER.
I'M HAVING A GREAT TIME! HOW ABOUT YOU?
ME TOO!
THANKS FOR COMING WITH ME!
AND THANKS FOR TEACHING ME HOW TO SET UP AN OPERATING SYSTEM.
CHUCKLE!
AWWWWWWWWWW!

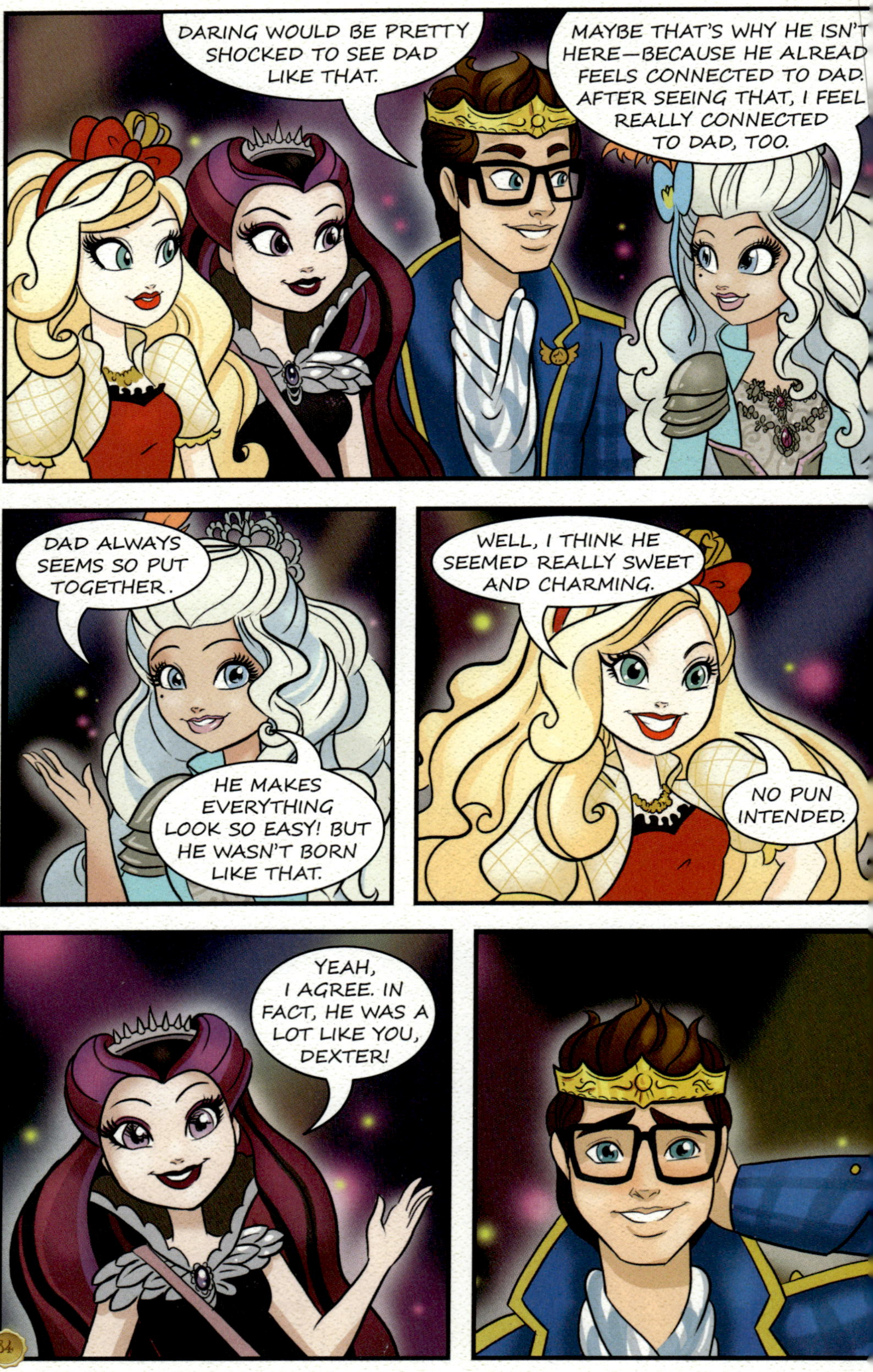
DARING WOULD BE PRETTY SHOCKED TO SEE DAD LIKE THAT.
MAYBE THAT'S WHY HE ISN'T HERE—BECAUSE HE ALREAD FEELS CONNECTED TO DAD. AFTER SEEING THAT, I FEEL REALLY CONNECTED TO DAD, TOO.
DAD ALWAYS SEEMS SO PUT TOGETHER.
HE MAKES EVERYTHING LOOK SO EASY! BUT HE WASN'T BORN LIKE THAT.
WELL, I THINK HE SEEMED REALLY SWEET AND CHARMING.
NO PUN INTENDED.
YEAH, I AGREE. IN FACT, HE WAS A LOT LIKE YOU, DEXTER!

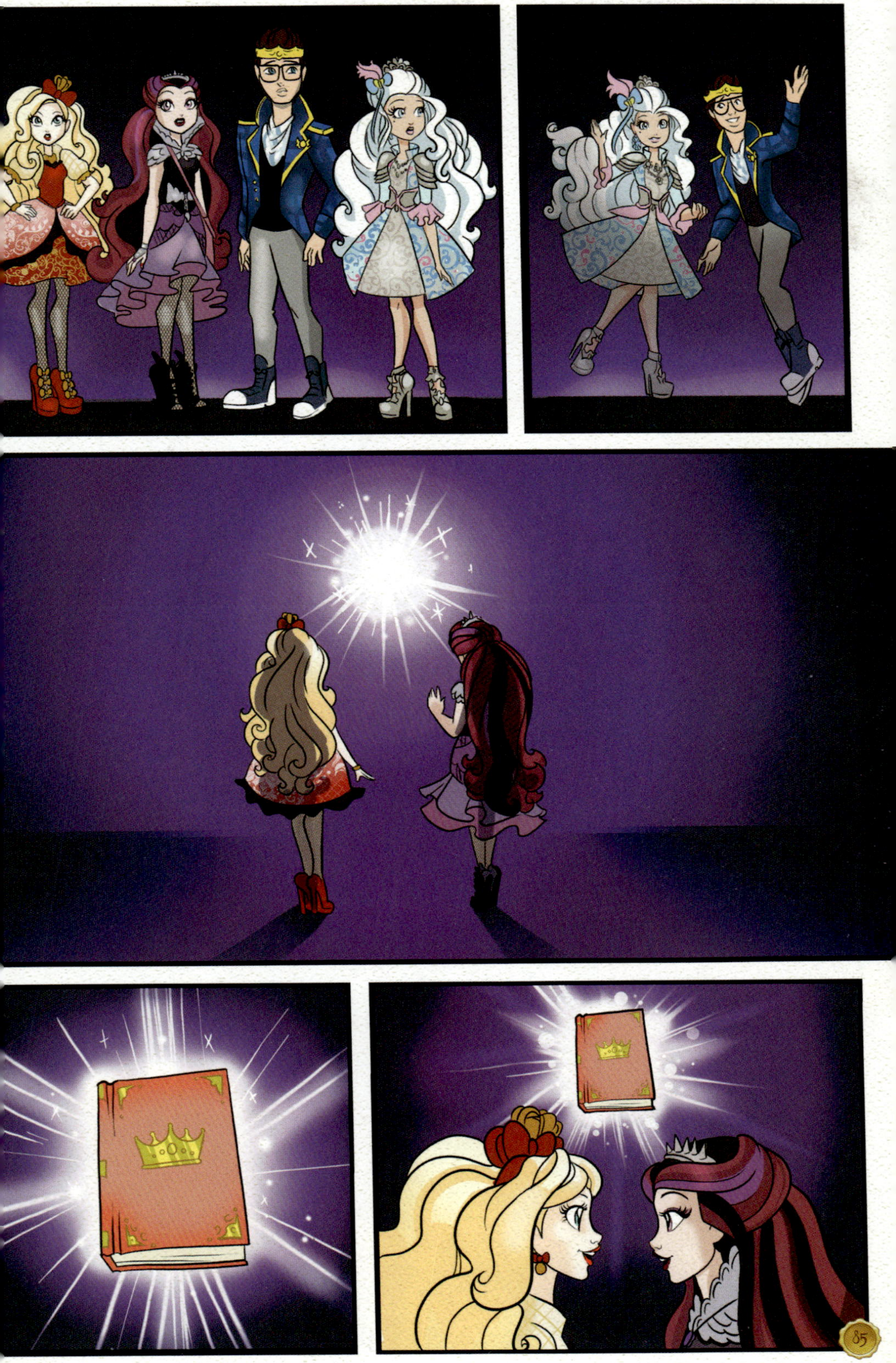

Story Six: Snow White & Evil Queen

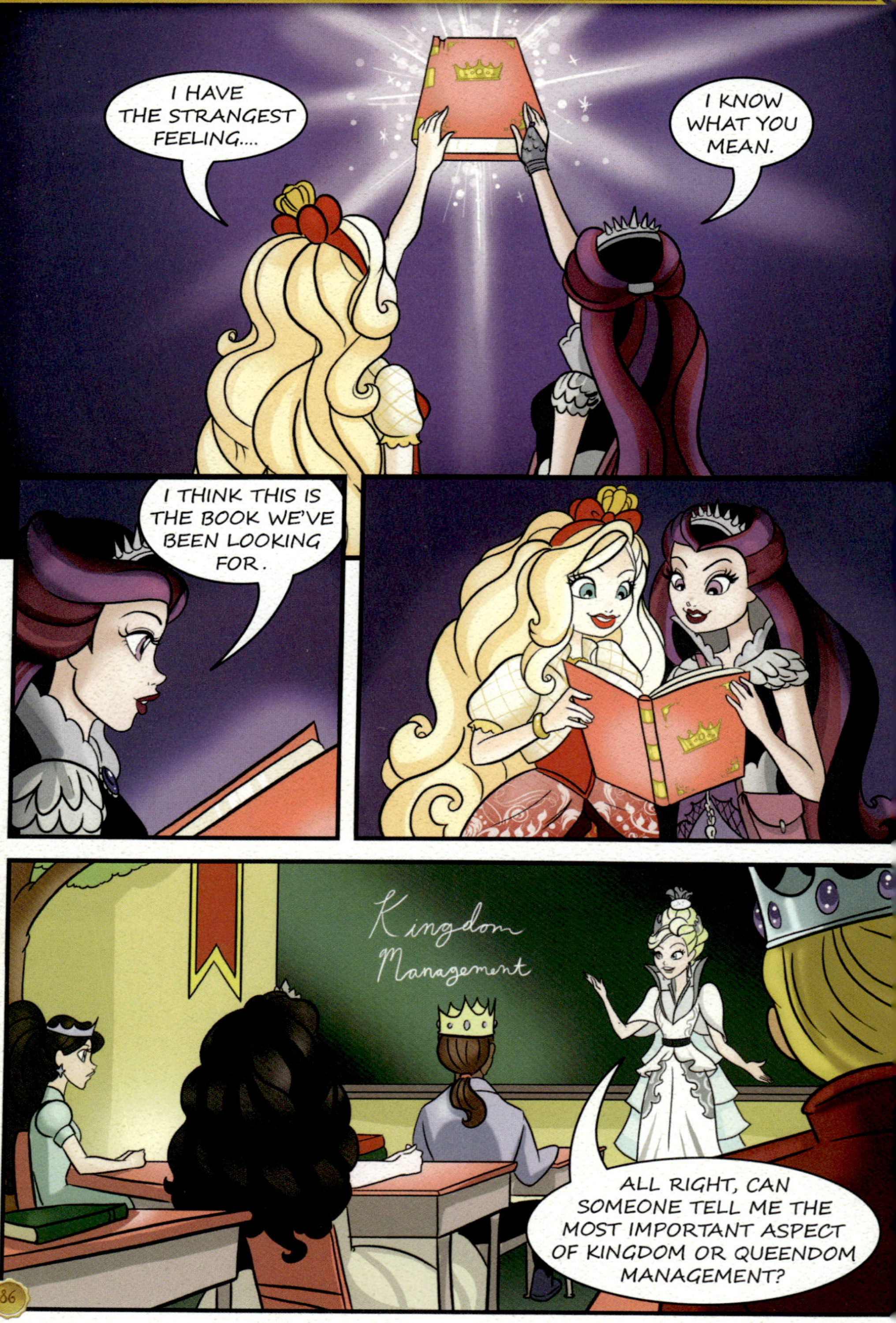

I HAVE THE STRANGEST FEELING....
I KNOW WHAT YOU MEAN.
I THINK THIS IS THE BOOK WE'VE BEEN LOOKING FOR.
Kingdom Management
ALL RIGHT, CAN SOMEONE TELL ME THE MOST IMPORTANT ASPECT OF KINGDOM OR QUEENDOM MANAGEMENT?

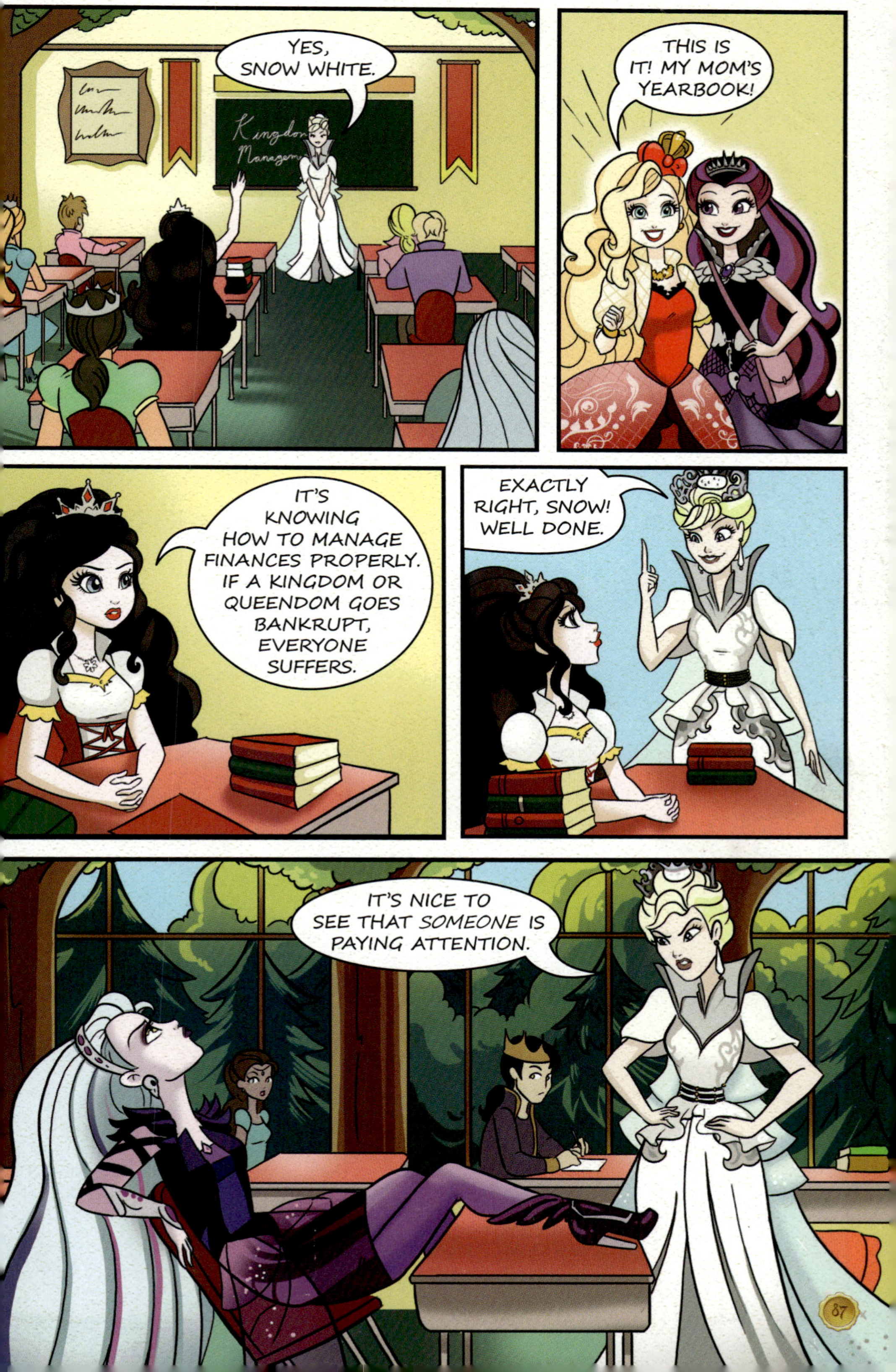
YES, SNOW WHITE.
Kingdom Managem
THIS IS IT! MY MOM'S YEARBOOK!
IT'S KNOWING HOW TO MANAGE FINANCES PROPERLY. IF A KINGDOM OR QUEENDOM GOES BANKRUPT, EVERYONE SUFFERS.
EXACTLY RIGHT, SNOW! WELL DONE.
IT'S NICE TO SEE THAT *SOMEONE* IS PAYING ATTENTION.

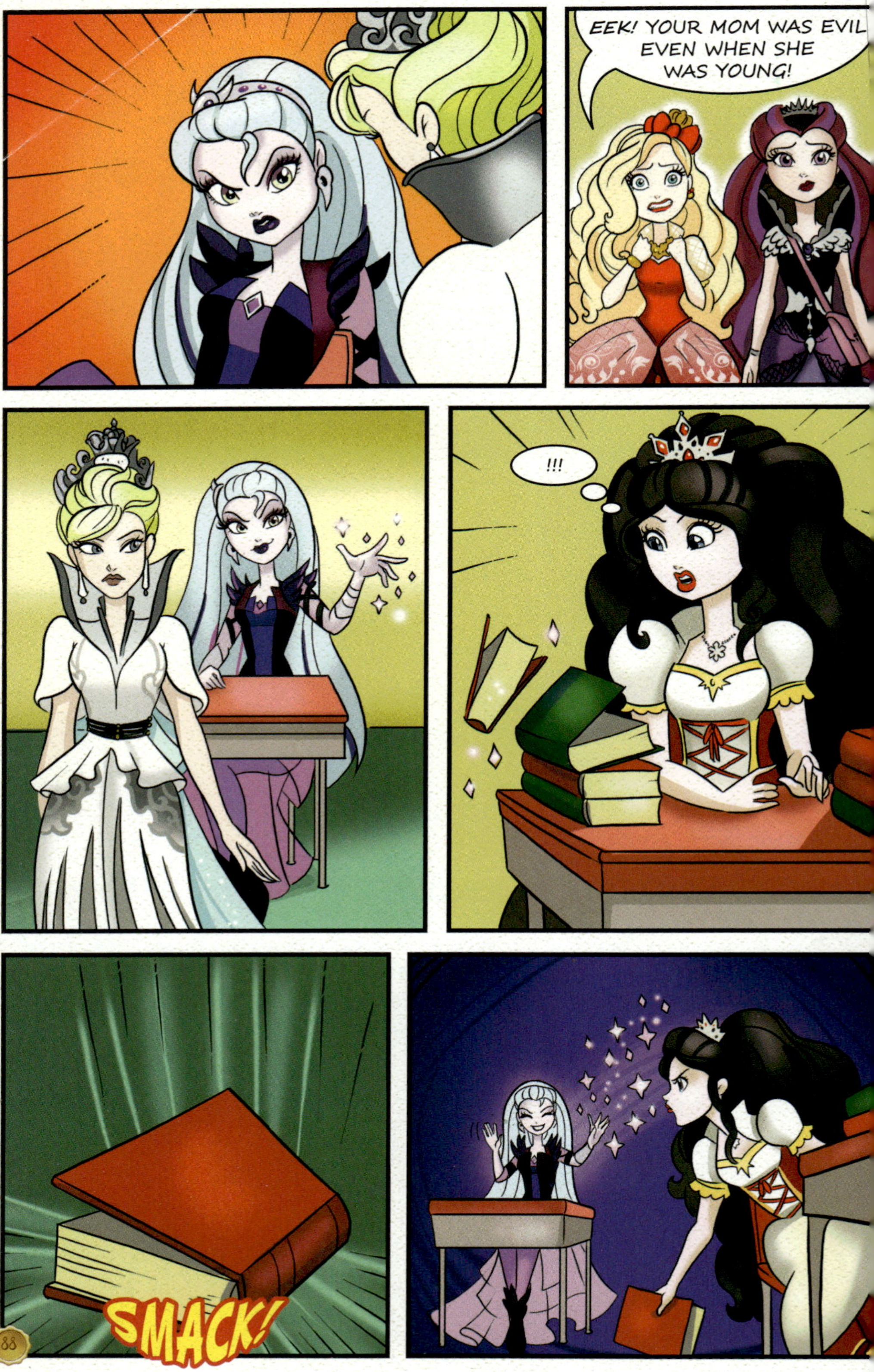
EEK! YOUR MOM WAS EVIL EVEN WHEN SHE WAS YOUNG!
!!!
SMACK!

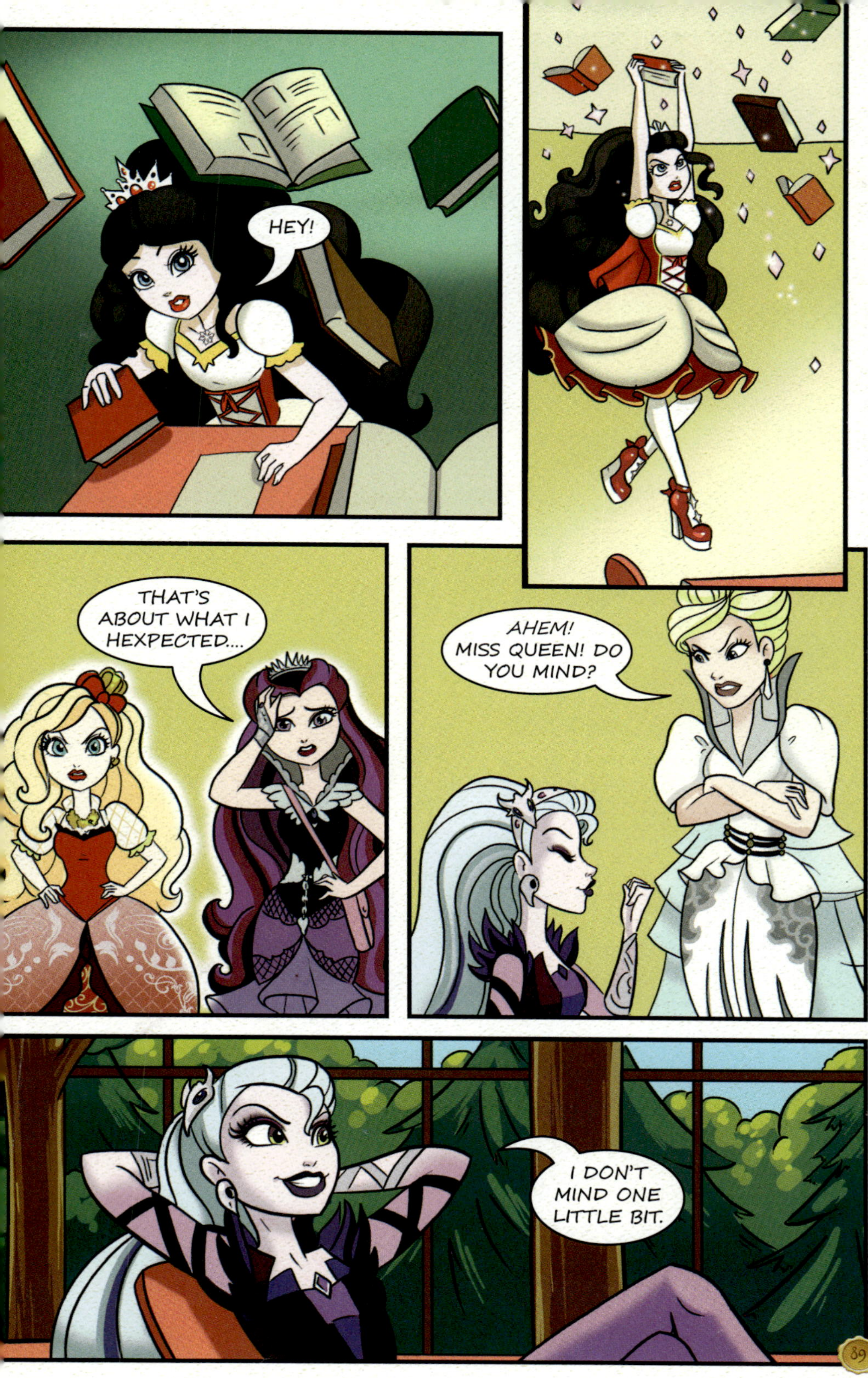
HEY!
THAT'S ABOUT WHAT I HEXPECTED....
AHEM! MISS QUEEN! DO YOU MIND?
I DON'T MIND ONE LITTLE BIT.

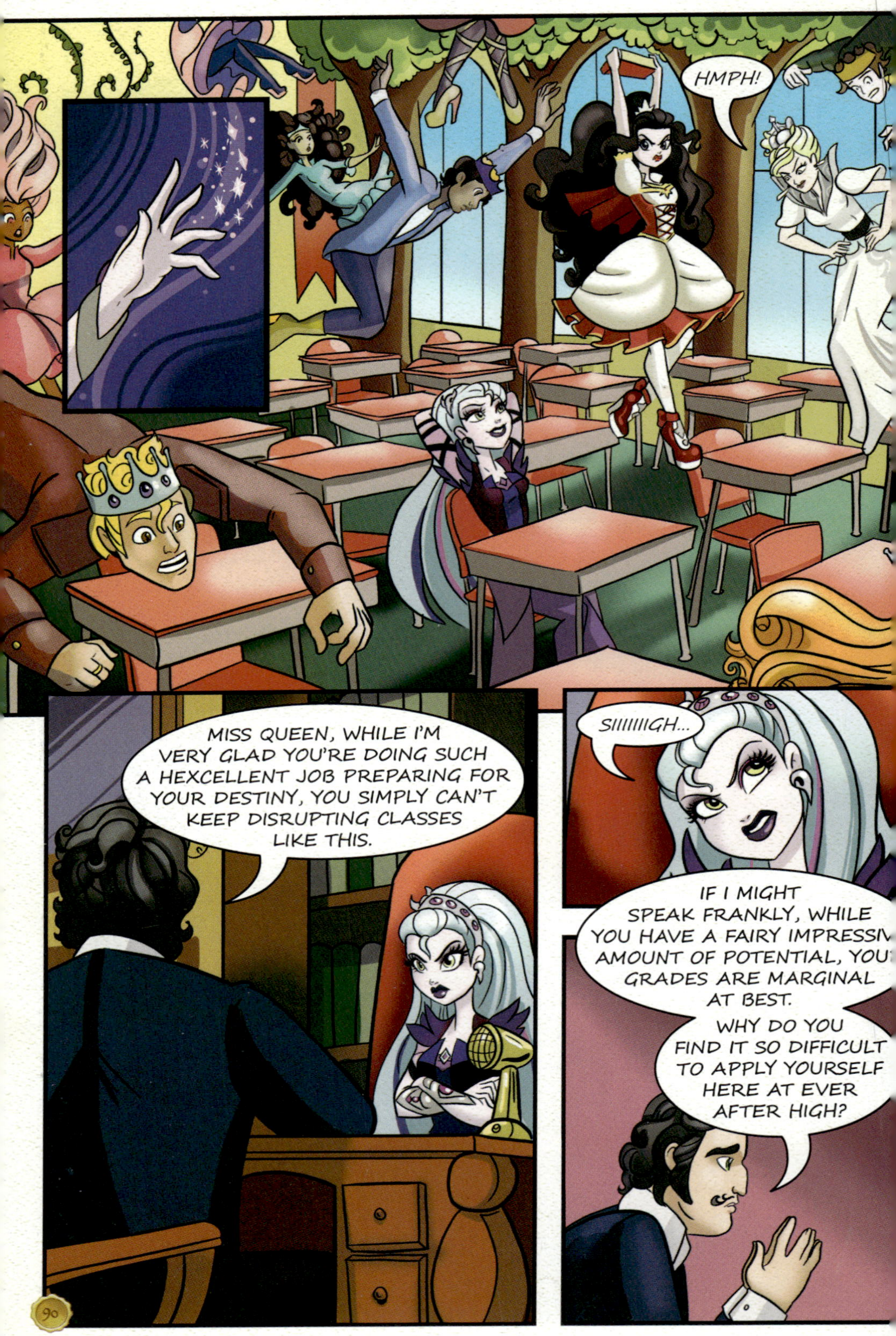
HMPH!
MISS QUEEN, WHILE I'M VERY GLAD YOU'RE DOING SUCH A HEXCELLENT JOB PREPARING FOR YOUR DESTINY, YOU SIMPLY CAN'T KEEP DISRUPTING CLASSES LIKE THIS.
SIIIIIIIGH...
IF I MIGHT SPEAK FRANKLY, WHILE YOU HAVE A FAIRY IMPRESSIV AMOUNT OF POTENTIAL, YOU GRADES ARE MARGINAL AT BEST.
WHY DO YOU FIND IT SO DIFFICULT TO APPLY YOURSELF HERE AT EVER AFTER HIGH?

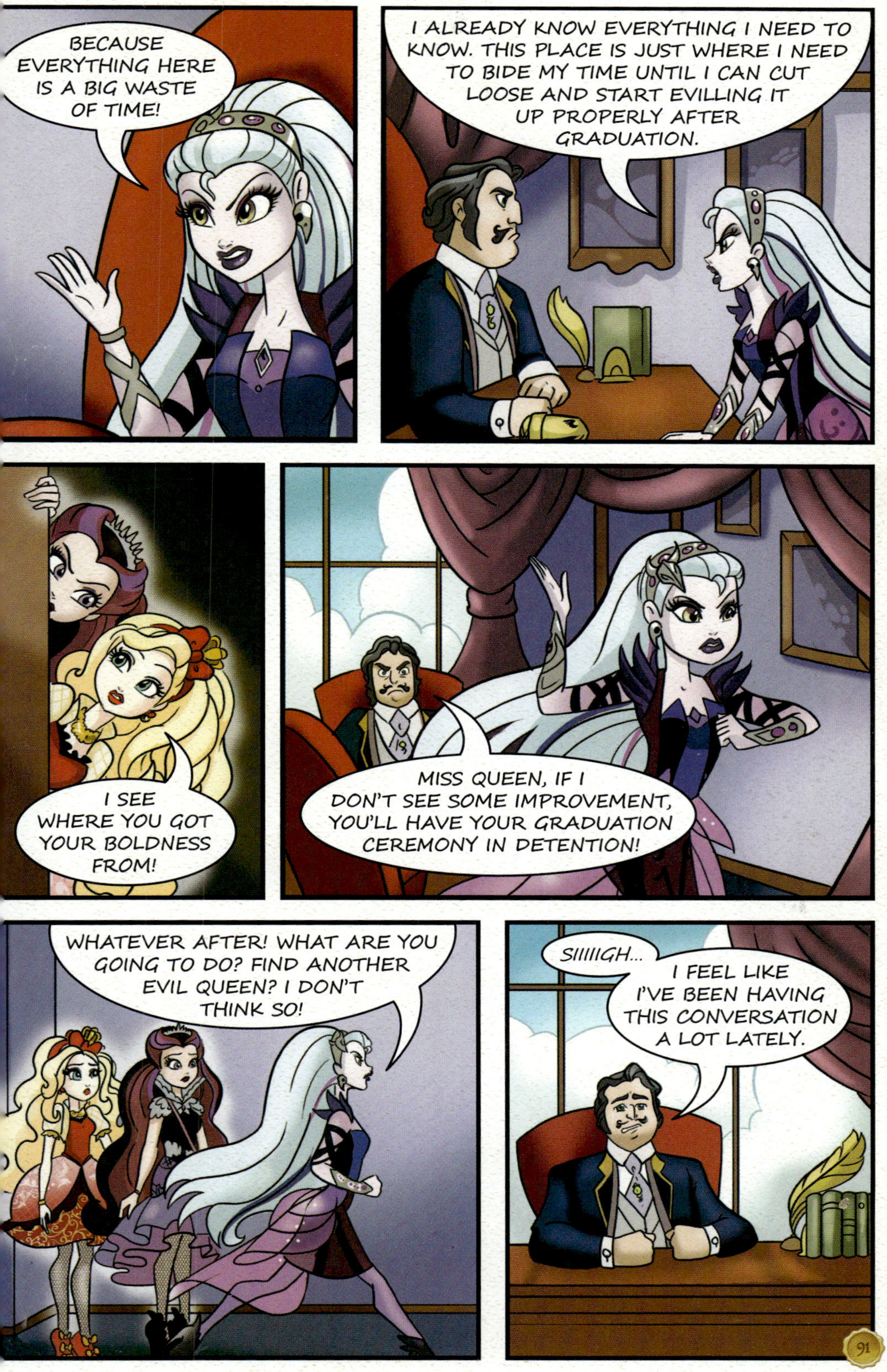
BECAUSE EVERYTHING HERE IS A BIG WASTE OF TIME!
I ALREADY KNOW EVERYTHING I NEED TO KNOW. THIS PLACE IS JUST WHERE I NEED TO BIDE MY TIME UNTIL I CAN CUT LOOSE AND START EVILLING IT UP PROPERLY AFTER GRADUATION.
I SEE WHERE YOU GOT YOUR BOLDNESS FROM!
MISS QUEEN, IF I DON'T SEE SOME IMPROVEMENT, YOU'LL HAVE YOUR GRADUATION CEREMONY IN DETENTION!
WHATEVER AFTER! WHAT ARE YOU GOING TO DO? FIND ANOTHER EVIL QUEEN? I DON'T THINK SO!
SIIIIIGH...
I FEEL LIKE I'VE BEEN HAVING THIS CONVERSATION A LOT LATELY.

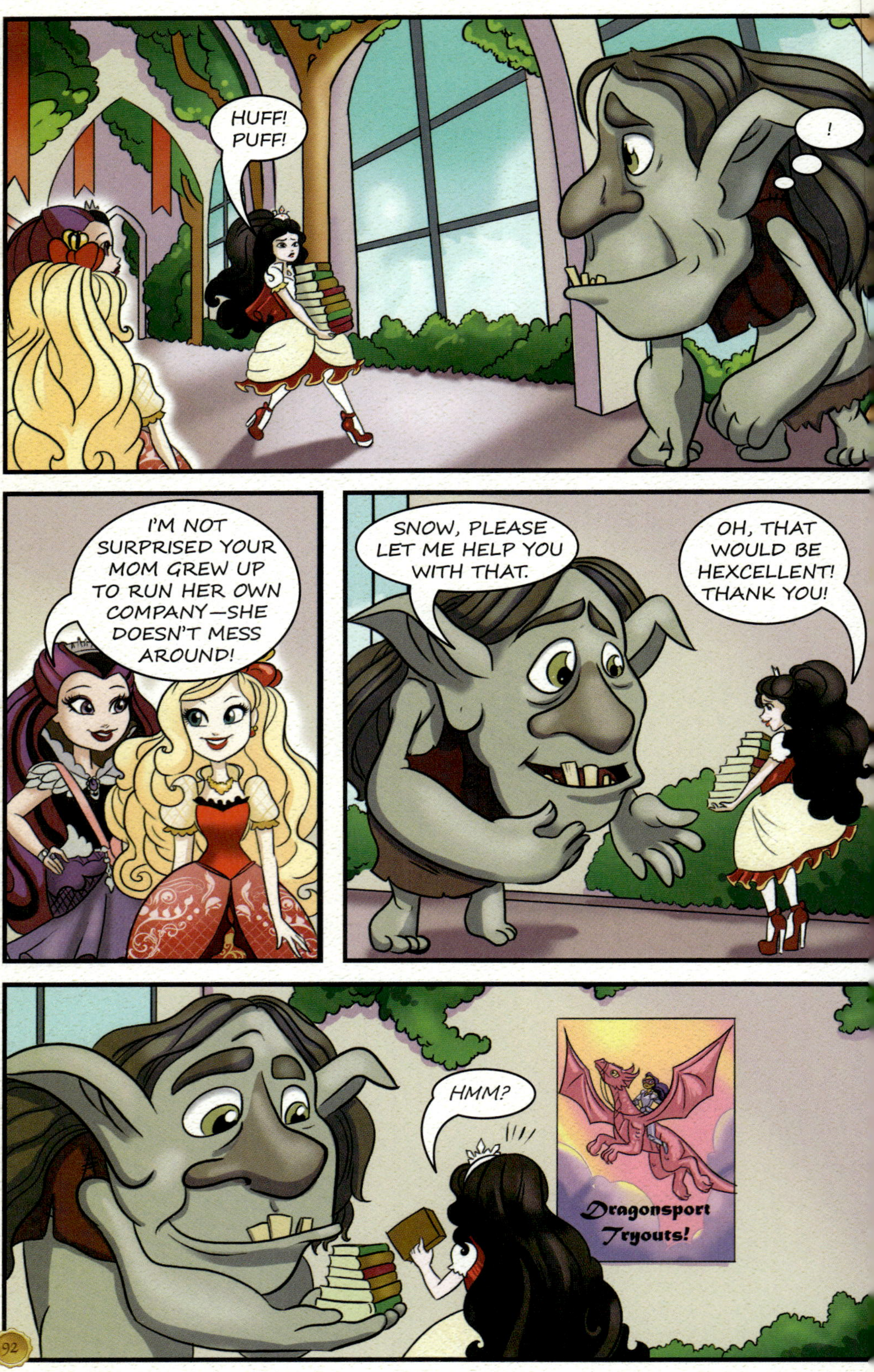
HUFF! PUFF!
!
I'M NOT SURPRISED YOUR MOM GREW UP TO RUN HER OWN COMPANY—SHE DOESN'T MESS AROUND!
SNOW, PLEASE LET ME HELP YOU WITH THAT.
OH, THAT WOULD BE HEXCELLENT! THANK YOU!
HMM?
Dragonsport Tryouts!

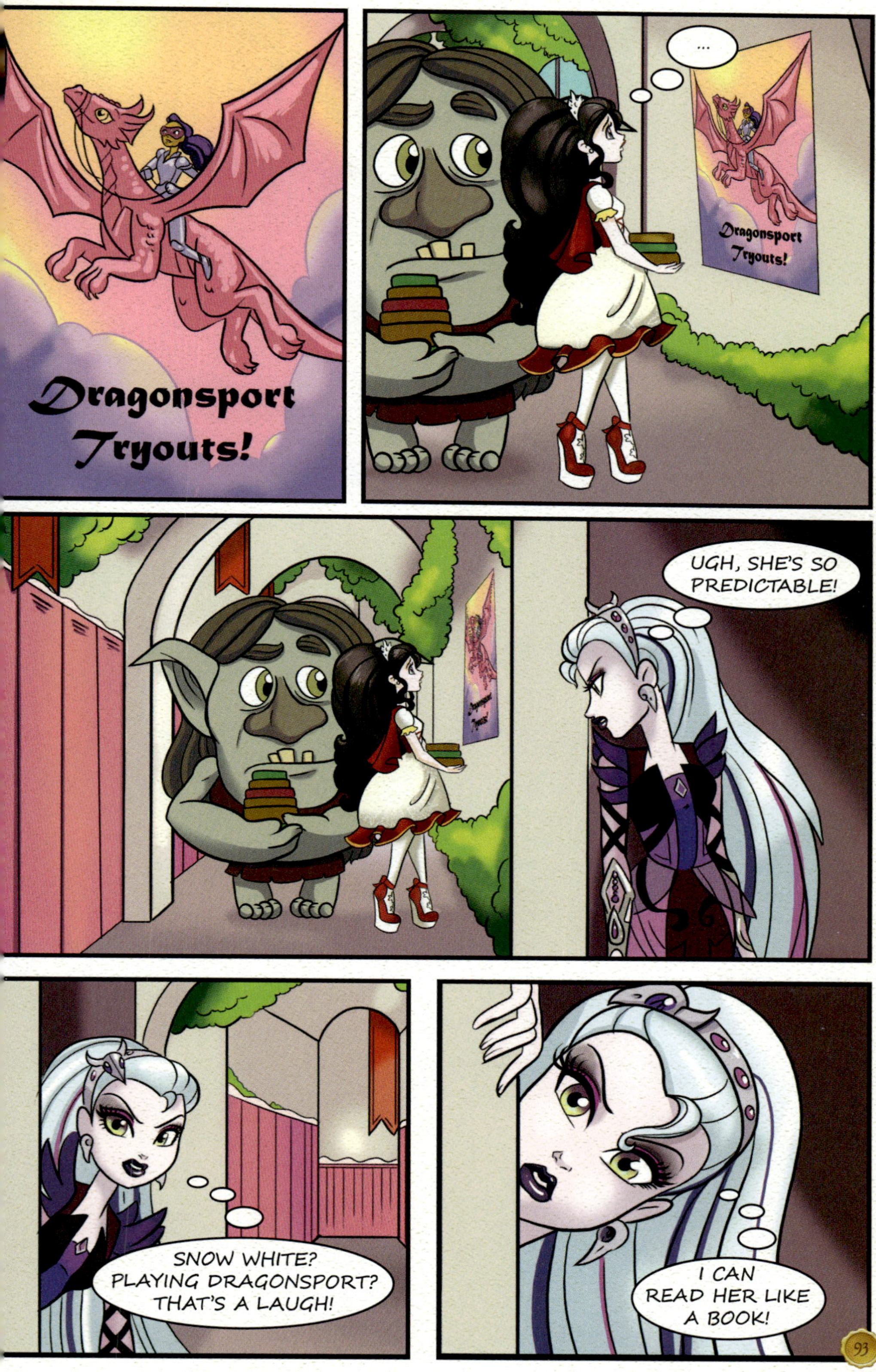
Dragonsport Tryouts!
...
Dragonsport Tryouts!
UGH, SHE'S SO PREDICTABLE!
SNOW WHITE? PLAYING DRAGONSPORT? THAT'S A LAUGH!
I CAN READ HER LIKE A BOOK!

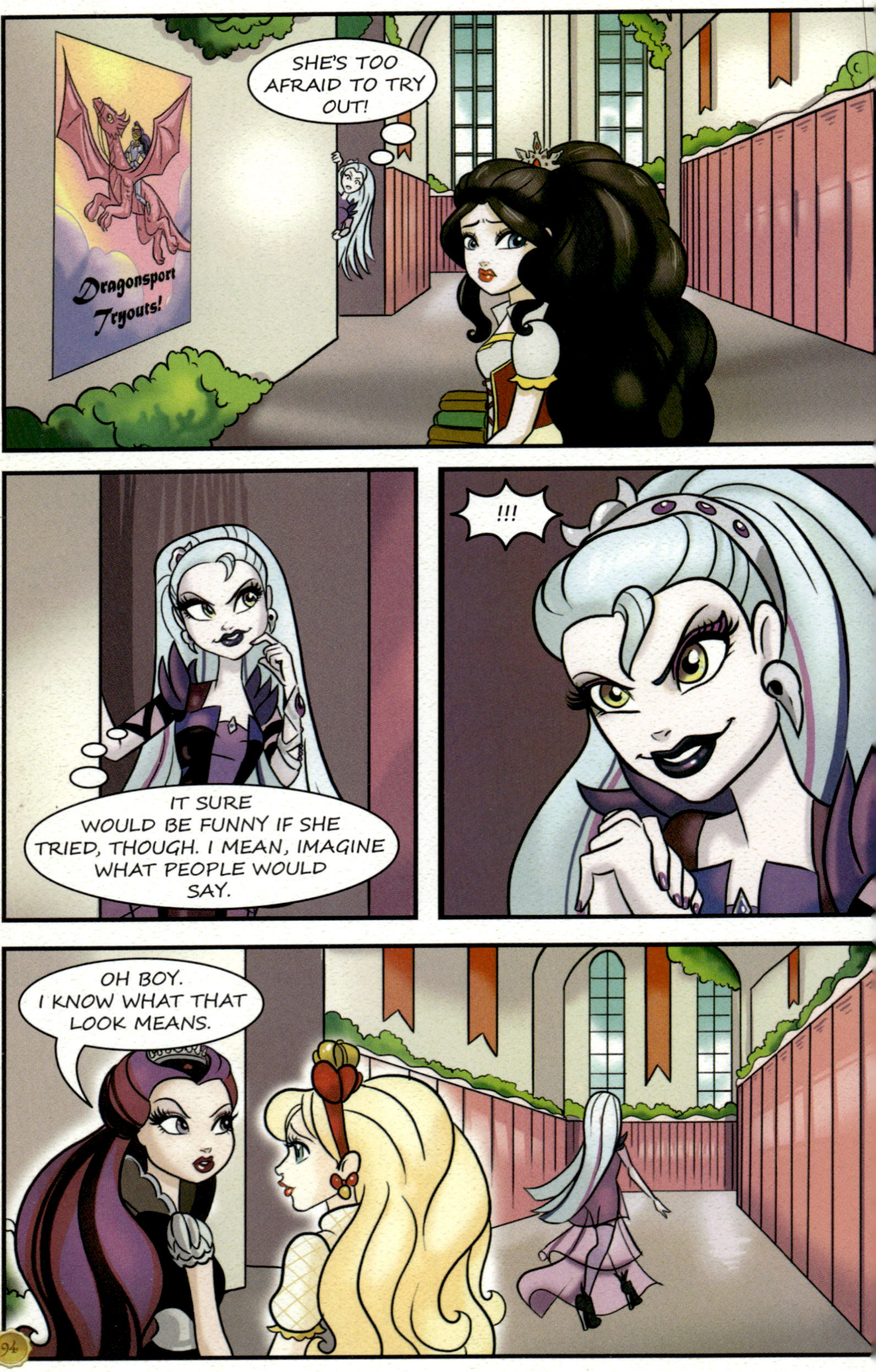
Dragonsport Tryouts!
SHE'S TOO AFRAID TO TRY OUT!
IT SURE WOULD BE FUNNY IF SHE TRIED, THOUGH. I MEAN, IMAGINE WHAT PEOPLE WOULD SAY.
!!!
OH BOY. I KNOW WHAT THAT LOOK MEANS.

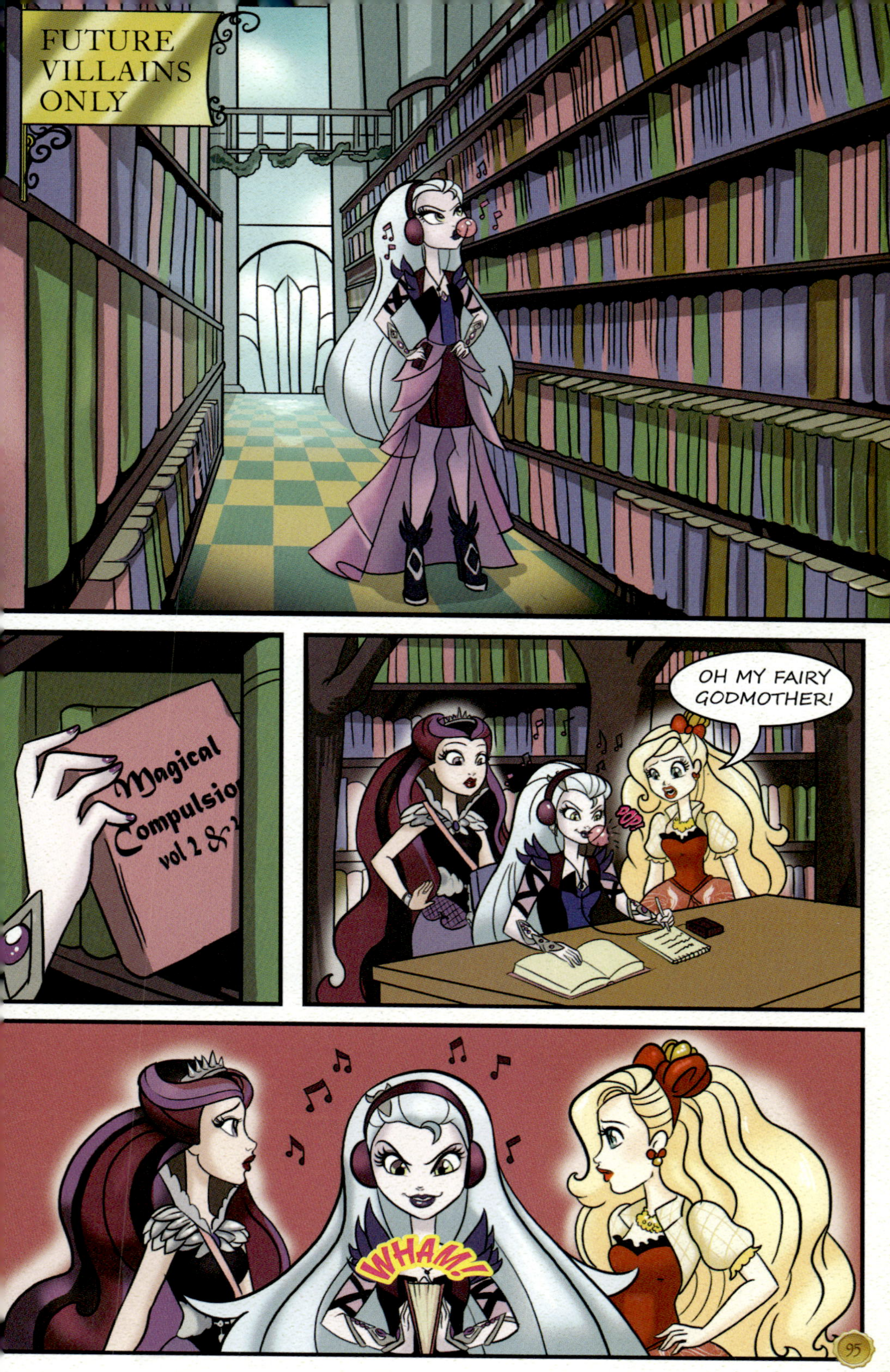
FUTURE VILLAINS ONLY
Magical Compulsio
vol 2 &
OH MY FAIRY GODMOTHER!
POP!
WHAM!

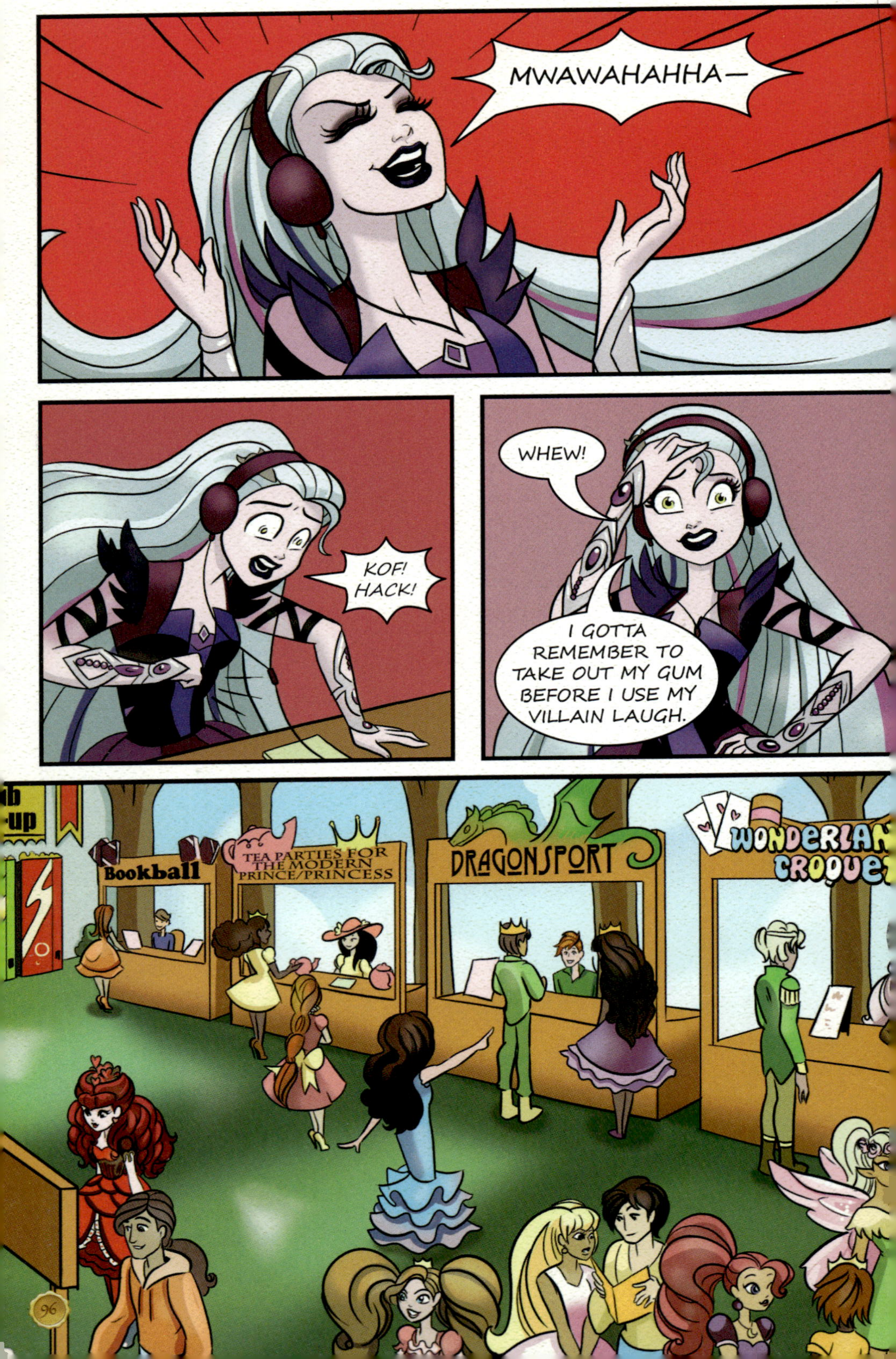
MWAWAHAHHA—
KOF! HACK!
WHEW!
I GOTTA REMEMBER TO TAKE OUT MY GUM BEFORE I USE MY VILLAIN LAUGH.
Bookball
TEA PARTIES FOR THE MODERN PRINCE/PRINCESS
DRAGONSPORT

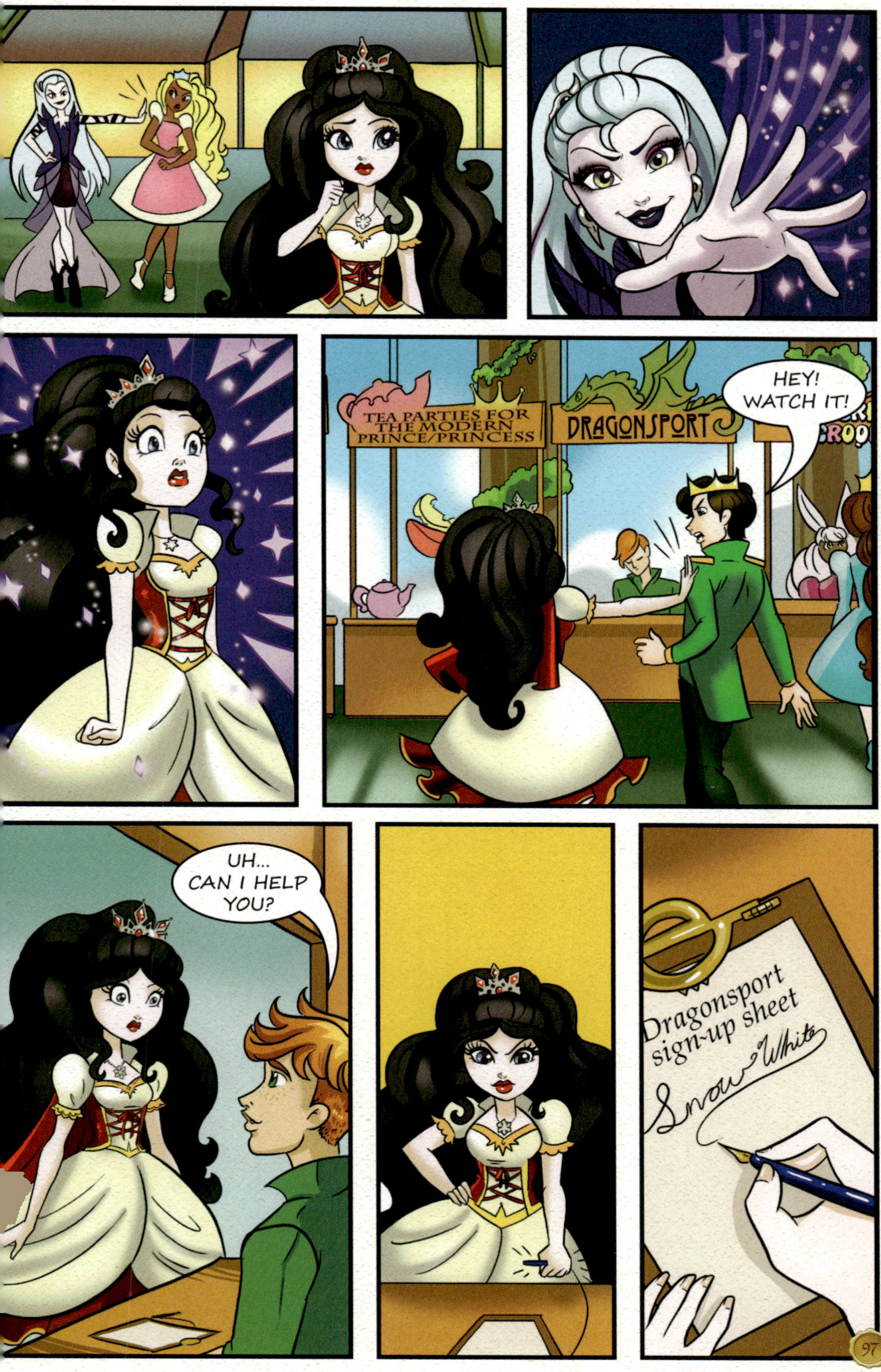
TEA PARTIES FOR THE MODERN PRINCE/PRINCESS
DRAGONSPORT
HEY! WATCH IT!
UH... CAN I HELP YOU?
Dragonsport sign-up sheet
Snow White

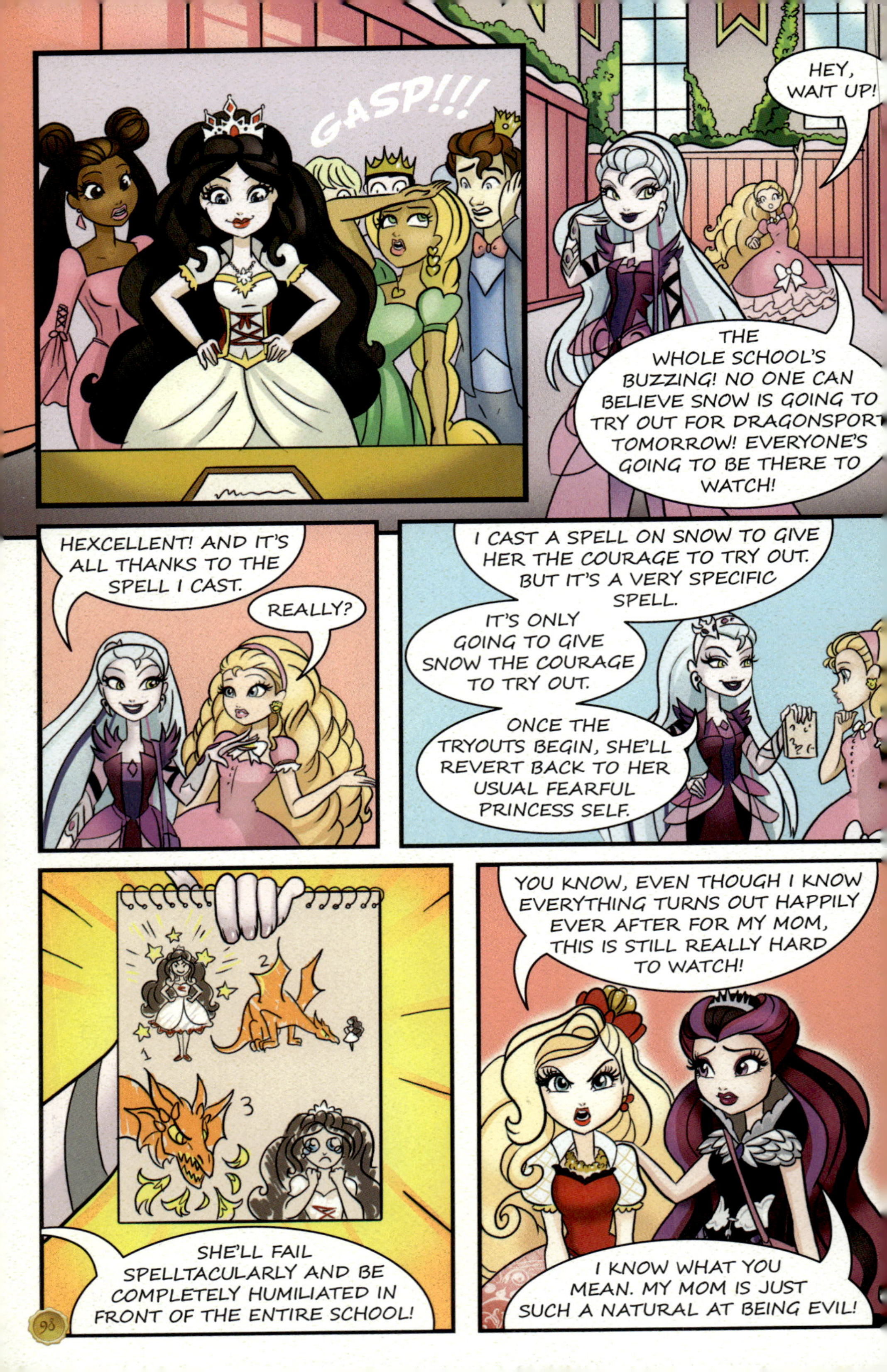

GASP!!!
HEY, WAIT UP!
THE WHOLE SCHOOL'S BUZZING! NO ONE CAN BELIEVE SNOW IS GOING TO TRY OUT FOR DRAGONSPORT TOMORROW! EVERYONE'S GOING TO BE THERE TO WATCH!
HEXCELLENT! AND IT'S ALL THANKS TO THE SPELL I CAST.
REALLY?
I CAST A SPELL ON SNOW TO GIVE HER THE COURAGE TO TRY OUT. BUT IT'S A VERY SPECIFIC SPELL.
IT'S ONLY GOING TO GIVE SNOW THE COURAGE TO TRY OUT.
ONCE THE TRYOUTS BEGIN, SHE'LL REVERT BACK TO HER USUAL FEARFUL PRINCESS SELF.
SHE'LL FAIL SPELLTACULARLY AND BE COMPLETELY HUMILIATED IN FRONT OF THE ENTIRE SCHOOL!
YOU KNOW, EVEN THOUGH I KNOW EVERYTHING TURNS OUT HAPPILY EVER AFTER FOR MY MOM, THIS IS STILL REALLY HARD TO WATCH!
I KNOW WHAT YOU MEAN. MY MOM IS JUST SUCH A NATURAL AT BEING EVIL!

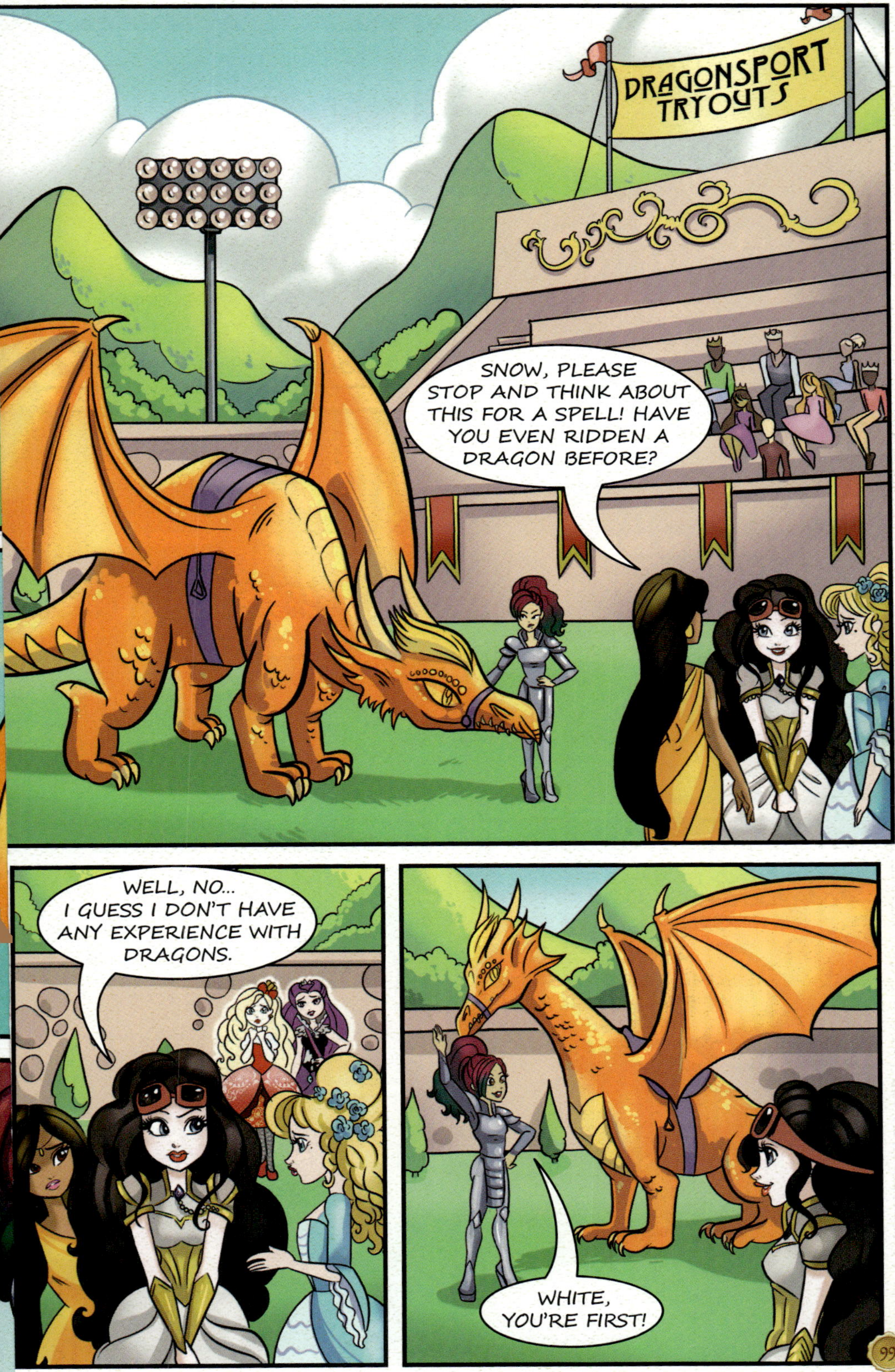
DRAGONSPORT TRYOUTS
SNOW, PLEASE STOP AND THINK ABOUT THIS FOR A SPELL! HAVE YOU EVEN RIDDEN A DRAGON BEFORE?
WELL, NO... I GUESS I DON'T HAVE ANY EXPERIENCE WITH DRAGONS.
WHITE, YOU'RE FIRST!

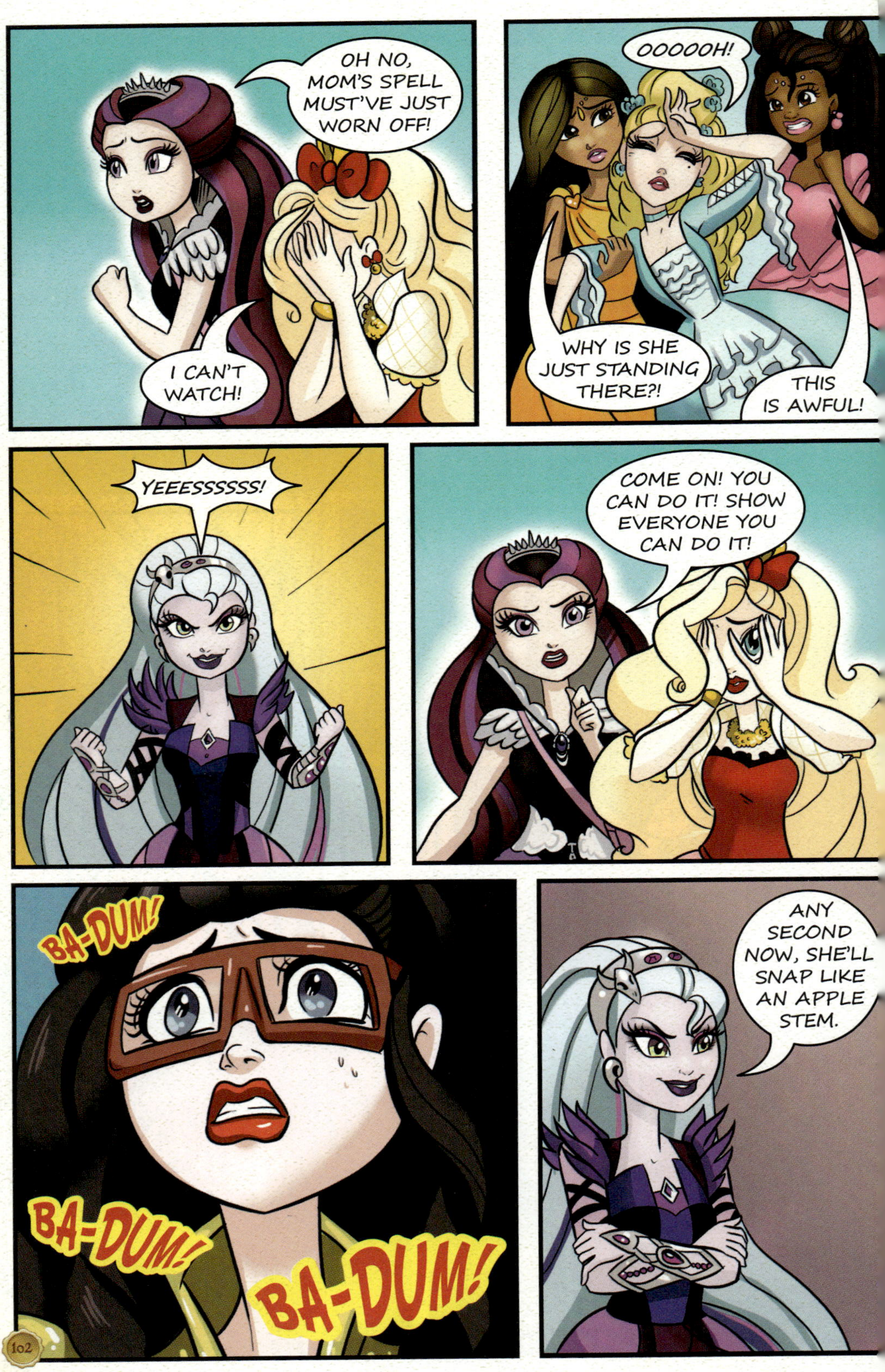
OH NO, MOM'S SPELL MUST'VE JUST WORN OFF!
I CAN'T WATCH!
OOOOOH!
WHY IS SHE JUST STANDING THERE?!
THIS IS AWFUL!
YEEESSSSSS!
COME ON! YOU CAN DO IT! SHOW EVERYONE YOU CAN DO IT!
BA-DUM!
BA-DUM!
BA-DUM!
ANY SECOND NOW, SHE'LL SNAP LIKE AN APPLE STEM.

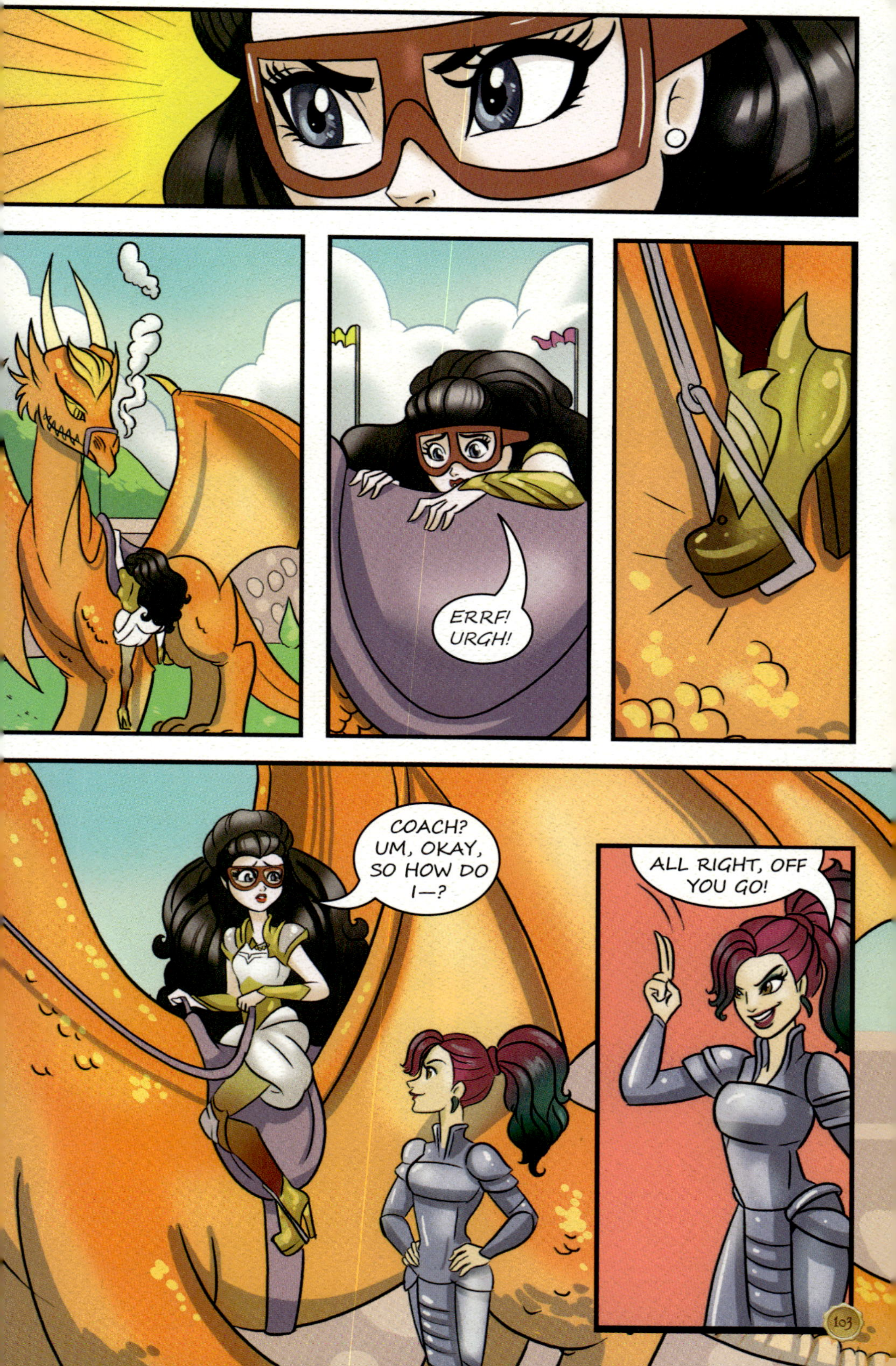

ERRF! URGH!
COACH? UM, OKAY, SO HOW DO I—?
ALL RIGHT, OFF YOU GO!

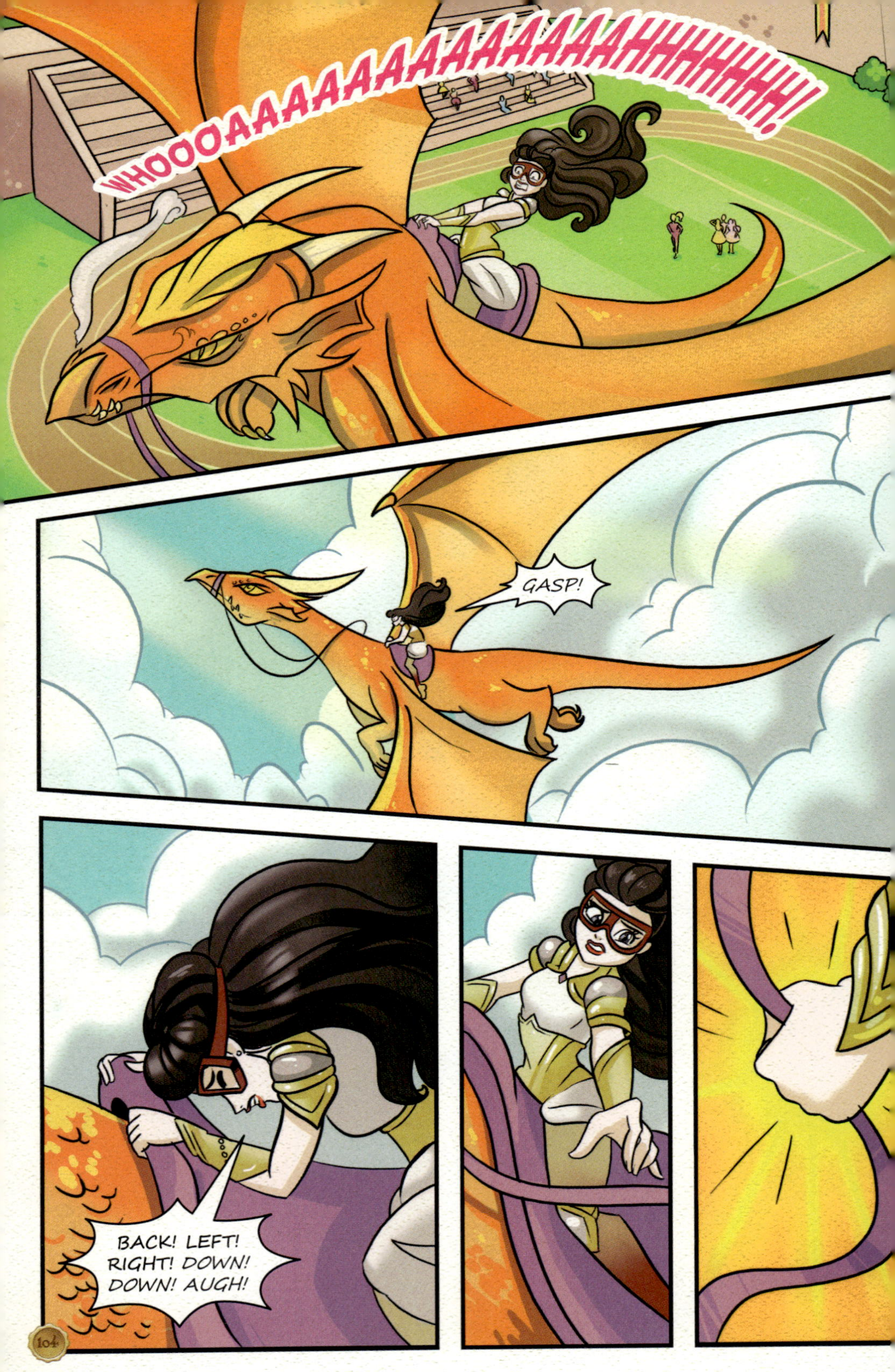
WHOOOAAAAAAAAAAAAAAAAAHHHHHH!
GASP!
BACK! LEFT! RIGHT! DOWN! DOWN! AUGH!

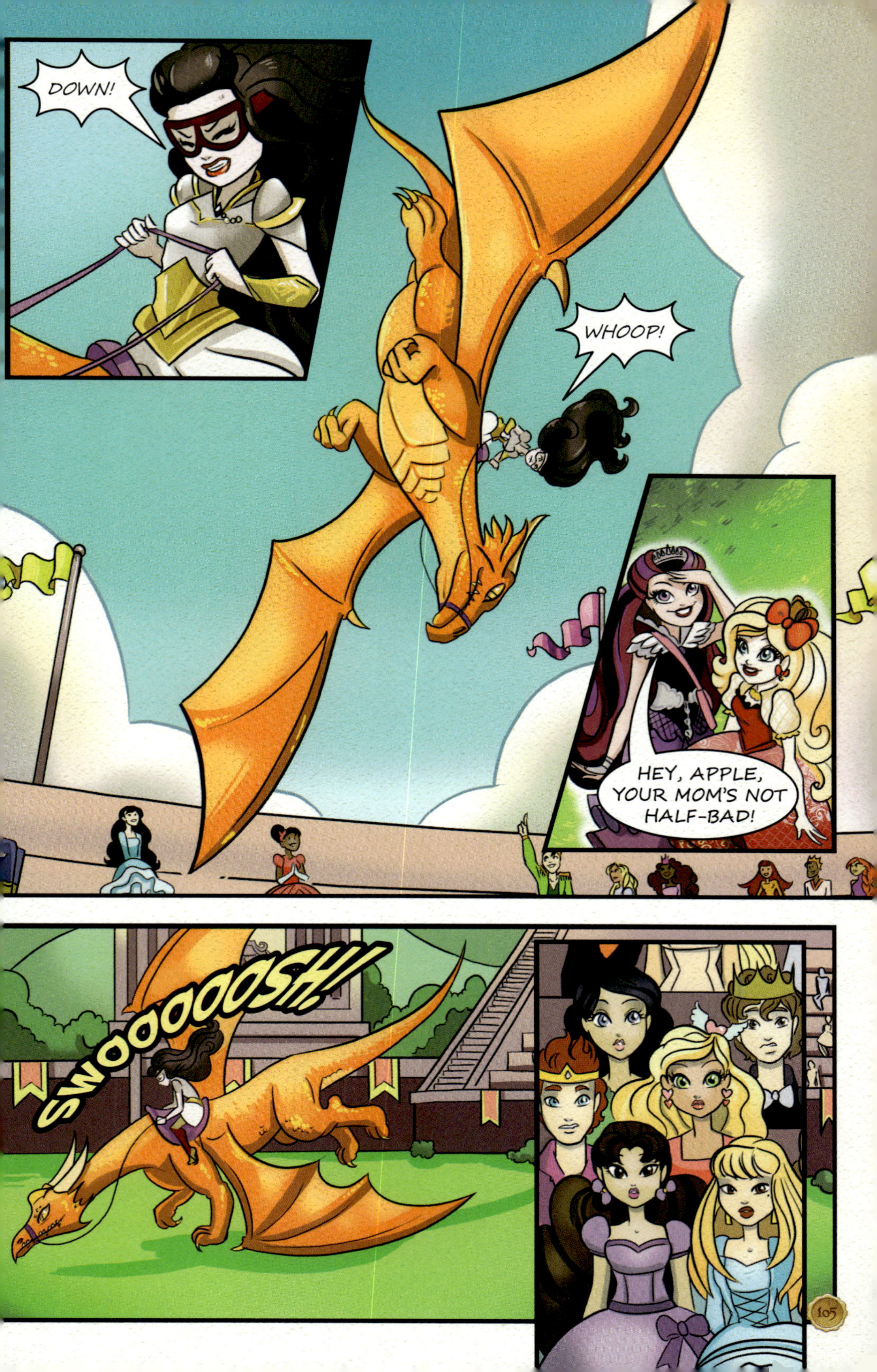
DOWN!
WHOOP!
HEY, APPLE, YOUR MOM'S NOT HALF-BAD!
SWOOOOOOSH!!

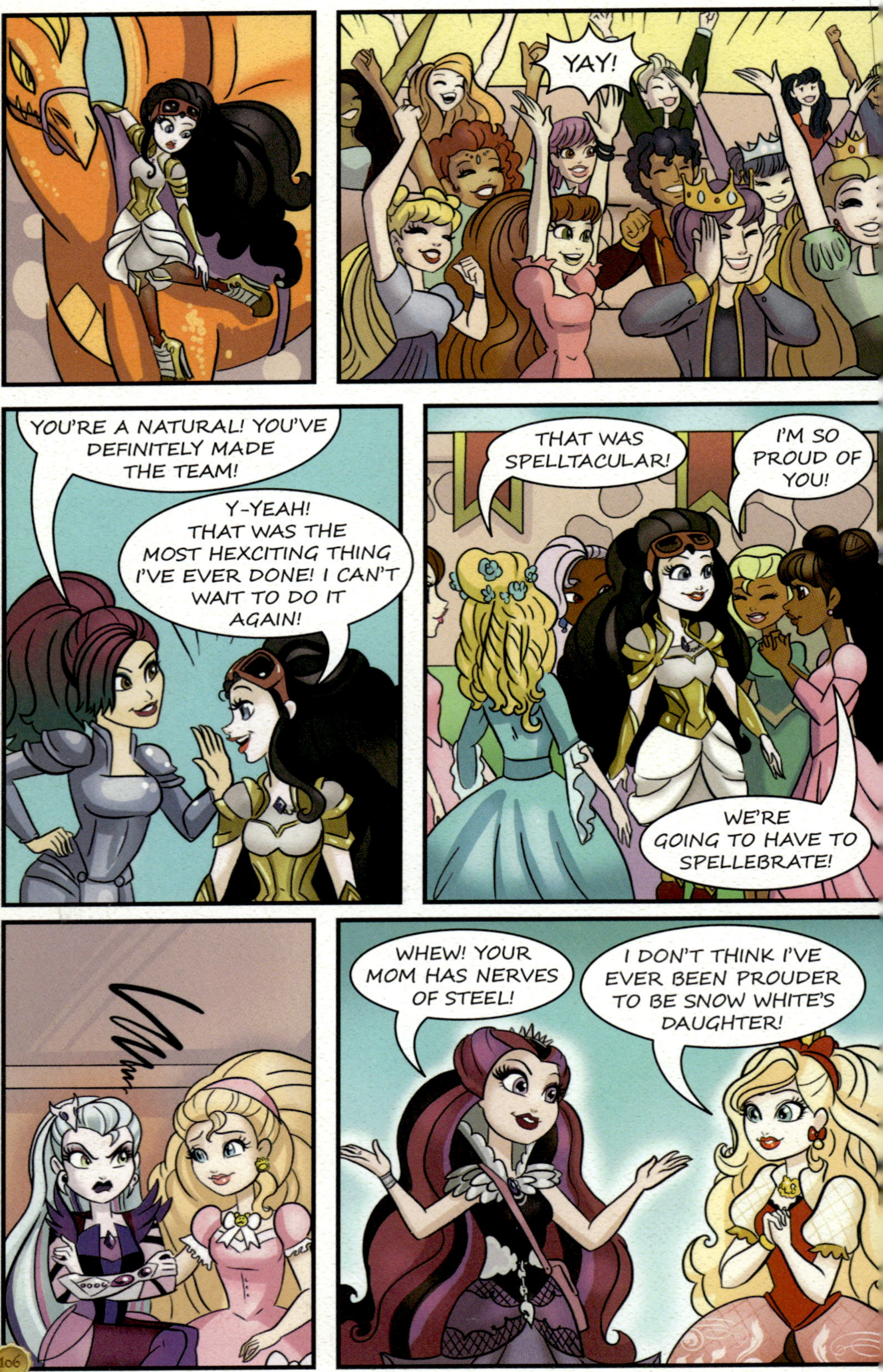
YAY!
YOU'RE A NATURAL! YOU'VE DEFINITELY MADE THE TEAM!
Y-YEAH! THAT WAS THE MOST HEXCITING THING I'VE EVER DONE! I CAN'T WAIT TO DO IT AGAIN!
THAT WAS SPELLTACULAR!
I'M SO PROUD OF YOU!
WE'RE GOING TO HAVE TO SPELLEBRATE!
WHEW! YOUR MOM HAS NERVES OF STEEL!
I DON'T THINK I'VE EVER BEEN PROUDER TO BE SNOW WHITE'S DAUGHTER!

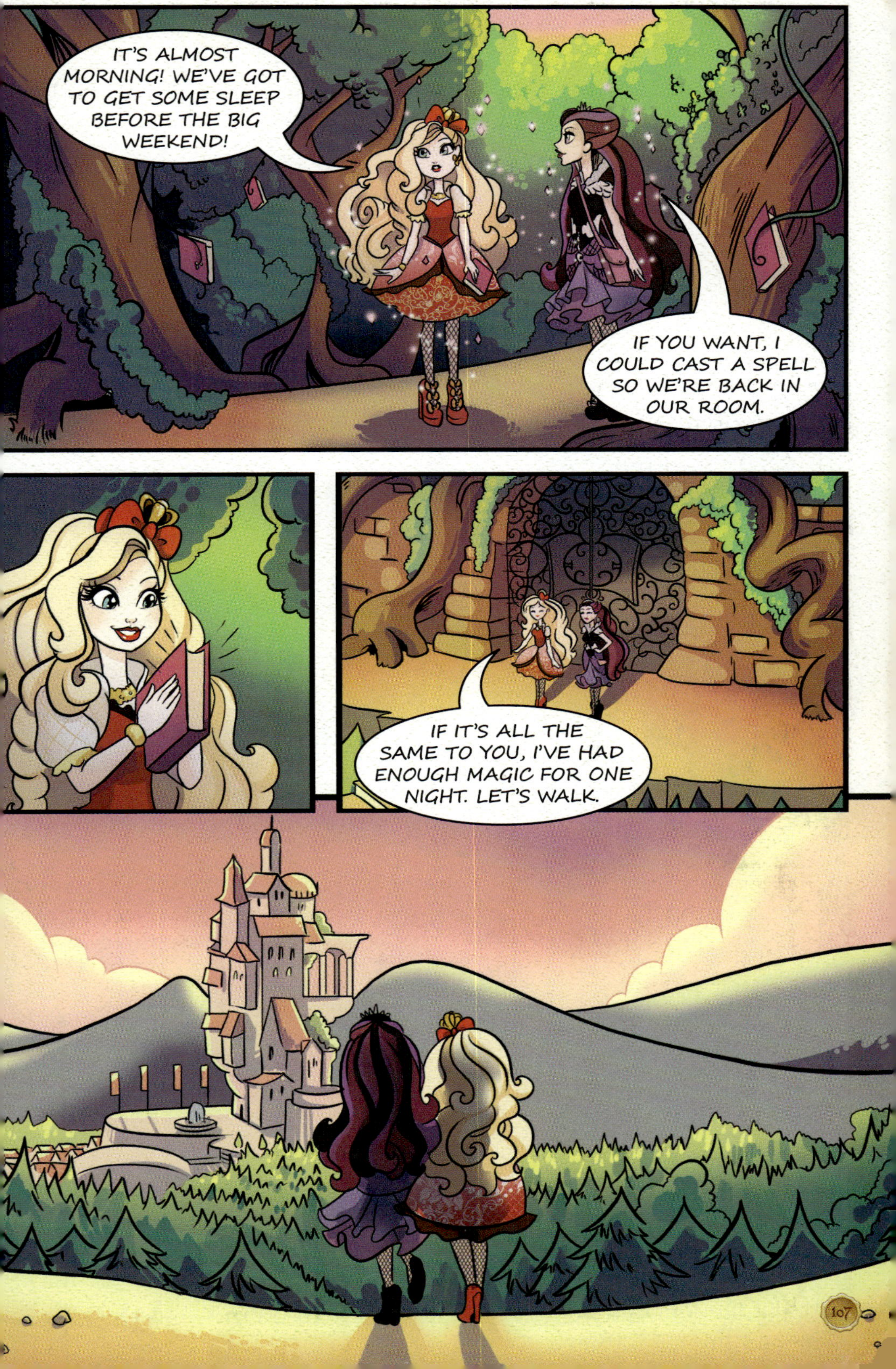
IT'S ALMOST MORNING! WE'VE GOT TO GET SOME SLEEP BEFORE THE BIG WEEKEND!
IF YOU WANT, I COULD CAST A SPELL SO WE'RE BACK IN OUR ROOM.
IF IT'S ALL THE SAME TO YOU, I'VE HAD ENOUGH MAGIC FOR ONE NIGHT. LET'S WALK.

Story Seven: Reunion

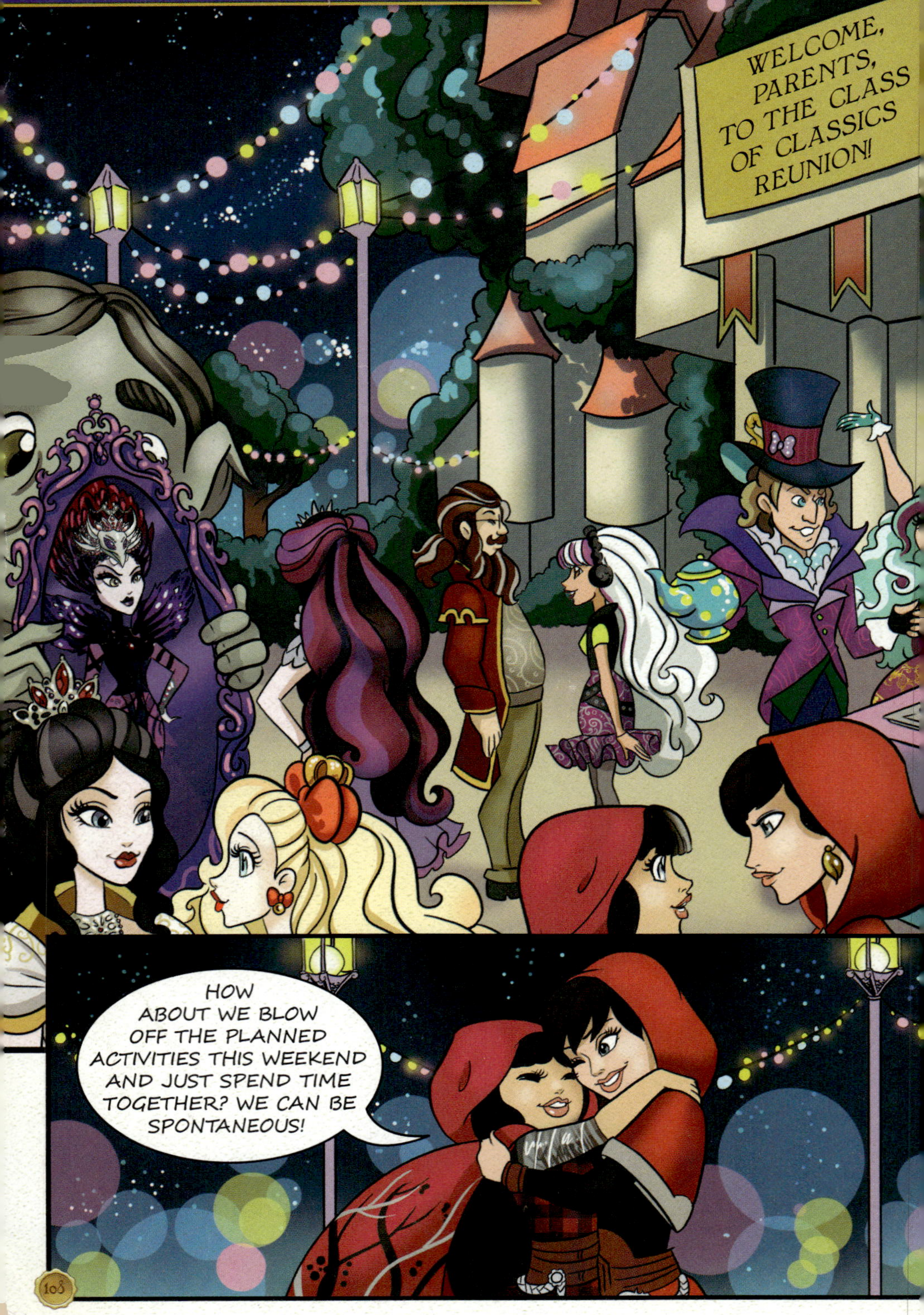
WELCOME, PARENTS, TO THE CLASS OF CLASSICS REUNION!
HOW ABOUT WE BLOW OFF THE PLANNED ACTIVITIES THIS WEEKEND AND JUST SPEND TIME TOGETHER? WE CAN BE SPONTANEOUS!

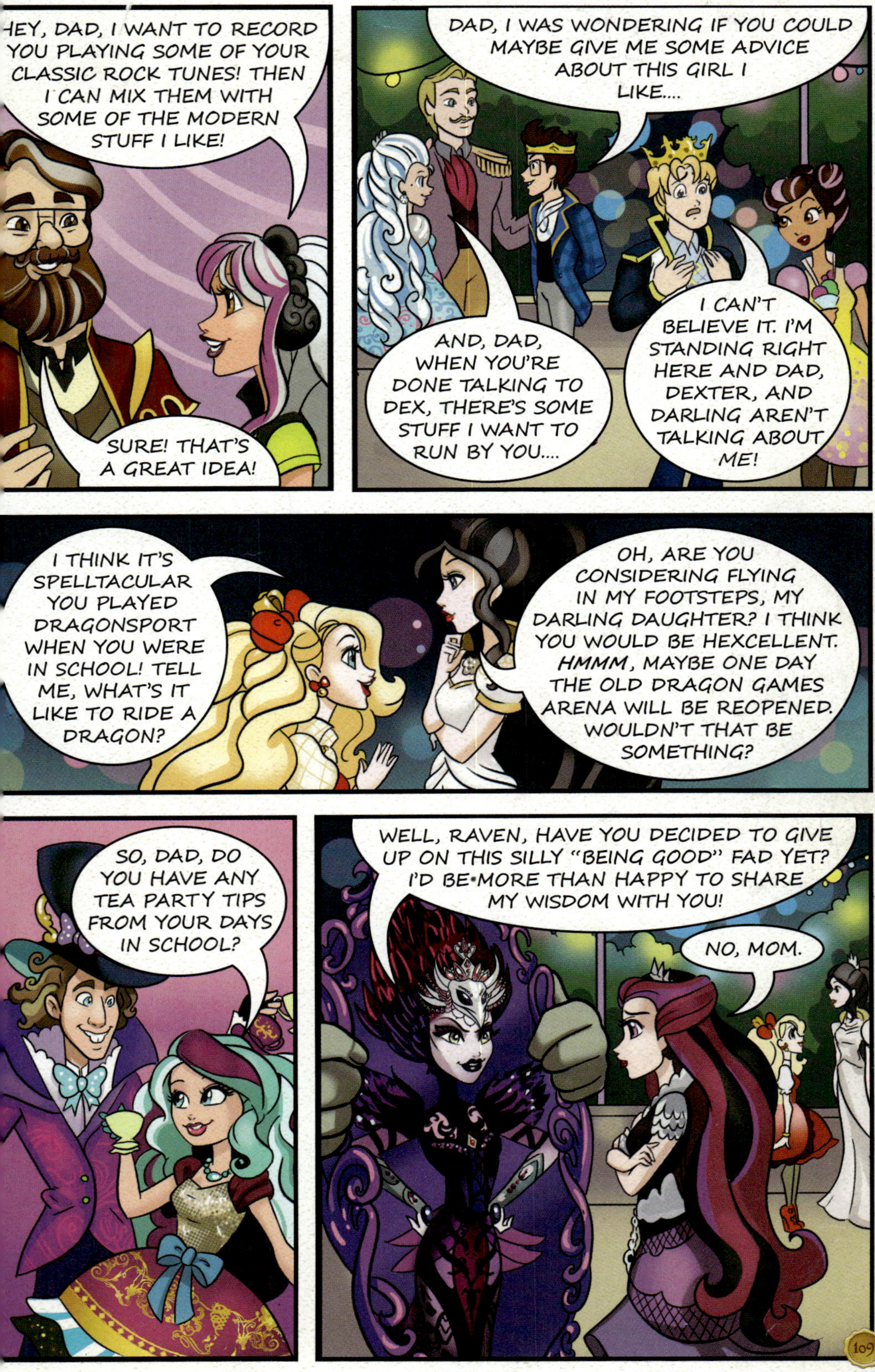
HEY, DAD, I WANT TO RECORD YOU PLAYING SOME OF YOUR CLASSIC ROCK TUNES! THEN I CAN MIX THEM WITH SOME OF THE MODERN STUFF I LIKE!
SURE! THAT'S A GREAT IDEA!
DAD, I WAS WONDERING IF YOU COULD MAYBE GIVE ME SOME ADVICE ABOUT THIS GIRL I LIKE....
AND, DAD, WHEN YOU'RE DONE TALKING TO DEX, THERE'S SOME STUFF I WANT TO RUN BY YOU....
I CAN'T BELIEVE IT. I'M STANDING RIGHT HERE AND DAD, DEXTER, AND DARLING AREN'T TALKING ABOUT ME!
I THINK IT'S SPELLTACULAR YOU PLAYED DRAGONSPORT WHEN YOU WERE IN SCHOOL! TELL ME, WHAT'S IT LIKE TO RIDE A DRAGON?
OH, ARE YOU CONSIDERING FLYING IN MY FOOTSTEPS, MY DARLING DAUGHTER? I THINK YOU WOULD BE HEXCELLENT. *HMMM*, MAYBE ONE DAY THE OLD DRAGON GAMES ARENA WILL BE REOPENED. WOULDN'T THAT BE SOMETHING?
SO, DAD, DO YOU HAVE ANY TEA PARTY TIPS FROM YOUR DAYS IN SCHOOL?
WELL, RAVEN, HAVE YOU DECIDED TO GIVE UP ON THIS SILLY "BEING GOOD" FAD YET? I'D BE MORE THAN HAPPY TO SHARE MY WISDOM WITH YOU!
NO, MOM.

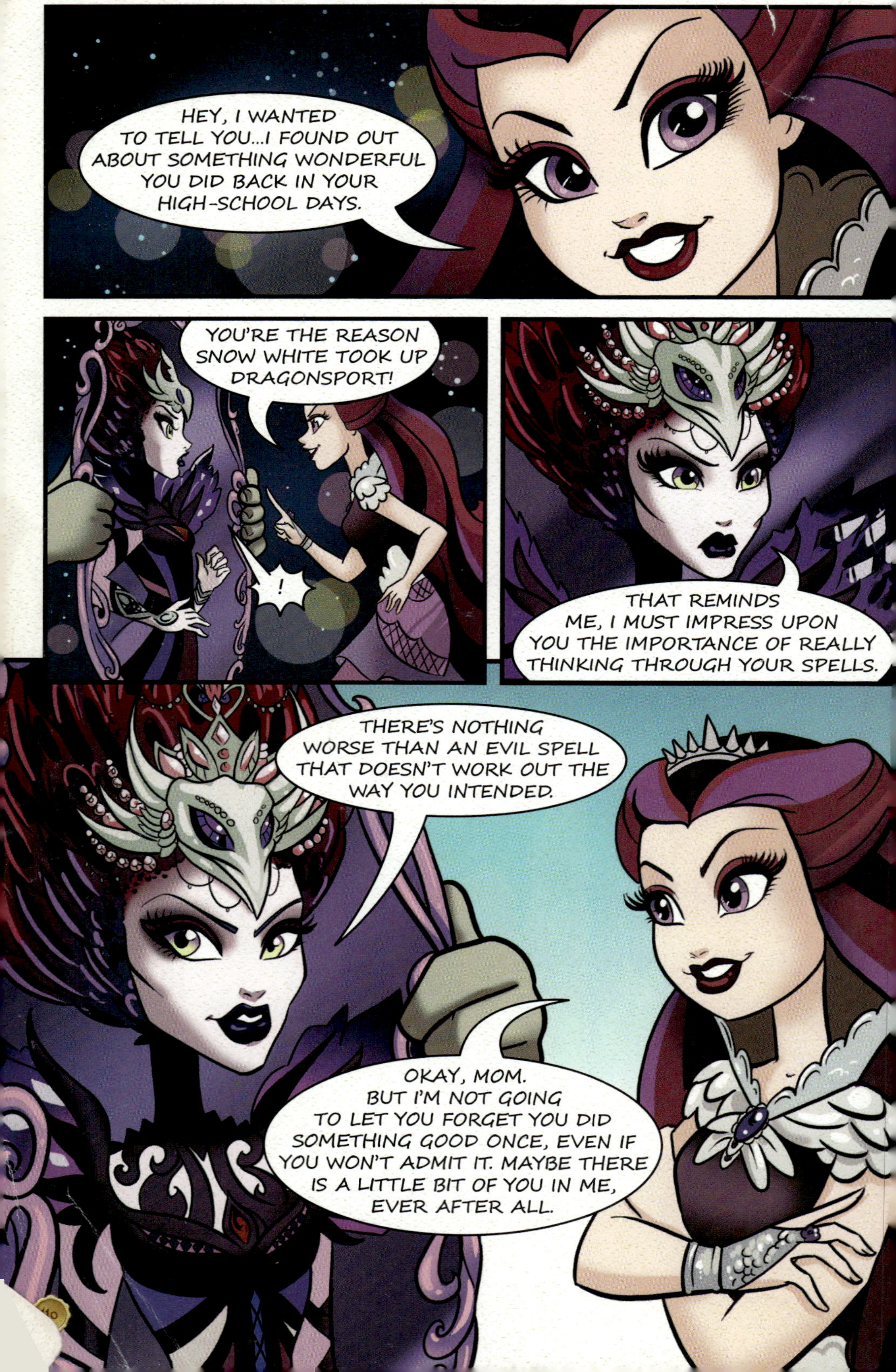
HEY, I WANTED TO TELL YOU...I FOUND OUT ABOUT SOMETHING WONDERFUL YOU DID BACK IN YOUR HIGH-SCHOOL DAYS.
YOU'RE THE REASON SNOW WHITE TOOK UP DRAGONSPORT!
!
THAT REMINDS ME, I MUST IMPRESS UPON YOU THE IMPORTANCE OF REALLY THINKING THROUGH YOUR SPELLS.
THERE'S NOTHING WORSE THAN AN EVIL SPELL THAT DOESN'T WORK OUT THE WAY YOU INTENDED.
OKAY, MOM. BUT I'M NOT GOING TO LET YOU FORGET YOU DID SOMETHING GOOD ONCE, EVEN IF YOU WON'T ADMIT IT. MAYBE THERE IS A LITTLE BIT OF YOU IN ME, EVER AFTER ALL.